Barbara Howe lives on the third rock from the sun, while her imagination travels the universe and beyond.

Born in the US (North Carolina), she spent most of her adult life in New Jersey, working in the software industry, on projects ranging from low-level kernel ports to multi-million-dollar financial applications. She moved to New Zealand in 2009, gained dual citizenship, and now works as a software developer in the movie industry. She lives in Wellington, in a house overflowing with books and jigsaw puzzles, and wishes she had more time time to spend universe hopping.

**Reforging series by Barbara Howe
available through IFWG Publishing**

The Locksmith (book 1)
Engine of Lies (book 2)
The Blacksmith (book 3)
The Wordsmith (book 4)

Reforging: Book 4

The Wordsmith

By Barbara Howe

The Wordsmith

All Rights Reserved

ISBN-13: 978-1-925956-92-4

Printed in Garamond and Goudy Old Style typefaces.

IFWG Publishing International
Melbourne

www.ifwgpublishing.com

Dedicated to

Maria Kelly
Rebecca Fraser
Brenda Quinn
Lynne Street
Grace Bridges
Donna Garzinsky
Margaret Ellis
Lee Murray
Dan Rabarts
Tim Jones
Carla Morris
Noel Osualdini
and other editors I've known but whose names I've forgotten,
and all the other legions of editors I've never met,
who take messy drafts and work magic
on them to make them readable.

Acknowledgements

I'd like to thank Gerry Huntman, Maria Kelly, Catherine Archer-Wills, and the others at IFWG Publishing Australia involved in turning The Wordsmith into a real book. Letha Etzkorn, Jo Leary, and Tim Jones have also given me valuable encouragement and support, but my most crucial supporters have always been my husband, Art Protin, and daughter, Lucy Howe. Without them, none of this would have happened.

Anger Management

"Whatever happens, lad, for God's sake don't lose your temper." Granny Mildred reached across the guildhall's kitchen table with her wand and poked Duncan Archer in the chest. "Remember what Her Iciness said."

"That if I hit anybody, I'll be punching myself, too. Not likely to forget that." Duncan helped himself to more beans with one hand, and held out his mug with the other. Hazel poured without taking her eyes off Mildred.

Mildred said, "Don't go punching that brand new marble fountain the duchess put in either—"

"Frostbite. What—"

"Watch your language, sonny."

"When did—"

"This past May…and it'll hurt you worse than you hurt it if you hit it with your bare hand. Stay away from the duchess and her good-for-nothing son. You're on the Fire Warlock's business; act like you belong there and know what you're doing. Be polite to the duke, even if he keeps you waiting for hours, like his dad used to do with your uncle."

Hazel's frown deepened. "Duncan's pulse rate has doubled since you started talking, Mildred. Are you trying to make him angry before he even gets there?"

"Nae, just giving him some advice, since he doesn't seem to be in any hurry to leave."

"That does it." Duncan grabbed his hat and stomped through the healer's hall to the tunnel—the one the duke's servants used, not the one ending in the duchess's sitting room. He ducked through and came out between the stables and carriage house, with a long walk ahead up a gravel drive to the manor house.

He'd never been up this drive before. Gardeners had cut a dozen bushes on each side into fancy shapes—a duck here, a squirrel there. The duchess must have thought they looked pretty. They looked pretty silly to him. If the duke trimmed them, Duncan wouldn't care, but the gardeners' wages came out of Abertee's rents and taxes—money that could have been keeping the roads in repair and feeding widows and orphans. Duncan pulled his hat lower and fixed his eyes on the end of the drive.

The marble fountain between him and the house was taller than his head; no way could he miss it. Abertee's stone was granite, so the duchess couldn't even argue she was supporting the local quarries. Figuring what it would cost to haul something that heavy up the coast made his head hurt. His eyes hurt, too. The yellow marble looked foul next to the grey manor house.

To be fair, the duke was a decent sort, but dim and spineless. It was his wife who had scared Duncan's Uncle Will so bad he'd get the shakes talking about her. And the duke's son, Lord Geoffrey, had invited that earl's whelp, Lord Edmund, north for the hunting. If Lord Geoffrey hadn't known Lord Edmund was hunting Abertee's finest lasses, Duncan was a stuffed goose.

He took a deep breath and unclenched his fists. His business was with the duke, not the duchess or her son. He was not going to lose his temper. He wasn't going in the servant's entrance either, and if she didn't like it, all the more reason not to.

The lion's-head knocker on the front door stared down its nose at him. He snarled and reached for it, but the door swung open, pulling the knocker out of his grasp.

L ucinda Rehsavvy slumped against the cushions on her drawing room's sofa and frowned at Earl Eddensford's footman. "Try again," she said, "I couldn't hear you."

"Yes, Madam Locksmith," was all she could make out, as the footman repeated his message, word for word, in the same inaudible mumble.

Lucinda clenched her jaw and counted to ten. She would not yell at the sweating, twitching messenger. He'd probably never met a warlock before, and losing her temper wouldn't help. It was not his fault the prolonged recovery from her injuries made her irritable, or that the tales told by the constant parade of angry and frightened commoners asking for the Fire Guild's aid made her seethe.

The nursemaid by the window playing with her son, and Tom Russell, the Rehsavvys' secretary writing letters at his desk, were members of the Fire Guild, and neither lived their lives in perpetual rage. Lucinda didn't have to either.

"Pretend I'm your deaf grandmother. Try again."

The footman started his message the third time, a bit louder. "Earl and Lady Eddensford humbly request—"

The fire roared. Another warlock charged out, shouting, "Hey, Lucinda!"

The nursemaid screamed and grabbed little Eddie, who squalled. The footman jerked around with wide and staring eyes, and fell over a footstool.

The warlock—her adopted brother, René—bent to help the man up. "Sorry, didn't mean to scare you." The footman rolled away from the outstretched hand and scuttled backwards towards the door.

Lucinda snapped, "When will you start looking to see who's there before you come popping out of the fireplace?" Then at the nursemaid: "Of course Eddie cried, with you screaming like that. Get used to it, or stop calling yourself a fire witch."

"Yes, ma'am." The nursemaid carried Eddie out of the room with her nose in the air.

René said, "Lucinda, you'll want—"

"Hold on a moment." She turned to the footman, who was climbing to his feet in the hall. "Start over, please."

He shouted his message, without taking his eyes off René. "Earl and Lady Eddensford humbly request the Warlock Locksmith's presence today at afternoon tea. Lady Eddensford further instructed me to say she is sorry about the short notice and she knows you tire quickly, but it's urgent and she needs you, and the Fire Warlock would want to know. I am to wait for a response."

Lucinda chewed on her lip. "Was there anything else? Did she act worried?"

"That was all, ma'am."

Scrying in the fire gave no hint what might be behind the invitation. Her stepsister Claire, in her sitting room, stabbed at her embroidery, using the wrong colour thread on a strawberry leaf. The Earl paced up and down a gallery, frowning. A bit on edge, otherwise normal.

Lucinda's mind's eye had not yet fully recovered. Using magic made her head throb. She needed a nap.

René rocked back and forth on his heels. "Lucinda, you've got to see this."

"You are annoying, you wretch." She waved a finger in the footman's direction. "One moment, please. All right, René, what is it?"

"I can't show you with all these people around. Guild Council business."

Slipping into the telepathic channel sent a needle of pain lancing across her temples. *At least tell me what it's about.*

There's somebody walking the challenge path—

You petrified this poor man over someone walking the challenge path? She hit René square in the chest with a blast that knocked him sprawling into the fire. The footman screamed and bolted.

"For once, Irene, just once, you ought to lose your temper and tell him what you really think."

Irene van Gelder peered at the healer in the dim light filtering through the bedroom window's closed shutters. "Pardon?"

"You heard me." The healer's touch soothed her headache, but the words threatened to bring it back. "You're good at keeping what you feel to yourself. Too good. But you've got a cartload of anger bottled up inside, especially at Enchanter Paul. He probably thinks you're grateful for that job at the school."

"A proper air witch never gives in to fits of temper or other violent emotions."

Granny Beatrice snorted. "You won't get out of the fix you're in without making a fuss. Your job is making you ill. Stand up for yourself. Take lessons from the Fire Guild if you have to."

"Oliver's Fire Guild friends drifted away years ago, and Mother would be mortified if anyone connected to her acted like a fire witch."

The healer pulled her hand away and glared at Irene with her fists on her hips. "What's that mean? Loud and obnoxious? Or do you mean if you acted like a witch who knows what she's worth, instead a doormat? Your mother didn't do you any favours; her idea of *proper* is a second-rate merchant's dim wife, with no ideas in her head besides keeping her husband happy, rather than a real witch." Granny grinned. "She'd have been scandalised if you'd turned out to be an earth witch."

The patterns in the wallpaper demanded Irene's attention. "She does consider most Earth Guild talents to be rather…"

"Crude? Vulgar? Bawdy?"

"Er…unrefined."

"Oh, spare me, please. If I can't be bawdy, what's the point?"

Gillian asked, "Granny, what's *bawdy*?"

Granny poked a finger at the younger of the two girls perched on the bed's footboard. "You two. You're going to grow up to be witches, so act like it. Be proud of yourselves. Hear me? And learn to take care of yourselves. Those old fairytales that end with 'happily ever after'—that's a lot of hogwash."

"True," Irene said. "They never mention the girl whose handsome prince dies on her a few years later, leaving her with children to feed and clothe."

Granny said, "Everybody ought to know how to earn money for themselves, even if they've snagged a prince. Even a prince like your papa is a man, after all."

Miranda said, "What's that mean?"

"Living with them is a pain in the arse. They snore. They drop muddy boots in the middle of the floor you just mopped. They sweat, and stink, and fart…"

Irene's laugh had a hysterical edge. "Oliver used to joke that the best thing about being an enchanter was that he could knock out an enemy warship with one fart."

Granny grinned. "Oh, Lord, I miss that boy. I bet he never said that to your mother."

"He did. She almost fainted."

Granny cackled. "His farts were so powerful the mere thought of them could knock a woman unconscious."

She was still chucking when she left. She stomped back in, scowling, a few minutes later. "You changed the subject on me, and I forgot what I needed to say. These headaches of yours are getting worse, aren't they?"

Irene studied the wallpaper.

"Aren't they?"

Irene said, "Yes, ma'am."

"They're getting to be more than I can cope with. I can send you to an earth mother, but the help she could give would be temporary, too. Between your anger and your job and those voices, it's a wonder you can still get up and walk around. If you keep on like this, you'll kill yourself. If you were a fire witch I'd go yell at the Fire Warlock for you—he respects earth witches. I'd even take on Her Chilliness—she's at least fair. But your Air Guild is so touchy about interference I'd do more harm than good if I bearded Enchanter Paul. I don't see any way around it. You've got to stand up for yourself."

Irene's headache returned, full force. "Oliver used to say that, too. But the guild has already rejected my claim, many times. How does one convince them that suppressing a talent to tolerate one's work makes one ill, when they don't believe that talent exists?"

Words on the Wind

The butler said, "Please come in, Master Duncan. The duke said to show you in as soon as you arrived. Follow me."

Duncan closed his flapping jaw and lurched after the butler, eyeballing statues and paintings on the way. He'd seen the like in the Fire Warlock's Fortress, but he'd watched those witches and wizards put their lives on the line for the whole country, and didn't begrudge them their luxuries. They earned their keep; the duchess didn't.

A crackling fire made the duke's sitting room as hot as a forge. The duke shivered, despite gloves, hat, and two wool blankets draped around his shoulders.

He brightened as Duncan walked in. "Master Duncan, I'm glad to see you." After asking a few polite questions about Duncan's plans to reopen Will Archer's smithy, the duke got down to business. "I understand you know which girls Lord Edmund, uh… That is, the young women that he, um…"

"Which ones he ruined, you mean."

The duke flinched. "Yes, them."

"I've talked to them." Duncan fished the paper out of his pocket and went through the list of names, telling the duke what he knew about them and their families before handing the paper over.

The duke backed away from it. "If I gave you money for them, could you…"

"Nae. They want 'I'm sorries' in person, more than they want money. Though money will help. And the Frost Maiden said you wouldn't get warm if you didn't make an effort."

"Oh." The duke pulled the blankets tighter.

Duncan snorted. The duke was in his fifties—about time he started acting like a grownup. "Besides that, the Fire Warlock told me to report to him on everything you've been neglecting. You haven't kept up the roads or looked after orphans like you ought, but every man, woman, and child in Abertee has been yammering about other things you haven't been doing, till I have a list as long as my arm. Not sure I believe it all. Tell me what you are supposed to do for us."

Wrapped in his blankets, the duke looked like a sheep overdue for shearing. Bleated like one, too. "But I don't know."

"Eh? What do you mean, you don't know? It's in your charter."

"What charter?"

"Uh…" Duncan's jaw hung open. He closed it. "Everybody who's anybody has a charter. The guilds, market towns, and, I thought, you aristos."

"But what is it?"

"It's a list of the rights and privileges that come with being a duke, and the duties that go along with them. Yours would have the king's seal, since he's your liege lord. The Air Guild would have written it up on parchment with some magic to not rot."

"I've never seen anything like that. The retired Fire Warlock told me I had to pay guards to patrol the roads. The duchess was furious but the king said I'd better go along with it, so I did. He and the Fire Warlock didn't agree on anything else. You lot keep harping about the roads, but Dad and the king both said you were getting above yourselves and not to pay any attention. The duchess said I'd better not think of spending even a penny on you rabble. Sorry, those were her words."

"Both the Frost Maiden and the Fire Warlock say taking care of the roads is one of your duties. Who would you rather have mad at you, your wife or the Frost Maiden?"

The duke hunkered down further into the blankets and didn't answer.

Duncan rolled his eyes. "Ice me if I can see why you're afraid of your own wife, especially since you've gotten on the Frost Maiden's wrong side once already. Tell your wife to go fight Her Iciness instead of you. If you took the money you'd spend on one party and spent it on the roads, you'd make a big difference, and folk in Abertee would start to calm down."

The duke leaned forward and whispered, "I'd be happy if I never had to give another one of those frostbitten parties. If both Officeholders say I have to spend money on the roads, maybe the duchess won't be angry with me."

"The highway north out of Crossroads is in the worst shape. If you hire a crew to start on it right away, they can make a dent on the worst bits before the weather turns bad."

Behind Duncan, somebody snarled, "Who do you think you are, tenant, telling us what to do with our money?"

A little rooster of a lad—the Duke's son, Lord Geoffrey—sauntered in with a walking stick and a curling lip. Behind him his uncle, the Red Duke, looked like a cat pouncing on a mouse. A third man, a clerk, staggered under a stack of books. Duncan gave the clerk a hand.

Lord Geoffrey tapped his foot. "Answer the question, you frostbitten tenant, or I'll have to teach you your manners."

"I'm a master swordsmith and your elder. Mind your own manners."

The clerk choked and bent over his books. The White Duke bleated. His son went white and swung his walking stick at Duncan's head. Duncan took it away, then grabbed him by his waistcoat and held him at arm's length. All he could reach was Duncan's arm, and his swings didn't do it any damage. Duncan wouldn't get into trouble with the Water Office for that.

The Red Duke went purple. He shouted something about Duncan's head getting too big.

"Aye," Duncan said. "My head's already so big my hats are custom made."

"I hear your sister's getting married soon. Perhaps her lord should exercise the right of first night."

Duncan grabbed the Red Duke with his other hand and hauled him into the air with a roar. The duke yelled back. Neither aristo looked scared, like they ought to with an angry fellow Duncan's size ahold of them. He stopped just in time from knocking their heads together. He didn't need a sore head, too.

A door in the near wall led to a closet. Duncan carried them in and dropped the son. He staggered. Duncan shoved the Red Duke at him and they both went down. Duncan slammed the door on them and stood with his back against it, his arms crossed over his chest, and glared at his overlord.

The White Duke said, "Geoffrey's not that bad, really. He didn't know what Lord Edmund was doing."

"Like hell he didn't. He knew damned well, and you did too, you—"

A pair of guards thundered down the hall, skidded to a stop, and saluted. "We heard yelling, Your Grace." They still heard yelling, and banging on the closet door, too. "Is there a problem, sir?"

With the blanket pulled around his face, all that showed were the duke's eyes. He looked at Duncan, then at the guards, then back at Duncan.

The first guard said, "Your Grace? Master Duncan?"

The duke waggled his fingers at them. "Master Duncan is giving the Red Duke a long overdue lesson in manners. Go back to your posts."

The guards grinned and left.

Duncan said, "Both of them called me a tenant. Everybody knows the Archers are freeholders. You better set them right."

The clerk looked up from his books with a white face. He opened his mouth. Closed it again. Swallowed.

Duncan said, "What is it, man? Speak up."

The clerk swallowed hard again. "That's what they were coming to tell you, and why I was carrying these ledgers. I'm sorry, Master Duncan, but according to the duke's records, you and your brother aren't freeholders. You're tenants."

The Rehsavvys' front door slammed behind the fleeing footman. Tom dropped his pen and let out a belly laugh. Lucinda rubbed her eyes and groaned.

René dusted himself off, grinning. "I remember somebody arguing with Quicksilver that we didn't need to use much force in our practice sessions."

"I'm a fire witch," Lucinda said. "I lose my temper sometimes." She glanced at the clock. Two o'clock. Plenty of time for a nap before tea. "Tom, send a message to the Eddensfords saying I'll be there."

"Close the door on your way out, and don't let anyone else in," René said. "Because, I swear, she'll blast me again if she doesn't see this."

Tom grumbled, "I want to know, too," but complied.

As soon as the door closed, Lucinda said, "I understand being the new Keeper of the Challenge Path is exciting, and supplicants are more interesting than the other problems we have to deal with, but those are more urgent. I don't have time for every new supplicant."

René glowered. "This one's different. I mean it." He waved at the fire. "Look at him."

A boy, younger than René, stared at a tree: the very same abomination of a pine tree Lucinda had climbed less than four years ago. Four years that felt like a lifetime.

The boy was unusually well dressed; his reaction to getting his clothes ripped and sap-covered could be entertaining. "So?" she said. "Who is he?"

René hopped from one foot to the other, his glower deepening. "You're not using your mind's eye."

"It hasn't fully returned yet. Using magic wears me out." Lucinda turned her mind's eye towards the fire. A bright purple aura denoted high-ranking nobility. "Who? No, wait, it can't be. The crown prince? Walking the challenge path?"

René grinned. "See? You'd have given me grief if I hadn't shown you."

"But what's he want?"

"I don't know; he hasn't said anything. The lieutenant at the gate was so shocked he didn't do a proper job of grilling him."

"If the Warlock accepts his quest, what will that do to relations with King Stephen?"

René shrugged. Lucinda didn't need her mind's eye to watch the prince climbing the tree for a bird's-eye view of the maze. As he swung onto a higher branch, his sleeve caught on a spike and tore. He stared at the rip for a moment in tight-lipped silence, before continuing up the tree with a set face.

Lucinda said, "Takes you back, doesn't it? I was so angry about my ruined clothes I swore I'd see the Warlock no matter what, and demand a new dress for my troubles."

René laughed. "Me, too. Not a dress, though. The only clothes I had were the ones I was wearing."

"Is it fair, to watch him like this? It feels like eavesdropping."

René shrugged. "I have to keep an eye on everybody walking the challenge path, so I can rescue them and send them home if they get into trouble. Besides, the royals are used to people staring at them. They always have staff around, and just ignore them. The servants might as well be furniture."

"Maybe you're right." Lucinda crossed her fingers; the prince's grim determination captivated her. His struggle with the pine tree must have been painful, but his expression gave nothing away. She exhaled when he reached the ground, and started through the maze; she hadn't realised she'd been holding her breath. "When he's through—assuming he makes it—take him directly to the Fortress rather than the Guild Hall. We don't need rumours spreading before Beorn's had a chance to figure out what he wants."

"Yeah, makes sense. I'd better go. Got to keep an eye on His Highness."

"The prince or the lion?"

"Both." René stopped with one foot in the fire. "We might not ever find out what he wants."

"I know. You can't make him tell unless he wants to. That doesn't mean you won't ask."

He grinned and disappeared into the flames. She watched the prince's progress: his soaking in the lily pond, his wide-eyed hesitation in the doorway with the Fortress towering over him, his confrontation with the lion. When the lion charged, the prince stood his ground in silence, neither moving nor screaming, and waited for the lion to come to a snarling stop a few paces away.

In a quavering voice, he said, "Nice kitty." The lion roared; the boy flinched. "Not a nice kitty. You're a fearsome beast. The king of the jungle. I hope you like that better. Now let me pass."

The lion shook its mane and roared.

The prince's jaw worked. In a moment he said, with no shake but in too high a pitch, "I order you to move aside." The lion didn't budge.

The prince took two steps towards the lion, and holding out an arm, pointed stiffly to one side. "Move aside and let me pass." It finally sounded like an order.

The lion strolled away in the opposite direction. The prince, facing forwards but watching the lion out of the corners of his eye, plodded towards the gate where René was waiting.

A brisk walk along the shore eased Irene's physical discomfort, but did little for her emotional turmoil. Her hands over her ears muffled the roar of wind and surf, but could not block the whispers the wind carried.

Irene…

For nearly three years, the winds had carried tormenting whispers, sometimes dozens a day, sometimes none for weeks at a time. This past summer they had stopped for nearly two months, encouraging her to hope they were gone for good, but they crowded back as thick as ever in September.

Promises…

The whispers were, as usual, mere breaths, too faint to carry tonal colour or emphasis. Those had long since lost their power to shock, but half a dozen times, no more, Oliver's distinctive baritone had called as if from the next room. On one occasion, a pot of boiling water had slipped from her hands, scalding her.

Oliver would have been appalled. He had been her champion, her protector. Whenever he was away, he would send messages on the breeze: *Irene, I'll be late for dinner*, or *Irene, I'm coming home.* Those had been reassuring.

I promised…

Many old tales depicted wizards and witches magic-bound to keep rash promises even after death. The more powerful the talent, the stronger the fetters would be, the tales said, and Oliver had been in the highest rank.

"As soon as the book is ready, we'll take it to the Company of Mages," he had said. "They'll understand. You won't have to take any more rubbish from the Air Guild. That's a promise."

You promised…

She broke her own rash promise to him within three months of his death. "Stand up for the children," he'd said. "You know what they need. Don't let Paul or your mother or anybody else make decisions for you. Promise me that."

Those promises had no weight now. She was not an illiterate peasant, misled by lurid fantasies. Oliver, an expert in magical theory, had scoffed at the stories, saying the magic of death was deep, powerful, and more fundamental than anything a wizard could invoke in making a promise.

Irene believed ghosts were nonsense, but Granny Beatrice preferred that explanation to the alternative, and had no patience with residents of Airvale who, out of misguided kindness, called Irene mad.

Under the brow of the looming headland, the path turned back towards the Hall of the Winds. Higher on the shore, several schoolboys taking an unauthorised holiday jeered. The ringleader, the White Duke's younger son, was a nasty piece of work, capable of sending whispers on the wind, and sadistic enough to enjoy it, but not proficient enough to reproduce Oliver's rich tones. Nor had Irene told anyone other than Granny Beatrice and Enchantress Winifred about the unfulfilled promises, and both of them kept secrets.

The boys blew sand and pebbles, and laughed as they drove her out of range.

"Frost you, Oliver," she muttered. "Why don't you haunt them instead?"

Lost in the Tunnels

The pounding and yelling on the other side of the door Duncan leaned against made the latch rattle. He put a hand out to quiet it. "That's claptrap. We Archers are freeholders, or I'm Jack Frost."

The clerk said, "Yes, sir, but the ledgers for the past forty years list everyone in Nettleton as paying rent, not taxes."

"Show me."

He flipped open the book on the top of the stack, and pointed. "Here."

Duncan read a line with his father's name: *Callum Archer, rent paid.* Duncan read it again, twice.

The clerk said, "This is from ten years ago, long before the recent uproar. As long I've kept the tallies—sixteen years—I've been telling the duke that couldn't be right. The older records are in a locked muniments room, and the duchess has the keys, so I've never had a chance to check them. It's probably a transcription error."

"A what?"

"A mistake. Some clerk years ago could have copied the wrong line from one year's ledger to the next."

The pounding stopped. Duncan leaned forward to glare at the White Duke. A solid shove behind him pushed the door open a few inches. He shouldered it closed. "What is this rot?"

The duke said, "If they've been wrong for forty years, it's not my fault. Besides, it's just words. Rent or taxes, what does it matter?"

The clerk gawked. Duncan shoved the book at him. "I'm going to see the Fire Warlock. You explain it to him."

"Gee, thanks," the clerk mumbled.

"And tell me what you know about the duke's charter."

He shook his head. "Never seen it. I've wondered where it is."

Duncan stepped away from the door. It flew open and the two men fell out, the duke's son landing on top of his uncle. The Red Duke came up with a bloody nose. Duncan's nose was fine. He grinned, and left.

His grin faded before he stepped outdoors. They couldn't force him out of Abertee without running afoul of the Fire Warlock, but they could force his brother's family out to get back at him. No wonder the Red Duke had looked so pleased with himself. Duncan jogged toward the tunnel with his fists tight. He'd choose getting kicked by a horse over having to tell his brother Doug he didn't own the Archer farm. Duncan had been kicked—he knew.

He hadn't been to the Fortress by himself yet, but Hazel had shown him the way two days ago. Getting there was easy—through the door at the end of the hall in the Earth Guild House, take the first right, count three doors and take a left, then another left into the Warren. Wander around the Warren a bit. Then duck through one tunnel to the Fortress. There was no way he could get lost.

He got lost.

There were doors aplenty, but none he remembered. He opened one and came out into an Earth Guild house south of Paris, giving the healers a fright. Once over their surprise, they fussed over him and brought out coffee and cakes. An hour later they stood at the tunnel mouth and he repeated their directions word for word, twice, before he left.

He got lost again.

The next door he opened led to an old granddad healer in Derbyshire who told Duncan his life story over tea. When he started to give directions, Duncan stopped him and made him lead the way. A moment later they were in the Warren.

The granddad went home and Duncan ducked into the tunnel to the Fortress. It didn't go there. His back ached from walking stooped over, and his head and elbows hurt from banging the walls every other step. Back in the Warren, after asking another witch for help, he cornered an earth father.

"The Fire Warlock said the Earth Guild agreed to let us—his agents, I mean—use your tunnels, but they're sending me everywhere but where I need to go. If it's some fool's idea of a joke, it ain't funny." A crowd of upset witches and wizards was gathering. Duncan stopped yelling. "I've been trying to get to the Fortress for hours now. I've got news for the Fire Warlock, and he's not going to be happy about me wasting time."

The earth father said, "No one would deliberately mislead you. You must have forgotten a step. Review the path from Abertee to the Fortress with Granny Mildred."

Duncan leaned over him. "You don't understand. I don't get lost. Somebody used magic to make me go the wrong way."

The earth father put a hand on Duncan's arm. "Calm down. I believe you when you say you don't get lost easily. That doesn't mean you don't occasionally make mistakes, and it's easy to become confused in the dark. Especially if your mind is on other problems, as I can see yours is." He steered the smith towards the Fortress. "Tell me what's bothering you."

He listened while Duncan talked about his problems: the lying ledgers, and how he wasn't getting any time alone with his lass or a chance to work in the smithy with every man, woman, and child in Abertee queuing on his doorstep, with one sad story after another, until his head was stuffed full and his heart was about to explode.

The Warlock wasn't in his study, but Duncan hadn't expected he would be. They reached the bottom of the Fortress stairs with Duncan still talking. About needing a second-in-charge to keep the smithy running while he was out on the Fire Warlock's business. Cousin Jock—him that could add two and two and get three, or sometimes five—was a hard worker and a good smith, but he'd starve on his own. He might do, but only if Duncan had the final say on hiring and firing and setting prices.

The earth father gave him some advice for dealing with the crowds, and for sounding out Cousin Jock, then turned back to the Warren. Duncan headed into Blazes to see the Locksmith.

The townie waiting to see the Locksmith would have let Duncan go first, but her clerk wasn't having any of it. "Wait your turn," he said, so Duncan cooled his heels in the hall, and wondered how she kept her temper with people dropping their problems in her lap every day.

A lass carrying a little tyke came along and stopped at the sitting room door. She put the little fellow down; he toddled over to Duncan and held out his arms. "Up!"

Duncan picked him up and swung him around. He giggled, so Duncan sent him flying, straight up. The lad crowed. The nursemaid screamed. The door opened and a woman snapped, "Stop that."

Duncan had caught the little fellow and was swinging for another toss. He stopped in mid-swing. The tyke howled. The Locksmith stood in the doorway, scowling.

She said, "For pity's sake, his father sends him flying all around the house. Go on, Master Duncan, toss him again. He won't be happy until you do."

Duncan breathed again and went back to tyke-tossing.

The nursemaid pouted. "Warlock Quicksilver makes him fly with magic."

The Locksmith said, "Master Duncan won't drop him, so leave them alone. As much as he likes to fly, he may turn out to be an air wizard." She yawned like a cat. "Toss him a couple more times, then come in and close the door."

Duncan handed the tyke back to the nursemaid and followed the Locksmith into her sitting room. She looked better than the last time he'd seen her—having eyebrows again helped—but still too skinny for comfort. She slumped into a chair and put her feet up.

"What's your trouble?" She closed her eyes, and he figured she'd be asleep before he stopped talking, but when he got to the part about the ledgers she opened her eyes and sat up straight.

"Fool! Not you, Master Duncan. Your duke almost started a riot in July trying to evict your brother, and the Fire Warlock raked him over the coals."

"Aye, and the Frost Maiden turned him into an icicle."

"Is he so idiotic he'll try it again?"

"No, ma'am. Not by himself he wouldn't. It's the rest of the family— his wife and son and brother-in-law—that are stirring the pot. The Frost Maiden didn't hurt them—she just pissed them off, and they're looking for revenge. The duke doesn't have the gumption to stand up to their bullying, and they can't see that it'll hurt them if Abertee goes up in flames."

"Lord Geoffrey had better be careful. Causing trouble when he's not in charge is as good as begging the Fire Office to burn him."

Duncan's gorge rose. He'd once seen a man burn to death, and didn't want to ever see that again. "Would it decide to burn him before or after he drives Doug and Jessie out?"

She made a face. "Let's not find out."

Before he had a chance to ask how they could avoid it, the Fire Warlock walked out of the fire.

18

Opportunity Knocks

The Fire Warlock bellowed, "What do you mean there's no charter?"

Lucinda winced, remembering the fleeing footman. "Beorn, easy…"

Master Duncan shrugged. "The duke's never seen one. His clerk hasn't either."

"But…but," Beorn sputtered, "there had to be a charter. Tell me I'm right, Lucinda."

"Absolutely. All the major noble families had them. They were pre-requisites for the Fire Office shields."

"That's what I reckoned," Master Duncan said. "And it ought to list everything he has to do."

"Of course," she said. "If he had no responsibilities towards the people in his domains, he wouldn't be given the power of life and death over them."

Beorn chewed on the end of his moustache. "Maybe he told the truth. Could be he's never seen it. His duchy's been around for centuries."

She said, "Plenty of time for a piece of parchment to be misplaced, forgotten…"

Beorn snorted. "Hidden, you mean. The recent ones would've hated it, and without the king enforcing it—"

"Enforcing it, my arse," Duncan said. "The king and the old duke told him to ignore everything us commoners said about what might be in it."

"Yeah. Well. No wonder they got away with hiding it. Even an idiot of a duke would know that without the king's help, the Fire and Water Offices couldn't do anything to them."

"But now Her Ici—er, the Frost—that is, since you lot fixed the Water Office…"

"Yep," Beorn said. "The new Water Sorceress can hold his feet to the fire. We hope. Er, well, I guess not to the fire."

Duncan said, "Hold his tongue to the cold iron railing?"

Lucinda cringed. Beorn shuddered. "God, what an awful idea."

"It's no worse than getting your feet burnt."

"Sure it is. I don't know why. It just is."

"What now?" Lucinda said. "Send a witch or wizard to hunt for it?"

Beorn grabbed his hat and turned towards the fireplace. "Charters are the Air Guild's territory. I'd better go talk to Enchanter Paul."

"Wait. Master Duncan wasn't through."

"Burn it," Beorn said, "there's more?"

"Yes. You'd better sit down."

After Duncan related his encounter with the White Duke's son and brother-in-law, there was a long silence as Beorn tugged at his beard with his eyes closed. Finally he said, "I had hoped I wouldn't have to worry about Abertee anymore, with you as agent, and Sorceress Lorraine having cooled things down. Guess I was naïve."

Lucinda said, "It would be rather ironic if full-fledged war broke out in the place we thought would be the calmest."

Duncan said, "I don't know about ironic, ma'am, but it would be funny, in a sick sort of way."

Beorn said, "The Red Duke is one of the king's closest cronies. They'd love for our experiment with agents to fail. We'd better look through those records, charter or no. I'll talk to the duke—the white one—first, and get his approval. He won't turn me down. Come on, Duncan."

Lucinda said, "Don't forget there's a supplicant waiting to talk to you."

"He's waited this long, he can wait a bit longer. Might be good for him."

The two men disappeared into the fireplace. She looked at the clock, and sighed. She was due at the Earl's for tea in an hour, and she still hadn't had a nap.

A fountain of flame erupted on the Hall of the Winds' portico. A normal person would have panicked. Irene gasped and backed into the wall. Two men, either large enough to unnerve the most stolid, emerged from the column of fire.

"Sorry, Irene," the Fire Warlock said. "I don't like scaring people, but

Paul gets pissed off when I jump directly into his study. Something about soot on the carpet."

"It's of no consequence, Your Wisdom." Her voice squeaked. A curtsey was out of the question; her knees would buckle. "An air witch has few opportunities to become as inured as Fire Guild talents do to hotfooting warlocks."

He grinned. "Some of them never get used to it, either. Most women scream." The other man nudged him. "Oh, yeah. Irene, this is Master Swordsmith Duncan Archer."

"Of course," she said. "There can be few others in Frankland of your stature."

"And this is Irene van Gelder, Enchanter Paul's daughter-in-law."

Master Duncan asked, "Why didn't you? Scream, that is."

"Mother would never forgive one of her family for drawing attention in such an offensive manner."

"You're joking."

"She's not," the Warlock said. "I did look first. I thought you were headed in. You must have turned around just as we jumped."

"Pacing can help one gather one's thoughts."

"I'm never ready to face Paul, either." He walked past her, but stopped at the door. "Say, Irene, Ollie told me once, long time ago, about some of the things you can do. We've got a problem and it just occurred to me that you could help, if you're willing."

"Yes, sir."

"You haven't heard what it is yet."

"No matter. I'd rather do favours for the Fire Warlock than for anyone in Airvale."

He grunted and held the door for her.

A decade earlier, Warlock Arturos had left an impression on Irene of a genial, relaxed giant. As Fire Warlock, he was still genial, but sitting on a chair edge, turning his wand over and over in his hands while describing the problem with the ledgers, he looked as relaxed as an overwound clock.

The Air Enchanter said, "I agree, a search through the White Duke's older records should find evidence to either confirm or contradict the recent ledgers. Clerks sometimes make mistakes, and the older receipt books may tell a different story. There may also be other records such as letters or bills of sale, and the church registries of births, deaths, and marriages. Searching shouldn't be difficult. Anyone with sufficient education, talented or not, could do it. Why do you need the Air Guild's help?"

"Because," the Fire Warlock said, "I'm hoping we can find his charter, too."

"If," Irene said, "the charter still—"

The Enchanter said, "Most charters were hidden or destroyed in that frenzy two hundred years ago."

The Fire Warlock glared. "Your Office protects them. How could they have been destroyed?"

The Enchanter returned the glare. "The Great Coven never imagined members of your guild deliberately throwing them into the volcano."

"Just because the parchment or paper they were written on was burnt doesn't mean they don't still stand, since only one side wanted out. I thought you could recreate any contract still in force."

"We can, but it's difficult, and we've had to postpone many things since the war. And imagine the nobility's reactions if we started pulling charters from thin air full of stipulations they find repugnant."

"They wouldn't believe us. That's why we need to find at least one."

"Please," Irene said, "if it—"

The Enchanter said, "I agree. I'm sure some still exist, and finding one intact would be ideal. I simply am not confident you'll find that one at the White Duke's manor in Abertee."

"It's his family's oldest manor. The other districts they control were added to their domain one at a time, over the centuries."

"If the charter is still intact—and we don't know that it is—it could be anywhere in the country by now."

Master Duncan said, "You sure won't find it by yelling at each other. Get somebody to look."

The Fire Warlock grinned. "Too bad I can't bring you along to the Fire Guild Council meetings to keep us on track. I'll get Sven to take this on, but I want somebody from the Air Guild, too. Sven could do it by himself, given the time, but we don't have the time. This is important enough I don't want him overlooking something in a rush, and the Air Guild's ways of searching are different from the Fire Guild's. With talent from both guilds, we're more likely to find whatever there is to be found."

The Enchanter said, "I'm of two minds about this. If it is so important, I would rather assign a member of the Air Guild Council."

Irene said, "No, please, this task—"

"Perhaps Enchantress Winifred…"

Winifred? Irene's nostrils flared. *Surely not.*

The Fire Warlock said, "No. Definitely not. She'd draw too much attention. I don't want the duke's family getting wind of the charter hunt, and finding it before we do. Besides, she'd be bored silly, and waste time flirting and driving Sven to distraction. If we can do it with someone less visible, we should, and from what Ollie said…"

Danger be damned. Irene said, "The school staff are unlikely to even notice my absence."

The Fire Warlock stood. "Good. Come on, Irene, let's go talk to Master Sven."

The Enchanter said, "If not Winifred, then perhaps Enchantress Carla, but she has been ill…"

The Fire Warlock squinted at Irene. She threw up her hands. "You want someone invisible?"

He scrubbed a hand over his face. "Look," he said, through clenched teeth. "You keep telling me the Air Guild's top ranks are overworked. Irene's a level three, and if she's not working on contracts or treaties…"

"Oh…fine," the Air Enchanter said. "You may have Irene's help in this endeavour. Just let me have a moment alone with her."

The Fire Warlock and Master Duncan stepped out onto the portico. Irene hid her fists in her pockets.

The Enchanter began trimming a new quill. "I am uneasy about this venture, but while I have doubts about Master Sven's competence as a mage, he should be capable of finding the evidence the Archers need without your help. If the charter is there, which I also doubt, no magical talent would be needed to flip through a stack of documents and find it. So you may go, but if you spend too much time in bed with your headaches, I'll find someone else to replace you. I will not let you embarrass the Air Guild. Good day."

Lucinda was groggy from her nap and running late. The witch in Gastòn's Fire Guildhall was not helping.

"You could hire a carriage," she said. "But it's at least a twenty-minute drive to the earl's palace. Maybe more."

"No good. I'll jump through the fire, if I can remember what the place looks like." She had been there twice, but had seen so many grand houses in the past three years they blended into one another. All she was sure of in the earl's home was the kitchen.

She could not have picked a worse spot. Women screamed, men yelled, crockery smashed. Fleeing servants knocked over a table and spilled food across the floor.

The din drowned her apologies. Within seconds the only other soul left in the kitchen was a scullery maid hiding behind a bench.

Lucinda peeked under the bench. "I'm sorry. I'm here for tea. Could you please show me the way?"

She still hadn't coaxed the maid out of hiding when Claire flew into the kitchen.

"Lucinda! I'm so glad… What in heaven's name…?" She gazed at the mess with wide eyes.

"My fault. I scared your servants."

Claire's hands flew to her face. "Oh, this is awful. The household was already on edge, and all that food, and the dishes, and, oh…" She sobbed.

Lucinda's face burned. She snatched up broken crockery and scattered cutlery while explaining. Claire dropped her hands and laughed. She sat on a stool Lucinda had just righted and buried her face in a frilly excuse for a handkerchief, laughing while tears rolled down her cheeks. The scullery maid gaped at her mistress around the end of the bench.

"Stop it, Lucinda," Claire gasped. "The servants will clean up. Oh, dear, I shouldn't laugh at you. Them. Whoever." She stifled another peal in her handkerchief.

She led Lucinda to a drawing room where the earl was waiting. He greeted her politely, looking sideways at his giggling wife. Lucinda explained about the disaster in the kitchen, but he cut her off in mid-flow.

"No matter. We are grateful you could come on such short notice." He stammered slightly and his hands trembled.

They sat at a table laden with a silver tea service and the earl sent the servants away. Claire calmed enough to chat about the children for a few minutes, long enough for Lucinda's face to cool, but neither host nor hostess touched the teapot or plates. The Earl rose and went to the door, and then, apparently satisfied that no one loitered outside, closed and locked it.

Lucinda abandoned a description of her son's latest accomplishment, and stared.

Claire said, "I'm sorry about the secrecy, Lucinda, but our other guest insisted."

"Your other guest?"

"Richard's aunt."

"Richard's aunt?"

"Someday, Lucinda, you really should study Frankland's noble families."

The earl picked up the tea service. "If you please, madam, we will withdraw to the next room."

"Thanks a lot," Lucinda muttered at Claire, and followed the earl.

Green velvet drapes, pulled almost closed, let in little light. A woman in a cloud of lace stood by the window, her hands bunching the material to hide her from the street. The earl coughed. The woman released the fabric and turned away from the window. Lucinda gasped, and curtsied.

"Thank you, Madam Locksmith, for coming. As one mother to another, I beg you for your help," Queen Marguerite said, "with my son."

Warning Signs

The painting on the wall opposite Irene in the Fire Warlock's study was a glowing masterpiece worthy of closer inspection, but the man seated underneath outshone it. While the Fire Warlock explained about the ledgers, and the search he wanted conducted, Sven Matheson drew her eyes. A decade ago other young women in Oxford had vied for his favour, but Oliver had so captivated Irene an elephant dancing across campus would not have drawn her notice. That younger Sven had left her with an impression of a gangling youth with a weak chin, ill-fitting, cheap clothing, and an aversion to giggling girls.

Enchantress Winifred's breathless admiration had implied his looks had improved, but Irene had not expected this Adonis. He had put on muscle, he carried himself with grace and confidence, and his bespoke suit complemented his fair looks. The thick, neat beard gave his face a different, stronger shape. No wonder Winifred had raved. Whichever of his admirers had claimed him was a lucky woman.

The Fire Warlock said, "Before we left the duke's, I threw spells on the whole place to keep any papers from getting burnt up or otherwise damaged."

Sven said, "I see. The duke may have agreed to the search, but you're expecting resistance from the rest of the family."

Irene tore her eyes away from Sven and focused on the Fire Warlock.

He said, "Right. They want revenge on the Archers, and they won't like this search. If they figure out you're searching for the charter—a charter, mind you, that some ancestor hid, or tried to destroy—they'll like that even less. What do you know about them?"

Sven shrugged. "Only the basics. Charters are Air Guild territory."

"I meant the Richardsons."

"Who?"

Irene said, "The White Duke and his family."

The Fire Warlock said, "Go on. You may know as much about them as I do."

"Only by reputation, and it's an unsavoury one. The duchess, her brother the Red Duke, and her two sons are all minor Air Guild talents. The school staff breathed a collective sigh of relief when the older son graduated. He and his brother are among the most self-centred, ill-mannered wretches we've ever been burdened with. They tormented the staff as well as the other students."

Sven said, "I'm not surprised. Enforcing discipline among the students from the noble ranks is a problem at all the guild schools."

The Fire Warlock grinned. "I'd loan you Warlock Flint for a few weeks, but he'd scare everybody at the school, including the teachers."

She said, "Don't underestimate the Richardsons. If they can't destroy the records, they'll have no qualms about using intimidation or outright violence to prevent a search."

"Yeah." He tugged at his beard, and glanced at her sideways. "That's why I'm asking Sven to take this on, and I wanted to talk to both of you out of Paul's hearing. There's some risk involved, but you already figured that out. Irene, if you back out, I won't hold it against you."

Kind of him not to say *"Irene, you coward!"* Under normal circumstances she would never go anywhere near the Richardsons, but an assistant to a flame mage ought not be in serious danger. She said, "What's your opinion, Master Sven?"

"I am in the Fire Guild's service. I can't refuse the assignment." He added, with a smile, "Not that I'm worried. What can minor air wizards do against a level four flame mage?"

"Burst your eardrums with noise, or throw things on the wind."

He shrugged. "I can maintain shields against both for hours. The shield against flying objects will stop anything short of an arrow, and only a level five could raise a wind that hard."

Master Duncan said, "What about swords?"

"I can block a sword, but would rather burn the man before he comes close enough to swing at me."

"Sven can put up a good fight," the Fire Warlock said. "He blasts me regularly when we practice together. He's got enough magic to take care of himself, and Irene, too."

"He'll have to," Irene said. "My talent is useless when it comes to violence." The Air Enchanter had expressed doubts about Sven's competence, but she had reason to distrust the Enchanter's judgment. Oliver had respected Sven, and if the Fire Warlock said he was capable, why would an air witch argue otherwise?

Master Duncan said, "Why didn't you want the enchanter to hear this?"

The big wizard took a deep breath and blew out through his moustache. "There are more nobles in the Air Guild than in the other guilds put together. Paul acts like it's one big happy family, and says I exaggerate the dangers of training those idiots to use their magic…"

Irene said, "He doesn't know the half of what happens in his own guild. Go on."

"He keeps reminding me you're short-staffed, and how many air wizards died during the war protecting Frankish ships. He's still pissed about the Air Guild taking the brunt of it when the Fire Guild's supposed to be in charge of Frankland's defences. Since he lost Ollie, I can't really blame him."

"No? If he had taken Warlock Quicksilver's warnings to heart, we wouldn't have lost so many." After a short silence while the three men contemplated her, she said, "If he did understand the danger involved, you think he would refuse the Air Guild's help? And you're tired of us airheads shirking our responsibilities?"

The Fire Warlock looked disconcerted. "Since you put it that way, yeah."

The painting above Sven's head drew her attention. "Forgive my faux pas; it's bad form to criticise one's own guild."

"That never stops us. I'd been hoping you'd agreed with Ollie. I know he didn't see eye to eye with his old man about what your responsibilities are."

Eye to eye? The disagreements had been so serious father and son had not spoken during last the five years of Oliver's life.

She said, "You do remember, don't you, that a brave air witch is as rare as a fire witch wearing pearls?"

"So I've heard, but look, Irene, the duke's already lost one run-in with the Frost Maiden. He won't give you trouble. The guards answer to him, not to his son, and nobody in his right mind pisses off a flame mage. The situation could blow up, but it doesn't seem likely. I expect you'll spend a few weeks rummaging through boxes of papers and crawling through attics, and the worst that's likely to happen is you'll get dust up your nose and cobwebs in your hair."

A lifetime's experience with seers made his attempt at reassurance no more satisfying than Sven's. It didn't matter. An opportunity this good might never come again, and life in Airvale was killing her, albeit silently and slowly. She took a deep breath, and exhaled. "Let me help."

Queen Marguerite wanted a warlock's help with her son? Lucinda gaped, and the queen flushed.

"Please, sit," she said, "and I'll explain."

Lucinda perched on the edge of the sofa, putting a hard rein on her impulse to bombard the queen with questions. The earl set down the tea service and left, closing the door behind him, leaving the two women alone.

The queen said, "You'll understand my father's experiences in his youth led him to develop strong opinions about governance."

Lucinda searched her memory for a name, a title. No luck. "Your Majesty, I don't remember what happened to him. Could you remind me?"

"Of course. I shouldn't have presumed you would know Prince Lorenz's full life story. He came to Frankland at the age of fifteen, after an insurrection drove his family from their kingdom. The shocking ingratitude of the rabble to their rulers made a lasting impression on him. He didn't want that bloody uprising repeated in his adopted country."

Lucinda had her wits about her again. "Yes, Warlock Quicksilver said your father…" Calling him one of the few noblemen in Frankland with more sense than God gave a squirrel might be impolitic. "He said he corresponded with your father for many years, and respected his opinions, although they didn't agree."

The queen smiled. "Some of their exchanges did grow rather heated. They agreed on little, other than each had the best interests of Frankland at heart, and both believed most of the nobility are imbeciles."

Lucinda choked on her scone.

The queen's smile broadened, then withered. "My father disagreed with the king as much as he disagreed with the Fire Warlock. In his last years he became convinced we would not avoid a disastrous civil war. And that is why I am here, today, asking for your help."

She stared down at the table, lost for a moment in her own thoughts. The delicate china seemed out of place under her sombre gaze.

"You see," she said, "King Stephen has no interest in children. He turned the responsibility for our son's education over to my father, who undertook the task with a good will. My father believed that leaving Prince Brendan in the hands of the other nobles and staff in the royal household would create a self-indulgent, spoiled brat, and he was determined to counteract their influence. He intended to produce a true nobleman, in every sense of the word."

The confident queen crumbled. "But now my father is dead." She played with a ring, twisting it around and around on her finger. "On his deathbed he exacted a promise from me I was reluctant to give, and now wish I could repudiate." She held out her hands to Lucinda as if pleading. "Please, you must understand."

Shaking her and saying "*Get to the point!*" would do no good. Lucinda laced her fingers together tight enough to hurt, and waited.

The queen said, "I don't like the position he put me in. If Stephen finds out, he will be angry. Very angry. I have been making excuses to myself for not doing this before now. But it wasn't until the trial…" Her hands clenched convulsively, then sprang apart. She lifted her teacup, splashing tea into the saucer, then grasped the cup with both hands. The shaking subsided to a mild quiver, but her long, elegant fingers were as rigid as claws. "The trial convinced me I must keep my promise. And so, I am asking for your help, Warlock Locksmith."

"What do you want from me? What did you promise Prince Lorenz?"

The queen shrank back, like a child expecting a reprimand. In a voice so quiet Lucinda had to strain to hear her, she said, "That I would engage the Fire Warlock Emeritus in training my son to be the next king."

The Newest Supplicant

"Yes, Your Majesty," Lucinda said, "King Stephen will be angry. Oh, dear."

Training a prince! What an opportunity for the Fire Guild, but what a pity for the prince. No wonder he had sported a look of hurt resignation all the way through the challenges. To have his mother send him to serve a man his father considered a mortal enemy must be both painful and bewildering at such a young age.

What a pity for Queen Marguerite, too. Where had she found the backbone to defy the king? A chill finger walked down Lucinda's spine. What revenge would he take?

She said, "I'm sure my husband will help with the prince's education in every way he can, but isn't sending Prince Brendan to Blazes a bit drastic?"

The queen's brow furrowed. "Good heavens, yes. They must meet here, and that will be risky enough."

"Your Majesty, where is Prince Brendan?"

"In the palace, having tea with his tutor, I presume, as he usually does at this time."

"His tutor must be racing around the palace, trying to find his errant charge. Less than an hour ago, the prince was in the Fortress, waiting for the Fire Warlock."

The teacup smashed on the table, splashing tea on the queen's skirt. She buried her face in her hands, and rocked in her seat. "Oh, dear God, no. This is dreadful. What has he done?"

"He walked the Fire Guild's challenge path."

"Why? In heaven's name, why?"

"I don't know. I'd hoped you could tell me."

She peered at Lucinda over her fingers. "You're a warlock. You can find out."

"No, ma'am, not unless he wants to tell me. A supplicant's quest is a secret between him and the Fire Warlock, unless the supplicant says otherwise."

She lowered her hands, revealing features drained of all colour. "What will I do? When Stephen finds out he will blame me. Oh! The Fire Warlock doesn't have to accept him. He could send him home."

"Don't hold your breath. If his quest is reasonable, the Fire Office won't let the Fire Warlock reject him. And even if he did… The prince has been gone most of the day. Won't there be questions raised about where he's been?"

The queen nodded. Her hands twisted together in frantic motion and she shivered. "What will I do?"

Lucinda grasped her hands and warmed them. "Your Majesty, how did you get here without anyone knowing?"

"My earth witch cut a tunnel from my chambers."

"Is it a private tunnel? Not connected to any of the others?"

"Yes. She said it wouldn't be safe, otherwise. I trust her. She's standing guard, telling everyone I'm too ill for visitors."

"Good. Go home, and stay in your room. Don't come out until tomorrow. I'll send word that Prince Brendan is in the Fortress. Someone should have done that already." Someone, namely René, would catch some heat for that oversight. "Don't let on that you already knew, and stay out of sight until the king's had some time to recover. Blame it all on your father, since he's dead and the king can't do anything to him. Pretend you don't know what he taught your son. I hope that helps."

"Yes. Yes, it will. Thank you," she whispered. "Promise me you'll look after him while he's there."

"Yes, ma'am, I promise. And you've kept your promise to your father; the responsibility is our own shoulders now. If there's anything else I can do for you, send messages through the earl."

"Thank you."

Lucinda released the queen's hands and she fled.

Duncan stepped into the tunnel from the Warren to Crossroads, and stood hunched over in the dark, with the walls and ceiling closing in to squeeze the breath out of him.

That was no good. Letting the tunnels scare him was a good way to get panicked, and if he panicked he really could get lost. He retraced the path Hazel had shown him. Two rights, past three doors, a left, and he stepped into the healers' guildhall in Crossroads. He gave the door a hard stare, then went looking for Hazel and Granny Mildred.

Granny Mildred scowled. "You think the tunnels were making you lost? That's silly, lad. It's easy to get lost on your own."

"That's what the earth father said, too, but he's wrong. I don't get lost."

Hazel looked up from her cooking. "Which earth father?"

Duncan leaned closer and got a nose-full of frying sausages and onions. "Mmmm." She yanked the pan away before he drooled in it. "The jug-eared middle-aged one."

Mildred said, "Father Martin. He knows his stuff. If he said you were lost, it's a pretty good bet you were lost, sonny."

Hazel frowned. "Father Martin is an excellent healer, but he's not an authority on everything. Duncan's telling the truth when he says he doesn't get lost."

Duncan mouthed a kiss. She smiled.

Mildred said, "Oh, sure, I can believe that's what he thinks. But thinking something's so and having it be so aren't always the same thing."

"I got lost once," he said, "when I was a wee lad. Scared the dickens out of me. I swore then I'd never get lost again, and I haven't in the twenty-odd years since. Until today. Today I got lost three times, with directions even an aristo could have followed. It doesn't make sense. Plenty of times I've been confused about just where I was, or which direction I was headed, but that's not the same as lost. I've always made sure I could get back to where I'd been. Whenever I've gotten confused, I'd back up to where I'd known where I was, and start off again."

"Wow," Hazel's eyes were round. "I could use that talent."

He waved a hand. "That's not magic. Just using my head."

"But mental models are the basis for all magic."

"Eh?"

"You have more talent than you think, but never mind. Tell us more about what happened in the tunnels."

"Today I couldn't back up. I'd turn a corner and know it wasn't right, but the tunnel behind wasn't the same one I'd come from. It's not completely dark—I could see that the doors and gaps for the other tunnels weren't in the same places. And I'd had my hands on the walls. I felt different kinds of rock. I swear, somebody or something was using magic to get me lost."

Mildred opened her mouth, then shut it without saying anything.

Hazel said, "We can test it out. You start for the Warren by yourself, and I'll come along behind a minute or two later. With a trail that fresh I'll have no problem finding you."

"Let's do that, then. Tomorrow." Duncan rubbed his aching neck. "If I went in there again today I'd have to crawl on my hands and knees."

Beorn's voice filled Lucinda's head, demanding to see her, now. He met her on the balcony outside his study, closing the door behind him.

"It's about that supplicant," he said. "I need your help, and Jean's, with him."

"You'll tell me what he wants?"

"No, he'll tell you himself—as soon as Jean gets here."

"Dragging out the suspense, are you?"

"Sure thing. Patience is a virtue. Develop some."

"This is a warlock talking? You have less than I have. But while we're waiting, let me tell you about our latest problem."

He leaned against the wall and yawned. "We already have more than I can handle. Go ahead."

Lucinda's description of her tête-à-tête with the queen brought him back upright, wide awake. "She's right to be scared. Stephen will look for a scapegoat, and she's the prime target. It's bad news for us, too. She has more sense than the rest of his advisors put together, and if he stops listening to her…"

They waited in silence until Jean arrived. Lucinda had had a nap; her husband had not. There were bags under his eyes and no bounce in his step, but he managed a smile. "What an unusual state of affairs, the fearsome and omnipotent Fire Warlock, locked out of his own study."

Beorn snorted and pushed the door open. "Our newest supplicant's in there. I need your help with him."

Lucinda took Jean's arm, and pulled when he stopped square in the doorway. Beorn gave him a shove, and he walked forward like an automaton as the prince rose to face them. Lucinda curtsied; Jean started and bowed.

Beorn said, "I told His Highness you two would help with his quest, so he's agreed to share it with you. In fact…" He clapped a hand on Jean's shoulder. "You'll do most of it."

Without taking his eyes off the pale and rigid boy, Jean said, "Most of what?"

Beorn nodded at the prince. "Go ahead, Your Highness. Tell him."

The boy flicked a glance at Beorn and one at Lucinda, then went back to staring at Jean. "Your Wisdom, I want to learn how to be a better…" He flushed. "I mean, I don't want a civil war. I want to learn how to be a good king."

Be Careful What You Wish For

The prince's flush deepened under Jean's stare. Jean echoed, "You want to learn how to be a good king?"

Lucinda frowned at Beorn. "You could have warned him. Of course we'll help." She pushed Jean into a chair. He sank into it with a deep sigh. The prince bridled.

She said, "What's the matter?"

He said, "No one should sit ahead of royalty."

"Oh. Well, I'm sure you're tired, too. Sit." The affronted prince remained standing. "Was walking the challenge path your idea, Your Highness? Or your grandfather's suggestion?"

"Grandfather said the hardest task I would have as king would be making courtiers tell me news I had to hear but they knew would upset me. I know he's right. Mother and Father have been arguing ever since the trial, and she goes to her room and cries, but no one will tell me what about. Grandfather said I should listen to the Fire Warlock and the Warlock Emeritus. He said I didn't have to take your advice, but I had to at least listen, because you'd enjoy telling me facts I didn't want to hear."

Beorn snorted. "'Enjoy' is not the word I'd use, but never mind. Go on."

"It was my idea to walk the challenge path, because I thought Father would forbid it if I asked to talk to you."

"Indeed so," Jean said. He had recovered from his shock, but was regarding the prince with some perplexity. "Prince Lorenz was wise to teach you that lesson early. Your grandfather and I were…not friends, but neither were we enemies. We were sparring partners, perhaps, or opponents at a game with living chessmen. One only learns to fight well with a worthy adversary. I, too, shall miss him."

The boy looked startled, but the rigid set of his shoulders eased. He sank onto the sofa behind him. "Will you accept me as a supplicant, then, Your Wisdom?"

Jean's brow creased. "Of course. How could we not?"

Beorn said, "Sorry, I should have said that already. You passed all the challenges, and I approve of your quest, so you're staying. We do have a big question, though, about what to teach you, and how."

Lucinda said, "You two wizards can argue that tomorrow. Tonight, an early supper and bed would do us all good, so let's deal with practicalities. Do you know about the conditions?"

"Yes, ma'am. I must dress below my station, and spend the next year doing demeaning labour."

She gritted her teeth and gave Beorn a dark stare.

He stroked his moustache, hiding a smile. "He can work with the other boys managing the food stores."

"That's reasonable." She congratulated herself on not letting exasperation creep into her voice. "It's hard work, but vital to the Fortress's functioning, and no honest work is demeaning. Warlock Snorri did his year's service there, and it's on a par with the cooking I did during mine."

The prince's eyes grew round. "Warlocks doing a year's service? Why? You didn't have to."

"We didn't know we were warlocks. Snorri was too young, and my talent was hidden. We both walked the challenge path, and I enjoyed working in the kitchen with Mrs Cole, the housemother."

Beorn winked at her from behind the staring boy.

Jean said, "Another condition is that no supplicant may have special privileges or use a title. During your service, you will not be called Prince Brendan or Your Highness. Addressing you by your second name, Alexander, will be more appropriate."

"Why? To punish me for being born royal?"

The two men locked eyes for a moment, then Beorn said, "No, it's the other way around. It's to stop us from punishing you for being royal. Otherwise, we'd overload you with as-you-call-it demeaning work to balance out your privileges. If you don't stick out over the other supplicants I'm less likely to mistreat you."

The boy gawked at him.

Jean said, "It is also for your own protection from the commoners. Given the current mood in the country, you will be safer if your special status draws no attention, as the usual shields the Office provides to members of the royal family are in abeyance during your year of service."

The prince's head jerked up. "I'm not shielded?"

"No, not since you entered the park with the maze."

The last vestiges of colour drained from the boy's face. "You mean...the lion...could have..."

Lucinda pushed him prone. "Lie down. We don't want you to faint."

"I'm not a coward. I'm not!"

Jean said, "We never thought you were."

The boy gave him a blank look. "You didn't?" He attempted to sit up, but Lucinda held him down with a hand on his chest.

"Lie there," she said. "You've had a shock and need time to recover. Anyway, you weren't in serious danger. The lion's been charmed not to hurt anyone."

Beorn coughed. "Uh, Lucinda, that's not quite so. He's well fed, and he's been charmed to not bite anybody, but he's still young and frisky. Likes to play. If he'd decided Prince Bren—uh, Alexander—was a new toy, he could have mauled him pretty bad."

"What? Since when?"

He shrugged. "Since pretty much forever, I guess. Why do you think the Keeper of the Challenge Path always meets supplicants at the gate? We keep an eye on Fluffy, but he's fast, and things could get out of hand."

She screeched, "Fluffy? You named that monster Fluffy?"

He gestured. "'Cause of the mane, you know."

Lucinda saw red, and not just the wizard's own mane.

Jean laid a restraining hand on her arm. "Lucinda, my dear."

She shook him off, and yelled at Beorn, "You have as much hair as that lion does. How would you like it if I called you Fluffy?"

His eyes lit. "Would you? I'm mighty tired of scaring people. It'd be nice to know somebody sees I have a soft side."

"Soft side, my foot. Your soft spot is in your head, if you think a lion is a good pet."

"Children..." The reprimand in Jean's voice was now unmistakable. She crossed her arms and glowered at the grinning Fire Warlock.

Alexander's eyes were as big as saucers. Lucinda shuddered. The rash promise she had made his mother had become monstrously harder to keep.

Jean said, "We have digressed, but I would understand why this revelation upsets you, my dear. A test of bravery must of necessity involve danger. The magic would not work without it. I assumed you understood that."

"I do, but…I made it through that challenge, but it…he…that beast terrified me. It would have given me nightmares if you hadn't assured me it was harmless."

Jean's brows drew together. "I beg your pardon, my dear, but I would never have said so."

"But… Oh, I must have said he'd been charmed not to eat people, and you didn't contradict me. You didn't say he'd been charmed not to hurt them. I believed what I wanted to believe."

Beorn said, "I won't tell anybody you're afraid of Fluffy. The guards are convinced, to a man, that you and Sorceress Lorraine are the bravest women in Frankland. As brave as Quicksilver and Master Duncan. I'd hate to disillusion them."

"But that's just it. That lion was something scary I didn't have to be brave about. I'm sick and tired of being brave. Bravery makes you do things that hurt. Bravery stinks."

Jean stroked her cheek. "There is little you now need fear on your own account, my love. Neither drowning nor fire less than a lightning bolt will harm you. Should you encounter the lion again, you may jump through the fire and away."

"Or yell at him," Beorn said. "Like you yelled at Sven and me in the Crystal Palace. He'll scramble for cover with his ears laid flat and his fur bristling. I guarantee it."

"We would have to acquire a new lion," Jean said. "Our friend's pet would no longer be fit for the position after such trauma."

She laughed, and dabbed at trickling tears. "How reassuring. I mean, to know I can appear brave by terrifying everyone around me even more. How uncivilised." She stood. "It's time for supper."

"Wait," the prince said. "I don't understand. Why do the guards think you're brave? What did you do?"

Beorn roared, "What do you mean, what did she do? Where've you been for the last month?"

The boy flinched, but thrust out his chin. "You've no right to talk to me like that. I've been stuck like a baby in the nursery wing in the palace, wondering what's happening, but the adults ignore me. I know people aren't telling me things. That's why I'm here. Stop yelling and tell me."

Beorn mumbled, "Sorry. Didn't anybody tell you she unlocked the Water Office so it could be rebuilt?"

The prince flicked a puzzled glance at Lucinda. "Yes, but…"

Jean's eyes were as hard as stone, his lips a thin line. "But they told you she did so for the warlocks' pleasure."

"I know it wasn't just that, but…"

Beorn said, "They didn't tell you, did they, that it almost killed her and Quicksilver and Sorceress Lorraine. Or that, going in, none of them believed they would live through it."

The boy's eyes seemed about to pop out of their sockets. He swallowed and shook his head.

Jean said, "We did so for the same reason you came here today. None of us wants to see our homeland reduced to smoke and ashes."

The Rehsavvys' house lay dark and quiet. Snores, and the soft creaking of beds as sleepers shifted positions, drifted from the servants' quarters. René lay on his stomach with his cheek on the edge of the bed and one arm dangling. In the next bedroom, the prince lay on his back with a firm grip on the counterpane. He had been touchingly grateful for Lucinda's company at bedtime, and for the story she told about Charlemagne.

Across the hall, she lay with her head against Jean's shoulder and cursed her aching right arm, still not quite full length. Twenty-three was too old for growing pains.

The only other person still awake was her husband, staring at the dark canopy over their heads.

Jean?

Yes, love?

Will he—Alexander—be safe if we sleep?

This house, with spells layered one on the other by generations of accomplished warlocks, could withstand anything short of an army or a riot, and we would have fair warning before either catastrophe. He is safer here than in the royal palace.

Then he's not in danger, even without the shields?

Neither here nor in the Fortress, but he will be exposed to danger on the path to the

Fortress gates, or elsewhere outside the Fortress.

Why? Or why him any more than any supplicant? With a lock hiding his purple flame, why would anybody notice him?

Because no magic spell will protect him from his own behaviour. He is a prince, and he will act like one. Do not delude yourself that he will not be noticed, or that speculation will not run rampant.

Jean?

Yes?

You've warned me about making rash promises…

Yes?

I made one today.

Tell me.

I promised the queen I would look after her son while he's here.

"Ah." He let out the word on a long sigh, and kissed Lucinda's forehead. *That was impetuous, love, but not unwise. You will not bear this burden alone. Even without your promise, you and I, and sometimes René, must keep watch over him. We cannot afford to lose him.*

If the path is dangerous, should we move into the Fortress? The thought dismayed her. As reassuring as the Fortress was, the house was hers, and they had only recently settled in after being on the move for two years.

No. That would draw attention, as surely as if we stood in the guildhall and shouted the news. We may have to reconsider, but for now we will remain here. We must be vigilant, my dear, but I am not overly worried about his safety.

Oh? Then why can't you sleep?

He was silent for so long she thought he might not answer. *So many times, I have wished to train a prince while he is still at an impressionable age. As the old adage goes, be careful what you wish for, for you will surely get it. Here we are with a prince in our house, and the task ahead of us is daunting, to say the least. You may think it odd I am more nervous about teaching a mere boy than I was in facing the Empire's wizards, but I am. The outcome is less certain, and more significant.*

Can we convince him to swear the Great Oath?

His grip on her shoulders tightened. *We must try. I cannot escape the conviction we are approaching a confrontation between Beorn and King Stephen that will be disastrous for both men. If we do not convince Alexander to take the oath, he, like his father, will view the next Fire Warlock as his mortal enemy.*

Heroes, One and All

"As to your assignment…" Jean paused and frowned at his coffee cup. The prince scanned the table. Lucinda handed him the plate of sausage and bacon, and he helped himself without looking at her.

René scowled. She handed him the plate next and he said, a bit too loudly, "Thanks, Lucinda."

The prince did a double take, and flushed. "Thank you, Madam Locksmith," he said, "for handing me the sausages."

"You're welcome. And here in my home, I'd prefer you call me Mrs Rehsavvy."

"I beg your pardon?"

She sighed. The poor boy would have more shocks before the day was over. "Madam Locksmith is rather a mouthful, don't you agree?"

He looked doubtful, but said, "Yes, ma'am. I'll try to remember."

And she must remember to call him Alexander. Even thinking of him as the prince would be to risk marking him out as special. But he was special; how could she ever forget that, after the promise she had made his mother? The twin horns of the dilemma pressing against her temples made her head throb.

Jean continued as if there'd been no interruption. "You will be working with three other supplicants, all several years older, managing the Fortress's food stores. The young man currently in charge will be leaving within a month when he completes his year of service."

Alexander said, "Then I will take charge when he leaves."

Jean frowned. "Certainly not. Whatever gave you that idea?"

Alexander returned the frown. "I'm a born leader. I should be in charge."

"You will find, if you study the lives of illustrious kings, that even the ones with natural authority needed training in leadership roles. Their talents did not blossom overnight."

"Then I should be in charge, to get that training."

"Perhaps, but you have had and will have many opportunities to command; few indeed could deny them to you. The boy next in line has had none. He has been waiting six months for this opportunity, and will not achieve what he desires if it is denied him. It would not be fair to him or his fellow supplicants for you to skip ahead of them."

Alexander scowled at Jean, the sausage lying forgotten on his plate. "But if he hasn't had any training, he'll give bad orders. What am I supposed to do if he gives an order I don't agree with?"

Jean's eyes danced. "Ah, a quandary. Tell me what you expect of a subordinate when you issue a bad order."

Alexander flushed. "I don't give bad orders."

René snickered.

Alexander's flush deepened. "Except for Mother and Grandfather, no one has ever contradicted…"

After a moment's silence, Jean said, "If your subordinates are too intimidated to voice objections, you must have other ways of recognising when you have erred. Thank you, you have further convinced me this assignment is appropriate. You will be better able to recognise your subordinates' reactions to careless or harmful orders if you have had those same reactions yourself."

Alexander stabbed his sausage and stuffed too large a portion in his mouth. He chewed in silence, his glaring eyes never wavering from Jean's face.

Lucinda's day had gotten off to a bad start. The nursemaid had given notice and walked out before Lucinda left her dressing room. Katie, her lady's maid, had accepted with good grace the news that she would have to care for little Eddie.

"Oh, *her*." Katie tossed her head and sniffed. "We're better off without her. You'll see, ma'am."

Downstairs, the kitchen had been empty and cold. The cook and scullery maid had not bothered giving notice. Lucinda didn't mind fixing breakfast; she did mind the disrespect. Matt, Jean's valet, helped. She grumbled that if he left without giving notice she would scorch his butt on his way out.

He grinned. "No, ma'am. I'm a real fire wizard. I wouldn't leave without telling you more than you want to hear about everything you're doing wrong."

After breakfast, Jean escorted Alexander to the Fortress to introduce him to the other supplicants. She watched them go. From her vantage point on the second floor balcony, she also observed several wizards on their way to the guildhall veering away and casting worried glances at the house from the far side of the street. A dog, ambling along, reached the corner of the house, yipped, turned, and sped away in the direction it had come. An examination of the protection spells on the house revealed a new and ludicrously powerful aversion spell, the most sophisticated she had so far encountered. She couldn't make out the terms.

"Thank you so much, Beorn," she muttered. "Will you help me replace the servants? No, I didn't think so."

A survey of the house showed Eddie and Katie in the nursery laughing over a game of peekaboo. Matt and Tom were in the kitchen arguing over which one had offended the nursemaid. In the dining room, René was eating toast and dribbling jam onto a textbook on aversion spells. The footman had disappeared. So had the cat. Across the street, Jean was regarding the house with a look of growing consternation.

Oh, God: Jean! Lucinda hurtled down the stairs and collided with René in the hall. The door opened as she reached for it, and Jean stepped in.

"Thank God," she said. "It didn't keep you out."

"Certainly not. I devised it. It is the spell I used to filter applicants for staff positions before we began our travels, and that I cast on our sleeping quarters every evening until Edward arrived." Lucinda and René exchanged blank looks. "Neither of you noticed?" Jean tut-tutted. "I thought I had trained you to always seek out spells in a new residence, but perhaps that was after I had to abandon its use when I could not find a wet nurse it accepted."

"What does it do?"

"Grossly oversimplified, it rejects anyone who, in a crisis, will value their own comfort over the good health of the state of Frankland—using my definition of good health, of course."

"Wow," René said. "That's…"

"Impressive? Thank you."

"Eddie," Lucinda said. "And Katie."

"Along with the Fire Eaters, latent heroes and heroines, all. May they never be called upon to demonstrate the truth of the spell's judgment."

"If it had rejected Eddie…"

"We would have awoken in the early hours to a screaming, inconsolable child, and I would have had unkind words with our friend Beorn. I may yet, over his slapdash spellcasting, and his failure to warn me he intended to use it." Jean smiled at her. "Relax, my dear. Edward will be a son to be proud of."

"That's reassuring. I think. But now…"

They trailed him down the hall. He said, "I have narrowed the focus so it will not frighten passers-by, but the exodus of half our staff will set tongues wagging."

"And all the people coming here to report problems…"

"Yes, we must deal with that complication immediately." Tom and Matt broke off their argument as the three warlocks filed into the kitchen. "Thomas, Matthias, my apologies, but with the reduction in staff we must reorder the household." Jean poured a cup of cold coffee and frowned at it. Steam rose. "Matthias, you will assume the footman's duties. Thomas, report to the guildhall and from there, assess the petitions for the Fire Warlock's aid. Summon a warlock only for the most urgent."

"Yes, sir," Tom said. "It's because of the prince, isn't it?"

Jean choked on his coffee.

Tom said, "See, I told you so. That's why His Wisdom got rid of the cook, too."

Matt said, "Give credit where it's due. Katie spotted His Little Highness first."

Lucinda took the cup from Jean so he wouldn't spill coffee while he coughed. "We should have realised they would place him; all three were in the counter-conspiracy and got a good look at him in Paris."

René said, "Other guild members were there, too."

Jean sighed. "And I was not overly worried about his safety. Well…" In short order they were gathered in the nursery, with Jean inducting everyone left in the house into a new conspiracy to protect Alexander's identity.

"But, sir," Katie said, "if we can't tell anyone who he is, what do we tell them?"

"That's easy," René said.

Jean regarded him with a raised eyebrow. "Oh? Enlighten us."

"Say he's a minor nobleman with a duke's self-conceit, and the Fire Warlock sent him to us to knock his head down to size."

"Tell me why a minor noble would elicit an aversion spell of such intensity."

"That's easy," Lucinda said. "Say Warlock Snorri was showing off and overdid it. Everyone in Blazes will believe that."

"Hey, I'm not sloppy."

"But you are conceited," Matt said. "His Wisdom sent you here to get your head knocked down to size. Didn't you know that?"

René glowered. Jean's eyes danced. "Odd you should object to claiming ownership of that spell. Everyone who felt its effects will be awed."

"Come on, Your Wisdom," Matt said, "you're not helping."

René opened his mouth, and closed it again without responding. Tom and Matt left for the guildhall and market with eyes alight and grins on their faces.

The mood among the three warlocks was not so light, as they retreated to Jean's study for further discussion. Jean's hair, still so short it felt to Lucinda's touch like fur, was growing in with a touch of grey at the temples. Always too thin, he was now skeletal, and the dark circles under his eyes had not faded.

"Jean," she said. "How can you take on anything else? Exhaustion is killing you."

"No, my dear, I will not let it. This is too important. I said we will re-order this household, and we will. We cannot let the merely urgent forever distract us from more important long-term goals. We will reserve time for Alexander, and to ensure adequate rest. We returned to our guild duties before recovering fully from our ordeal, and our zeal has hindered our performance. I must be of sound body before resuming René's training as a lightning wielder, and we cannot let that lapse for long."

"I've been getting tetchy about that," René said, "but Lucinda said not to bother you, what with all the troubles…"

"Thank you, but with the commoners appeased, the strife is diminishing. Beorn and I had already discussed shifting some responsibilities onto other shoulders. As for you, my dear, you will have duties here at home."

"That's obvious," she said, "With the cook and nursemaid gone…"

"And impossible to replace at this juncture. You, with Katie's help, must abandon your other duties and shoulder the roles of housemother and housekeeper. I trust you will not mind the change."

"Mind? You trust I won't mind?"

"Don't look so happy, Lucinda," René said, "or the spell will push you out of the house, too."

She snorted. Jean laughed. "No, my young friend, the spell does not operate in that fashion."

"Housemother," she said. "What should I do?"

"Follow your instincts and inclinations. Read to Alexander, or tell him stories. You have a large repertoire available from the centuries when kings and warlocks were still allies. Your choice last night was an excellent start. As for you, René, you will still answer to the Fire Warlock's demands, but will also assist in watching over Alexander whenever he is outside the Fortress or this house."

"Why do I have to be a babysitter?"

Jean said, "Bodyguard, my young friend, not babysitter. Alexander has already demonstrated he is more capable of rational thought and moral purpose than most adult noblemen. We cannot afford to lose him, and he must come to trust you. As future Fire Warlocks, it is more critical that he trust you and Lucinda than that he trust me."

To Impress a Mage

Sven was waiting for Irene on the hillside behind the Hall of the Winds. He brushed aside her apology, saying he hadn't wanted to keep her waiting, as if an outcast air witch's time mattered.

The door to the Earth Guild tunnel assaulted her eyes and ears with flaking green paint and creaking hinges. He held it open for her, saying, "Not used very often, I gather."

"Being underground terrifies most Air Guild talents, and those it doesn't frighten won't admit it for fear their colleagues will shun them."

"It didn't appear to bother you."

They were already threading through the maze of the Warren by then. "No one accuses me of being typical. And as for being shunned…" She shrugged.

"I inquired about permission for you to travel through the tunnels on your own, but the Earth Guild said no. Only the Earth and Fire Guilds may use the tunnels without escorts. That seems unnecessarily restrictive, since you would be on the Fire Warlock's orders, but…"

"An air witch would get lost on her own, but it is unfortunate you have to come out of your way."

"The Fortress and Airvale tunnels are side by side. Escorting you isn't an imposition. The imposition… I had hoped to resume teaching after the Water Office reforging, but the Fire Warlock has a habit of reorganising other people's lives for them. The members of your guild tend to have more ordered lives than members of mine. I hope this disruption won't be hard on you."

Irene and her daughters had danced last night in the girls' bedroom. "Oh, Mama," Gillian said, "you won't have to cry over those nasty essays anymore. Wishes do come true."

Oliver had tended towards grand gestures and hyperbole, but her talent for understatement had amused him. She smiled. "It will be a pleasant change."

The butler clasped his hands behind his back and gazed at a point in space several yards beyond Sven's left shoulder. "Her Grace, the Duchess, gave orders for you to be escorted by guards at all times."

Irene had expected insults to be thrown at her, but so blatant an affront to a mage left her gasping. Sven pivoted, looking down his nose at the four guards closing in on them. They studied him with a good deal more concern.

Sven turned back to the butler. "I don't fault you for carrying out your mistress's orders, but you will convey to her that she offends the Company of Mages, the Fire Guild, and the Air Guild; Mrs van Gelder is the Air Enchanter's daughter-in-law."

The guards' attention focused on Irene. She winced.

"Of course, sir," the wooden-faced butler said. "She also gave orders you are to have your dinner in the kitchen, with the servants."

Sven's eyes narrowed and his lip curled. Irene pre-empted his retort. "Good. We're underdressed for dinner with a duchess. Is there anything else?"

"No, madam. If you will follow me."

The guard's heavy tread echoed off the corridor walls. She kept her eyes fixed straight ahead. Glancing over her shoulder would have been an admission of intimidation.

The clerk's office, a dingy ground-floor cubbyhole, was jammed with a desk and two chairs. The guards followed them in.

Sven growled, "Back up, and stay in the corridor. You have to give us enough room to work."

The sergeant held his ground. "Her Grace don't want you walking off with any papers. She said we have to have two guards watching each of you while you're here. That means we've got to get in here where we can see you."

Sven leaned down, nose to nose with the guard. "I am a flame mage. Only warlocks outrank me. Pick whom you would rather argue with, Her Grace or me."

Sweat beaded the guard's lip but he didn't move. "You, sir."

"You're joking."

"No, sir."

Five minutes later, they were arranged to Sven's satisfaction. One guard, squeezed between boxwoods outside, looked in over the shoulders of the guard sitting on the sill of the open window. The sergeant sat in the doorway with the fourth guard in the corridor behind him. Irene was trapped between the desk in front, shelves behind, Sven on her right, and the guard in the window on her left. His knees were wedged against the left arm of her chair. Maybe there was a benefit to being a failure as an air witch. Most Air Guild talents would have gone berserk in such tight quarters.

The clerk, who introduced himself as Andrew Henderson, was the only one with room to move. "The most recent ledgers recording rents and taxes are in the shelves behind you, ma'am. The oldest ones are on the top shelves by the door. Oops! Sorry, sir."—He'd stepped on Sven's foot—"We also have receipts paid for the upkeep of the various properties, and other correspondence. Of course, these are the most recent records. The older ones, that'll be most helpful, are locked in the muniments room, and Her Grace won't let you in until you've seen everything here."

The sergeant interrupted. "Yup, that's what she told us, too. You have to do your magic on each of them books in here before we let you in there."

Mr Henderson sighed. "I suppose she imagines you'll give up before long. Where do you want to start?"

Sven looked at Irene. "With the newest ones and work backwards?"

"Sounds reasonable," she said.

The clerk reached behind Irene, pulled out a ledger, and opened it to a bookmarked page. "This is the section for Nettleton. The Archers are here."

To Irene's eyes, the clerk's fine, elegant hand was a pleasant change after endless pages of childish scrawls. Sven opened the book at the front, thumbing through the pages. "I want to examine this one page by page for anything else pertinent. Stop me if I go too fast."

"This is fine. Go on."

The clerk and the guards watched with avid curiosity. When he finished, Sven asked, "Is there anything else you need?"

"No."

He handed the ledger back to the clerk. "We're done with this one. Next, please. The rest will go faster."

The clerk looked surprised. "What…" He stopped with a glance at the guards and shrugged. He reshelved the book and took down the next.

The sergeant, however, said, "Wait a minute. Ain't you going to work some magic on 'em?"

Sven and Irene exchanged glances. Together, they said, "We did."

Her fingers flipped pages in the next ledger faster than Sven had done, but slow enough to avoid missing a page. Summoning a breeze to fan them would have been faster, but she needed her limited power for inspecting the text. The prospect of exhausting her magic troubled her more than the guards did. Failure on this search would see her back in Airvale, opportunity lost.

She pushed the second ledger towards Sven. He paged through that one while she scanned the next two. She stifled the urge to ask in front of the guards how his magic worked. Her mind should be on her task, not his.

They worked steadily all morning. Her pace through the ledgers felt like sap rising, but at first the stack of scanned books rose, waiting for Sven to take his turn. Sometime in late morning, the stack stopped growing. Sven took the next book, held it in his hands with his eyes closed while she scanned another ledger, then handed it to the clerk without opening it.

He caught her watching him, mouthed 'Later', and took the next from the stack.

By dinnertime the stack was down to one ledger. She rubbed her temples. Why had she, a level three nobody, imagined she could impress a mage?

Mr Henderson led Sven and Irene to an empty spot at the end of the long table in the kitchen. The rest of the duke's staff gave them a wide berth.

"They aren't unfriendly," the clerk said. "They're just scared to be seen talking to you. They know Her Grace will find out."

"Why her," Sven asked, "and not the duke?"

The clerk snorted. "That milksop? He's scared of her, too. She's ruthless. She'd stab her own child in the back to get her way. With the Fire

Warlock looking over her shoulder she can't treat you two as bad as she treats other commoners, but she'll come as close to it as she can, and she'll punish anybody who gives you the time of day. She's had people whipped, branded—you name it—for less."

Irene said, "Doesn't talking to us put you in danger?"

The clerk's smile was bleak. "Not for the moment. She was already furious with me for suggesting to Master Duncan that the older ledgers might tell a different story, so when the Fire Warlock put spells on the place to protect the records, he put one on me, too. She can't do anything to me until you've finished your search." He dropped his voice to a whisper. "I don't have a wife or children, and I send most of my pay to my mother in Edinburgh, so I'll help as much as I can. All I want in exchange is for you to let me leave with you when you're through. Help in getting out of Abertee safely is all I need."

Sven said, "I'm sympathetic to your plight, but reluctant to promise anything. Promises wizards and witches make have an unfortunate inclination to twist into shackles that neither person intended. I will say it's a reasonable request, and we owe you for your help."

"Fair enough. I'm willing to risk it to see her taken down a peg. She's hurt too many people. If I can help the Archers and help you squelch her to boot, I'll count that as something to be proud of. I just hope it's not a wild-good chase. Maybe the Archers really are tenants."

"No," Irene said, "They're freeholders. That was obvious as soon as you opened the first ledger."

Rent and Taxes

"If paying rent implies tenancy," Irene said, "while paying taxes implies owning the land, then the Archers are freeholders. Whoever first wrote 'rent paid' instead of 'taxes paid' made a deliberate choice to record the wrong word. They are being cheated."

Clerk and wizard gaped at her. Sven recovered faster. "How can you tell from one page?"

Her fingers knotted together. "Because the colours are wrong."

"I beg your pardon?"

Mr Henderson's eyebrows drew together. "Debts are recorded in red, otherwise it's all black ink."

"My talent brings the words, the very letters on a page, to life, glowing in vivid colours. What colours appear varies depending on my focus. A well-constructed sentence shows itself in violet, even though on closer examination the individual words may be in unrelated colours. Mistakes and clumsy phrasing appear in a rather putrid muddy yellow, lies in a bright lime green painful to the eyes. When looking for specific words, such as Archer and Nettleton, those words pop off the page and dance before my eyes in bright pink—a pink not reproduced in any ink available in Frankland.

"On the page you showed us, listing the monies collected from the farmers in Nettleton, the entire column reading 'rent paid' was in that lime green." Could she afford a demonstration? Yes. The word *rent*, in inch-high green letters, hung in the air above the table. "The colour was faint, faded with time and many copies, but someone, in the not too distant past, knowingly wrote 'rent' where another word belonged." The word floating between the two staring men faded away. "The same pattern appears in all the ledgers we have looked at so far, and the colour is brighter in the earlier ledgers.

"Please, eat, before your food gets any colder."

The clerk started and looked at his half-empty plate. Sven pushed his aside and leaned forward on his elbows. "Are you sure it was deliberate? Perhaps it was a simple mistake."

"Wrong colour. That would have been yellow."

He gazed into the far distance. "My stars, so much from a few words on one page."

He hadn't called her a liar. Not yet, anyway. For a few minutes, the clerk ate in silence. Irene toyed with her fork.

Sven said, "Haven't there been other air witches and wizards with similar talents? I recall something from the histories…"

"Yes, it isn't uncommon in the Air Guild's top ranks. One in five enchanters and enchantresses have had it to some degree, but there are no records of anyone else below level four being blessed with it." She was pleased that her voice stayed steady.

The clerk said, "If there are ledgers in the muniments room that have 'Great-Granddad Archer, taxes paid' in them, what colour will you see that in?"

"Bright pink. It may briefly flash gold to show that the lie has been corrected."

"What about you, Master Sven?"

He grimaced. "I had imagined I would wave my wand around the room and find all the references to the Archers, but the ledgers are full of them. There must be hundreds in this district. I hadn't realised they were so prolific."

"They're that, all right," Mr Henderson said, "And outspoken. They take up far more than their fair share of the space in the other records."

"Argh. The ledgers are easy, because they're regular. I built a mental model of the information in the first few ledgers, focusing on the name Archer. With each succeeding ledger, I simply compare it with my existing model for any changes pertaining to the Archers or Nettleton. I've been fine-tuning the model as I go, so each comparison is a little faster. Before the day ends I expect to cover the last shelf of ledgers in a few minutes."

Mr Henderson finished and left, promising to return shortly. Irene's mutton chop, never her favourite dish at the best of times, languished in a pool of watery gravy. On reaching the muniments room, would Sven sweep through in a quarter of an hour, while she plodded through one shelf?

"Mrs van Gelder?"

She started. "Sorry, Master Sven."

"Please, call me Sven. Ollie wouldn't have appreciated formality amongst friends."

"No, he wouldn't have, but…" Irene's mother would not approve of such familiarity with a fire wizard. "Fine, then. Sven it is."

"And you won't mind if I call you Irene? Good." He smiled. "If I understood what you said, you can search as fast as you can see the pages. The content doesn't matter—or doesn't matter much. Is that right?"

She sent the plate holding the repulsive chop skidding down the boards. "Yes. You would notice, wouldn't you, if the other thing we're searching for was hidden between the pages of a ledger?"

"Of course. It doesn't seem likely, but if it is there, I couldn't miss it. It would be as attention-getting as a torch in a dark cellar."

What did he need an air witch for? "That's a relief. Missing a page is a worry, but if you're sure you would catch it perhaps I can search a little faster."

"Really? You are good. You'll be done in the clerk's office while I'm still sifting through the first box of letters."

"Pardon?"

"This isn't a race, you know."

"No," she said, "but you'll be ahead of me before long."

"I won't stay ahead. The ledgers are easy, because they all have the same organisation. The other records won't be as regular, and the correspondence will be highly irregular. The other thing we're looking for is more likely to be there than amongst the ledgers, so I'll slow down to a crawl again when we reach the correspondence."

"That makes you the tortoise?"

"No. I'm the hare, jumping between fast and slow. If you maintain a steady pace, you're the tortoise and likely to win."

"You said it wasn't a race."

He grinned. "Not between the two of us, no. But it may be a race between my head and my stomach, if I'm faced with another mutton chop as wretched as this one."

The lad mending a broken stile hard by the road to Nettleton got a good look as Lord Geoffrey and his guards went past. As soon they were out of sight, he ran for the copse where he had hidden a horse, and kicked him into a gallop for Crossroads. He reached the smithy late morning, and began talking so fast the words tumbled out one on top of another.

"Whoa, lad," Duncan said, "Slow down. You're not making sense."

"They're going to Nettleton, Master Duncan, like you said they would. The duke's son and half a dozen guards."

Duncan nodded, placing each guard as the lad described them. There were decent sorts among the guards—many lads joined because the pay was good, and they needed a steady job—but some got their fun bullying the folk they were paid to protect. With the Fire Office's shields, Lord Geoffrey didn't need any guards along, but he favoured the bullies. Duncan wasn't surprised at the ones he'd picked to beat the Archers into cowering if they gave him any backtalk.

There'd been far too much of that lately. About time somebody put a stop to it.

When Lord Geoffrey and his guards reached Nettleton, Duncan and his brother Doug were waiting for him. Several hay wagons parked along the side of the track forced the guards to ride single file past the church. As Lord Geoffrey's horse stepped into the square, the lads at the front of the first wagon rolled the barrow they had ready into the path of the first guard's horse. The horse balked. At the end of the line, a cart rolled into place, boxing in the guards.

Two dozen farmers joined the men already at either end of the church. None of them carried weapons, but pitchforks and quarterstaves leaned against the walls within easy reach.

Lord Geoffrey pulled his horse around to stare at the guards. "What is the meaning of this?"

The first guard tried to force his horse through the knot of men, and brought his whip up. Doug grabbed his arm and pulled him half off the horse so that the guard was fighting for balance. Old Malcolm yanked the whip out of his hand.

Duncan said, "We're just trying to keep the peace, and make sure nobody gets hurt."

"Let go of my guard!"

Doug looked at Duncan. Duncan shrugged. Doug let go. The guard fell sideways onto a wagon. Something cracked, and the guard whined like a beaten dog.

"Oops," Doug said. "Sorry about that."

"How dare you attack my guards!"

Duncan said, "Attack the guards? Look at us. You're nuts if you think the Frost Maiden will believe a bunch of unarmed farmers attacked armed guards, on horseback to boot."

Lord Geoffrey sputtered, his face as red as the Fire Warlock's beard.

"Besides, we're trying to help. Meeting you here saves you the trouble of climbing yonder hill. If it has aught to do with those ledgers, I reckon the other farmers in Nettleton would like to hear it, too."

"You know perfectly well it does."

Doug said, "Go ahead. Tell us."

"The Fire Warlock said we had to prove you're tenants to evict you. We have proven it. Everyone in Nettleton is a tenant, and we want you Archers off our land. Now!"

Doug said, "The Fire Warlock said you have to give us three months."

Duncan said, "And he said yesterday you haven't proven it to his satisfaction. If you evict anybody before those magic folk have looked through your books, it might as well be theft."

Lord Geoffrey said, "I'm tired of your insolence. That's 'it might as well be theft, *sir*'."

"I'm glad you agree with me, and that you're seeing I deserve some respect."

Lord Geoffrey gave the laughing farmers the evil eye. "You are all tenants. I can evict every one of you."

"I'd like to hear what your mum says when she finds out how much tax money that'll cost you."

Lord Geoffrey went purple. "The Fire Warlock said to give you three months. Very well. Lord Edmund delivered the eviction notice on July seventh. October seventh is three months. If you aren't out then, I'll burn you out."

"Are you done?"

He sputtered a moment more. "Yes."

"Good." Duncan yelled so all the guards could hear. "When we let you go, you're going to turn around and go back the same way you came.

You aren't going to hurt anybody here. If you try, we've got an earth witch who'll spook your horses and make them throw you. Got that?"

"Yes, sir!"

"Good. Let 'em go, lads."

Before Mr Henderson had pulled down the next ledger after dinner, the guard outside the window cleared his throat. "Excuse me, ma'am?" Six heads swivelled. The man's face reddened. "Uh, ma'am, the wizard said you're the Air Enchanter's daughter-in-law. I was wondering, uh, were you Enchanter Oliver's…"

"Yes," Irene said, "he was my husband."

"Sorry, ma'am. I don't mean to upset you, or nothing."

"You won't. It's been three years. What would you like to know?"

"Not that so much as… Well, you see, ma'am, my brother's a sailor. He says Enchanter Oliver saved him and his mates from the Empire's wizards driving their ship up on the rocks. If there's anything I can do for you, ma'am, I'd be happy to do it, so long as I don't get in trouble with Her Grace."

Oliver would have been pleased. Irene thanked the guard, but could see nothing he could do without risking his position.

The clerk's office had been warm but bearable in the morning. After dinner the room became stifling. A guard snored. Sven yawned four times over a single ledger. Using more magic would tire Irene sooner, but it could serve double duty.

The zephyr's delicious coolness revived everyone. The men stared as it fanned the ledger's pages.

The sergeant grunted. "I wondered when one of you was going to do some magic we could see."

Sven said, "The world's fastest tortoise. I'd better hurry."

They gave the clerk no respite, flying through ledgers as quickly as he could bring new ones down and reshelve the ones they had finished. By late afternoon, he was using one hand and holding the small of his back with the other, but made no complaint.

The breeze died halfway through a ledger. Irene moaned.

The nearest guard said, "Are you all right, ma'am?"

"Burn it," Sven said. "The Fire Warlock warned me not to overwork you. If I've given you a headache…"

She rubbed her eyes. "No, no. It isn't that." She turned pages by hand, but the colours had faded to black. "This work is draining, and I'm only a level three witch."

"I'm sorry. I should have paid more attention."

The clerk said, "There's a sitting room across the hall, ma'am, with a sofa. You could lie down and rest."

"No, really, this is fine."

Sven said, "For you maybe, but not for the rest of us, without a breeze. You can slip out, and take a pair of guards with you. I'll finish the last shelf while their shape is still fresh in my mind."

From across the hall she watched him slide his wand along the last shelf, no longer even needing to touch the ledgers. Picturing him as a hare in a tailored suit amused her, but did little to break the spell his good looks had cast. Was it true that a fire wizard's hands were always warm? Sometimes Oliver had come to bed with hands like ice.

Such thoughts were dangerous. He wore no ring, but he was too fine a man to be unclaimed. On their way back through the tunnels, casting around for a safer topic, she said, "The duchess' failure to acknowledge our presence is in character, but one would have expected Lord Geoffrey to harass us."

"Yes, it seemed odd. It worries me a little." Sven shrugged. "We've made a good start. I'm more confident we'll find the evidence the Archers need since you confirmed that they are freeholders. Thanks."

They reached the exit to the Hall of the Winds. As she started down the path he called, "Ollie used to say you were the Air Guild's finest witch. I'm starting to see why. Cheers!"

She had learned to act is if she had recovered from losing Oliver, but this casual reminder of better days caught her by surprise. She fled down the hill with an aching heart. When she reached her mother's house, the girls came running.

"What happened, Mama?" Miranda said. "We thought today would be a good day."

"You don't understand, sweethearts." She knelt and gathered them into her arms. "Today *was* a good day. The best since your papa died."

Once Lord Geoffrey and his guards had left Nettleton, the women came out of hiding. The village had a little party, with a lot of backslapping and kissing and hugging and grinning, right there in the road. The Archers didn't mind, but weren't in the mood for it. They retreated to the farm, mulling over Doug and Jessie's choices: Lord Geoffrey had ordered them to leave, the Fire Warlock had ordered them to stay.

Jessie asked, "Can those witches and wizards find anything in less than three weeks?"

"Iced if I know," Duncan said. "I'm sorry I made it worse. He might have given you until the middle of December if I hadn't shot off my mouth."

Doug shrugged. "One week was all we got to start with. Moving now, before the weather gets bad, will be easier than in December."

Duncan and Hazel left after supper. He went through the tunnel first. A moment later he was in the Crossroads guildhall, frowning at the tunnel door.

Hazel stepped though. "You didn't get lost."

"No, but I've been hopping through the tunnels in Abertee by myself without any trouble, and I got back from the Warren last night without any problem either. I got lost going towards the Warren or the Fortress. Could we try that?"

"Sure. Go ahead. If you get lost, stop and wait for me to catch up. A problem with the tunnels will be easier to fix if we know where it goes wrong."

"Yes, ma'am." He walked through the door, took the first right, counted three doors, and turned left. He walked a few feet forward, and his right hand ran out of wall.

The tunnel on his right shouldn't have been there. He peered ahead, but couldn't tell if there was a tunnel on the left. Better not find out. He sat down and waited.

And waited.

And waited.

Ice it, he hated those frostbitten tight spaces. What was taking Hazel so long?

He wasn't nervous. Yet. Time always crawls when you're waiting for something, and in the dark, without hints like shadows moving, he couldn't tell how much time had passed. He sang a few drinking songs, then slow hymns, then the longest song he knew—all twenty-seven verses he could remember. He sang them all through again, slower.

He stopped singing and listened.

A mouse scrabbled some ways away. Water dripped somewhere nearby. If Hazel hadn't said to stay put, he would have been opening doors.

His eyes had adjusted to the dim light. The tunnel to the right sloped downhill, ending in a door, with a glimmer coming in under the bottom. He hugged his knees, staring at that door. Running down that tunnel and charging out into the light seemed like the best idea in the world.

Hazel had said to wait. He had a full belly, and it had been a long day. He lay on the tunnel floor and buried his face in his arms to block out the sight of the door.

The light coming in under the door was stronger, like moonlight. Duncan must have slept for several hours. The noises had stopped, even the dripping water. He opened his mouth to call, thought better of it, flattened his back against the wall, then gripped the rock with both hands, holding his breath and listening. Nothing moved.

Dark places and tight spaces had never scared him. Warlocks and sorceresses did, and after the riot in Blacksburg, angry mobs, but not much else. But now he was a mouse, and a cat waited to pounce as soon as he gave away where he was.

He stood, moving slowly to not make any noise, and stepped into the right-hand tunnel. Gravel slipped under his feet. He fell and slid into the door, knocking it open. He cursed and grabbed for the tunnel walls as his arse slid on through and out into empty air.

The Tunnel Door

Duncan came to a stop with his chest halfway through the tunnel door. Loose gravel slid past. He never did hear it land.

The tight quarters he'd been cursing saved him. He was stuck. He would've had to turn sideways to fit through. He kicked, but his feet dangled in mid-air.

He reached further in, using his bit of earth magic to dig handholds in the wall, and inched back into the tunnel. Hauling his arse over the edge scraped skin off his back, but after that it was easy. Once he was all in, he sat up to get a good look at where he'd almost gone.

As far as he could tell—he wasn't about to stick his head out—the door opened out high up in a cliff wall. The tunnels must have taken him clear across the country into South Frankland, because the mountains on the other side of the valley were the biggest he'd ever seen, with tops already covered in snow halfway through September. In the light of the full moon, they were gorgeous. And cold—as cold as the Frost Maiden at his trial.

The mountains called to him. The open door said, Come on through, you'll be free of these frostbitten tunnels. You won't have to worry about Doug anymore, or get pissed off at the aristos. No more worries, ever.

Magic tugged at him. He shuddered, and couldn't move, up or down.

"Duncan?" Hazel called, from far away.

The spell broke. "Here," he yelled. He climbed into the cross-tunnel and lay face down, digging his fingers into the cracks.

Hazel came running, and knelt beside him. He wrapped an arm around her waist, and buried his face in her skirt. She stroked his hair and said soothing things.

"Duncan, I'm so sorry. You were right. Your trail ended in a wall, so there had to be magic involved. I've been looking for you for hours. Mildred's looking, too, and a couple of others who are good trackers. What happened?"

He told her about the door into empty space, and the magic. The tunnel door creaked in the breeze. He would've crawled away, but couldn't leave that devil's door swinging open. He'd never be able to live with himself if somebody else fell through it.

Hazel had gone stiff while he talked. "But Duncan, they told us at the Earth Guild School that the tunnels are as safe as…as…well, as a healer's hall. Guild members have been using the tunnels for centuries without getting lost or hurt. If this is a trap, it should have caught somebody before now. This isn't new."

"How old is it?"

"No one else has been here for years. Let me see what I can tell about it."

She edged into the tunnel. He kept a good grip on her so she wouldn't go sliding. She wouldn't stick in the door like her big ox of a sweetheart did.

She felt around with her wand, then sat quiet for a few minutes, before climbing out. "It's at least five hundred years old, maybe a thousand, or even older, and no one else has been in it for centuries. Even stranger, a fire wizard set the trap. Why would a fire wizard set traps in our tunnels? Why would we let him?"

Duncan shifted to sit with his back to the wall, staring down at the open door. Hazel shivered, and he pulled her against his chest to keep her warm. "A fire wizard, you say, and old enough to date back to the Great Coven."

"Yes. Why?"

"The old stories say the Earth Mother built the Fortress for the Fire Warlock, but they don't say what he did for her. Maybe he set traps in the tunnels to protect the Warren."

"From what? The Fire Warlock protects the whole country. Why would the Warren need anything special?"

"My dad said the Warren and the tunnels were started hundreds of years before the Great Coven. They built the Fire Office later because we were under attack from all sides. Think what would've happened if an army had gotten into the tunnels and made it to the Warren. They could've wiped out all our healers and run free over the whole country. We'd've been newborn lambs beset by wolves. It would've made sense for the Fire Guild to set traps. There could be traps scattered all over the tunnels."

He shouldn't have done his thinking out loud. She started shaking as hard as he'd done while hanging betwixt and between in the tunnel.

"Whoa," he said. "It's all right. That didn't happen. The Earth Guild wasn't wiped out—not anywhere close."

"But Duncan, if there are traps in the tunnels, why does the Guild Council keep telling us they're safe? Why haven't guild members gotten caught in them?"

"Er… What could you tell about the spell on the tunnel?"

"Not much. I couldn't read it."

"I bet the tunnels are safe, for earth witches and wizards, anyway. Before the Fire Warlock asked to let his agents use the tunnels, the Earth Guild never let anybody through unless they were sick or hurt, or going somewhere with a guild member. I used to think it was snotty of them, but maybe they set out to make sure nobody got hurt without giving the game away. The traps would know who belongs here and who doesn't. You could've walked past this one a hundred times and never known, until I stumbled into it."

"Oh, Duncan, I'm so sorry."

He kissed her, and tasted tears. "Sorry for what?"

"I never dreamed you were in real danger. You could've been dead or dying, and I didn't hurry. I should've gone to the Guild Council and insisted they look for you." She buried her face in his shoulder.

"Hey, now. It's all right. You found me. No harm done. And you wouldn't have had any luck rousing the guild. They wouldn't've believed you any more than Granny Mildred believed me. I bet the Fire Warlocks and Earth Mothers forgot about the traps ages ago, or they wouldn't have let me use the tunnels. The Fire Warlock's protected us so well for so long that nobody worries about things like that anymore. Look at the guards. They had no idea they were riding into a trap in Nettleton."

She laughed. "They did look silly."

Thank God he'd finally managed to say the right thing. "We'll tell the Earth Mother and the Warlock in the morning, but is there anything we can do now? He won't be happy if the tunnels kill off his agents."

She turned towards the swinging door. "I can put an aversion spell on it, but it may not be strong enough."

"You could put a lock on the door."

"I've never done a lock spell. I suppose I could use a weight spell on the latch, to make it too heavy for anyone without earth magic to move. Yes, I'll do that."

She slithered into the tunnel. He hauled her back. "You're not going down there."

"I have to close the door. If we leave it open, someone could just fall through."

"Aye, like you. Forget it."

"But Duncan, I—"

"You couldn't reach the latch without hanging out over the edge."

"But Duncan, I—"

"I'll do it."

"But the compulsion spell…"

"It went away when you called. I'm fine now."

"Are you sure?"

"Yes, ma'am." He skidded down the slope, keeping a grip on the walls, and came to a stop, upright this time, against the lip. "See, I'm fine." He reached out, caught the latch, and the spell caught him.

This time it didn't tell him he'd be happy if he stepped out the door. This time it said he was going to fall, and nothing he could do would stop it. The latch tugged at him, and he couldn't let go. He was fighting to keep from leaning out further, and losing.

Hazel's hand touched his arm. "Earth grips you. You will not fall."

He was an oak tree, with roots grabbing so tight nothing could knock him over. "Yes, ma'am," he said, and pulled the door closed.

Beware the Fire Guild

Gale force winds off the bay whipped Irene's skirts around her legs and churned her hair into a knotted mess. She kept a solid hold on the railing as she climbed the stairs leading to the Earth Guild tunnel.

Two steps from the top, Oliver's voice called, "Irene!"

The shock knocked her off balance. A gust bowled her over; only her grip on the railing saved her from tumbling the full flight. She crouched against the support, whimpering.

Another voice—a clear, strong soprano—called from above: "Irene!"

This was no figment of Irene's imagination. The intensity of the wind dropped, as her only friend in the Air Guild made a graceful landing on the top step. A bubble of calm surrounded them; a few feet away, tree branches whipped in the wind.

"Irene, are you all right?" Enchantress Winifred knelt beside her. "I saw you fall."

Irene took stock. "My left wrist is sprained and there will be bruises, but it could have been a lot worse."

"No kidding. You could have broken your neck. You were lucky."

"No one else in the Air Guild calls me lucky."

Winifred helped her to her feet, but she wasn't ready to face the wind yet. "Are you here for today's Guild Council meeting?"

"Yes," Winifred said. "Much to my regret. I'd rather do anything else than listen to those old bores."

"Why come, then? Rumour says you never do."

"Before the war, I didn't. Now, with so few left, Paul won't let me beg off. He threatened to hold the council meetings in my house if I didn't come."

"Oh, dear. If he had threatened Oliver with that…"

"He knew it wouldn't have worked. Ollie would have hauled you and the girls away on a day's outing and left them to fend for themselves in your parlour, whether you liked it or not. But that's not your worry. Where are you headed in such weather?" Winifred smiled at Irene's hesitation. "If you don't want to tell me, that's fine. If it's anything interesting I'll find out at the council meeting."

"That's true," Irene said, and described the search.

"Charters, eh? Sounds like a wild-goose chase to me. I'm glad he didn't stick me with that job, although that Sven is to die for." Winifred rolled her eyes up and sighed.

"Don't you prefer men with biceps the size of hams?"

"I do, but I'd make an exception for him, as long as he keeps his mouth shut. All he talks about is dusty old history and magical theory. *Gah!* More your type than mine. Maybe…" She stopped in mid-sentence, her mouth half open, eyes unfocused.

Interrupting a seer in a trance is a bad idea. One waits. Winifred's eyes focused into an incredulous stare. Irene backed away, but Winifred grabbed her left wrist and shook it. Irene stifled a yelp.

"Irene, be careful," Winifred said. "Don't take refuge in the Fortress."

"Why would any air witch do that?"

"I don't know. But it's a trap."

"You're jumping to conclusions. What did you see?"

Winifred retreated, shaking her head.

Irene reached for her sleeve. "Tell me what you saw."

"If you ever spend a night in the Fortress, you'll never sleep anywhere else. Do you understand? You'll die there." Winifred broke free from Irene's grasp and sailed away on the wind.

———⊙⚜⊙———

Sven was fighting to hold the tunnel door open when Irene staggered around the last bend. He started towards her with a cry. "What's wrong?"

"The door—" Too late: the wind slammed it shut.

He swore and yanked at it. Irene waited with her left arm pressed against her chest. She could offer no help; the wind buffeting her wrist made her see stars.

Sven wedged the door open and pulled her through, then let it slam. She slid down the wall into a heap on the floor. He knelt beside her with a ball of flame in his hand and looked her over.

She said, "The Fire Warlock said cobwebs in my hair was the worst that would happen. Ha!"

"What happened? You look terrible."

"Thank you. Are you always so complimentary?"

"Burn it, I didn't mean—"

"Of course you didn't. But I do. Look terrible, that is. I fell on the stairs."

"No wonder. Let's get you to a healer, and then I'll see you home."

She gave him a blank stare, ignoring the proffered hand. "Home?"

His brow furrowed. "Back to Airvale."

"Oh. Airvale isn't home."

His unsettled look deepened. "What?"

"I live there, but it isn't home. Hasn't been for years. Oxford was home, but the house was too expensive after Oliver died. Sorry, I'm babbling; you don't care about that." She put her sound arm down to push off from the floor.

"Here, let me help."

This time she accepted his aid, and let him pull her to her feet.

"I meant," he said, "you should take the day off, and rest."

"No! No, I'd rather not." She didn't dare. The Air Enchanter would assume she was shirking. An aching wrist was better than that.

They left the Warren with her arm in a sling and her thoughts in a whirl. Years ago, Winifred had predicted Airvale's blacksmith would die in the smithy. The man's wife insisted he sell the smithy and buy a farm. Three years later, the man's heart stopped while he was lambasting the new smith for a slipshod repair job on a harrow. Three years in which the former smith was miserable, and his family nearly starved, as he worked at something he had no aptitude for.

All foreknowledge was incomplete. Surely one could discover an alternative interpretation for this new prediction, if one thought hard enough.

A sullen, shifty-eyed man replaced the guard who had offered Irene his aid the previous day. Sven gave each of the others a hard look, but didn't comment.

She worked at the desk, as before, finishing the ledgers before starting on the correspondence. The first few letters were ordinary—unrelated to the Archers, and written by another nobleman's clerk. Someone, that is, with an education, and whose profession demanded his writing be legible and lucid. They were easy on her eyes, with little emotional content.

A dozen letters in, she flinched and dropped the sheet of paper. When her vision cleared a moment later, the men were on their feet, the sergeant pushing Mr Henderson out of the way to bend over her.

"Here now, ma'am, what happened? What hurt you?"

She flipped the page over, hiding the lurid writing, and blinked away the afterimage. "It's fine… I'm sorry to have startled you, but one doesn't expect letters like this." She pushed it towards Sven. "An instant's glance is too short to take in the subject matter, but it was written by someone barely literate in a murderous rage. The emotional burden is overwhelming."

Sven flipped it over and read it. Mr Henderson craned to read upside down. "You got that dead-on, ma'am," he said.

Sven handed him the letter. "Lock this away somewhere," he said, and returned to his box of correspondence.

Irene paged through the correspondence with a trembling hand, hoping not to encounter any more such obscenities. Between Winifred's prediction, the letter, and the sore wrist, focusing on her work was a struggle. The physical presence of the wizard working beside her, shoulder to shoulder and knee to knee, added an additional distraction. Glancing up while handing on another sheaf of papers, he met her eyes, and smiled. If her presence disturbed him, he didn't let on.

Irene's mother would have been outraged to see her crammed into a tight space with a fire wizard. Not that anything would happen; they were better chaperoned than when Oliver had courted her. Four guards and a clerk would witness all.

Several boxes of correspondence later—Sven was still on his first box—a truculent voice from the corridor made her start. "Out of the way, you brutes! Let me see what damage they're doing to our property."

The guards at the door scrambled. Mr Henderson followed them into the corridor. Lord Geoffrey strutted in like a bantam cock. Sven bowed. Irene, unable to rise, greeted him politely. Lord Geoffrey sneered. Sven's eyes narrowed. Lord Geoffrey pushed past him and sat in Sven's chair.

"Mother will be relieved when I tell her this search through our records is a formality, and won't help our cheating tenants. Obviously, the Air Enchanter doesn't believe you'll find anything. If he did, he wouldn't have sent the Air Guild's most notorious fraud, would he?"

Cold Mutton Stew

Insults about Irene's decade-out-of-fashion dress, less-than-perfect teeth, or the frizzy tangle passing as her hair would not have surprised her. A thrust so close to the bone did. Why would a duke's son be aware of a level three commoner?

Oliver had advised her to project an air of confidence even when ill at ease, but doing so was not as easy as he claimed. No one had ever doubted his abilities. When Sven subjected her to a shocked stare, her self-confidence shrivelled to the size of a mustard seed and rolled away under the desk.

Lord Geoffrey leaned back in the chair with his hands behind his head and rested his feet on the box of papers Sven had been sifting through. "Go on, get back to work. Don't let me stop you."

Sven stood next to him with a sheaf of papers in his hand, scowling.

Meaningless, drab squiggles covered the papers in Irene's hands. Her breathing was shallow and her hands trembled, but retreating further would have required crawling into the lap of the guard in the window.

Lord Geoffrey lowered his arms, and laid a hand on her thigh. Sven snatched a box off a shelf and shoved it into the aristocrat's lap.

"Oof!" Lord Geoffrey let go of Irene and grabbed the box.

Sven pulled the desk away from her. "This room is too crowded. Guards, move the correspondence into the sitting room across the hall. We need more room to work."

Several deep breaths while leaning on the sitting room's windowsill steadied Irene's nerves, but the relief lasted less than a minute; her trembling resumed when Lord Geoffrey sauntered over and leered at her bodice.

Sven yanked him away and shoved him into a chair. "Stay there."

Lord Geoffrey lunged for the fire wizard and fell with the chair stuck to his clothes. Sven waved for the guards to set the chair upright. Lord Geoffrey shouted obscenities at him.

"And shut up." Sven turned his back and set to work, ignoring shaken fists and wordless snarls.

"Where do you want this, ma'am?" a guard asked.

Irene gestured towards the window. The guard set the card table under the sill, out of Lord Geoffrey's line of sight. She could not be as nonchalant as Sven about the violent emotions on display; hers were as violent, although better hidden. The urge to cry and a desire to strangle the conceited wretch, both reactions anathemas to an air witch, vied for control. Lord Geoffrey's opinion of her did not matter; Sven's did. After an hour's struggle to regain a calm focus on her work, her pace was still too slow.

Promises...

The whisper shattered her concentration. She waited, unable to work. Sven rubbed his ears and glowered at Lord Geoffrey. A moment later, Lord Geoffrey rubbed his own ears. Sven smiled and bent back over his work.

Irene, you promised...

With a dry mouth and pounding heart, she stared at Lord Geoffrey's back. A level two wizard could produce these colourless whispers, but how could he have known what to say? And as for reproducing Oliver's captivating baritone, impossible. Only someone who knew him well could have gotten the timbre right, and Oliver had left Airvale a decade ago. Lord Geoffrey would never have met him.

Irene...

Sven looked up, scowling.

If this reprehensible excuse for a nobleman was her torturer, he should be stopped, but her talent was useless for this. If only one had a weapon...

She stifled a laugh. She had a weapon, a mundane one.

She sang—off key, with a tonal quality like fingernails scraping on a slate. Lord Geoffrey clamped his hands over his ears. The other men winced. The whispers stopped. Sven's scowl dissolved into a grin.

Her mother would have berated Irene for embarrassing the guild with her sham of a singing voice, and would have fawned over Lord Geoffrey, the greater embarrassment.

Bury her mother. Irene drew out the final notes twice as long as the song called for.

A few minutes of quiet followed, then the whispers began again. Irene sang a ballad extolling one of the Earth Guild's commoner heroes. Sven bent over his work with his face turned away and his shoulders twitching. By dinnertime Irene's throat was raw, but she was once again working at full speed.

Sven made a show of casting spells on the boxes and stacks of papers spread throughout the sitting room and office. Before they left, he addressed Lord Geoffrey. "You may get up and talk once we're in the kitchen, but if you interfere again with our search, or are disrespectful of Mrs van Gelder, I'll make your seat hot with you glued to it." He offered her an arm. "Shall we see what culinary delights await us today?"

The serving girl ladled mutton stew from a bubbling pot. The stew was tepid and congealing when she set their bowls on the table.

Irene said, "Lord Geoffrey is chilling our stew."

"That's a silly trick to play on a fire wizard." Sven reached for her bowl. A moment later it steamed. He grinned. "Eat up."

The stew wasn't any more appealing hot. She choked down a spoonful.

Sven leaned forward, frowning. "He was taunting you with those whispers, wasn't he? I heard them, but couldn't decipher them. I hope you don't mind me asking what they were about."

"No, not at all." Three mouthfuls later, she dropped the spoon into the bowl and pushed it aside. "And you mustn't mind not getting an answer."

"Demands that I mind my own business aren't usually so diplomatic." He toyed with his spoon. "About the earlier incident this morning... I didn't mean to be rude, but I didn't want to discuss it with the guards listening."

"Pardon?"

"That letter."

"Lord Geoffrey drove that from my mind. What was it about?"

His smile was a bit crooked. "I should have let well enough alone." He glanced at Mr Henderson. "Could you explain?"

The clerk glanced around the kitchen. Sven said, "I'm blocking our voices. No one else can hear."

"Well, then. The father of a young woman Lord Edmund ruined wrote it, threatening to kill Lord Edmund and the Duke and any other noble he could lay hands on."

Irene said, "Oh, dear. The poor man."

Sven said, "Who else besides you and the duke know about it?"

Mr Henderson said, "Just Granny Mildred, the local healer. She calmed the fellow down and knocked some sense into his head. I convinced the duke not to send guards after him."

"A humane choice, in my opinion."

Irene asked, "But if he really is a threat?"

"He probably isn't, with a healer at work on him, but you understand I have to inform the Fire Warlock."

Mr Henderson frowned, then shrugged. "Yes, sir. The Fire Warlock's judgment is better than the guards'. Speaking of the guards... They said Lord Geoffrey was in Nettleton yesterday, giving the Archers their eviction notice."

Sven nodded. "We expected that."

"Yes, sir, but things didn't go as he planned. Master Duncan made him look like a simpleton, not that that's hard, and the only person hurt was a guard with a couple of broken ribs. His lordship lost his temper and ordered the Archers out by October seventh."

The grin lighting Sven's face vanished. "The seventh's less than three weeks."

"Yes, sir."

"How many boxes of papers are in that muniments room?"

"Lots. The records in my office only go back forty years. The records in the muniments room go back centuries."

"We can finish in your office this afternoon." Sven pushed away his half-eaten stew. "Let's get back to work."

Lord Geoffrey didn't return after dinner. Neither did the whispers. Irene raced through the correspondence, only occasionally stopping to rest her eyes after a painful letter. In this larger room, without the need to stir a breeze, her magic lasted until late afternoon. It died with only one box of correspondence left. Sven was several boxes behind.

She rubbed her eyes, and read.

With the correspondence done, Irene's growling stomach and aching arm demanded attention. She rested her head on her arms. Sven looked drained, too. Well past her usual suppertime he said, "That's it for today. Let's go."

Lord Geoffrey had left a surprise for them on their way out: their hats had been stomped flat, and the badge ripped from hers. No great loss; the three limp flags had been a constant reminder of her ineptitude.

The quartet of flames still flickered on Sven's hat. He glowered at them. "I hope you burnt his fingers."

They trudged through the Warren in silence, but at the tunnel to the Hall of the Winds Sven said, "You have children waiting?"

"They're at Mother's. They'll have already had their supper and be in bed by now."

"And what will you have for supper?"

"Cold leftovers." She forced a smile. "Not a hardship; no one praises Airvale for the quality of its cuisine."

"Right. Let's have a good meal together." He took her elbow and steered her in a different direction. "Because you and I need to talk."

She shook off his hand and marched through the tunnel he indicated, staring straight ahead. "Of course. You want to know why the Air Guild saddled you with a fraud."

Sven Finds Her Out

Sven emerged from the tunnel, straightening to his full height. "I am curious about your talents, but that isn't what I want to talk about. Although perhaps we'd better, since Lord Geoffrey's insult upset you."

Irene looked him in the eye. "What that insufferable beast thinks is of no consequence."

He frowned. "Of course it isn't. Why would I consider you a fraud?"

"Because he said…" Her gaze slid away from his intent blue stare. "Because the Air Guild think I'm one."

"What rot. Why?"

"Because I can't do anything a proper air witch can do, and nobody believes in the things I *can* do, and it's just awful."

He took her elbow again, with a firmer grip, and guided her along the corridor. They emerged onto a balcony hanging on a cliff face. It had no railing, and stairs as steep as ladders. She gasped, and froze.

"What's the matter? We're just going down the stairs."

"I'm a complete, utter failure as an air witch." A tear leaked from a corner of Irene's eye. She whirled to escape into the corridor. "A fall on these stairs will kill me."

He caught and held her. "I'm sorry. I'd forgotten about your fall. No wonder you're trembling, but you need something to eat. We both do, and the food here is excellent." He wrapped an arm around her shoulders and pushed her towards the stairs. "Hold onto me. You won't fall."

She clutched his cloak with one hand and the stair rail with the other. They stepped onto the stairs, and dropped like pebbles down the cliff face. She buried her face in his shoulder and shuddered.

The journey passed in a blur. Tears trickled down her cheeks. He steered her off the stairs and down a corridor, passing staring groups of scholars. How long would the rumour of a crying witch, arm-in-arm with a fire wizard, take to reach the Air Guild? How long before she dared venture out again in public in Airvale?

They lurched into a kitchen. Sven slammed the door on some curious scholar who'd had the poor sense to follow them. An elderly woman with a kind face pressed a glass of stout into Irene's hands. "Drink up, honey. It'll calm you down."

The beer was as nourishing as brown bread. Irene downed half the glass in one long swallow. A bowl of some thick, dark soup appeared, and a spoon was thrust into her hand. After the mutton stew at dinner, soup had little appeal, but habit raised the spoon to her lips. She burned her mouth shovelling in more.

"Sorry, honey, my fault," the elderly woman said, handing Irene an Earth Guild lozenge.

Sven cupped his hands around the bowl. "I'll cool it for you."

By the time Irene had wiped the last drops from her second bowl with a chunk of bread, she had stopped trembling. Sven watched from across the table; she stared at her bowl.

He pushed his aside. "I hope you don't mind eating in the kitchen. Unlike the duchess, we're not trying to insult you. We're more private here than in the dining room. Don't let Mrs Cole fool you." He waved a hand at the cook, bustling around the kitchen. "She finished her day's work hours ago. She's pretending to be busy so she can eavesdrop. She's housemother, and won't be happy until she knows what this is about." He pulled out the chair at the end of the table. "Come and sit down. Stop that annoying fussing."

Mrs Cole sat, giving him an affectionate swat with a potholder in passing, and winked at Irene. "There's no point in pretending. He knows me too well."

Irene said, "Housemother? Does the Fire Guild really let an earth witch in on its secrets?"

Mrs Cole dimpled. "I'll take that as a compliment, honey, since I was trying to make you feel better, but bless you, I'm a fire witch through and through."

"I beg your pardon. Fire witches are reputed to be...um..."

"Bad-tempered, rude busybodies? Plenty of us are, but we're not all like that. I admit I am a busybody, but I try not to be rude about it. I would like to know what's wrong, but if you don't want me to listen, I'll leave once I'm sure you're in better spirits and Sven won't make you cry again."

"It's all right if you stay, and he didn't make me cry. He's very kind, though he must be angry."

He growled, "I'm not angry."

"Quiet, Sven." Mrs Cole flapped a hand at him. "Yes, he's angry. He's just not angry at you, honey."

Irene risked a glance. "You're not?"

"No. I'm angry with anyone calling you a fraud. If that puts me at odds with the entire Air Guild, it won't be the first time the two guilds haven't seen eye-to-eye."

"But they call me a fraud because I'm nothing like a normal air witch." Her words, pent up for so long, tumbled out. "I can't touch or talk to another person at a distance. I can't follow the wind with my mind's eye. My senses of pitch and smell are poor even by mundane standards. The best I can do in summoning a wind is the feeble breeze I conjured yesterday, and it was tiring. It should have been trivial. I can't do anything a level three air witch is supposed to do. The flags on my hat won't even flutter. The one and only talent I have is in dealing with words on paper. That's it."

"In other words," he said, "you're a javelin."

"Yes!" she shouted. Sven and Mrs Cole both started. Irene clapped a hand over her mouth. "Sorry." Her head felt as light as a small child's drinking her father's ale. If she released the bowl, she might float to the ceiling.

"A javelin?" Mrs Cole asked. "What's that?"

Sven said, "Most witches and wizards have a wide, but shallow profile. They can do the things their guild expects from someone at their level, without having any special talents. A few will display talents aligned with the next level up in one or two areas, at the expense of something at their own level. A javelin is a witch or wizard with a narrower focus—"

"Sven," she said, "You're lecturing. Get to the point."

"I'm a teacher. What do you expect? The point is, a javelin 'spears through' the levels, and displays a single talent normally seen in witches and wizards two levels or more above them. The price they pay is the inability to do anything else at their own level."

"Why haven't I ever heard of such a thing?"

"Javelins are rare. It's unlikely you've ever met one before. All four guild schools focus on the practical arts. The staff don't consider it important to teach about javelins, if they've ever even heard the term themselves."

"They haven't," Irene said, "or they might have guessed why I was so different. I never heard it before Oliver encountered the term at Oxford."

Mrs Cole said, "But didn't they test you to find out what you could do?"

"They did, over and over again. But seeing letters and words in different colours, the only ability I knew of then, isn't demonstrable to someone else. They viewed me as Martha-the-social-climber's daughter claiming credit for a talent that had appeared before only in enchanters and enchantresses, and believed me either mentally unstable or trying to dupe them.

"The more demonstrable abilities associated with the wordsmithing talent developed later. If Oliver hadn't believed me, and searched through the histories after we married, I might never have discovered them."

Sven said, "But surely your ability to identify mistakes so easily…"

"They explained that away as not needing any talent. I read quickly, and they said it wasn't healthy for a girl to spend so much time lost in books."

Mrs Cole snorted.

Sven said, "But even without believing in your magic, surely they considered that a useful skill."

"A boy might have been praised, but how many forty-year-old men enjoy having twelve-year-old girls point out their grammar mistakes in class? My talent must have been rather obnoxious when it first manifested. By fifteen, self-defence had taken over. I stopped offering criticisms of anyone's writing, and hid in corners to escape attention. The staff stopped testing me and pretended I didn't exist."

Mrs Cole said, "Do you mean to say you went through a wizard's school without a single soul believing in you?"

"Winifred believed I had talent, and tried to help, but she doesn't really understand, and couldn't properly defend me. She was the only one."

Sven shuddered. Mrs Cole said, "Oh, you poor dear." She patted Irene's hand, and resumed fussing around the kitchen, wiping her eyes on her apron. Sven glared but didn't comment. A moment later she whisked away the soup bowls and replaced them with slices of apple pie. "If I have nightmares tonight I'll blame your teachers, not you. It's a pity we can't interfere in another guild's business—I'd give somebody a piece of my mind, if I could."

Sven said, "It's as well you're in the Air Guild. You might not have survived the Fire Guild School. Why didn't Ollie support you?"

Irene said, "He was two years older, and unaware of my existence until one summer on recess from the university, when no one else in a ring of admiring girls understood his jokes. Once he came courting, life was much easier. He didn't care, at first, about my supposed lack of talent, but when he understood, he was thrilled. He taught me theory and helped develop the other aspects, and I proofread everything he wrote. He had his own problems, of a different sort, with the guild, and after we eloped we never returned to Airvale. I made friends among the mundanes at Oxford and pretended not to care about the guild."

"No wonder his essays earned better marks than mine. And that book of spells was so good it was almost sickening."

A bit of pie stuck in her throat. Would praise for that book always be a stab through the heart? "It's late. You must be eager to go home."

"I am home."

"Pardon?"

"What's the matter? You look like I flamed your cat."

"It's nothing. Just…why would one… Never mind."

"Live here?" Mrs Cole said. "The Fortress is a fine place for old busybodies and confirmed bachelors."

"Oh, but… Never mind. If you didn't consider me a fraud, what did you want to talk about?"

"Oh, that. We need to stop doing overlapping work if we're to find that charter in two and a half weeks. Here's what I have in mind…"

"**M**ama," Miranda said, "please stay on key or stop singing."

"Yes, dear." Her daughter's justified complaint didn't spoil Irene's good spirits, nor did putting on her oldest dress, patched more than once, and tucking her hair under an ancient scarf.

Irene's mother frowned when she met her on the stairs. "How will you attract another man, dressed like that? You look like a drudge."

"Drudge is an accurate description of someone rooting through centuries-old dust and grime." Irene marched into the pantry and rummaged through the shelves. "An air witch should be capable of earning a living on her own, whether or not she has a husband."

Her mother sniffed. "You aren't making a good showing as a representative of the Air Guild."

If she had seen Irene the previous evening, crying in a fire wizard's arms in public, she would have ordered her adult daughter to bed without supper. Irene rolled her eyes. "Who will notice me? A clerk, a fire wizard, and a few guards."

"You never know who you might meet. A water wizard, now that would be a good match."

Irene stalked out, pausing at the hall mirror to tuck in renegade curls. Oliver had never commented on her clothes, but he hadn't married her for her looks. Winifred had curves; Irene had angles, even after two children. No one would accuse her of being a temptress.

Her high spirits, already faltering, sank further on nearing the stairs to the tunnel, but recovered on finding Sven waiting at the foot. She held out her bag. "We don't have to rely on Her Grace's wretched hospitality. Assuming you find cold ham, cheese, bread, and oranges more palatable than mutton."

He hefted the sack slung over his shoulder. "Roast beef, apples, oatcakes, and a jug of cider. We've enough for Mr Henderson, too."

He gave her his arm. They climbed the stairs without incident, and had a pleasant walk to the Duke's manor. Not even the wooden-faced butler blocking the way to the muniments room spoiled her good mood.

"I beg your pardon, sir," he said, "but my orders are clear. You are to remain here, in the entry hall, until Lord Geoffrey has eaten."

"Where is Lord Geoffrey?" Sven asked. "Finishing his breakfast?"

The butler stared straight ahead. "No, sir. I do not believe he has risen. He was up rather late last night."

"That's too bad, because my orders are not to let anyone interfere with our search. Mr Henderson, please lead the way."

The clerk and the wizard paced down the corridor. Irene scurried after them. The guards stomped down the hall behind her. The butler chased after them. "Wait, sir, you can't do this. Sir, stop!"

They stopped in a hallway in front of a padlocked door.

Sven said, "We will continue the search. You may unlock the door or stand aside while I break the lock. Your choice."

The butler said, "I can't unlock it, sir. Lord Geoffrey has the key."

Sven inserted the tip of his wand into the keyhole. "Everyone, back up. Mrs van Gelder, take cover behind the guards."

The butler said, "Guards! Stop them!"

The sergeant shrugged. "Our orders were to keep an eye on them and not let them take anything."

With a flash of light and a roar, bits of metal went flying, one of them hitting the guard in front of Irene. He yelped and clutched his arm.

Sven said, "Sorry. Should we summon a healer?"

The guard rubbed his arm. "No, sir. It'll be sore is all."

Sven lit the lanterns Mr Henderson had brought, and they filed in with the guards following. The room was windowless, with a narrow path running through a dozen rows of shelving. The light from the lanterns did not reach past the first two rows. A small table and decrepit chair occupied a narrow gap by the door. Boxes, ledgers, and beribboned stacks of papers thick with dust filled the shelves.

Sven directed Mr Henderson to bring Irene boxes, starting with the oldest and working forward, while he scanned the ledgers, working backwards from the most recent. She scrubbed dust from the furniture, and eased onto the chair. It creaked and wobbled, but held her weight. If she sneezed it might not.

They had been working for more than an hour when a voice from the corridor said, "What happened to the door?" A gentleman, dressed as if outdoors in midwinter in hat, coat, gloves, and muffler, stared at the door with a befuddled expression.

"The key wasn't available this morning, Your Grace," Mr Henderson said. "Master Sven—the Flame Mage—broke the lock."

"Oh? Is the key lost?"

"No, sir." Mr Henderson coughed. "Lord Geoffrey has it, and he wasn't up yet."

"Oh." The duke took another look at the door, then shrugged. "Get someone to fix it."

Mr Henderson did the introductions. The duke looked at Irene uncertainly. "You don't look like an air witch."

"Dust and cobwebs would ruin a good dress, Your Grace."

"Oh. Yes, I suppose so." He looked around, as if taking in the room for the first time. "What are you guards doing here?"

The sergeant said, "Lord Geoffrey told us to keep an eye on them."

"Oh. Well. But how can they work with you getting in their way? You two—" He waved in the general direction of a pair of guards. "Go away and do something useful. Stop bothering these people while they work." He walked down the line of shelves and back, looking perplexed. "Now, why did I…"

He spied the stack of parchments on the table and brightened. "Oh, I remember. That whatchamacallit Master Duncan and the Fire Warlock talked about—you know, the thing that lays out what I'm supposed to do—have you seen it?"

Mr Henderson said, "The charter?"

The duke said, "That's it. If you run across it while you're looking for stuff about the Archers, let me know. If I knew what I was supposed to do, I wouldn't have so many people bothering me, you see? Might be for the best."

He left, leaving the searchers staring after him, open-mouthed.

A Favour for a Mage

"I am sick to death of mutton." Mr Henderson layered ham on a slice of bread. "Mutton chops, mutton stew, mutton pie. It never ends. If I never have another bite of mutton after I leave here, I won't miss it."

He looked as pleased with Sven and Irene's simple fare as if it had included suckling pig and meringues. Irene was pleased to be eating in the sitting room across the hall from the clerk's office, away from the calculated ostracism in the manor's kitchen.

"Speaking of leaving here," Sven said, "what will you do then?"

"Look for work in Edinburgh. It won't be easy—I don't expect the duchess will let the duke write me a letter of recommendation—but I have enough money saved to last a while. I'll find something."

"I'd be happy to write a letter for you," Irene said. "Coming from a member of the Air Guild, that should help."

"Bless you, ma'am," he said. "That would. A lot. But you haven't been taking the time to read much. What can you say?"

"Quite a bit. You're meticulous, conscientious, well organised, and polite even under trying circumstances. Your handwriting is legible, you make few mistakes, and you don't cheat your employer. If I needed a clerk, I'd hire you."

He rocked towards her, beaming. She froze, but he settled back on the sofa with a deep sigh. What would she have done if he had kissed her? She bent to grab an orange as cover for her confusion.

"That's very kind of you, ma'am," he said. "Very kind. Can you tell all that from your magic?"

"Most of it." She slid a penknife under the rind and began peeling. "Certainly the parts about not cheating and making few mistakes. Your correspondence has been easy on my eyes, compared to much of what I've read."

Sven asked, "Does it hurt to read bad writing?"

"Yes. Lies and mistakes are painful. Writing by someone in the grip of violent emotion, even if it includes few mistakes, can also be painful. Combine the two, like that letter yesterday, and reading can be like gazing into the sun."

Both men winced. The clerk asked, "Do you enjoy reading anything?"

"Of course. My talent is often vexatious, but there's much by mages and other scholars that brings me pleasure. Oliver taught me enough theory to understand Rehsavvy, and I've read his entire oeuvre." She glanced up from the orange, and was startled by Sven's glower. What had she said? She abandoned the no-longer-appealing orange.

"Good for you," Mr Henderson said. "I started one of his books on magic but it was beyond me. I'll stick to his histories. So, what do you do for the Air Guild? Do you proofread the mages' work for them, or write spells, or what?"

"To my regret," she said, trying and failing to keep her tone light, "the Air Guild doesn't appreciate my talent. They gave me a job at the school, correcting children's essays."

Both men stared. "Tell me what idiot thought that was a good idea, and I'll flame him," Sven said. "No wonder you have headaches. What would you rather do?"

"Pardon?"

"If the Air Guild did appreciate your talent, what would you want to do with it?"

Her throat tightened. Sven's innocent question was as unsettling as Lord Geoffrey's hand on her thigh had been. When she could speak again, she said, "If we're through with dinner, we should return to work."

Mouse droppings and skeletons fouled the next box of documents. Irene was picking through shreds of parchment when Lord Geoffrey stalked in, his face livid. "What is going on here?"

Sven didn't turn. "We're searching, as we were ordered."

Lord Geoffrey made a rude gesture at his back, then sat on the table, blocking Irene in. He grabbed her chin and twisted her face up towards his. He opened his mouth, and breathed in a cloud of dust blown off the nearest shelf.

He coughed and sneezed, his eyes streaming. Still gasping, he choked out, "You'll pay for that, witch."

"Pardon? I couldn't have done anything. After all, you said I was a fraud."

He grabbed her hair and twisted. She shoved the table. He flailed and fell. Sven yanked him to his feet and pushed him out the door. "Don't come back until you're ready to apologise for assaulting Mrs van Gelder."

Lord Geoffrey shouted, "Guards! Get them off my property, now!"

The two guards rolled eyes at each other and inched towards Sven. He raised his hands, palms out. "I have nothing against either of you personally, but if you touch me or Mrs van Gelder, I will burn you."

"Yes, sir," the sergeant said. "Same here, but we've got our orders, too. Grab him, Johnny."

They lunged. Fire flew between the shelves and out the door towards Lord Geoffrey. Irene dove for the floor and cowered behind the overturned table. Scuffling, yells, and a scream were followed by the door slamming.

Silence. Sven pulled the table away from Irene and offered her a hand. "Are you injured?"

"Only my dignity." Her scarf had fallen off and her hair tumbled over her shoulders. She brushed it from her face with her arm, then noticed her sleeve was filthy. "I must look a fright."

He smiled. "You do look a bit dusty, but there's nothing frightening about it."

His own tunic, once blue, was grey with dust, and he had cobwebs in his hair. He set the table upright, and scooped up documents. Mr Henderson rescued Irene's scarf from the wreckage. "Looks like this got singed, ma'am."

"Sorry about that," Sven said. "I doubt they'll bother us again, but just in case, let's not waste this chance." He laid a ledger on the table. "Look at this."

Irene bent over the book. The words on the page flashed gold, then settled into a sublime pink. *Malcolm Archer, taxes paid.*

Irene's scarf would not stay on. It began slipping when they reached the stairs behind the Hall of the Winds, but she didn't dare release her grip on either the railing or Sven to fuss with it. When she turned at the foot to thank him, it completed its slide, evaded her hand, and landed in the mud. Sven picked it up by a corner and handed it to her.

She held it at arm's length. "My hair's already filthy, but one must set a limit somewhere."

He tugged at a loose curl. "Wearing your hair down suits you better. It's softer. Prettier." Her eyes widened, but he didn't give her a chance to respond. "Irene, I have a favour to ask. Would you…" He hemmed and hawed, holding his hands together behind his back like a schoolboy. "Listen, Irene, I know it's not fair to ask when you've exhausted your magic." He pulled a sheaf of papers from his sack. "But could you proofread some poetry I've written? Please?"

The White Duchess

"What do you mean, you were told to go home?" Duncan tossed an iron in the fire and glared.

The work crew foreman shrugged. "We had just got going good this morning when a couple guards trotted up and told us to go home. To quit working on the road. Her Grace's orders."

"She's got no right to give orders. The duke told me to hire a crew and put 'em to work."

The foreman shrugged again. "Aye, and I believe you, but she's got her hands on the purse strings. You should've known what would happen when she got wind of it. When the guards said she wouldn't pay us, the lads said they'd be fools to keep on working. They shouldered their tools and headed for the tavern."

Duncan gave the bellows a good, hard yank. Cousin Jock raised an eyebrow. "Better watch that temper, Duncan."

"How happy would you be if you couldn't spend more than five minutes at a time doing what you're good at? I can't do more than get into a good rhythm before somebody comes along with a new problem."

Jock grinned. "I'm glad somebody's dealing with the duchess, and better you than me."

Duncan marched into the tavern, and told the lads lounging there that their break was over and to get back to work.

"Aye," one said. "Will you pay us, when the duke doesn't?"

"The duke promised to pay you, and I'm going to hold him to it. I'm going to have a talk with the duchess, right now."

They grinned. One wiseacre said, "And what're you going to do? Dunk her in a horse trough if she won't pay? I'd like to see you try it, if you think you'd survive a second trial."

Duncan stomped out, grumbling. The foreman followed. "Be careful, Duncan. She's cursed people before—I don't doubt she'll do it again. And just how will you make her fork over the money?"

"Don't know, Jamie. I'm making it up as I go along. But look—get them back to work. I don't need you undercutting me. I can't hold the duke to his end of the bargain if the work's not getting done."

Dealing with the duke was one thing. Dealing with the duchess was something else. Duncan had never fought a duchess before, and she'd scared even Uncle Will. He chewed on Jamie's question without coming up with any answers as he cooled his heels for an hour and a half. He would bet she was sitting with her maids, laughing at him. He would've barged in on the duke, but if he walked in on the duchess while she was getting dressed, he'd be in trouble.

If she was trying to make him nervous, it didn't work. When the butler finally let him in, he was hopping angry.

She looked harmless enough, with her head bent over her sewing, for all that her chair looked like a throne. Then the door closed behind him. She looked up, and he almost wet himself. She scared him more than the Frost Maiden had. He backed against the door, and groped for the latch without taking his eyes off her.

She said, "Why are you here, vassal?"

He croaked, "The duke's supposed to pay for the upkeep of the roads…"

That was all he could get out. She watched him the way a cat watches a cornered mouse, knowing it can close in for the kill any time it wants.

She said, "I can be generous. Drop this nonsense about spending my money, and I will not curse your sweetheart and firstborn child."

He made the sign against the evil eye behind his back.

"Fool. Your worthless signs will not protect you. You bore me. Go, before I change my mind."

He yanked the door open and ran.

Whatever magic the duchess had used didn't last past the front door. Duncan reached the tunnel, slammed the door open, and headed for the Fortress.

He had no trouble getting there, this time. The tall mage, Master Sven, had checked out the trap Duncan had nearly fallen through, and agreed with his guesses about it. The mage couldn't defang the trap, he said, because he wasn't a warlock, and they were too busy, but it was safe for the Earth and Fire Guilds. The Earth Guild Council met, and on the strength of Duncan's ability to dig, dragged him into the Earth Guild, as an apprentice reporting to Granny Mildred.

So now, in addition to being a swordsmith and the Fire Warlock's agent, he was a two-bit earth wizard who could dig holes in the ground and nothing else. He was real proud of that, all right. Frost him if he knew when he'd have time to learn the rules and customs of two new guilds in addition to everything else. If those warlocks decided to even the score and drag him into the Fire Guild, too, he would chuck it all back at the Fire Warlock and tell him to find some other dupe to do his frostbitten work for him.

Duncan had cooled off and started thinking before he found the Locksmith in her kitchen. "Look, ma'am, we've got to pry the purse strings out of her hands, but it won't help for the Fire Warlock to go and yell at her because she'll claim he bullied her. You're the one that should deal with her."

"Why me?"

"'Cause you're another woman, you're younger than she is, and you don't look scary. Well, you are, but you look like you'd rather be feeding the little lads and lasses their breakfasts than flaming somebody. The gentlefolk will have a hard time believing that she'd be scared of you. They don't like her much either, from what I hear, and might laugh at her for letting you get the best of her."

"I see your point." She got a faraway look in her eyes. "Fine. Let's go see her."

Never, Ever, Lie to a Warlock

Lucinda set down her mixing bowl and untied her apron. "What was the duchess wearing?"

Duncan said, "How would I know?"

"You said you didn't dare look away. How could you not notice?"

He waved his hands. "She was wearing a dress. I don't know—a dress is a dress. It was blue. I think. What does it matter?"

"It matters because I don't want to overdress and outshine her—that wouldn't play well with not bullying her."

"What's wrong with what you're wearing?"

"A plain wool housedress? You have to be joking. The staff would think I'm a servant and I wouldn't get past the front door. I have to look impressive enough to be taken seriously, without overdoing it. You're not helping."

Lucinda climbed the stairs, grumbling about men's inability to see things in front of their noses. She had nothing close to the latest court finery—the current styles would have looked hideous on her—so she pulled on a dress of dark red silk she had acquired in Cathay. With a high collar and sleeves that fell a couple of inches below her wrists, it was simple but elegant, and exotic enough to demand attention.

When she returned, Duncan said, "Wow. You look like a real fire witch."

"I didn't before?"

"Uh, sorry, ma'am. I meant…"

She laughed. "Never mind. I thought they wouldn't know quite what to make of me in this."

"They'll know you're enough of a witch that you don't care what the men think."

"What?"

"You're not showing any skin, so you must not care about getting a fellow's attention."

"I am a happily married woman. I don't need another man's attention. But seriously, Duncan, is that all you men care about—how low-cut our bodices are?"

He shrugged. "That must be what those high-born women think, or they wouldn't wear dresses without any tops to them. They're not showing off their wares for other women."

"When have you seen a noblewoman without a bodice to her dress?"

"Well, I didn't mean that, quite. But the duchess… The only thing I can figure out was holding her top up was a little witchcraft."

"You said you didn't notice anything about her dress!"

"You asked how she was dressed, not how she was undressed. Uh, ma'am, remember you aren't trying to look scary…"

Walking the serene avenue from the tunnels to the duke's manor house soothed Lucinda's frazzled nerves. A well-executed boxwood squirrel caught her attention, to Master Duncan's evident annoyance.

She said, "What a pleasant garden. The topiary here is lovely."

"Topi-what?"

"The shrubbery trimmed into fanciful shapes. It's a very old art form—we got it from the Romans, I believe."

"The Romans should've kept it."

She ignored him for the rest of the walk.

"Why are you letting your wife make you look like a limp dishrag?" Lucinda tapped her foot and frowned at the White Duke. "You made an agreement. She doesn't have the authority to renege."

He hunkered down in his chair, staring at the floor and pulling his muffler tighter around his shoulders and ears. "She threatened to curse me. My toes would rot and fall off if I didn't do as she said."

Duncan and Lucinda shared a dumbfounded stare over the duke's head. She said, "Nonsense. You're the one the Fire Office shields. Any curses thrown at you will bounce off."

The duke looked up. "What? You mean the Office shields against curses, too?"

She resisted the urge to grab the fool's shoulders and shake him. "What do you mean, *against curses, too?* That's the primary purpose of the magical shields. The spells against physical violence were thrown in as an afterthought, and frankly, they're half-baked. The shields against malicious magic are much better."

The duke's eyes went wide. "I didn't know that. Why didn't anybody ever tell me?"

"Someone should have. Every Frank should know this. Master Duncan knew, and he's not a noble."

"Aye," Duncan said. "The Fire Warlock promised me the same shields as long as I'm his agent, so her threats didn't bother me, once I was out of range. I figured she'd hurt herself if she did try to curse me or mine. That's the way it always worked in the old stories. You should've listened to them."

The duke said, "My mother claimed they were sops for ignorant peasants and wouldn't let the nursemaids tell them."

Lucinda said, "Ignorant peasants, my foot. Duncan knows more about your position than you do. Maybe you should hire a minstrel to tell you stories at bedtime."

The duke brightened. "I could, couldn't I? I'd like that."

"I guess you don't know about the magic on your money, either."

Both men looked blank.

She sighed. "If you, as duke, designate a sum to be used for a specific purpose on behalf of your subjects, that money can't be spent on anything else. Anyone who tried to use it for other purposes would be burned."

"Really?"

"Yes, really. So you will count out the money, right now, to pay for the roadwork you've already agreed to."

The duke sent for a clerk, and while the three of them put their heads together, debating a fair amount to set aside, Lucinda gazed out the window, admiring the view over the formal gardens. When they finished, she told the butler, "Tell Her Grace to come here at once. We—the duke, Master Duncan, and I, the Warlock Locksmith—must talk to her. I have other obligations, and will not be kept waiting."

The butler looked to his master for guidance. The duke said, "Go ahead, tell her that. But don't be surprised, madam, if she doesn't come."

"I don't know why not. She's in her sitting room with her attendants, doing embroidery. She isn't busy."

The butler rolled his eyes at Lucinda. The duke said, "She resents anyone telling her what to do."

"All the more reason to inconvenience her occasionally."

The butler cast another pleading look at the duke, who said, "Go on, tell her." The trembling butler left.

The duke joined Lucinda at the window, looking more cheerful than she had yet seen him. "Do you like my garden?"

"Yes, Your Grace, it's as picturesque as any I've ever seen."

"Thank you," he said. "The duchess doesn't like it. She's been badgering me to tear it up and start over. She says it's too old-fashioned."

"Topiary has gone out of style, hasn't it? It's a shame. I like it. If you like it, keep it."

"I will. Work in the garden is all I've ever really wanted to do, but nobody ever lets me dig in the dirt. They tell me I mustn't get my hands dirty—it's not dignified—but they let me trim the topiary. The squirrel's my favourite—I won't let anyone else touch it. Do you like it?"

"Yes, very much." After a few minutes' chat on garden design, she said, "Time's up. Follow me." They met the whimpering butler in the hall. He gasped as she breezed past him. Master Duncan and the duke followed her into the sitting room. The butler and the clerk listened from the hall, out of their mistress's sight.

The women's heads bobbed up from their embroidery. The duchess said, "Who are you? How dare you barge into a private room without permission?"

"You heard the butler. I am a warlock, under the Fire Warlock's orders. You—"

A wave of terror bounced off Lucinda's mirror shield, and the squawking harridan collapsed into a squeaking mouse. Her women stared. Hands holding needles and floss hung forgotten in mid-air.

"Stop it," the duchess begged, curling into her armchair with her hands over her eyes. "Who are you? You should be scared of me. I'll do whatever you want, just make it stop."

Lucinda said, "You stop it. I'm using a mirror shield spell, that's all. You're scaring yourself."

The terror spell went on. The duchess cowered in her chair, crying.

"Oh, for heaven's sake, I can't stand this." Lucinda threw a lock on her. The duchess straightened, gasping and dazed.

Lucinda said, "You can dish it out but you can't take it. Rather, you could dish it out. You won't be scaring anyone, ever again, with that perverted glamour spell. You won't be interfering, either, with agreements between the duke and the Warlock's agent on how money is to be spent. The duke designated the bag of coins Master Duncan is carrying to be spent on the roads, and it will be."

The duchess snapped out of her daze. "I say it won't be."

"Oh? Master Duncan, give her the bag."

He leaned in with the bag at arm's length and dropped it on the table beside her. She looked at it uncertainly.

"Go ahead," Lucinda said. "Try using the money for something else. Give some to one of your attendants."

The duchess reached into the bag, then screamed, flinging a coin away from her. Duncan picked it up, turned it over in his hands, and shrugged.

She said, "You enchanted this bag—"

"Not I," Lucinda said. "This magic protects and supports any nobleman. Any money he designates for a purpose on behalf of his people will burn any thief."

"How dare you call me a thief!" She glowered at Lucinda, then her expression went slack. "My spell. What happened to it?"

Lucinda repeated, "I put a lock on it. You can't use it, ever again."

"I am an air witch. How dare you interfere with the Air Guild!"

"Interfere? You attacked me, remember."

The duchess snarled, "I curse you, you wretched hothead. Your hair will fall out—"

"Too late. I'm wearing a wig; I don't have any hair. Besides, you don't have enough power to curse a warlock on Fire Guild business. I'd be surprised if you even have the talent to curse a mundane."

An attendant said, "She gave a maid boils, and one of the footmen running sores."

"Did she? That's not air magic." Lucinda frowned at the duchess. "Did you hire an earth witch to throw curses for you?"

She scowled. "Of course not. I am quite capable of throwing curses myself."

Lucinda breathed fire. "Fool. Do you imagine you can lie to a warlock and not suffer for it?" She had let this idiot box them both into a corner; it would be disastrous to let the wretch dull one of the Fire Guild's most potent weapons. Drawing herself up to her full height, Lucinda thrust her wand out like a sword and intoned:

> *What is done cannot be undone.*
> *What is said cannot be unsaid.*
> *If you spoke to me words untrue,*
> *I command all your mischief return now to you.*

Boils and running sores spread across the duchess's exposed skin. She screamed. Her attendants scattered. The duke stared at his wife with undisguised revulsion.

Lucinda retrieved the money. "Come on, Master Duncan. We're done here."

In the entrance hall, she handed the bag to the clerk. "Count out the first week's wages so Master Duncan can show it to the road crew as proof of the duke's good faith, then put the bag back in the strongbox. Just because it would burn anybody who isn't authorised to handle it doesn't mean it's a good idea to leave it sitting out. Pay for the work done at the end of each week until the bad weather settles in. Whatever hasn't been used by New Year's can be used for other purposes without penalty." She eyed the duke, who had followed her. "In the future, set aside the money as soon as you and Duncan agree on something. That will save everybody grief. And don't bother sending for a healer. Find the earth witch who cast the curses for her, pay her to remove them, and report her to the Earth Guild afterwards."

"Yes, madam," he said. "And, madam—thank you."

On their return to the tunnels Duncan and Lucinda stopped, by unspoken mutual consent, to examine the squirrel.

He said, "I never will understand the gentry. All the power he's got, and everybody bosses him around. Telling him he can't get his hands dirty. What a load of...well, you know what. And letting his duchess hag-ride him. Things should change for the better once word gets out that she can't scare anybody anymore."

"Can't scare anybody? Don't be naïve. A duchess doesn't need magic to hurt people. She's not through scaring people—not at all."

"But if he's not scared of her…"

The hairs at the back of her neck rose. "You think he isn't? She won't give up without a fight, and she's been bullying him for—what?—twenty, twenty-five years. Bullying or being bullied—neither habit is easy to break. You and Hazel better keep on eye on them, or she'll make his life hell."

"That reminds me, ma'am. The Fire Warlock said we—his agents, I mean—would have the same shields as the nobles. So why did her scary spell work on me?"

She chewed on her lip. "Good question. I'll ask Jean. He'll know."

Jean, when asked, blinked at her. "The White Duchess did what?"

"Terrified Master Duncan with a negative glamor spell, and he's supposed to be shielded. He stood up to the Fire Warlock, but this level two airhead sent him running."

"He is shielded. Paul, Sven, and I together went over the wording of the contract the king signed. The king, and only the king, has the authority to override the shields on a specific nobleman, but the contract disallows unilateral overrides for our agents."

"What does it say?"

"The agent, once appointed… *Drown it!*" He turned on heel and marched to the fire. Several moments frantic search revealed the duchess complaining to the king years ago about the power the Abertee blacksmiths exerted over her husband. The king responded by telling her to do whatever was necessary to counter the Blacksmiths' Guild's bad influence. "Use your magic if they step out of line," he said. "That's an order."

"Bad influence?" Lucinda said. "My God. Calling the man trying to keep the peace a bad influence is…"

"Asinine." Jean straightened up from the fire. "Locking away her talent was a good tactical manoeuvre, my dear, but may have an unfortunate strategic impact."

"You're saying today was a Pyrrhic victory? I felt that, too, but why?"

"You caught her by surprise today; she had not known she was fighting a war. Now she does."

Rumours

"Aversion spells, shields, traps…" The glowing quartet of flames on Sven's hat bounced above the garden path, stopping at the gate. "It's as safe as I can make it without attracting unwanted attention, but I can't protect your garden against missiles thrown over the wall."

"Of course not. One wouldn't expect that," Irene said. "Thank you for what you have done. Mother is a strong enough air witch to protect herself and the children from airborne threats, if convinced of the danger."

"That rock that hit you this morning ought to convince her. It could have broken a bone."

Irene's arm still ached, despite a healer's ministrations. "Showing her the bruise won't do any good. Her sense of self-worth depends on her position in the guild. She would throw me to the dogs rather than accuse any recognised air wizard of misbehaviour."

"That's…just…"

"Wilful blindness?"

"Appalling. Especially with small children involved. I don't want to worry you any more than you already are, but…"

"She did, at least, take the threatening letter mentioning them seriously, while castigating me for having brought it on myself by turning my back on the Air Guild."

"Oh, wonderful." He was silent for a moment, then said, "You don't seem eager to abandon the search."

"I'm not eager to return to drudgery at the school, or to prove that threats work. They would torment me further for the sheer pleasure of it."

"That's true, but you shouldn't call yourself a coward."

"You haven't met Mother. She will scare me witless if she discovers me in the garden after dark with a fire wizard."

White teeth gleamed. The gate creaked open. "Fine. I can take a hint."

"Douse your hat, or rumours will be all over Airvale by morning."

The glow disappeared. "I'll meet you here at first light—don't leave the garden by yourself. Be safe."

The gate clicked shut behind him. Irene trudged up the path to the supposed safety and comfort of her mother's house. On the top step, something squished underfoot and stank. Like Sven's aversion spells, the action of yanking her skirts aloft came a little late. With a sigh, she stepped out of her shoes and went on into the kitchen, where Susan, the maid, greeted her with "Phew! What happened? You smell like a privy."

Irene explained about the gift on the top step—"a reminder of what the Air Guild thinks of me"—and sent the maid upstairs for clean clothes. When decent again, Irene left the kitchen, and found her mother waiting with an expression of icy disdain at the top of the stairs.

"Young lady," she said, "I have had enough of your contempt for propriety."

"Pardon?"

"I do not approve of conspiring with fire wizards against our own guild, but I have held my tongue. I will not, however, condone flagrant misconduct. Have you no morals?"

"Mother, what are you talking about?"

"You know perfectly well what I am talking about."

"I have no idea." Irene's knuckles on the bannister had turned white. Susan peered at them around the kitchen door.

Mother said, "You are setting a terrible example for your children."

"You're not setting a good example, either, accusing me of a crime without telling me what it is."

"You have no right to speak to me like that. And I will not demean myself by repeating such vile gossip." She turned her back and swept away.

Irene waited on the stairs until her voice was under control. Was there truth to the neighbours' whispers her father died young to escape from his wife? Irene retreated to the kitchen, where Susan was making a noisy display of setting out pots and crockery for the morning.

"Put down those dishes," Irene said, "And tell me what Mother's angry about."

"Oh, ma'am, you don't want to hear it."

"How can one defend oneself against unknown charges?"

"There's gossip going around..."

"That was obvious. Details, please."

Susan sang. A catchy little ditty, using an old, familiar tune, with well-chosen rhymes and vivid imagery, it would be easy to remember. Neither of the duke's sons had enough wit to have written it, but Irene could guess which of their friends was responsible. The author would have deserved her compliments, if not for the subject matter: an allegation that she, false air witch, had seduced Flame Mage Sven Matheson, driving him into such a frenzy of desire that he made the wildest of promises while ripping her clothes off in public.

"Thank you, Susan." Irene should have expected it. The Richardsons were not known for fighting fair, and she was an easy target.

"Begging your pardon, ma'am," Susan said, "but you did ask. But, ma'am, you shouldn't worry. No one in Airvale would believe you would do something so... so..."

"So improper?"

"So bold."

No one but Mother. The rest of Airvale should jeer at the idea Irene had enough magic to seduce a mage, but logic was not often the Air Guild's strong suit. She sighed. "I'd rather break my oath to the Air Guild than embarrass myself in such a fashion."

"Yes, ma'am. Goodnight, ma'am."

Irene had stepped into a pile of shit, for certain, and not all of it on the back steps. The standard advice the Air Guild offered when a member was slandered in the course of duty was to act unconcerned and let the guild take the rumourmongers to court. The guild would protect you, they said.

And pigs might fly.

At least no one outside of the Air Guild had ever heard of her. In a few months no one beyond Airvale would care, or remember. Irene would do what she should have done long ago: return to Oxford and scrape out a living proofreading undergraduate's essays. A lonely life of genteel and obscure poverty was the best to be hoped for, as no one who cared about his reputation would have anything to do with her.

Sleep, like Mother, avoided her. She was waiting at the garden gate long before first light. When Sven arrived, the faint pre-dawn light was strong enough to show the thin line of his mouth and set of his jaw.

Irene turned away. "You've heard the song."

"Yes. It's a pity you've been subjected to such rot."

They walked in silence. They were halfway to the duke's manor before he added, "I won't blame you if you say you've had enough, and quit."

"Would that help, or would it just give weight to the rumours?"

"Probably the latter."

"Then let's carry on. Finding the evidence to call them to account will be the best revenge."

The other guests' whispers and the space they left around the cohort of witches and wizards didn't bother Lucinda. She understood why they'd been invited, and she would have work to do before the day ended, but she was with friends, and she loved weddings.

She settled into the pew with a sigh. Her strength was returning, but she tired faster than she used to, and it felt good to sit down. She studied her hands while they waited. The fingers on the right were the proper length again, although thinner than the ones on the left. She wore gloves because the skin tones were so different—her right hand was as pale as a newborn's. A noblewoman would have considered it perfect, and worn a glove only on the left. Having grown up engaged in gardening and outdoor play, to her it looked uncanny.

The beaming bride processed in on her brother's arm. Lucinda blocked out worries over Frankland's problems, and gave herself over to enjoying the ceremony. The sweating groom stammered through his vows. She couldn't fault him for nerves, with brothers-in-law the size of elephants.

Too soon it was over and the wedding party swept out. Over the hubbub of happy voices in the church came the sound of horses—lots of horses. The chatter dwindled. The crowd parted to let the three witches through. The wizards trailed after them. Lucinda reached the church door as the White Duke's son reigned in his horse in front of Maggie and Will.

He must have brought with him every guard in his father's employ. The troop, riding three abreast, stretched down the road and around a hill. The arrogant brat sneered, "It's your lucky day, wench. I'm in time to exercise my right of first night."

The groom jerked convulsively. Lucinda grabbed his arm.

"Don't," she hissed as she pushed past him. "It's my prerogative."

"Nonsense," Lucinda said aloud. "That's a fable some blue-blooded swine invented to excuse rape. There has never been such a right."

The brat stared as if he couldn't believe his eyes and ears. "Who the hell are you?"

"The Warlock Locksmith, as you could tell from my hat if you had any sense."

Lucinda thought if he'd been a fire wizard he'd have flamed her. "I know my rights," he snarled. "The Fire Guild can't interfere in a nobleman's affairs with his own people."

Lucinda's witch friends stepped up beside her, one on either side. The guards started backing their horses.

Sorceress Lorraine said, "Did you understand nothing of the trials? The Water Guild does not condone hunting women for sport."

"It's a shame we can't let him try," René said.

Lorraine's head snapped around, brows lowered, nostrils flaring.

He said, "It would improve the quality of the next generation of nobility if the Water Office gelded him."

The duke's son turned purple. The watching cattle and sheep breeders roared.

Lucinda raised a hand. Thunder rumbled. The churchyard went quiet save for the thud of retreating hooves.

"A pleasing thought," she said, "but not fair to Maggie and Will. You—Lord Whoever-you-are—you and your guards are not welcome here. Any still in sight after I count to three will meet the forces of fire, water, and earth. One."

The guards wheeled their horses. The nobleman snarled and cursed at them.

"We should have invited Enchantress Winifred—" Hazel said.

"Two."

"—To make it unanimous."

"Three."

Needles of ice pelted Lord Geoffrey in the face. A tongue of flame hit him in the chest. Sleet and fireballs like wasps stung the fleeing guards. The ground shook. The horses bolted, scattering in all directions. The crowd cheered as they disappeared.

"I feel awful," Hazel said, "scaring horses like that. Some of them may not make it home."

"Pity," Douglas Archer said. "About the horses."

I rene said, "Are you sure the Earth Guild won't mind us using their library?"

"Quite sure," Sven said. "Access to every guild and college library in Frankland is one of a mage's privileges, and there's a long-standing tradition that gives the Fire Guild Council free run of the Warren's public spaces."

"They haven't been as welcoming towards the Air Guild."

"That's true," he said. "Would you prefer the Fortress?"

"No. Those stairs…"

"Then the Warren will have to do."

The few people about late on a Sunday afternoon greeted them politely. No one laughed, leered, or recoiled, as the guards and servants had at the duke's. If these members of the Earth Guild had heard the song, they gave no sign of it.

If only that nasty little ditty hadn't embedded itself in Irene's memory. Sven treated her with the same gallantry as before, but the lyrics hung, unmentioned, between them, and it was evident he was deeply angry. For days they had engaged in little conversation not related to the search or the most general of topics. She inspected every word before it left her lips, expunging any hint of flirtation or innuendo. Anything personal was fraught with traps.

Sven led her through the deserted library to an alcove with a small fireplace. He lit a fire, then fiddled with the lamp, turning it up and down, and then up again. Stalling.

Irene pulled the few poems she had had time to read from her handbag. The first three pages were violet, purple, and deep blue. "These are lovely. A pleasure to read."

"You've made plenty of comments."

"About minor things. Word choice here and there, punctuation and meter in a few places. The first had a structural problem, but it can be fixed."

He sagged against the chair back. A slow smiled formed. He nodded at the two pages still in her hand. "What about those?"

The topmost sheet, titled simply *Grief*, glowed in deep red, like embers, with flickers of yellow and orange. "This was more difficult to read. The colours are hard on my eyes."

His face fell. "You didn't like it."

"Oh, but I do."

"But if it's full of problems—"

"There are no more problems in this than in those others."

He frowned. "But…"

"The emotional content makes it more difficult to read, and more rewarding. Those are good; this is better. Those are cerebral—enjoyable, but not gripping. But this one—about your father? Read once, it is unlikely to be forgotten. It described my emotional state in the weeks after Oliver died. You've captured the anger over losing someone you love as well as, or better than, anything else I've ever read."

"I'm a fire wizard. Anger is an emotion I know well."

"Sven, this is superb. You have to publish. It would be a crime to keep it to yourself."

He blushed. What must it do to one, to have one's emotions always on public display? There was something to be said for being an air witch.

The last poem lay face down. "And then there's this one."

His eyebrows drew together, but he didn't interrupt.

"Sven, this is perfect. There is nothing I can improve upon, which is as well, because it seared my eyes. Save it to be published posthumously. Publishing it now would expose too much of your soul."

Turning it over exposed the flaring colours, perfection's royal purple fighting the greens of envy and jealousy and the orange and reds of anger. Heat rose from the page. His face, so open moments before, closed, his eyes hooded, his expression guarded.

"The witch and the other fire wizard from the first stanza are unknown to me, but they are probably well known in the Fire Guild. Don't show them how jealous you are. And the second stanza—it's about Oliver, isn't it?"

His eyes blazed, and he turned away. "What makes you think that?"

"You were at university together, but Oliver was admitted to the Company of Mages six months before you were."

He faced the fire. The muscles in his face worked, his nostrils flaring, his jaw clenching.

She didn't add, 'And Oliver was a hero and you're not'. Oliver had died rescuing a shipload of sailors from the Empire's wizards. But Sven wasn't a warlock. He wouldn't be called on to give his life for his country. Thank God.

Sven's voice was tight, the words clipped short. "Ollie used to claim he was too lazy to be a mage, but that book of spells proved him wrong. I couldn't blame them—he deserved it." He lurched to his feet. "You're right—I won't show it to anyone else. I shouldn't have shown it to you. Forget it."

He snatched the paper from her hands, threw it into the fire, and stalked from the room, leaving her gasping. She was sitting on the hearthrug, watching the fire, when he returned.

"I'm sorry." His voice still sounded strained.

"So am I." He had no idea how strong her regrets were.

He said, "Thank you for reading my poetry. It means a great deal to me that you say they're good."

As they walked towards the tunnels, she fingered the fragment hidden in her pocket, that she had snatched from the fire. It would cost her a day's magic to recreate, but she would. There was enough left. Her guilty conscience would not let this masterpiece vanish. The title on the charred remnant burned in her mind's eye: *Always Second Best*.

The Charter

With one day left before Lord Geoffrey's deadline for the Archer's eviction, he should have been harassing the searchers, but he had not appeared. The guards who usually dogged them had disappeared at dinnertime and not been replaced.

Mr Henderson started when addressed and showed signs of a stutter. Irene's breathing was rapid and shallow. Her holiday was over. With the duke's younger son still in Airvale, returning to the guild school would be hazardous as well as unpleasant.

They finished by mid-afternoon. As Sven and Irene followed Mr Henderson across the width of the manor house, Sven's head swivelled at every open door and passageway. He mouthed "Guards?" at her. She shrugged.

In the duke's study, Sven spread the documents across the desk. "Ledgers showing the Archers paid taxes. The deed granting land in the Upper Tee Valley to a troop of soldiers for their services in a foreign expedition. A letter from your great-aunt to your grandfather complaining about the arrogant freeholders in Nettleton…"

The duke peered at them with befuddlement on his pudgy face. He dropped the last document and pulled his gloves back on. "What does all this mean?"

"The evidence is in the Archers' favour, Your Grace. You can't evict them."

"I didn't think we could. If it were that easy, Grandfather would have kicked them out sixty years ago. He always said they were infernal nuisances."

"Maybe that's why the ledgers were falsified," Mr Henderson said. "To make it easier for someone later to evict them."

The duke sighed. "It's just as well. I'd rather deal with a few Archers than have everybody in Abertee queuing to carp at me. Is that all?"

"No, Your Grace," Sven said. "Mrs van Gelder also found the charter, or, rather, what's left of it."

The duke brightened, but his face fell when he saw the blackened scrap of parchment. "Good heavens, what happened to it?"

"One of your ancestors burnt it, I believe."

He turned it around in his hands. "I can't read it. I can't even tell for sure which way is up."

Irene said, "It's in Latin, in a script that fell from favour six hundred years ago. See, here it says, "The duke shall," but the rest of that line is illegible. Further down—here, Your Grace—it clearly says 'via'. Something about roads."

"So those nuisances in Nettleton were right all along, were they?" He pulled the muffler tight around his neck. "But if that's all you can tell, I still won't know what I'm supposed to do."

"The charter can be repaired, Your Grace."

"Really?"

"May I show you?"

"Oh, please do."

With a blank paper resting on the parchment, she drew on every speck of power she had, concentrating on seeing the charter as it had once been. It was a moment's work, and little drain, to copy onto the paper the lettering still legible on the parchment beneath. Filling in the gaps between legible phrases was harder, but the words appeared at the same rate as if one copied them manually.

Then from the edges, working outwards, she groped for words no longer having any physical trace. The charter had been written so long ago that every word, every letter was a struggle, and ink flowed across the paper at the pace of a schoolboy first learning his letters. After two lines, she was suffocating. She abandoned the effort, wheezing.

The men pressed her to sit, and would have summoned a healer, but she insisted none was needed. "I'm tired, that's all. This work is draining."

Sven picked up the paper, eyes flicking back and forth between paper and parchment. "This is impressive. Very impressive."

The duke said, "How long will it take to do the whole thing?"

Irene said, "A week, Your Grace. Possibly two."

"What does it say? Is it the charter?"

Sven said, "Oh, yes. We're missing a sentence or two at the beginning, but it starts with 'agreement with King Richard on behalf of the people of Abertee. The duke shall have the right to...' and then it lists your rights. Further down it says, 'In return for these privileges the duke accepts these responsibilities', and the first one is 'For the furtherance of commerce the duke shall maintain two highways, one running north and south, the other east and west, through Abertee'."

"The duchess won't be happy about that. Not one bit." The duke waved them away. "Come back when the whole thing's done. Don't bother me again until then."

As they left, Irene could have sworn he was laughing to himself.

Sven helped Mr Henderson with the bags he'd hidden by the tunnel entrance. When they emerged in the Warren, the clerk said, "I couldn't talk back there, because I didn't know who was listening, but there are rumours making the rounds. One is that you found the charter. Don't ask me how anyone guessed that. I didn't give it away."

Sven said, "Didn't think you had."

"And the kitchen staff said Lord Geoffrey's taken all the guards, without telling the duke, to burn the Archers out tonight."

"He gave them until tomorrow. He can't get away with that."

Irene said, "They always have so far."

"If they're headed for Nettleton, Master Duncan can hop through the tunnels after they reach Crossroads..."

Mr Henderson said, "The road to Nettleton from the manor doesn't go through Crossroads, sir. They'll cross the Upper Tee at Drayman's Ford and ride north. They could be in Nettleton before Master Duncan gets word."

"*Drown it!* If he doesn't request the Fire Warlock's help..."

The clerk's stutter became more pronounced. "I'd d-d-do it, sir, on behalf of the Clerk's Association, but I'm r-r-running away from Abertee, sir. Do I count?"

"Would you leave Abertee if you weren't afraid of the duchess?"

"No, sir. I like the duke and I have friends there."

"That ought to count. Follow me!"

They hurried through the Fortress tunnel. The Fire Warlock's study was cold and empty.

"Of course he's not here," Sven said. A fire sprang to life in the fireplace. Sven knelt and began calling names.

Mr Henderson said, "What…"

Irene grasped his arm. "Shh!"

After calling a dozen names with no responses, Sven jabbed the fire with his wand, scowling. After a few moments, he shot upright with an explosive "*Frostbite!* That weasel's timing stinks. There's a riot in South Frankland and I can't get their attention. Come on!"

They raced through the tunnels to the door above Airvale. "Here," he said, shoving the stack of documents at Irene. "You two, take these to Enchanter Paul. Tell him about the charter, and about Lord Geoffrey. He can demand a warlock's attention. I'm going back to Abertee."

With a swirl of cloak he was away, running for the other tunnel.

Halfway through Mr Henderson's story, Enchanter Paul leaned back in his chair and closed his eyes. A moment later, he raised a hand. "Stop. A warlock will be here in a few minutes. You may tell the whole story then. Meanwhile, let me see what you unearthed."

Irene handed him the documents, holding back only the partially recreated charter, and he spread them out on his desk. He interrupted her description. "I had not expected anything from this venture. I shall have to commend Master Sven for his perseverance and attention to detail."

"I found—"

"You, too, Mr Henderson. Thank you for your assistance."

"Yes, sir," the clerk said, glancing sideways at Irene.

The enchanter examined the scrap of parchment. "How extraordinary— to think that someone tried to destroy it, and hid the scrap that survived. The problem, of course, will be to convince the White Duke that it is real…"

"Sir," Irene said, "he does believe it, after I—"

"And to recreate it."

"Sir, I've already begun—"

He waved aside the paper she held out. Taking a fresh sheet from a drawer, he laid it on the parchment. With the full power of the Air Office at his command, ink flowed across the page faster than anyone could write. In less than two minutes, the complete charter lay on his desk.

Bitter gall rose in Irene's throat. Her partial copy fell to the floor.

"If we can convince the nobles this is real," he mused, "finding other charters may be more important—and more urgent—than I had imagined. I should assign someone with real talent…"

"Sir, I found the charter. I—"

"Perhaps Enchantress Winifred…"

Irene slammed the ledger on the table. "Sir, listen to me!"

For the first time that day—no, for the first time ever—he focused on her. "Enough, woman! Be silent."

Her protest made no sound. Shock and pity showed on Mr Henderson's face. Her remaining shreds of pride would not let her cry before witnesses. She blundered for the door.

A Volcano Erupts

The air witch was blind with tears, and slammed into the half-open door. Lucinda winced, and yanked it further open. The air witch fled. Lucinda marched towards Enchanter Paul. "Was that necessary?"

He had the decency to look discomfited. "My dear Locksmith, forgive me for subjecting you to such an unpleasant little scene, but Irene has a tendency to overreact."

"Overreact, my foot. She had something to say and you never gave her a chance. If someone treated me like that I'd flame them."

He flushed. "I'm afraid she has a long history of emotional instability and self-aggrandisement. To indulge her by listening to her stories doesn't help."

The clerk tugged at his collar and bent to pick up the crumpled paper the air witch had dropped. "Your Wisdom, it doesn't seem fair to commend Master Sven and not commend Mrs van Gelder, too. She found two bits of evidence for every one he found, and she found the charter. She could recreate it, too."

Paul raised a hand wearily, motioning the clerk to stop. "Nonsense. I don't think she was deliberately pulling the wool over your and Master Sven's eyes, but she is deluded about her abilities. I can believe she found the documents through speed reading and luck, but recreating the charter from a fragment is enchanter-level magic, and she doesn't have the talent—any talent."

Lucinda forgot about the riots. She forgot about the clerk. She saw Enchanter Paul through a red mist. The crackle of burning enveloped her. "The Fire Warlock believes this search is crucial to maintaining the peace in Frankland, and you sent someone you consider unqualified?"

A cat's mewing on the portico outside sounded loud in the sudden hush. With lowered brow and thin lips, Enchanter Paul bore a remarkable resemblance to Warlock Flint. "You forget yourself, young lady. You have no right to address me in such a manner."

Lucinda leaned on his desk with both hands flat on the polished wood. She lowered her voice, but didn't quench the fire. "You forget I am the Fire Warlock's apprentice and privy to his counsel. You will not silence me. If the Fire Warlock burns out soon, as seems increasingly likely, you will answer to me while the present crisis lasts. The rebuffs I've gotten from some members of the Air Guild when we've asked for help have dismayed me. They don't take the situation seriously. Now I understand why."

He ground out through gritted teeth, "We are short-staffed. Let me remind you that with our responsibility for protecting sailors we lost more wizards during the war than the Fire Guild did."

"Let me remind you I have risked my life in Frankland's service, more than once." She twitched the charter out of his hands and scooped up the other documents. Maybe he wouldn't notice the scorch marks on his desk until after she left. "If or when I am Fire Warlock, I will not hesitate to use every last man, woman, and child in all four guilds to keep Frankland from tearing herself apart, if that's what it takes. Because, if we are in such dire straits that I am Fire Warlock, God knows we'll need all the help we can get."

She turned towards the door, and came face to face with the pale, trembling clerk. He bolted.

Drown it. She shouldn't have said all that with a mundane listening.

She stalked to the door without looking back. "Good day, Your Wisdom."

"Come out from behind that wall," Lucinda said. "I am angry, but not at you."

A pair of eyes peeked around the corner of the building. "Y-Y-Your Wisdom…"

"Don't call me that. I'm not the Fire Warlock. I pray I never will be."

"Yes, sir. Ma'am, I mean." The head recoiled into the shadow of the wall like a turtle into its shell. "Oh, dear…"

Despite her boiling temper, Lucinda had to laugh. "I won't flame you;

I came here to talk to you. You have a problem to report?"

The clerk edged out, exposing his head and shoulders, and described the situation in Abertee.

"Good man," she said. "Thank you for bringing it to our attention." She concentrated. The clerk had stepped out of the wall's shadow when she opened her eyes. "I've informed the Fire Warlock. Thank you also for your aid in the search for these documents, and for standing up for Mrs van Gelder."

"Ma'am... Uh, what am I supposed to call you, ma'am?"

"Either Madam Locksmith or Mrs Rehsavvy. I prefer the simpler title."

In a shaking hand, he held out the paper the air witch had dropped. "Mrs Rehsavvy, ma'am, would you look at this? I watched Mrs van Gelder make a start on recreating the charter, and it looked like magic to me. She said it would take a week or two, because she wasn't powerful enough to do it all at once, so it's not as impressive as what he did, but all the same... I don't understand why the Air Guild don't think she's a witch. She impressed Master Sven, and he's a mage."

"Master Sven's opinion is enough for me. I intend to find out why Enchanter Paul is such an ass. I may have to give him another piece of my mind." The magic guilds weren't supposed to interfere in each other's business, were they? Well, she'd see about *that*! "But not tonight. There's more than one crisis tonight, and I don't have time. Where's your home?"

"Edinburgh, ma'am."

"Good. Edinburgh is quiet. So far. Go to the tunnel mouth and wait. I'll send someone to escort you through the tunnels. Don't go into Airvale. With so many nobles in the Air Guild it's not safe."

"Yes, ma'am. Thank you, ma'am. Ma'am, if you ever are Fire Warlock, I think you'll do fine." He turned towards the tunnel, but immediately turned back. "What about Mrs van Gelder? She lives in Airvale."

"*Burn it!* No, it's not safe for her either. The Fire Warlock should never have put a level three witch at the mercy of enemies in her own guild. What was that frosted fool thinking?"

The last Lucinda saw of the clerk as the flames rose was an open-mouthed gawk. He was too shocked to be frightened.

Mother's Worst Fear

Irene's flight from the Hall of the Winds was without thought or direction. Deep in the pines, burning lungs brought her to a stop. Attempting to speak confirmed her suspicion the Air Enchanter had not lifted the order to be silent.

Returning to Airvale in this condition was out of the question. Miranda and Gillian wouldn't understand. They would only know that the past week's disgraces had intensified. Rumours were rife: Irene was conspiring with the Fire Guild in forging evidence to cheat the White Duke. Sven wasn't fit to be in the Company of Mages. Irene's two daughters were not Oliver's children.

Susan had refused to repeat any more. Mother's neighbours shunned her.

Irene sank onto a drift of fallen needles in the dark forest and made no effort to wipe away tears. Mist became drizzle, but the cold and damp didn't prod her to move. Why move when she had nowhere to go?

"Mrs van Gelder?"

A woman's voice woke Irene from a near-stupor. A young witch, cupping a flame in the palms of her hands, bent over her. Irene's few encounters with fire witches had been with bad-tempered crones dressed to intimidate, but this woman, dressed in plain wool, was not long out of her teens. The sounds issuing from her mouth meant nothing. Something about warlocks and riots. Nothing that mattered.

This witch would tell her friends about the mute air witch crying in the rain. Another reason for the Fire Guild to laugh at the Air Guild. Another reason for the Air Guild to hate Irene. She bent over and pulled her hood tighter.

"…said not to let you go back to Airvale."

Not return to Airvale? Irene lifted her head and mouthed questions. The fire witch looked blank. After a few awkward moments while Irene waved at her throat, the fire witch squealed, "Somebody ordered you not to talk and then didn't take the spell off? That stinks. Speak to me."

"Thank you," Irene breathed.

The fire witch beamed. "Good. I wasn't sure it would work—I've never done that before. You want me to give whatever churl did that to you a hot arse?"

Tempting as it was, a fire witch berating the Air Enchanter on Irene's behalf, hot arse or not, would not earn her any favours. She shook her head. "Who are you?"

"Katie Underwood. I work for Mrs Rehsavvy. She's worried about you."

"Who?"

"The Locksmith. The warlock that married the retired Fire Warlock, remember?"

Irene's nose was running, but her handkerchief was already sodden. Wiping her face with her wet sleeve didn't help. The fire witch handed her a dry handkerchief. Irene mumbled thanks and blew her nose. "Why would the Locksmith concern herself with an air witch?"

"Because of Master Sven."

Sven. That song. Irene froze, and stared at the fire witch over the handkerchief.

"He told Mrs Rehsavvy the Air Guild were wasting your talent, and if they hurt you now it would be our fault."

Irene breathed again and stood. "He said that, did he? He's right."

The fire witch brushed water from Irene's cloak. "So you won't mind not going home to Airvale tonight?"

"Mind? If I never again set foot in that odious den of malicious rumourmongering, that barren wilderness of egotism mimicking polite society, that..." The fire witch stared. "Oh, dear. Please don't repeat that. Airvale isn't home, but I've nowhere else to go."

"That's all right, ma'am. You can sleep in the Fortress tonight, and we'll sort things out tomorrow."

Irene gasped, "The Fortress?" She backed away and fell over a root.

"Easy, ma'am," the fire witch crooned, and helped Irene to her feet. "If you'd rather not go to the Fortress, there are other safe places."

"Safe places? Mother's house has the normal spells against robbery, and Sven—Master Sven—added some to the garden. Now that we've finished the search, there's no point in harassing us. It should be safe."

"No, ma'am. That's what I was saying. The nobles are going berserk. They want revenge, and the usual spells won't hold up to a mob."

"My children," Irene squawked. "In Airvale."

For a frozen moment the two women reflected horror at each other. Then Irene's feet were in motion, sliding down the hillside in the deepening dusk, her mind racing to catch up. A bramble blundered into her way. She fought, but it ensnared her.

"Wait!" The fire witch slashed thorns away with a flaming wand. "Let me go first so we can see."

They stumbled onto the path and flew along it to the edge of the woods. The fire witch doused her wand. "Better not attract attention…"

"Your hat."

"Oh, yeah." The glowing trio disappeared. They paused, listening. Noises and moving lights in the town centre indicated more activity than normal for an autumn evening.

They ran, skirting the edge of town, keeping to the cover of fences and hedges. Irene's mother's house was serene; lamplight shone through unbroken windows. The street was quiet, the noises from the square hadn't grown louder. They hung on the garden gate, throats burning, sides heaving.

"Mother…"

"Bring her, too."

"She'll never leave…" Irene shook her head—too out of breath to explain that Mother would face down the Frost Maiden before abandoning Airvale. "And especially not with a fire witch."

The fire witch doubled over with a wheezing laugh. "Could be worse. If Mrs Rehsavvy had sent a fire wizard, your mother might think you were eloping."

"Her worst nightmare. But witch, wizard—doesn't matter. She won't let the girls go."

The fire witch pushed the gate open. "Leave her to me."

If Mother chose to stay in the house, that was her prerogative. The children's safety was Irene's first concern. Odds were, Mother wouldn't notice them creeping in and out. The Air Enchanter had rudely reminded Irene this evening of her invisibility; a dramatic entrance was beyond her reach. Mother had not spoken to her in a week, giving orders through the long-suffering maid. Susan could relay a message after they left, warning of danger.

Irene squared her shoulders and marched in. Susan met them in the hall. She shrieked, and backed into the hat stand, knocking it over. The girls came running, and squealed.

"Mama," Miranda screeched, "what happened?"

Mother appeared. "Dear God, Irene. You look dreadful."

Irene's dress was ripped, soaked, and muddy. The thorns had left scratches, her hair and eyes were wild, her face flushed and tearstained, and she was out of breath. Dreadful was, for once, accurate.

"Susan, tell Irene she looks like..." Mother's eyes lit on the woman behind Irene. "A fire witch in my house. Irene, what is the meaning of this?"

The fire witch's tone was polite. "Warlock's orders, ma'am—"

Irene knelt before the two staring girls. "Go upstairs and grab your cloaks—"

"For your daughter's safety. The Fire Guild—"

"Young woman, this is not amusing—"

"We'll send for clothes tomorrow. Gillian, bring your doll. Miranda, your songbook—"

"—don't want her to suffer for what she's done for us."

"Done? Irene's antics are not—"

Irene said, "We're leaving Airvale tonight."

"You most certainly are not!" Mother snapped. "Stay where you are."

"No time." The fire witch swung her wand towards the stairs. "Move."

The girls ran. Irene followed. Mother advanced on the fire witch like a siege engine. When Irene came back downstairs moments later, shoving Sven's poetry and Oliver's miniature into her handbag, Mother was staring down the full length of her aquiline nose. The shorter fire witch returned the glare with her arms crossed and her chin up. She spoke quietly; Mother shouted about her impertinence. Susan gaped from the kitchen. The girls scooted past Mother towards the door.

"Miranda, Gillian," Mother said. "Go upstairs at once. Do you hear me? I will not let you be subjected to the Fire Guild's bad influence."

The fire witch's eyes bulged. "All the lies your guild's told about your daughter, and you're calling the Fire Guild a bad influence? Oh, for Heaven's sake, shut up and listen."

Mother gasped and clutched at her chest.

"Airvale's not safe," the fire witch said, "and yelling won't make it so. You can stay or you can come with us—your choice—but Mrs van Gelder and her children are leaving."

Miranda grabbed Gillian's hand and pulled her out the door. Irene chose not to see Gillian sticking her tongue out at her grandmother.

"You should be proud of your daughter," the fire witch continued. "Master Sven said his job would have been impossible without her."

Irene grabbed Susan's cloak, shoved it at her, and pushed her outside. Through the half-open door she heard, "And you're nuts if you think a three-flag airhead can countermand a warlock's order by acting like a fire witch."

Irene peeked around the door. Mother was white and swaying.

The fire witch said, "You can talk now."

Mother screeched like a teakettle on the boil.

Irene towed Susan down the path. "Go spend the night with your brother. You'll be safe; they're not interested in you."

"Yes, ma'am." Susan vanished in the dark.

At the gate, Irene stopped to listen. Mother was still screaming. Miranda was humming. Shouts from the town centre were growing louder. Lights bobbed towards them. A hand tugged at her sleeve. She slammed the gate on her left hand.

"Sorry, ma'am," the fire witch said. "Didn't mean to startle you. You'd better run." She handed Irene a wand with a glowing tip. "Wait for me at the stairs; I'll catch up."

A man on crutches could run faster than Irene's six-year-old daughter. She carried Gillian and prayed her heart and lungs would not give out before the mob caught them. The distant voices did not follow them, but she couldn't risk slowing down.

The fire witch wasn't even breathing hard when she rejoined them. "As mobs go, it's a damp squib." She sounded disappointed. "Half a dozen drunken louts with not enough sober magic between them to set fire to a cat. Or whatever nastiness airheads—uh-oh, sorry ma'am—whatever air wizards get up to."

"Throwing things, usually." Irene set Gillian down and massaged throbbing fingers.

"They may break some windows, but they won't get in the house. Your mother is safe enough. I left a surprise for them."

"What sort of surprise?" Miranda asked.

"Hot feet." The fire witch picked up Gillian. "Let's go."

They climbed the stairs with no sign of anyone following, and slackened their pace.

Irene said, "Mother's worst criticism has always been to compare me to a fire witch. Thank you for enlightening me as to why she dislikes the Fire Guild so much. And thank you for standing up for me."

The fire witch snorted. "I live with the Fire Guild. I'd rather take on the whole Air Guild than have a warlock angry at me."

"Well, yes, the Fire Warlock is more dangerous than my mother."

"Oh, *him*. He's an old softy. I meant Mrs Rehsavvy."

A small child's furious howl greeted the van Gelders as they stepped through the Rehsavvy's front door. The two girls clapped their hands over their ears.

"Wait here," the fire witch said, and ran. She returned a moment later with a red-faced, howling toddler in her arms. "Just in time. Mrs Rehsavvy was about to combust."

Miranda said, "He sounds hungry."

"We'll fix that." They followed the fire witch into a large kitchen. Irene took the child and manoeuvred him into a high chair while the fire witch swung a soup pot over the flames.

Irene said, "Miss, er…"

"Underwood. But call me Katie, ma'am."

"That wouldn't be right…"

"Don't see why not. The Fire Guild don't stand on ceremony much, and besides, you outrank me."

Clearly she was misinformed. Too weary to argue, Irene said, "Fine. Katie. Are you the nursemaid? Cook? Or…?"

Katie laughed. "Nanny, lady's maid, sometimes cook. General dogs-body these days." She flung bowls and mugs onto the table and dove into the panty.

Gillian said, "I thought you were a fire witch."

"I am, and a good one, too." She emerged from the pantry with a loaf in one hand and a bowl of pears in the other. She shoved the bread at Miranda, the pears and a knife at Irene, and returned her attention to the soup pot. Irene and Miranda fed chunks of bread and pear to the howling child. He stopped howling. The storm clouds in the girls' faces faded.

Katie added, "And grateful for the privilege of working for two of the most important people in the country."

Miranda said, "Can't they afford a nursemaid?"

"Of course they can." She gave the soup a good stir. "There was a nursemaid. She…" Katie gaped at Miranda. Soup dripping from her spoon sizzled in the embers. "I clean forgot. I never… You shouldn't have…"

"Shouldn't have what?" Irene said.

"What happened to the nursemaid?" Gillian said.

"She left. The…uh…the Fire Eaters scared her away."

Irene froze. "Fire eaters?"

Gillian goggled. "Fire eaters? Can we watch?"

Katie dropped her spoon back into the pot and resumed stirring. "They don't really. They're just fire wizards. But they do shoot flame around."

"And you said they live here?" Irene's voice rose. "If my girls aren't safe here—"

"Mama, don't be silly," Miranda said. "The Fire Warlock protects women and children. If you don't give him more pear, he'll start howling again."

The absurdity of Warlock Arturos throwing a tantrum over fruit startled Irene. "Pardon? Oh." The toddler had thrown the bread on the floor and was reaching for the pear, just out of reach. Irene cut more chunks.

"She's right, ma'am," Katie said. "Warlock Quicksilver won't let anyone hurt you here. If anybody flamed a guest, it would bounce back and burn the one that threw it, just like in the Fortress. This is one of the safest places in Frankland. The only place safer is the Fortress."

That statement did not reassure Irene as much as Katie obviously intended. If this was such a safe place, why did the nursemaid leave?

In a few minutes, Miranda and Gillian were settled in the Rehsavvy's dining room, taking turns feeding the little boy, and devouring a second supper of hot chicken soup, fresh bread with butter, pears, and a platter piled high with more pastries than Irene could name. Katie led her to a sitting room to meet the Locksmith. Irene stifled a gasp; her first impression—that the Locksmith was crawling into the fireplace—was incorrect, but she was sitting on a footstool, close enough to the flames to singe her eyebrows. The boy with her was not so eager; he stood to the side, all but his eyes shielded from the heat behind a fire screen.

"Ma'am," Katie said, "Mrs van Gelder is scared of the Fortress, and all her relatives are in Airvale. Where should I take them?"

Without looking up, the woman with her head in the flames said, "The Warren's safe."

"Please," Irene said, "The Earth Guild don't welcome air witches."

The Locksmith reared back from the fire. "You're here? In this house? I thought Katie meant Blazes."

Katie said, "Her two girls are here, too." The Locksmith gawked.

"I beg your pardon." Irene's curtsy was rather stiff. "I didn't mean to intrude."

The Locksmith scrambled to her feet and returned the curtsey. Even in the dim light, her blush was obvious. "That wasn't what I meant. You and your children are welcome here. It's just that this house is, uh…"

Like the other fire witch, this woman was young and plainly dressed, with no jewellery other than a wedding ring and a string of lustrous pearls. Pearls? Irene groped for a chair and sat down. The two witches bent over her.

"Are you all right, ma'am?" Katie said.

"Alexander, please fetch the brandy," the Locksmith said. "Have you had any supper? What happened? You didn't look like this earlier."

"She fell into brambles in the dark," Katie said. "We had a fight getting her out."

"And left them battered and bloody, waving little flags of truce," Irene said.

The Locksmith eyed the holes in Irene's skirt. "I see. Well. You've had quite a day, haven't you?" She thrust a brandy snifter at her. "Katie, put her in the blue bedroom."

The brandy sloshed around the glass. The Locksmith steadied it. Irene gulped and gagged. "We don't want to impose."

"Nonsense. We have space, the Fire Guild is in your debt, and I want to talk to you when I have time." The Locksmith gave no opportunity to interrupt. "Sorry I can't now; the Fire Warlock is yelling at me to get back to work, so it's either here or the Crystal Palace or the Warren, because I don't know where else is safe tonight. I'd rather you stayed here." She settled back down on her footstool, facing the fire. "Katie, make sure she eats, and gets a warm bath. Find some salve for those scratches." She waved at the fire. It roared. The other two women were dismissed.

Katie stared at the back of the Locksmith's head and jammed her hands into her armpits. Sweat beaded her upper lip. This young woman, whose eyes had glowed with the light of battle at the approach of the riotous Air Guild, rolled her eyes at Irene, whites showing. "Ma'am?"

"The Crystal Palace terrifies me, too."

Katie relaxed. "I'll get the blue bedroom ready while you eat supper." She steered Irene into the dining room, placed a bowl of soup and a thick slab of buttered bread before her, and ushered the drooping children away.

It was silly to be frightened of Blazes. The Fortress didn't reach out and ensnare people, and who better to protect Irene and her children than a warlock? Returning the rest of Sven's poetry would be easy. More to the point, they could go nowhere else. After the excitement and exertion of the past two hours, Irene's mind and body were shutting down. Her stomach craved the food, but the effort of lifting spoon from bowl to mouth exhausted her remaining willpower. When she had eaten all she could, Katie guided her, unresisting, up the stairs. After looking in on the sleeping girls, Irene wallowed in rose-scented bathwater, and fell into a blissful stupor as Katie anointed her scratches and bruised fingers. Her eyes were half-closed when Katie doused the light.

"Thank you," Irene murmured. "The Fire Guild have no reason to befriend air witches, but you've been very kind."

"I admit I wasn't thrilled when Mrs Rehsavvy sent me after you. Warlock Quicksilver keeps telling us not to let preconceptions blind us, and he must be right. I thought air witches were cowards, but now that I've seen how brave you are, I can't help but respect you. Good night, ma'am."

The door clicked shut. Irene stared into the darkness, eyes wide open, wondering what could have given a fire witch such a mistaken impression.

War

Duncan was eating supper with the two grannies when Master Sven charged out of a tunnel, yelling. By the time Duncan figured out what Sven was going on about, Hazel and Mildred were pulling bottles of salve out of cupboards and shoving bandages and burn cloths into sacks.

"Take all the burn medicine," Mildred said. "There's more at the smithy, if anybody comes in tonight needing them."

Hazel said, "We may also need to deal with sword cuts, puncture wounds, broken bones, who knows what else. The three of us can carry enough bandages. Splints can wait."

"What do you mean, *three?*" Duncan said. "Master Sven and I are going. You and Mildred are staying here. We'll send anybody who gets hurt to you after it's over."

"Duncan, don't be silly. You'd have to carry anyone badly injured, and it would take too long. It will be better if I'm there."

"Didn't you hear what he said? It's going to be dangerous. I don't want you getting hurt. You're staying here."

A few minutes later, as they ran through the tunnels, Duncan grumbled to himself: how can you win a fight with somebody who doesn't argue, just smiles like you're the sweetest wee lad she's ever seen and keeps on doing what you tell her not to? At least she hadn't gotten angry at him—she could knock him back on his arse with her little finger, for all he must've weighed three times what she did.

Nettleton looked peaceful, with the houses closed up snug and warm, and lights shining as folk went on with their suppers and putting the little tykes to bed. Duncan opened his mouth to yell, but closed it again. Hazel dropped to the ground, muttering, and rubbed her hands in the dirt.

Sven said, "Maybe I'm worried over nothing."

Hazel said, "No, you're right. There are horses coming upriver. About two dozen."

Duncan grabbed Sven's arm. "The Fire Warlock's not coming?"

"He can't. A riot in a city takes priority. More people would get hurt."

"But I'm telling you we need his help. I've done what I'm supposed to. Can we fight back?"

"You shouldn't have to. I have the authority to override Lord Geoffrey's orders."

"There's one of you, two dozen of them, and they aren't thinking straight. Can you block swords and arrows coming at you from all directions?"

"No."

Duncan was making him sweat. Too bad. They'd all be sweating before long. "If the guards do you in, we're on our own. How much trouble will we get in if we fight back?"

Sven intoned, "As a Flame Mage in good standing, I give you permission to defend yourselves, your community, and your property. If this decision is wrong, I accept responsibility." He sounded like he was reciting a spell.

Hazel hissed, "Listen."

The two men raised their heads. The sound of hooves carried up the valley on the cold, clear air.

Sven said, "But you can only fight back. Understand? Whoever starts the fight—they're dead."

"Gotcha," Duncan said, and let him go.

"Which one's your brother's?"

Duncan pointed, and Sven ran. Hazel waved her wand at the church, setting the alarm bell ringing. Duncan bellowed. Doors popped open. When Duncan reached the farm, leading a dozen men armed with quarterstaves and pitchforks, the guards, carrying lit torches, were already pouring into the yard. Somebody had learned something from the farce at Maggie's wedding—most were on foot, leaving their horses on the track.

Master Sven's roar echoed across the valley. "In the name of the Fire Warlock and by my authority as Flame Mage, I order you to drop your weapons and leave peacefully."

Duncan winced. It would have been better if the mage hadn't sounded out of breath. For a moment, everything seemed to stop. Lord Geoffrey, still on his horse, faced Doug and Sven. The guards—the worst of the lowlife scum the duke had hired—flanked a stranger with fire on his hat.

The torches went out. Lord Geoffrey shouted for his wizard to relight them, and for the guards to fire the house and barn. Some guards yelled that they didn't want trouble with the Fire Guild but others yelled back at Master Sven. Duncan sidled closer, but their horses milled around between him and the house. In every direction, torches flamed to life, and went out again.

Fire flew at Sven, and bounced off. A guard's bow blazed. He screamed and hurled it away. Flames licked across the line of guards. A few panicked and ran. The horses bolted. Duncan dove behind the low stone wall, ducking flying hooves.

After several horses thundered past, he stuck his head up. Lord Geoffrey yelled for somebody to deal with that frostbitten fire wizard. Sven stood before the open door with the kitchen fire behind him, looking like a warlock.

Or like an easy target. As Duncan drew breath to yell, an arrow hit Sven in the chest. He staggered backwards, twisting sideways. Another arrow hit and he dropped.

The guards went berserk. Torches blazed. Fire flew in all directions. Duncan hurdled the wall and waded in, laying men out with his quarterstaff.

The fodder in the barn went up in a ball of flame. Screaming livestock added to the din. Something in the house had caught, too. Jessie and the screaming bairns huddled against the wall behind Doug.

The men of Nettleton put up a good fight, but they were losing. Duncan cleared a path towards the house, but there were still two guards with torches between him and Doug when Doug went down. Then fire flowed out of the house and barn, and across the guards still standing. Lord Geoffrey's fire wizard burned like a torch. A voice thundered, "Fly, fools, or die."

Wherever the Warlock was, Duncan couldn't see him. Hazel crouched beside Sven. Screaming guards ran away trailing fire. In seconds the fight was over.

Doug tried to stand, but one leg buckled. He wasn't at death's door, anyway, not like little Billy Martin. Duncan dropped his staff and clamped a hand around Billy's arm, and the blood stopped shooting out. Hazel came running to patch him up.

Duncan said, "Where's the Fire Warlock?"

She said, "He's not here. That was Sven."

"How'd he do all that with those arrows stuck in him?"

"He wasn't unconscious. He couldn't concentrate because of the pain, until I reached him. Now, I need you to pull the arrows out, so I can fix him up proper."

Duncan had never pulled an arrow out of a man before. He snapped off the fletched ends, rolled Sven over, braced a knee against his back, and got a good grip on one of the shafts. "Ready?"

Hazel held Sven's hand. "Ready."

Duncan yanked. Sven fainted. His pain burned through Hazel's chest. She screamed.

Yanking the second out was worse, because they all knew what was coming.

Duncan said, "For the love of God, Hazel, I hope you never ask me to do that again."

"For the love of God, Duncan, I hope I never have to."

It was two in the morning before the injured men and surviving livestock had been tended to and Nettleton quieted enough to think about sleep. Jessie, with silent tears trickling down her cheeks, took the bairns down the hill to spend the night with her mum. Doug watched them go with a look on his face that said if Lord Geoffrey were a commoner, he'd be dead inside a week.

Duncan was inspecting the ruins of the barn when the Fire Warlock did show up.

"What's the tally?" he said.

"On our side, two men dead. Half a dozen others wounded, but Hazel says they'll recover. The house is a mess, but fixable. The barn and everything in it are gone. The rest of the village will help out, but it's going to be a long, hungry winter for everybody."

"On their side?"

"Seven guards and one fire wizard dead. Lots of others with burns, but they didn't stick around for healing. We don't know what happened to Lord Geoffrey—Hazel thinks his horse dragged him away after the barn went up."

"All right," he said, "I'll look for the brat when I leave here."

They walked across the yard, and the Warlock flipped the dead wizard over with his toe. Duncan leaned over the rock wall and heaved. When he could talk again, he said, "What was he doing here, and with them?"

"He was a good-for-nothing nobleman whose blue blood meant more to him than the two flames on his hat. We've got a few in our ranks causing trouble, like Lord Geoffrey and his ilk in the Air Guild. It's just as well Sven dealt with this one. He wouldn't look half this good if I'd gotten ahold of him."

In the house, Hazel sat on the floor, half asleep, her head lolling against the charred sideboard. Doug sat on the settle with his hurt leg up and a whiskey bottle in his hand. Sven lay on a singed mattress, with a pair of aunties fussing over him. They quieted down and backed away when the Warlock pulled up a stool beside him.

"What the hell happened? I wasn't worried about you—there were only a couple dozen of them."

Duncan had to bend down to hear Sven's reply. "I gave them a chance to disperse. I don't like burning people. You're going to tell me I'm stupid."

"For being humane? Don't be an ass. And don't mind me," the Warlock said gruffly. "You did fine, even with getting shot. I'm mighty glad you're still with us. I'll take you back to the Fortress—"

Hazel's eyes snapped open. "Don't move him!"

The aunties gasped, but the Warlock acted like a girl a third his size yelling at him was nothing unusual. "Sven, what do you say?"

Sven breathed, "Leave me be."

"All right. You're in better hands here with Granny Hazel than you would be at home." The Warlock turned and looked at Doug. "Somebody from the Water Guild will be coming to see you—"

Doug's bad leg thumped onto the floor. He pushed himself upright. "We were defending ourselves, Your Wisdom. They've no right—"

The Warlock pushed him back down. "Let me finish. You're the injured party, and the Water Guild are on your side. When they get here, the only thing you'll be feeling is righteous indignation. If they scare you, then shut up and let Duncan talk. You two are going to charge the duke, his wife, and his son with everything you can think of. Attempted murder, arson, theft—I don't know what all, but we've got the charter and proof that you're freeholders—thanks, Sven—and there ought to be a lot to charge them with. Sven can help figure out what. Right, Sven?" The mage waggled his fingers. "I'll take that as a yes. The point is, the Frost Maiden and I both want the duchess hauled into court. That greedy, selfish hag is the biggest troublemaker of the lot. She's gotten her way for far too long, and I want her taken down a peg. A dozen pegs. You with me?"

The Archer brothers answered together. "Yes, sir, Your Wisdom."

The Fortress Beckons

"**W**ho are you, fair lass, and why are you haunting my wife's kitchen at this ungodly hour?"

This emaciated figure with blood-shot eyes and dark stubble was the revered Fire Warlock Emeritus? Common sense argued that Irene should run from the drunken vagabond rummaging in the Rehsavvy's pantry. She curtsied instead. "Irene van Gelder, Your Wisdom. The Locksmith invited us to stay. I'm an early riser, and the pastries in the pantry called to me."

She had abandoned her bed after lying awake for an hour, fretting over worries exhaustion had squelched the evening before. How could she and her children stay here with the Fortress looming over the town? Where would they go when they left? Who would hire a witch without a recommendation from her guild?

"Is it time to rise?" he said. "I am finishing my supper. I am surprised by, but not averse to, more guests. My wife's reasons are sound, whatever they may be. Please forgive me if I am incoherent; I am a trifle weary."

He staggered across the kitchen, holding an apple tart in a trembling hand. The stench as he passed drove Irene backwards, but he stank of smoke and sweat, not sour wine. His voice was as clear and steady as Enchanter Paul's.

"Of course, sir. I beg your pardon for disturbing you."

That elicited a short laugh. "You hardly did that, young lady. Please, sit. I am almost done. Van Gelder? Oh, yes, Enchanter Oliver's widow. My wife relayed the message you had uncovered the White Duke's charter. That is excellent news, and we sorely need good news at this juncture."

Irene's breath escaped on a long sigh. "Thank you, Your Wisdom. Sir, what is happening? Miss Underwood said the nobles were rioting, but she didn't know any details. Your wife was too busy to talk."

"There were riots in London, Rouen, and Manchester, and isolated acts of violence in other districts." He leaned his head on the heel of his hand and closed his eyes. "Frankland will be a long time recovering from the wounds. I am afraid neither of us will be good hosts. You may have to fend for yourselves for several days."

"I'm sorry, sir. You don't need a houseful of guests to deal with now. We'll withdraw to the Warren, if they'll have us, and remove one annoyance."

He straightened, almost smiling. "That offer was spoken with a conspicuous lack of enthusiasm. No, stay. Please, I insist. Anyone who can abide this house is most welcome."

"Is something wrong with it?"

"Not at all. Merely an eccentric aversion spell." He patted her arm. "Think no more of it. Master Sven's description of your talents piqued my interest, and I would talk to you at length when I have time. Further, have you any talent as a story teller?"

"Pardon?"

"We are educating another houseguest, the boy Alexander, in Frankland's folklore and heroic sagas. Could you tell tales, or read to him? With the other members of the household at the Fire Warlock's beck and call, and Master Sven hors de combat, there is no one…"

His voice echoed in her head. The room darkened and spun.

"Steady, girl." Warlock Quicksilver bent over her with a hand on her shoulder. Her hands, already battered, hurt from a death grip on the table.

She whispered, "Sven?"

"He was shot twice through the chest last night, but the healer says he may make a full recovery."

"May?"

"One arrow shattered a rib. I know no more than that. I am not a healer."

"But Sven's not a warlock." Her voice rose. "He's not a warlock. Somebody should have gone to help him."

"Who?" The bleakness in Quicksilver's expression made her turn away. "Every warlock was on duty in cities with far more innocent souls than live in the Archers' village. Many lower-ranking guild members were injured. Several died. My wife cried herself to sleep an hour ago for not going to their aid, but the Fire Warlock ordered her to stay here, coordinating actions. Nor would Master Sven have welcomed her assistance. I warned him, years ago, that to aspire to the title of Flame Mage was to put his life at risk in the service of his country, as surely as if he had been a warlock. He understood, and accepted that risk."

Irene stared at her hands in silence until regaining control of her voice. "I'm sorry, sir."

"I am sorry, too," he said. "For him and for you. I did not know you had an attachment to him. Mourning two such fine men is a burden no one should have to bear."

She sat at the table, staring out the window into the grey nothingness of pre-dawn, long after Quicksilver had stumbled from the kitchen and climbed the stairs.

The children were Irene's saviours that morning. Alone, she would have sought a dark corner and dissolved into a useless heap, but their need to be fed, clothed, and educated forced her to remain engaged. They wandered into the Rehsavvy's library in search of paper and pens. She threw open the shutters and stood transfixed, forgetting the children, their lessons, Sven, and everything but the Fortress.

They had arrived, disoriented, in the rain the previous evening, and noticed nothing other than their immediate surroundings. The library, at the rear of the house, looked across several rows of cottages and onto the Fortress's southern face. Morning light, coming from an autumn sun far to the south, cast a golden glow over the curtain wall and filled the north-facing room with a cool brilliance. A ray of sunlight, glancing off something high above, dazzled Irene's eyes. While the girls practiced their penmanship, the sight of the shining citadel, Frankland's defence and supreme refuge, held Irene spellbound. The Fortress's comforting solidity, dwarfing the town, drove both Winifred's warning and the homicidal stairs from her mind. She yearned to leave Airvale behind for good, and to move into this beckoning stronghold offering her a haven, a home.

The van Gelders spent most of the chilly day by the warm oasis of the library fire. The Rehsavvy's collection of tales and sagas, well rounded for Fire Guild adherents, provided ample entertainment after they finished the girls' lessons.

Warlock Quicksilver had not said why he wanted someone reading to his young guest, but it didn't matter. Miranda and Gillian could make room for another listener. He had not said, either, what stories the boy was already familiar with, but warlocks would tend to choose heroes with affinities for the Fire Guild. Introducing a few Air Guild heroes might be beneficial.

The Locksmith appeared late-morning, sporting red-rimmed eyes. She handed Irene a manuscript, *Synthesis and Antithesis: The Origins of Polyelemental Spellcraft in the Merger of the Braided and Equilibria Traditions* by Jean Rehsavvy, and asked her to proofread it at her leisure, then settled into a sofa in the drawing room and began issuing orders through the fire. A half-dozen weary fire wizards came and went, came and went. The first few times, Irene watched over her shoulder, but they exhibited no more rash behaviour than air wizards.

The fire wizards returned the scrutiny with questions in their eyes. Irene tensed when a pair leaned in the door, listening to Miranda singing over an arithmetic exercise, but after a moment one grunted, "I'm glad somebody's happy today," and they went on their way. After that, they paid the van Gelders no more attention than they paid the furniture.

Alexander returned from the Fortress in early afternoon, and listened to Irene read from *King Alaric the Air-farer* for an hour. He appeared despondent and lost in his own thoughts at first, but his attention sharpened as the enchanter king outtalked, time and again, the less-than-brilliant seventh Fire Warlock.

News arrived that Sven was in good spirits, and the healer expected him to walk home through the tunnels in a few days.

"Mama," Miranda pleaded, "when you sing, please stay on key."

In the late afternoon Irene sent the children out to play in the garden, and stood on the patio as the setting sun turned the western face of the Fortress golden. Behind her, a voice said, "I never tire of this sight, but it is odd an air witch finds it compelling."

Warlock Quicksilver looked and smelled a good deal more respectable, although he still appeared to be a man teetering on the edge of exhaustion.

Irene curtsied. "It seems to be calling to me, sir, telling me not to fear it."

Together they watched until the light faded, then he turned to go.

"Your Wisdom," Irene said, "thank you for the letter you wrote me after Oliver died. It meant a great deal to me, that you took the time to be kind."

"Thank you, my dear. I deemed his death a grave loss to Frankland, and I did not even know, then, of the existence of that book of spells. One can only wonder what such a monumental talent could have produced had he lived."

Had anyone been watching, his disappearance in a burst of flame would have been reason enough for Irene to cringe.

"Help yourselves." The Locksmith pushed a platter of cheese scones, still warm from the oven, across the kitchen table towards the van Gelders. "Dinner will be a while yet, and I doubt you had enough breakfast."

"Thank you, ma'am." Miranda and Gillian attempted to swallow theirs whole. Irene chided them for their poor manners, and nibbled at hers.

The Locksmith laughed. "I'm glad you enjoy my cooking, but you'll choke if you don't slow down. We won't let you starve, although I am sorry you've had to forage for yourselves in the pantry. I feel guilty about inviting you here and then ignoring you for three days."

"Don't," Irene said. "Katie's soups are delicious, and your cold leftovers are better than many fresh dishes served at Airvale dinner parties. My clothes will become too tight if we stay here long."

"Would it be so bad to let them out? You're awfully thin."

She was accusing Irene of being thin? A neighbour in Airvale who had seen the Locksmith before her wedding had sniffed that she enjoyed her food a bit too much. It was difficult to believe this hollow-cheeked figure, clad in a too-loose dress, was the same woman. Talents who rely on heavy magic use in their day-to-day lives seldom gain weight, but if she didn't cut back soon she could kill herself.

The girls finished their scones and wandered away. The Locksmith continued working on dinner, setting a knife to chopping carrots and parsnips, before getting down to business. "Why does Enchanter Paul dislike you so much?"

Not the question Irene had expected, but one easier to answer, because she'd had a decade to consider it. "He blames me for Oliver's failure to be the perfect son, although they were at odds long before we eloped, and for stealing Oliver away from Enchantress Winifred. Mother didn't help by boasting about my big catch."

"Ouch."

"The Enchanter thought he would outlive Oliver—he was right—and wanted to train an enchanter grandson to be the next Officeholder. The odds would have been better if Oliver had married Winifred."

The Locksmith snorted. "Better, maybe, but not guaranteed."

Irene shrugged. "It hardly matters, since I couldn't even produce a son. The Enchanter doesn't seem to consider his granddaughters worth his time."

The Locksmith scowled. "I used to consider Paul the epitome of polite behaviour, but I'm about fed up. The way he ignored you was outright offensive."

"He probably didn't mean to be. He doesn't seem aware when he does so."

The Locksmith looked up from the peas she was sorting and studied Irene for a moment. "You've produced a surprisingly unemotional analysis about someone who's treated you like dirt. How do you manage that?"

"Three nights ago it would have been impossible." Irene picked at her scone. "Being away from Airvale is calming, and introspection is useful. It's easier to deal with one's own life by standing aside and viewing it as if one is an outsider. Is that surprising? Isn't an undemonstrative, emotionally detached loner with a tendency to overanalyse everything a stereotypical description of an air witch?"

"I thought the whole point is that your talents aren't typical."

"That's magical talents. Personality traits aren't the same."

The Locksmith grinned. "I know. People called me a fire witch long before we knew I had any talent. But I'm a little confused. I thought air witches were—forgive me, please, I know this is a sweeping generalisation— were flighty, lazy pleasure-seekers given to wild mood swings."

"That's the other extreme, and Winifred's a good example. Both types are well represented in the Air Guild ranks. The Air Guild as a whole seesaws back and forth between the two. The undemonstrative, detached side, exemplified by the Air Enchanter, is in the ascendency now. That's a good part of why many members of my generation, Oliver and Winifred included, left Airvale and resist all attempts to pull them back."

"So you and Oliver were opposites? How well did that work?"

"It worked." Taking a large bite of scone gave Irene a moment's respite. "He relied on me to give him focus and tame his turbulent energies. He gave me wings. As for wild mood swings, the past three weeks have given me enough to induce motion sickness."

"Not surprising, given all the duchess and her spoiled children have thrown at you. We shouldn't have gotten you into such a mess. Look, Irene—you don't mind me calling you Irene, do you? No? Good. *Mrs van Gelder* seems too formal for a guest in my own house. And you'll call me Lucinda."

"That wouldn't be proper, ma'am. You outrank me."

"Not by much."

"My talent is level three, and you're—"

"I'm a mage's wife, and you're a mage's widow."

Irene stopped chewing.

The Locksmith said, "You never considered that?"

Irene shook her head. Oliver's induction into the Company of Mages had been a shock, and years too late to disturb ingrained habits, nor would drawing attention to his ascension have been wise. The mystery was why this had never occurred to Irene's mother.

The Locksmith said, "Sven and Jean—Quicksilver—are furious over the Air Guild's lack of respect, and Sven doesn't lose his temper often—as fire wizards go." She slammed a cleaver down on the table. "It pisses me off, too."

God help Irene if the Locksmith was ever angry at her. Katie's reluctance to antagonise her seemed prudent.

The Locksmith sniffed. "Paul doesn't seem to understand that slighting you is a slight on his son's judgment."

"You mean, like a husband who insults his wife to the point where one starts to wonder why he was so stupid as to have married the woman in the first place?"

"Exactly. It holds true for wives, too, you know."

"No doubt. For a mage, the Enchanter relies too much on others' opinions, but perhaps you're overreacting a wee bit? A witch deserves some respect in her own right. Politeness to my face for Oliver's sake wouldn't prove they weren't still laughing at me behind my back."

"Maybe not, but even a mundane married to a mage deserves better. At the very least, the other three guilds would have given you a comfortable stipend to live on."

A stipend? Irene's fingers crushed the remains of the scone to crumbs. "One could put up with muffled derision."

"Yes, I imagine one could. Now look, Irene, I don't want to offend you, but I really want to know. Is there any basis to the gossip about you and Sven?" She blushed. "Never mind. Forget I said anything."

Irene toyed with the crumbs, surprised only in how long it had taken her. "You mean, could my magic entice a mage into a frenzy? Absolutely not."

The Locksmith stared at Irene through narrowed eyes.

"Except in my daydreams," Irene added.

The Locksmith smiled and began quartering a chicken. "That I can understand. I only meant, do you enjoy each other's company? I'd like to see him happy. I certainly didn't believe the rumours. The notion of Sven making a fool of himself in public over anyone is ludicrous. It's just annoying that the Air Guild won't lift a finger to spread news that would help Frankland, but vicious gossip is everywhere within hours."

"It's annoying, too, that the Air Guild are the most susceptible to our own lies."

"Really? But…" The Locksmith gaped. "You can't mean some of them actually believe that garbage."

"Yes."

Her face darkened. She straightened, snarling, with her knife in hand. Steam rose from the damp chicken. "You've convinced me. I don't know what we can do for you, but we will help you, protocol be damned, and if Paul complains about my interference in Air Guild business, I'll scorch more than just the frostbitten fool's fancy desk. What do you say to that?"

Irene sat without moving, her eyes following the bobbing cleaver. "That would be lovely, Lucinda."

Fraud

"That lock you put on the White Duchess?" Beorn dropped onto the sofa in Lucinda's drawing room and put his booted feet on the low table. She stifled a rebuke. It had been his house, his table, and a few more scratches wouldn't make much difference.

"You're going to have to take it off," he said.

"What?" Concerns over the furniture's condition flew out of her head. "Are you mad? That woman's a menace."

"Yeah, but she's threatening to take you to court."

"A lawsuit?" The butt of her wand banged on the table. She picked it up and ignored the new dent. "Against me?"

"Against you. And if you plead special privilege for acting as my agent, against me, too."

She crossed her arms and glared.

"Look, Lucinda, I don't like it either, but I don't have the time for that right now. You don't have time for it either. She can't afford to cause more trouble in Abertee, not with the Water Guild already picking over her life with tweezers, and we've got plenty of other problems to deal with."

She tapped her foot and disdained replying.

"And King Stephen and Enchanter Paul have shoved their oars in, too. Stephen says it was appallingly rude to treat a duchess like an impertinent scullery maid—hey, don't hit me—and Paul was already steaming before you went and left scorch marks on his desk. Now he's really pissed off, and complaining right and left about the Fire Guild's interference in Air Guild disciplinary matters. They both want her to have her witchcraft back immediately—yesterday, if not sooner. Don't look at me in that tone of voice. I'm just trying to make the best of a bad deal. If throwing them a bone helps, I'll do it."

"Fine. Just fine. I'll unlock her, and she'll go back to scaring everybody in sight. Do you want that on your conscience?"

"What'd you expect? She's fighting with the weapons she has, and the courts have been the nobles' playground for centuries."

"And I, for one, will laugh when the Water Office metes out the justice she's due on all those charges the Archers brought against her."

"Well, as to that…" He blew out through his moustache.

"Don't tell me there's another problem."

"There is." He rubbed a hand over bloodshot eyes. "She was under orders from the king. And yeah, I know she talked the king into giving her those orders, but still… She's ducking behind him and the duke. Since she's only a level two witch and married to a duke, the law says he's at fault for not keeping her in line, and it's up to him, not us, to discipline her. The only way to get at her is through the duke, and anything we do to him to hurt her is going to hurt him a lot worse."

"Are you joking?"

"I'd be a damned sight happier if I was."

"But… That's ridiculous. Asinine."

"Yeah, and maybe someday we can get the law changed. But not now. Not in time for this trial. I'm beginning to wish…"

"Wishing's dangerous," she said.

"I know. But we'd be better off if I'd gotten to Abertee earlier. Even those noble asses know not to cross the Fire Office. Any grumbling about the dozen I torched the other night they're keeping to themselves. But I'm too soft-hearted. Handing that bastard Lord Geoffrey over to the Water Guild instead of killing him then and there was a mistake."

"Because they'll go berserk again when the Frost Maiden executes him?"

"They will, if it comes to that, but it may not. Why do you think I had the Archers bring charges, instead of making the charges myself?"

"I hadn't considered. Uh, wait… Because if you bring charges, they're on record as coming from the Fire Warlock, and the Office won't let you withdraw them?"

"Bull's-eye. But Douglas Archer, farmer, can withdraw them, or negotiate for either lesser charges or reduced sentences. If we play our cards right, and toss out the heaviest charges, she might not have to execute him. If we can make him harmless—strip him of rank and privilege, slap one of your locks on him, and leave him to rot in a cell in the Crystal Palace—the Fire Office would tolerate that. It doesn't care about punishment; it only cares about threat."

"I see your point," she said. "I don't have to like it, though. That slime attacked people I care about; I'd rather see him iced. But with the upper class on edge, not killing him is a better strategic choice. So what are you worried about?"

"Remember I said, if we play our cards right. What happens if we don't?"

"She executes him, and the nobles go berserk."

"Or?"

"Or what? I must be tired. Not thinking clearly."

"You're forgetting King Stephen."

"Am not. He can't step in now and demand a harsher sentence, and why would he do that anyway?"

"You've got it the wrong way around. He can still step in and issue pardons."

Lucinda's wand slipped from nerveless fingers and rolled across the floor. The Fire Office would never let such a dangerous man loose to cause more trouble. If the king issued a pardon, the Fire Office would turn on the king. She made fish mouths without sound at Beorn.

"Right," he said. "The Fire Office calmed down in September, after Stephen accepted the verdict in Duncan's trial. But after this latest round of trouble, it's back to where it was, and looking for a target to burn."

He heaved himself upright and went to the window overlooking the town square. "And there's something else."

"Drown it. What else?"

He played with the catch on the window for a few moments before answering. "It doesn't make sense that things went to hell in so many places on the same day by accident. Jean and I are looking for evidence somebody was passing messages around. Arranging things."

"You mean a conspiracy?"

"Yeah, and that scares me. It felt like somebody was testing how hard they had to push to make the Fire Guild collapse. Or make me burn out."

How much more pressure could he take? Not much, she feared. He had not always been haggard, but she couldn't recall when. She would have laid odds he had not had eight hours sleep in the past four days. Neither she nor Jean had slept much more.

Beorn said, "I don't know why I thought I could find something Jean couldn't."

"You're the Fire Warlock. The one with the authority."

He shrugged. "Hasn't helped. But we're convinced something was going on. I want you to take a stab at it, too."

"If neither of you found anything, why do you think I will?"

"You read those locks nobody else could read. If somebody's using a lock to hide it, you'd be the one to find it."

"Jean can recognise a lock exists, even if he can't read it. But of course I'll look."

"Thanks." He grinned. "And get some sleep. Don't let worry keep you up nights."

The van Gelders had been at the Rehsavvy's five days when Warlock Snorri emerged from the library fireplace in the late afternoon with Sven in tow. Irene pulled a padded chair closer to the fire, and he eased into it. Lucinda fussed over him, and he waved the two women away, but it was clear the attention pleased him. Lucinda returned to her work in the kitchen, calling over her shoulder, "You'll stay for supper, won't you, Sven?"

She didn't wait for an answer.

Irene asked, "Was that an invitation or an order?"

He smiled. "Does it matter? Why do you think I came at this time of day?"

"The girls know you were a friend of their father's, and they have some questions for you. Would you mind?"

"Not at all, if you'll let me satisfy my curiosity first. I've heard rumours about an aversion spell Snorri put on this house, and I want to see it for myself."

"Uh, Sven…" Snorri said.

"Although I have my doubts about its effectiveness, since it clearly didn't drive an air witch away."

"Sven," Snorri said, "Leave it until after supper."

"I can't believe you're telling me to be patient. It won't take long." Sven leaned back with his hands behind his head and closed his eyes.

Snorri mumbled what might have been a curse. Irene frowned at him. He frowned at Sven, then pulled several embers from the fire and began juggling. Irene gasped.

"If I drop any," he said. "I'll quench them before they hit the rug. Promise."

She winced. "You're a warlock. Be careful about making rash promises."

He nodded at Sven. "He tells me that all the time. He wouldn't promise his own mother the sun will rise in the morning."

Sven opened his eyes. "You didn't cast this spell."

Snorri flung the coals against the back of the fireplace. "I never said I did. You've been listening to gossip."

Sven's eyebrows drew together. "Then why... Never mind." He resumed an expression of fierce concentration.

After a brief interval, Irene opened a book. Snorri retreated to the far end of the room and banged chessmen against their board.

Sven's eyes snapped open and he surged half out of the chair, yelling at Snorri, "What's the Fire Warlock doing? Lucinda told me she invited Irene here for her safety. Not to put her in danger!"

"Shut up, Sven. She's not—"

"And her children, for God's sake. You can't—"

"Nobody did. They were that way already—"

Irene flew between them, confronting Snorri. "Are my children in danger? If they're not safe here…"

"They're fine. Sven misread the spell."

Sven said, "I misread the spell? There's no—"

"No present danger. No need for heroics, or histrionics."

"But then, what—"

"It recognises latent personality traits, that's all."

Sven said, "Latent personality traits?"

"Well, anyone that would step between two shouting fire wizards…"

"Pardon? Oh!" Irene sidestepped. "My children. Promise me they're in no danger."

Snorri hesitated. Sven gave Irene a very odd look.

She grabbed Snorri's wrist. "Tell me what's wrong. For my children's sake."

He laid his other hand on her shoulder. "Relax. I can promise you that this house is one of the safest places in Frankland."

His voice was very soothing. She released his wrist and sighed. "Of course it is."

"The spell repulses visitors who don't meet His Wisdom's high standards of conduct, that's all."

"That's all?" Sven eased back into the armchair. "That's all? Wow."

"Look, Mrs van Gelder, I'm sorry we upset you. Forget about it. You'll feel better."

Sven mumbled, "You're getting far too good at that."

"I've had lots of practice lately." Snorri opened the door for Irene. "Didn't you want to introduce your girls to Master Sven?"

She blinked at him. After a moment her confusion dissipated. "Oh, yes, I did. Thank you for reminding me."

When she returned with Miranda and Gillian, they stared at Sven in silence as he attempted to engage them in conversation. She was about to chide them for their poor manners when Miranda abruptly came to life.

"Can you tell us stories about Papa?"

"What sort of stories?"

"True stories, about what he was like."

"I'm sure you've already heard lots of them."

"Yes," Gillian said, "But Papa's friends don't live in Airvale. Mama's stories are true, but she's run out of new ones. Grandmother and other people in Airvale tell us what they wish he'd been, not how he really was. I can tell. But you're a fire wizard, and you'll tell us the truth."

"Not even a brother or sister, or husband or wife, can tell you everything about another person. I can only tell you the parts of the truth that I know."

"That's good enough," Miranda said. "Tell us."

"Well…" Sven fingered his beard. "He played a prank once on a history lecturer, and the poor wretch never figured out what happened…"

He held them in thrall through supper with stories even Irene had not heard. Alexander, unnaturally solemn for a boy his age, relaxed and laughed. No one besides Irene seemed to notice the odd expression Sven's face sometimes acquired when looking at her or the girls.

Later, after tucking the girls into bed, she came downstairs to find Warlock Quicksilver, manuscript in hand, talking to Sven in the drawing room.

"Come," he said, "and sit with us, please. We invited Master Sven to sup with us tonight because, although the atmosphere is still volatile, the overt violence has abated enough to let me take an hour to consider your talent, as he and my wife have been insisting I do."

Irene perched on the edge of the sofa beside Sven, and squeezed trembling hands between her knees. Lucinda nestled next to her husband on the other sofa, facing Irene and Sven. The two boys, Alexander and Snorri, looked up from the chess board.

Snorri said, "Hope you don't mind me listening."

Alexander said, "You listen, and I'll beat you."

"You haven't yet."

The younger boy had a stubborn set to his jaw. "I will."

Warlock Quicksilver sighed. "Mistress Irene, do you mind? Snorri, as befits a warlock, suffers from insatiable curiosity. If I order him away, he will spend the next hour eavesdropping. It is simpler to let him listen."

"It's fine, sir, I don't mind."

"Now, then, my dear. My wife is correct in her assessment that the prohibition against interfering in another guild is a convention to preserve peace amongst the guilds, not a magically enforced rule. I do not yet know what, if anything, we can or should do for you, but wasted talent, particularly one such as Master Sven suggests you have, irks me. I trust you will forgive me if I value the judgment of a single flame mage over that of the entire Air Guild."

He did not seem to expect an answer, but Irene nodded. She, too, trusted Sven more than she trusted the Air Guild.

Sven said, "Tell him everything you've told me. He'll listen."

His support was gratifying, but traps lay in all directions. She talked, carefully, telling the Rehsavvys about her talent, her experiences with the school, and how she and Oliver had explored and developed her talents after they married.

When she finished, Warlock Quicksilver said, "I want you to demonstrate your talent for me."

The words "Yes, sir," danced in the air before him in gold letters. Lucinda "oohed" and clapped in appreciation.

The letters faded. Irene said, "That wasn't much of a demonstration."

"But it is in keeping with the descriptions of a wordsmith's abilities," Quicksilver said. The scrap of parchment from the White Duke's charter appeared in his right hand, Irene's partial recreation in his left. "I understand reproducing this much of the charter exhausted your reserves, but I want to see it done. Would two or three words be too much of a drain?"

"No, sir, I'm well rested today. I could do a little." She arranged the paper atop the parchment on the low table between the two sofas, then frowned at the paper, groping for the absent text. Her frown deepened to a scowl as seconds ticked past and the text eluded her. She was close to panic when she found one, and then a five-word phrase followed in smooth succession. She stopped, panting.

Quicksilver picked up paper and charter, and compared the two. "I am impressed. Quite impressed. In truth, however, I am more interested in the less demonstrable aspects of your talent. While you were upstairs, I read the corrections you suggested to my manuscript. I trust your description of how you recognise mistakes, but it does not matter. Magic or no, you did fine work. You could not have suggested the corrections you did if you had not understood the text. Have you written much of your own?"

She avoided the trap with a half-truth. "Yes, sir, quite a bit. Fairy tales and children's stories. My children are always begging for them."

"Does your talent help you with your own writing?"

"Of course, Your Wisdom. My own shortcomings are as obvious as others' are. My attempts require revising and rewriting, as anyone's does, because my talent doesn't supply the wording, although it does make improvements obvious. One apparently simple, four-line verse required three dozen revisions and hours with Dr Johnson's dictionary before the colours became pleasing."

"Persistent, are you? Good. Can you recognise mistakes in other languages?"

"Yes, sir. If I can't read the language—"

"How many languages can you read?"

"Nine, sir. But I can only speak four. If I can't read the language, mistakes are still apparent from the colours of the letters. That doesn't tell me what the mistake is or how to fix it."

"No, I would not expect that. Comparing two texts from different languages, can you tell if one is a true translation of the other?"

"Yes, sir."

"Even if you cannot read either language?"

"I've never tried that."

A sheet of manuscript appeared in one hand, a book in the other. He turned to a bookmarked page, then laid the book and paper on the table.

"Can you read either?"

"No, sir."

"Have you ever seen this book?"

"No, sir. The alphabet is new to me."

"The script is Devanagari; the language is Hindi. The manuscript is a translation of this page. What can you tell me about them?"

"There are inaccuracies in the original: here, and here. The translator fixed one, here, but not the other, and introduced several other mistakes accidentally, here, here, and here. Further, the entire third paragraph is a deliberate mistranslation. For some reason, the translator lied."

He almost purred. "You could be a very useful young lady. Very useful indeed."

The spell book appeared in his hand, and he paged through it. "It is obvious now why Oliver's writing was so polished. Many authors would benefit from an editor of such calibre. This exquisite little book of spells, for instance—did you help him with the wording?"

Never, ever, lie to a warlock. She hesitated a trifle too long. He looked up, expression intent. There was nothing sensible she could say. He repeated the question.

Panic crept into her voice. "No, sir, I didn't help with the wording."

His eyes were hard. "You are evading the question."

The room was silent, except for the soft crackle of the fire. Lucinda and the two boys were still. Sven stared as if he'd never seen Irene before.

She recoiled from the warning in Quicksilver's voice. "Did you write these spells?"

"Yes, sir," she whispered, and cowered against Sven as Warlock Quicksilver slammed the book down onto the table.

"How dare you perpetrate this monstrous fraud!"

Irene Exposed

"Jean, stop it." Lucinda pushed between Warlock Quicksilver and Irene. "You're scaring the poor woman. What fraud?" Irene clutched at her skirt, and tried to hide behind her.

Quicksilver's voice battered her ears. "Fraud against the Company of Mages, over Enchanter Oliver's posthumous induction. If Enchanter Paul had not submitted the spells in this little volume as proof of Oliver's aptitude for scholarship, we would have rejected him. This book countered his deficiencies in other respects. Enchanter Paul believes this is his son's work, but it appears he was deceived. Mrs van Gelder, I demand an explanation."

Lucinda stepped aside. Sven provided no refuge. He leaned forward with his elbows on his knees, staring straight ahead, his body rigid. Snorri and Alexander hung over the sofa back, staring. There was no escape; she had to talk.

"There was no fraud intended. It was a mistake, Your Wisdom. Writing the spells was Oliver's idea. He had the ideas, but not the patience to do the writing and rewriting needed. I have the patience. He taught me theory, fed me suggestions, and tested the spells for me. He promised to take the manuscript to the Company of Mages. He said you would appreciate them, and understand, and could force the Air Guild to acknowledge my talents. But he died with the book incomplete."

She lost control of her quavering voice. "A copy of the manuscript must have slipped into the boxes of Oliver's papers shipped to the Air Enchanter when we left Oxford. It shouldn't have, but I was too overwhelmed then to sort through them. I don't remember the Air Enchanter ever asking me about it, but that may mean my memory is faulty, not that he didn't ask.

"Six months later, he announced to the guild that Oliver had been named a mage, and presented me the published book with Oliver's name on it. And then what could one do? He was grieving for Oliver, too, and was proud his son had finally settled down to do the solid work that he, his father, had wanted. Exposing the mistake would hurt my children; what could one tell them—either their father or their grandfather was a fraud? And my attempts at confrontation, with either the Air Enchanter or other guild authorities, have never ended well. If I did claim to have written them, would the Air Guild believe me so mentally unstable they would take Miranda and Gillian from me? If my own guild doesn't believe in me, why would the Company of Mages? What could one do?"

She tugged her scarf tighter and blinked hard at her shoes. The silence was as profound as it had been minutes earlier.

When at length Quicksilver spoke, his voice was gentle. "My dear Mistress Irene, I offer my most abject apologies. I jumped to the unwarranted conclusion you had deliberately inflated Enchanter Oliver's reputation."

"I would never dishonour his memory in that way, Your Wisdom."

"I beg your pardon?"

"He didn't want to be a mage. He wasn't willing to work hard enough to earn the distinction, and the additional responsibilities frightened him. It seems evident now that he had foreseen his own future, and a hero's death was enough for him. After he graduated, he said he intended to never write another research paper. He enjoyed teaching, but he preferred spending his free time outdoors with the children, not chained to his desk. He said he would leave that to Sven."

Sven's shoulders twitched, but he twisted away from her. They sat side by side on the sofa with an invisible wall between them.

Quicksilver said, "I regret the necessity of this question, but did you write Oliver's university essays for him?"

"It's a fair question, Your Wisdom. He wrote them and I proofread them. My understanding of theory was inadequate then to fix his mistakes. My current knowledge comes from what he taught me, or from reading on my own since. He practiced his lectures on me, and claimed I was his best student."

"He must have been a gifted teacher, even if his spellcraft was not as we imagined it." His voice was still gentle. "The integrity of the Company of Mages is a serious matter. I trust you will not take it amiss that I verify what you have said is true."

"No, sir. Oliver respected the mages and would have been furious over any question of the Company's integrity. You must investigate." Her eyes swam as the words were wrenched from her. "You've given me a fair hearing. If you tell me tomorrow or the next day I'm deluded, that I was merely a scribe and Oliver did create those spells, I'll stop fighting the world's opinion and turn myself over to the healers."

Sven, still leaning forward, twisted around to stare. His voice grated on her ears, though the words should have cheered her. "You aren't deluded. Everything you've said fits with what I know about Ollie and his relationship with his father. I wouldn't have accepted those spells as his work if Enchanter Paul hadn't insisted."

He glared at Quicksilver. "Go ahead and investigate, but it won't do any good. It won't help Irene with the Air Guild, and it won't squelch the might-have-beens over Ollie." He stood. "I'd better go away and cool off. I won't be good company for a while." He stalked from the room. A few moments later the front door slammed. Irene flinched.

"What's the matter with him?" Alexander asked.

Quicksilver and Lucinda exchanged glances. She said, "His ambition was to be his generation's pre-eminent mage. He's angry because he lost to Oliver, and Oliver didn't even intend to compete."

Snorri said, "How's he lost? He has plenty of time to build his reputation. Mages aren't expected to do their best work until they're in their forties or fifties, and without Enchanter Oliver around... Oh. Right."

"I still don't see," Alexander said.

"As Master Sven pointed out," Quicksilver said, "speculation will continue for many years, perhaps centuries, over what Enchanter Oliver could have achieved had he lived his allotted three-score and ten. Even if the truth about the book of spells is exposed, many will not hear the full story, or will choose to believe an enchanter must have written spells of such quality, not a level three witch. Enchanter Oliver will not be here to uphold his reputation, but he will also not be here to refute it. Master Sven will spend the rest of his years in competition with a ghost, a phantom, and that is a competition no one can win.

"Further, Enchanter Oliver was an undisputed war hero, and Master Sven is not." He raised a hand to forestall Snorri's interruption. "No, hear me out. Enchanter Oliver died in battle with our centuries-old enemy. No one, from king to scullery maid, disputes the claim he is a hero. But in a civil war, one man's heroism is another's treachery. Master Sven is a commoner, his actions were in the interests of other commoners, and in opposition to a noble. Our guild's view of him as a hero is not universally accepted."

Snorri glared at the older warlock from a prone position on the hearthrug, but didn't argue. Alexander chewed on his lip for a few moments before asking, "What do you mean, 'even if the truth is exposed'? You're a fire wizard. Don't you have to expose it?"

Quicksilver said, "Mistress Irene has handed us a conundrum of the first order. I have an obligation to the Company of Mages, certainly, but the Fire Guild's relations with the Air Guild are already severely strained, and outside interference in their affairs could be the breaking point."

Snorri jerked upright. "So what? Enchanter Paul is an ass. Let's take those snotty airheads down a peg or two."

"Thank you so much," Irene said.

He flushed. "Sorry. Didn't mean you. But they've treated you like—"

"Watch your language," Lucinda snapped.

"—like dirt."

"It's true, they have," Irene said. "If you can embarrass the Air Guild without further damage to my family or the mages, do what you will."

"Thank you, my dear," Quicksilver said, "for your concern for the Company of Mages. Nor do we want to increase the danger to you and your children."

Alexander asked, "What danger?"

"Most members of any guild would resent another member, particularly one they already believe to be a fraud, publicly embarrassing their guild head. We would not have to search far in the Fire Guild to find a hothead willing to torch her in revenge."

Snorri said, "And without a shield, she'd be dead. But we're talking about the Air Guild. They can kick up a good wind, but if she stays indoors, what could they do to her?"

Irene said, "Nearly anyone in the Air Guild can create a breeze, even indoors, strong enough to blow small objects in my face—objects like paring knives. I would be no use to anyone, blinded."

Alexander and Lucinda cringed. Fire crackled in Quicksilver's voice once again, but Irene did not flinch, as it was not directed at her. "We must not let such an atrocity happen. For Frankland's sake, as much as for yours."

162

The boys finished their game—Snorri won—and left for bed. Quicksilver motioned for Irene to stay. She slumped against the plump sofa cushions. Her eyes wouldn't stay open.

Neither adult warlock looked livelier. Lucinda leaned against her husband's shoulder with her eyes closed. He stifled a yawn.

"I do beg your pardon," he said. "We are all weary. Had I been more alert, I should have reacted to your admission by rejoicing that a talent of such calibre is still with us, rather than taking you to task. You need never return to the drudgery of marking schoolchildren's essays. Many scholars would benefit from your services, and both Sven and I will direct them to you." He smiled. "Although some texts they will ask you to edit may remind you more of your schoolboys' essays than a mage's writings. Have you any more shocking news?"

"No, sir. You've put me through the wash and hung me out on the line to dry."

"Soon I will let you retire, but I may not have an opportunity to talk to you tomorrow, and I have a request."

"What, sir?"

"As a member of the Air Guild, you are, I presume, familiar with the theory behind the King's oath."

"The one he refuses to take? Yes, sir."

"We need a variant of that oath for the Warlock's agents and noblemen in positions of authority."

"The nobles already have one."

"Yes, but theirs does not include the most important clause."

"Oh, of course, the part about being fair to all."

"Yes. I intended to work on a new oath myself, but have not had the time. You have the time and talent to do it for us. We need something pithy and memorable. A short poem would be ideal. Would you undertake this task?"

He was asking? She would have grovelled, begging for the opportunity. "Your Wisdom, I would be thrilled. Honoured."

"Good," he said, without moving. His eyelids drooped. "Bedtime then, for all, if my dear wife will deign to let me up."

Irene attempted to rise, but floundered in a quagmire of cushions. "One question, Your Wisdom. Do you want the mistranslation in the oath fixed?"

"Mis—?" He sat up, sending his wife tumbling, and stared at Irene with eyes wide open. "What mistranslation?"

The King's Oath

Two copies of the king's oath lay on the table in the Rehsavvy's drawing room—the original, in Latin, written over a millennium ago, and the newer version, translated into the vernacular three hundred years after the forging of the four Offices. Warlock Quicksilver scowled at the pages as Irene pointed to the line with the mistranslation.

"Right here, sir. Do you see?"

He nodded. His eyes, narrow and alert, flicked between them. "I know the translation by heart, and have read the original more than once. I should have noticed this difference."

"Not necessarily. It's a subtle distinction—a one word change, in a preposition, at that."

"A small difference, yes, but one with non-trivial consequences."

Lucinda peered over his shoulder. "I can't read Latin. Explain it to me."

Irene said, "It's in the line about the source of the king's authority. The translation uses the word 'from'—the original uses 'of'. As the oath reads now, it implies the king is separate from the people, and draws power from them to speak as their agent. In the original, the king was one of the people, and spoke with their voice."

"Yes," Quicksilver rasped. "A king who took the original oath would have greater authority than one who took the newer version. A king with level four or five magical talent would have power on a par with any Officeholder."

Lucinda wrapped her arms around him. "Jean, don't beat yourself up. You can't be expected to know everything."

He shook her off and began pacing. "Perhaps not everything, but this bears on the knottiest problem of our time—the role of our king and his relationship with the four Offices. I should have noticed. The long, slow decline of the royal family began more than six hundred years ago, but I attributed it to other causes—inbreeding, antagonism towards the Fire Warlock, et cetera. It never occurred to me there might be a magical explanation for the kings' declining power."

He shook his head, and threw up his hands. "One can only wonder what might have been if someone had noticed this mistake at the time of translation. Perhaps we would not now be in such dire straits."

"Your Wisdom," Irene said. "It wasn't a mistake. It was deliberate."

He halted. "Deliberate, you say."

"Yes, sir. The translator intended for the king's power to be diminished. I assumed the Fire Warlock and the Air Enchanter had conspired on it."

He stared at her for a long moment before resuming pacing. "If they did, there is no trace of such an accord in the Fire Guild's record, not even in the private journals only the Fire Warlock has access to. I shall ask Enchanter Paul what he knows. As for your question regarding the lesser nobles' oath, I must give the matter some thought. I do not foresee what the consequences might be. Let us proceed with the mistranslation. Further, I ask that neither of you mention the matter to anyone else."

Lucinda twisted around on the sofa to stare at him. "Why? It won't stay a secret after you tell the king."

He leaned against the sofa back, frowning down at her. The boys had left the drawing room door half open. In the silence, a door in the hall upstairs creaked.

Quicksilver said, "I do not intend to tell the king."

"Why not? You've been saying our biggest problem is his refusal to take the oath, and you want to convince him to do it. If he knew he could have more power, wouldn't he take it?"

"He would not believe me. He would construe the promise of enhanced authority as a desperate ploy on my part."

"What if someone else told him? Wouldn't the king believe Enchanter Paul?"

The stairs creaked under a light step. Miranda or Gillian looking for their mother? Irene attempted to stand, but the sofa had swallowed her.

"Consider, my dear," Quicksilver said, "the consequences of handing that fool of a king more power."

Lucinda said, "But, Jean, I thought you wanted the king to take the oath."

"I do." His mouth twisted into a wry smile. "But I have been reminded several times lately of the adage to be careful what one wishes for. I want him to take the oath as we know it. I would abolish the monarchy entirely before handing King Stephen this additional authority."

"We can't get rid of the monarchy until all four Offices have been rebuilt, and that's years away. What do we do in the meantime?"

"I do not know, my dear. Tonight, I am too weary to give the matter the rational thought it deserves. Let us retire and get a good night's sleep." Irene accepted his outstretched hand and let him pull her from the sofa.

He said, "But first, both of you—Lucinda, Mistress Irene—must give me your word you will not discuss this with anyone else, most especially not with Alexander."

Irene shrugged. "Yes, sir." This topic wasn't one she would discuss with a child anyway. "Thank you, and good night, Your Wisdom, Lucinda."

Opening the door brought her face-to-face with a boy with blazing eyes. Alexander brushed past her and marched up to Warlock Quicksilver.

"What's this secret," he demanded, "you don't want me to know?"

An Apology

"Sir," Warlock Quicksilver snapped, "eavesdropping is not behaviour befitting a gentleman."

"I didn't mean to. I was hungry again and was going down to the kitchen. You're keeping secrets," Alexander flared back. "That's not honourable either. You promised to tell me what I need to know. You better keep your promise."

For a moment the two of them, facing each other with crossed arms, jutting chins, and blazing eyes, looked so much alike Irene thought they could have been father and son.

Lucinda said, "You did make that promise, Jean. You have to tell him."

Quicksilver flashed her a venomous glare. "I am aware of that, thank you. Mistress Irene, may I introduce Crown Prince Brendan Alexander."

Her curtsey wobbled. "I beg your pardon, Your Highness. I didn't know."

"You were not intended to," Quicksilver said. "I regret to say my wife is correct. Please tell Prince Brendan about the mistranslation."

During Irene's explanation the prince glanced at the page, then resumed glaring at Warlock Quicksilver. When she finished the prince shrilled, "How dare you keep this a secret!"

Quicksilver stared him down. "Why should I inform you or your father? If, as you believe, I want to reduce the king's power, you cannot believe I would willingly tell you of something that would increase it."

"You were talking about getting rid of the monarchy, too. You can't think I like that."

Quicksilver shrugged. "That is no secret. I am surprised you did not know, as that was the source of my most intense disagreements with your grandfather. If you do not believe me, ask your mother."

"I will. I'll tell my father your secret, too."

Quicksilver drew a deep breath, held it, and let it out slowly without lightening his scowl. "Very well. I cannot stop you. Perhaps I was wrong to attempt to keep it a secret as it may not matter—your father may no more believe you than he believes me."

The prince made sketchy bows towards Lucinda and Irene without taking his glaring eyes off Quicksilver. "Good night." He ran out the door and up the stairs. No one else moved until they heard his door close.

Lucinda said, "Go to bed, Jean. I'll come upstairs in a few minutes with bread and butter for Alexander. He appears to have forgotten what he came down for."

"I'll do it," Irene said. "You two must be exhausted. Why else would neither of two warlocks notice him outside the door, listening?"

Quicksilver's eyes sparkled, no trace of anger in them. Lucinda's smile was a yard wide. "What makes you think we didn't?"

The service stairway carved into the rock behind the living quarters in the Fortress's middle tiers was narrow, stuffy, dimly lit, and apparently endless. Climbing six flights, after emerging with Lucinda from the kitchen fireplace, left Irene gasping. The scholar guiding her let her dawdle on a landing.

"With all the magic in this place," he puffed, "they ought to make these stairs move, too. Somebody with a sick sense of humour must have made them as inconvenient as possible so he could laugh at those of us who ride the outer stairs with our eyes closed and both hands clenching the rails."

"At least he gave us this sop. Have any Fire Warlocks been afraid of heights?"

He laughed. "They wouldn't have lasted long if they were. Well, come on. One more flight for you."

At the next landing, he pointed out the study door at the end of the corridor, then plodded up the last flight of stairs to the library. The door opened for her; Sven ushered her in, a model of politeness, but his face was an expressionless mask. He scooped books off a chair by the window. Irene blinked at the tottering stacks of papers. The room did not display the extravagant disregard for order of Oliver's study, but it wasn't the tidy microcosm of perfection that seemed more in character, either.

"I came to apologise," she said. Rain lashed the window, the weather as grey as her mood. "Until you asked me to read your poetry, this debacle seemed my private concern, not hurting anyone else. Oliver would have been mortified. He thought highly of you. When you graduated, he said you were destined to be a famous mage."

Sven's face softened. "I believe you. I'm happier knowing I had taken Ollie's measure, but it doesn't change the fact that he's now seen as an exemplary mage. He's set an illusory standard I can never live up to."

"I'm sorry."

He stared into the fire, arms folded across his chest. With a sigh, she rose to go.

Without turning away from the fire he said, "I'm sorry, too. It's hurt you worse than it's hurt me. It's not fair for me to be angry with you. I'm more angry at someone else, but you're here and he's not. Maybe someday I'll get over it."

"Anger at the Air Enchanter doesn't surprise me. Good day."

How could Sven forgive her, when her mere presence would always remind him of Oliver? Would he even try? He had no reason to. She trudged towards the service stairs with a leaden heart.

"Irene, wait."

"Sven?"

He stood in the doorway of his study. "Please, come back. You have a mistaken impression, and it's not right to let you continue with it."

He closed the door behind her, eased into his desk chair, wincing a bit, and returned to staring at the fire.

She said, "My mistaken impression?"

"I am angry at Enchanter Paul, yes, but he's not the wizard I'm most angry at."

"Do you mean Oliver?"

He shook his head. "I let you think that when we talked about that poem, but it wasn't about him. His induction into the Company of Mages didn't help, but the poem was about someone else."

After another long silence, she said, "The whole poem was about one person? Who?"

"Warlock Quicksilver." He slumped forward with his head in his hands, elbows on knees. "I'm glad I've had the opportunity to work for him. I learn so much from him, and he treats me as well as he treats other warlocks.

But the seers predicted he would die in the war, and he didn't. As long as he's alive, no one will ever come to me with questions about fire magic. They'll seek his advice first. I feel guilty for resenting the fact he's still here. I respect him, I like him, I know we need him. But why can't he just go away?"

The wretchedness in his voice tore at her heart. The rain beat on the glass, all but drowning out his mumbling. "The worst of it is… There was gossip… I should have been admitted to the Company of Mages before Ollie, but Flint blocked it out of spite at Quicksilver. Somehow a rumour spread that Quicksilver was holding it up because he didn't think I was good enough. He let Flint believe it so he'd stop opposing me. Quicksilver swore to me the rumour was nonsense, but Flint reminds me at every opportunity, and it gets to me. Sometimes I feel like an imposter, and if Quicksilver only knew, he'd have me kicked out. He's so far beyond me, it amazes me he could think I'm good enough."

The poem he'd written, *Always Second Best*, had seemed to burn through the paper. No wonder. And he'd said the poem, not just the second verse.

Teardrops of rain slid by on the other side of the glass. Irene said, "You lost the Locksmith to him, too. You're in love with her, aren't you?"

"I…was. Or thought I was. I'm not sure anymore. Maybe I just wanted to be. It's probably just as well. She has an annoying habit of winning arguments, and she's blood-curdling when she's really angry."

He rose, and came to stand beside her at the window. "I'm sorry. I shouldn't have upset you." He brushed her cheek with a gentle finger. "I thought you were crying."

"Air witches never cry."

"Of course not. Not even when they've had their sanity questioned, or when they're tired and hungry and facing something frightening…"

She pushed his hand away. "Sven, it's hopeless to compete with Quicksilver on his terms. Spend your energy where you're more talented than he is."

"Be serious. He's a warlock and I'm a level four. He's a hundred and fifty years old, and I'm thirty-one. There isn't anything I'm better at than he is."

"Yes, there is."

"What?"

"How talented a poet is he?"

"I don't know. I hadn't thought about it. He's done plenty of spellcraft—there are spells scattered through everything he's written on theory."

"Those are mnemonic devices, not poems. His sense of meter is good, but he hardly ever uses a rhyme scheme more complicated than AABB or ABAB. When was the last time you read a poem of his that wasn't a spell?"

"I, uh… I don't recall."

"There aren't any. He's written valuable essays on other people's poetry, but admitted in one that he can't write it himself, and has no interest in trying. Sven, you're a poet, and he's not."

He flushed. "Flattery will—"

"It's not flattery. This is my area of expertise. How many people in Frankland besides a few dozen scholars and the top ranks of witches and wizards are interested in, or can make sense out of, his books on theory? But the poetry you've written is universal. If someone in the Air Guild set your poems to music, the songs would be all over Frankland within weeks."

She picked up a pen and ink bottle from his desk and thrust them at him. He accepted them, looking dazed.

"Sven, you have to publish your poetry. The Air Guild have abandoned their responsibility for spreading news. My lamentable attempts don't express emotion as well as yours. Write about what happened in Abertee. Frankland needs to know."

He watched her leave with his soul in his eyes.

Justice Hall

Arrows thudded into Sven's chest. Irene buried her face in her hands and hunched over, shuddering.

The prince patted her shoulder. "It's all right, ma'am. They didn't kill him."

Bless the child. Watching the White Duchess and her son prove themselves rapacious, murderous savages hadn't been easy on him, either, but here he was, trying to comfort her, the adult.

An unremarkable air witch had no reason to attend this trial, but the prince had insisted on her company, and the warlocks had joined forces with him. "We'll go through the tunnels," Lucinda had said, "and you won't have to face the Crystal Palace in the daylight. It's not nearly as scary from the inside."

Her husband had been more persuasive. "I would prefer he stay here and watch the trial in the fire, but he has the right to attend, and I will not deny him. You have the education and understanding to explain the proceedings, and we will be otherwise occupied, nor should we draw attention to him. He trusts you, and I am glad of that. He will need an adult's comforting presence if there are any nasty surprises. Will you not come?"

So here they were, turning to ice on the topmost bench in Justice Hall. The revelation his father had ordered the White Duchess to block her husband from carrying out his responsibilities as duke had deeply shocked the boy. What consolation could Irene offer? That even at thirty, a parent's shortcomings could tear one's heart into little pieces? No comfort there.

Matt, on his left, reached over the prince's head and tugged her cloak collar higher. "I'm sorry, ma'am, that I can't stop you from shivering, but I'm only a level three and I can't keep myself warm in this frost—sorry, ma'am—in this arctic hellhole. But this part of it's over. We can hop back to the Fortress for dinner and warm up."

The battle scene in the magic looking glass had disappeared; it now reflected Justice Hall. Far below, Sven was bent over, clutching at his chest. Lord Geoffrey jeered at him. Someone should give the wretched beast the slap he deserved. Irene turned her eyes aside, watching the Water Guild Council process out.

A ripple of laughter drew her attention to the prisoner's bench. A guard was chasing after the departing Frost Maiden. The Duke and Lord Geoffrey had risen, but the Duchess could not. The Frost Maiden had frozen her to the stone bench for demanding a padded armchair like the one Sven occupied.

The armchair and footstool the Water Guild provided the Frost Maiden Emerita had come as no surprise to Irene. That they also so honoured three members of the Fire Guild did astonish her. "Our wounded heroes," the new Frost Maiden had called them.

They would need their heroes. Humiliating a duchess is not an exercise for the faint of heart.

Irene stood. "Yes, let's get warm."

A prince, even at the age of twelve, expects to get his own way, and with two Fire Eaters supporting him, Irene's reservations carried little weight.

Alexander said, "They're done with the magic mirror, aren't they?"

"Well, yes, but—"

"I want to be where we can hear. The top row is too far away."

"We can see better from further down, too," Tom said.

"Which also means they can see him."

Matt played with the tassel on Alexander's borrowed, oversized hat. "Nobody will recognise him. His Wisdom already saw to that."

What about Irene's visibility? Good sense lost to her desire to see. "Fine. Just not the first few rows."

They compromised on the end of the fifth horseshoe row, opposite the line of armchairs, and above the barristers' table, close enough for a good view of the low but heated disagreement between Warlock Quicksilver and the lead advocate. One of King Stephen's closest advisors, the barrister,

Lord Harold St John, was a minor air wizard with a reputation for being as pliant as obsidian. The noises of other spectators filing in, pulling on gloves and adjusting cloaks, drowned the argument, but regardless of its merits, His Wisdom might as well surrender now.

The prince pointed with his chin at the empty thrones dead centre. "My m—" He blinked and swallowed. "I thought the queen might come for the sentencing."

"She doesn't want to anger the king." Irene wouldn't be the one to inform the prince that the king had forbidden the nobles from attending what he called a charade of a show trial. She would leave that to Quicksilver.

The high-ranking wizards and witches reclaimed their seats. Irene ducked behind Tom, but Enchanter Paul did not glance in their direction. He settled in the first row with his back to them. Sven, smiling and invigorated, strolled in arm-in-arm with the Earth Mother. He nodded in Irene's direction. She gave a small wave of her hand and looked away.

Warlock Snorri climbed towards her, leaping from bench to bench.

She said, "There are stairs."

He grinned and dropped onto the bench behind her. "Stairs are boring. Quicksilver said you'd be explaining things to Alex. Mind if I listen?"

"Yes. Even whispering in his ear could draw too much attention."

"Oh, that's easy." He closed his eyes and frowned for a moment. "We can talk as loud as we want. Nobody but you and Alex and us fire wizards will hear."

Warlock Quicksilver turned on heel and marched to his place between his wife and the Frost Maiden Emerita. Lord Harold chortled over sending a flame mage away with a livid complexion and hard eyes. Irene wondered why embarrassing the Air Guild had ever concerned her. With idiots like him in their ranks, they deserved to be embarrassed.

Warlock Quicksilver caught her eye and shook his head. She should have stood firm for an inconspicuous spot on the top row. The gong sounded. Too late now; the trial was about to resume.

Guards escorted the defendants to the prisoners' bench. The duchess stomped in with a curled lip and glaring eyes, her son sauntered in, the whimpering duke crept in behind them. No wonder: he'd been here before, and emerged the worse for it. The scenes shown today in the looking glass evoked pity for the poor man. This disaster was his wife and son's doing; perhaps the Water Office would be kind this time. If not, Irene hoped, surely the twenty-five years he'd been married would count towards his time in purgatory.

The duke sat with his head in his hands. Lord Geoffrey twisted around to survey the room, and wink at his younger brother. Too bad the Frost Maiden hadn't frozen him in place. His incessant fidgeting throughout the morning had rubbed Irene's nerves raw. What a pathetic disgrace he was to the Air Guild. A proper air wizard would behave with the respect due the occasion.

Lord Geoffrey noticed her, laughed, and pointed her out to his mother. The duchess glared. Irene pulled her cloak tighter and her hat further down.

A whispering voice began the nasty little ditty wherein Sven ripped off Irene's clothes. She flinched. The fire wizards with her stiffened; other spectators were glancing around. Sven went livid. He started to rise, but Lucinda grabbed his arm and yanked him back down. Then a great roaring and crackling, as if unseen floodwaters warred with an inferno in Justice Hall, drowned the whispers.

The double doors opened. The Water Guild Council filed in. The roaring stopped. The voice continued singing.

"Lord Geoffrey!" the Frost Maiden snapped, "No harassment is permitted in this chamber. Desist."

He laughed at her. "You can't make me."

"Can't I?"

Frost rimed his hair and spread down his arms and chest. He bent over, shivering violently. His teeth chattered.

"Fine, you win." The singing stopped. Sven looked up at Irene. She looked away.

The trial resumed with the charges against the duke and duchess. The scales teetered, rose, and dipped, clearing the duke of malicious intent, but giving an emphatic positive response to the charges of gross negligence and dereliction of duty. With the newfound charter enumerating his responsibilities, one would expect no less, but his lawyers offered only token resistance. It couldn't be that the king accepted the wisdom of the rebuilt Water Office's judgements. Had disgust with the duke's shortcomings led the king to abandon him to the Water Office's tender mercies?

When the Frost Maiden summoned them to hear their sentences, the duke started and froze. His own son, the ungrateful whelp, gave him a shove.

He shuffled forward. The duchess moved like a puppet on strings, fighting the forces pulling her to a kneeling position before the Frost Maiden. Master Duncan came forward to stand with the duke.

The Frost Maiden frowned. "Who will stand with the duchess? It is not right that she should have no one with her."

The silence stretched out to an uncomfortable length before a soprano voiced drawled, "Oh, I suppose I'll do it." Enchantress Winifred floated down from the top row. "She is an air witch, after all."

Snorri said, "When did she show up? She wasn't here earlier."

Irene said, "Why would she attend at all? She despises the Water Guild."

"Your Grace," the Frost Maiden said, "You did not approve of your son's actions. Nevertheless, as duke, you must be held responsible. For more than twenty years you have informally abdicated your position. In return, the Water Office formally relieves you of that position. You will leave here today a commoner, without a nobleman's responsibilities or privileges. Your son, the new White Duke, will pay the compensation due the Archers for their losses. In addition, Abertee will be removed from your family's jurisdiction—"

"Rupert, you idiot," the duchess shrieked. "Look what you've cost us."

"Silence! Your protests can only make the sentence less lenient."

For a moment the two women, one alabaster white, the other splotchy red, exchanged glares.

The Frost Maiden turned back to the duke. "Mr Richardson, the manor house in Abertee is your ancestral home, but it is entailed to be the seat of governance in the district, and will transfer to Abertee's next overlord. You and your wife will live as pensioners in a small apartment in one of your family's southern holdings. That is all."

The soon-to-be former duke gaped at the Frost Maiden. "You won't make me colder?"

"No, sir, I will not."

"I don't have to throw any more of those frost—er, damned, parties?"

The Frost Maiden smiled. "You will not have the means to throw parties, and I doubt you will ever be invited to another one. If invited, you do not have to attend. Nor will anyone object if you take up gardening."

A slow smile spread across his face. "That's all?"

Her smile vanished. "Your Grace, you have not yet heard what awaits your son."

He paled, but she gave him no time to reflect. "Flame Mage Sven Matheson, Farmer Douglas Archer, Master Swordsmith Duncan Archer, as or representing the wronged parties, are you satisfied with this judgment?"

The three men held a whispered conference. Sven nodded at the swordsmith, who said, "No, ma'am. Two things, Your Wisdom. First, if the White Duke's not our overlord any longer, who is?"

"King Stephen will appoint a new overlord."

"Subject to my approval." The Fire Warlock leaned back and crossed his arms over his chest. "If I don't approve, it doesn't happen."

The swordsmith chewed his lip. He had reason to worry. Going without an overlord for years, while king and Fire Warlock haggled, had its own dangers.

"Well, we don't like that part, but we can understand it. The other thing is, you're letting her off too easy. And while I'm glad she won't be bothering us anymore, it's not right to let her loose on somebody else."

"Agreed. I consider this sentence too lenient for the heartaches she has caused, but it is in accordance with the law, and any further penalties imposed would affect her husband more than her."

"Now, ma'am, as to that: he wasn't a bad duke, when she wasn't hag-riding him, and he's one of us. I got awful homesick when I left Abertee, and I bet he will, too. Let him stay if he wants to. That house is so big whoever else lives there might not ever notice him."

The duke turned wide eyes on Master Duncan. "You'll let me stay?"

"Yes, sir. But just you. Not her."

The Frost Maiden said, "Mr Richardson, what would you prefer?"

He turned his back on his wife. "I'd like to stay in Abertee. Please?"

"You may. And speaking not as Water Sorceress, but as a neighbour, I wish you well."

"Thank you, ma'am."

The duke radiated relief and pleasure. His wife radiated rage. Despite a thickening layer of hoarfrost, she mouthed threats and shook her fist at all concerned. The hatred on display struck terror in Irene's soul. Duchess or not, Marie Richardson could still cause trouble, lots of it, and a homeless level three air witch was an easier target for revenge than the Frost Maiden in her Crystal Palace or a mage living in the Fortress.

"The worst that's likely to happen," the Fire Warlock had said, "is you'll get dust up your nose…" *Bury the man!* She had known better. Oliver had demanded she care for herself and the girls, not get into serious trouble. The judgment against Marie Richardson did not satisfy her, not one bit.

The Frost Maiden stood. "Sorceress Lorraine has requested an hour's adjournment to advise Lord Geoffrey's lawyers. I suggest you use the opportunity to warm yourselves. You will need it, before the trial is over."

The warmth imparted by a hot fire leached out as Irene's cohort reclaimed their seats. Enchanter Paul and the Frost Maiden Emerita were having no more success with Lord Harold than Warlock Quicksilver had had. This time Irene heard the end of the argument.

"Thank you for your advice, Your Wisdoms," Lord Harold said, "but we will pursue our own strategy."

"Of course, sir," the former Frost Maiden said. "Clearly you understand the law and the Water Office better than either the Air Enchanter or I could ever hope to." She sailed across the floor, her spine rigid, her face an icicle.

The Water Guild Council processed into the chamber in dignified silence. The reigning Frost Maiden, last in line, carried an hourglass. The duke fainted. The room went still. Metal clinked on stone as she set the hourglass on its plinth.

Nasty surprises, indeed. Irene wished His Wisdom had warned her. Matt looked exultant. How could he work for Quicksilver and still be that naïve?

The prince, staring, stammered, "They never…they wouldn't…they couldn't…" He lifted enormous eyes to her. "Could they?"

"They have, but not in centuries."

"But that's for when a nobleman murders somebody that matters."

"And that swine matters more than a mage?" Her shrill outrage overrode the wizards' growls. "Has he anything to commend him other than being born a duke's son?"

The prince flushed but raised his head and set his jaw. "The Company of Mages used to be all nobles, but now none of them are. He outranks them."

"You think they don't matter? Your Highness, you are mistaken. Once, ascension to the Company conferred automatic membership in the highest ranks of the nobility. Mages did not matter because they were noble. They were ennobled because they matter." Her breathing was rapid and shallow. She drew in a deep breath and held it.

Tom said, "You mean Warlock Quicksilver ought to be a duke?"

"Yes. No. For his services, he should be an honorary prince."

Snorri snickered. "That would piss him off, for sure. From what I've heard, Enchanter Oliver wouldn't have liked being a duke either."

"An outrage of that magnitude would have brought him back to haunt someone."

The poor prince looked horrified. Snorri murmured in her ear, "I didn't think air witches were so blunt."

"Diplomacy never helped me with the Air Guild, so why bother? You disapprove?"

"I'm a warlock, remember."

"Ssh." The legal manoeuvrings had begun. Translating the Latin was easy; explaining the lawyers' actions was not, as they left her increasingly bewildered. The charges against Lord Geoffrey were capital, of course, but lawyers always have wiggle room. Overheard conversations had convinced her the Fire Guild Council worried, and rightly so, about the repercussions on the fragile peace, and did not want him executed. Defanged, yes; executed, no.

But Lord Harold St. John, the prisoner's own counsel, was not playing along. He insisted on Lord Geoffrey being tried on the full battery of charges.

After the nobles' rout at Master Duncan's trial, did he really believe the Water Office had not changed? Risking a client's life on such poor odds was not a gamble a conscientious advocate should take. Or was he planning a show of strength, letting the king step in at the last moment to issue a pardon and snatch the convicted criminal from the Water Office's clutches?

If this criminal went free, there would be more riots.

The cold seeped into Irene's bones.

Chandeliers blazed. The weak autumn sun shining through the clerestory windows had faded to black before the questions were put to the Water Office. Silver scales hung in the balance, a figure of Sven, the Fire Warlock behind him, in one pan; Lord Geoffrey in the other.

"At the Archer farm, who had the overriding authority: Flame Mage Sven Matheson, or Lord Geoffrey Richardson?"

The pan with Sven dropped. The arm stood vertical. Lord Geoffrey had no authority. More questions received emphatic answers: guilty on all charges, including the minor charge of slander. His conviction would do Irene no good; not even the Water Office could erase an entire guild's memories.

Watching the scales was easier for her than looking down and meeting Sven's gaze. Again.

When the Frost Maiden summoned Lord Geoffrey to hear his fate, he sauntered forwards. "Why should I kneel? You've already said I'm going to be duke."

"You have a brother. Kneel!"

He went down on one knee with a thud, as if Master Duncan had shoved on his shoulders. He snarled at her. His trembling father crept forward to stand beside him.

Alexander was pale, and frightened. Tom and Matt looked ready to celebrate, but puzzled at the evident consternation emanating from the members of their guild council. Warlock Snorri was grim, and, at fifteen, seemed far more adult than the other two fire wizards in their early twenties.

Alexander said, "The king will come and pardon him, won't he?"

"Lord Geoffrey," the Frost Maiden said, "you have been found guilty of several crimes, foremost among them the attempted assassination of a mage, and disobedience to orders from that mage acting as the Fire Warlock's representative. For these, the Water Office has decreed you must die."

Snorri met Irene's eyes and shook his head. "The king won't come. Lord Harold wants a martyr."

"You have one hour in which to make your peace with your God, your family, and anyone you have wronged." The Frost Maiden turned the hourglass over and set it on the bench beside her. "I advise you to use the time well."

Battle Lines

At the first opportunity, Lucinda fled to the Warren, having no stomach for the chaos erupting in Justice Hall, and even less for the execution to follow. Other witches and wizards followed over the next hour and a half, drifting into the sanctuary of the Earth Mother's amber chamber, to sit in funereal silence or to pace the floors, as Jean had done ever since arriving. The trapped heat warmed their bodies, but not even the cheerful glow of lamplight reflecting off the honey-yellow walls, ceiling, and floor dispelled the chill in Lucinda's soul.

Mother Celeste and Sorceress Eleanor arrived together. "It's over," Mother Celeste said. "The Archer brothers are propping up the duke. Mr Richardson, I should say. They're taking him and his son's body home, and will organise the manor house staff for the burial. Enchantress Winifred offered to escort the duchess—er, Mrs Richardson. That was decent of Winnie, since no one even in her own guild likes the duchess much."

Jean said, "For decades I have dreamed of a day like today." He had not paused in his measured pacing. "My most fervent wish was for the Water Office to hold the nobility responsible for their foolishness, to remove the incompetents from their positions, and to punish them as firmly for crimes against commoners as for crimes against other nobles."

Lorraine said, "You have gotten your wish, Jean, and it is an unmitigated disaster."

Lucinda tensed, but Jean's temper didn't flare.

"Indeed," he said. "I should have been more careful in what I wished for. This is a catastrophe."

René said, "But I thought that's why we rebuilt the Water Office. What went wrong?"

Lorraine said, "You are correct, Warlock Snorri. This is what we hoped to achieve in the long term. Jean's wish has been my wish also. We expected a gradual shift the nobility would grumble about but acquiesce with, not realising the extent of the changes until too late to reverse them. Many, I believed, would neither notice nor care, being too dull to understand and lulled into complacency by their belief that because nothing had ever changed, nothing ever would.

"Instead, the Water Office shifted abruptly and decisively. Between last month's verdict on Master Duncan and Lord Edmund, and today's verdict on the White Duke and his family, even the dimmest of those dullards must see that. It still favours the aristocracy—it did not, after all, require the duke's family repay centuries of misused taxes, and the crimes damning Lord Geoffrey were attacking a mage and disobeying orders, not the attempted slaughter of a family with three innocent children—but the nobles will not see it that way."

"No," Jean said. "They see their privileges ripped away, and will fight with every weapon at their disposal to recover them."

"Until now," she said, "both nobles and commoners viewed the magical guilds as predominantly neutral, working to maintain order and the common good. But the battle lines have been redrawn, by this and other events of this terrible fortnight."

"Before today," Jean said, "individual nobles engaged in solitary panics and isolated rebellions. Now, they will unite against us. They cannot destroy the Fire Office, but if they kill all level five witches and wizards in any guild, Frankland will collapse in chaos. We are at war, my friends, and the attack that nearly killed Master Sven has shown them how vulnerable we are."

Fabric rustling and chairs creaking were the only sounds for several minutes. Lucinda started when Enchanter Paul cleared his throat.

"Two weeks ago," he said, "I would have castigated you for paranoia, but now I must admit you may be right. I never envisaged an attack of such violence on a fire wizard—a mage, no less—attempting to keep the peace. I still do not believe either the Earth or Air Guilds are in danger, but if an angry fool attacks a member of the Water Guild Council…" His voice trailed off.

Sorceress Eleanor said, "Go ahead, say it. If they succeed in murdering a single sorcerer or sorceress, the floodgates will open, and we are not well equipped to defend ourselves. Our entire guild will be swept away."

"Afraid so," Beorn said. "Those nobles that love their hunts will go hunting for bigger game. The asses will even brag about risking their lives protecting their class. Jean, it's time we told them about Plan B."

Heads turned, swivelling between Beorn and Jean. "Plan B?" Eleanor asked.

Jean sighed. "My friend Beorn exaggerates. We have no plan. We merely have an idea that Beorn, Lucinda, and I have been discussing for some time. I have misgivings about trotting it out now, as it needs time to come to fruition, and time we do not have."

Mother Celeste said, "Perhaps not, but I want to hear it. Go on, Jean."

Jean hesitated for a moment, frowning. "We have, so far, attempted to control the nobles through pressure on King Stephen. This has been a spectacular failure. Our idea is to turn the tables, and control the king through pressure on the nobles. We would show the nobles a modified version of the king's oath—an oath requiring them to be fair to all their subordinates—and offer a choice between swearing the oath or facing trial for neglecting their charters. As nobles acquiesce and take the oath, the pressure towards civil war will abate. The king may even eventually understand the oath is as advantageous to the nobles as to the commoners."

"That is an audacious plan, Jean," Mother Celeste said, "But, how? If we couldn't convince the king, how can we convince the nobles?"

He gave her a sardonic smile. "Like them, we are trapped in the belief that because nothing has ever changed in Frankland, nothing ever will. We now have two powerful weapons we have not had before, and we should not hesitate to use them."

"Two? The Water Office upholding the White Duke's charter is one. Some of them might view taking the oath as the lesser of two evils. What's the other?"

"The threat to abolish the nobility and royalty completely when we rebuild the Fire Office."

Shocked witches and wizards turned to stare at Lucinda. She winced. *Drown the man!* They had already discussed this, but to hear the prospect stated so baldly made her stomach knot and her palms itch.

She hid crossed fingers under her skirt. "Unlocking the Fire Office won't hurt me when I'm a fully fledged lightning wielder."

Jean raised a hand and waited as a clamour of voices swelled and then subsided. "Peace, friends. That event will not be for years yet, but the nobles need not know that. Nor am I proposing to abolish the nobility immediately. I would prefer to erode their power and privileges and let them wither, but that will take decades, if not centuries."

Enchanter Paul grated, "What are you suggesting, then?"

"That we use the threat as leverage to bring them under control. We have demonstrated we can rebuild the Offices; they will believe the threat. We can convince them that if they want their shields to continue, they must abide by our rules. Some, particularly in the lower ranks, would rather risk the king's wrath than ours. If we persuade a few, others will follow, and pressure on the dukes and the king will build from below."

"I see why you were reluctant to call it a plan," Paul said. "This sounds like wishful thinking to me. The Fire Guild can't possibly talk to all of them—not even the top ranks, much less the minor nobles—before they cause more trouble. The dukes won't give you any rest once they hear what you're up to."

Sorceress Eleanor said, "Do you have any better ideas?"

"No, I'm afraid I don't," Paul admitted.

"Then let's see if there's any way to make it work," she said. "I'd rather do something—anything—even if the odds of success are low, than wait in fear for an arrow out of the dark."

"To pull this off," Beorn said, "the Water, Fire, and Air Guilds will have to drop everything else, and work together, talking to the nobles, and hunting for charters where we have to, to light fires under the stubborn ones. And when I say everything else, I mean everything else. This is the only thing that matters right now, in the whole country."

Paul glowered, but didn't retort.

"Absolutely," Eleanor said. "It means life or death to the Water Guild. We will cast our lot with the Fire Guild and do everything we can to keep Frankland from collapsing."

She turned a pointed stare on Paul. His lips, already clamped shut, thinned further. Lucinda experienced a pang of sympathy for the bewildered nobles. That the Water Guild would side with the Fire Guild against the Air Guild struck her as bizarre, and she had initiated the change.

Hey, big sister, he's dreaming, isn't he? There's not enough of us between the Fire and Water Guilds.

Maybe if we could work with the Air Guild...

No chance.

Mother Celeste said, "It's life or death for all four guilds. How can the Earth Guild help? Charters and oaths aren't our bailiwick, but you can't do it without us being involved."

Dear old Mother Celeste. Lucinda blew her a kiss.

Beorn said, "What makes you say you aren't involved? Your guild's been working your arses off patching people up."

"When we treat wounds, it's too late. It's better to keep the peace, so we're not overrun with injured people."

"You got any magic potions you can feed them, to make them develop some sense?"

"If I had, I would have used it years ago."

"If only you did have medicines to give them," Lorraine said. "Sometimes their ridiculous notions and pond scum ideas spread like the plague."

"The plague," Mother Celeste breathed. "That's it. We can help. We will."

Jean pivoted, his eyes alight. "My dear Celeste, you are brilliant. We will have the time we need. You have tipped the odds of success in our favour."

Beorn looked at Lucinda. She frowned and shrugged.

"I'm tired," he said. "Explain it to me."

Mother Celeste's smile was radiant. "Quarantine."

The Fortress

Two poems lay on the blue bedroom's writing table. One, a clean copy of the revised oath, pleased Irene's eye in royal purple. The longer poem that her jottings for the past week had produced repelled her eye in muddy yellow. A lame effort, it contained a bare recital of facts, with little to make it memorable. She was scribbling corrections on it when Katie appeared with the morning's post.

"Mail for you, ma'am."

Though unexpected, the contents of the two letters were in character. The thicker one, a long diatribe from Irene's mother, castigated her for exposing Miranda and Gillian to the Fire Guild's corrupt and uncouth influences, and demanded their return to Airvale. Irene, however, was not welcome without an apology for her immoral behaviour. The only surprise was a postscript saying Winifred had asked for her, and had been appalled to learn she'd gone to Blazes. Winifred had begged Mother to remind Irene not to take refuge in the Fortress.

The second letter, a terse note from the Air Enchanter, said new demands on the Air Guild would leave the school understaffed. If Irene spurned his advice to resume her work there, he would give more credence to the stories she had an illicit lover. She should expect to lose her position, and he would not help her find employment in the future.

With the letters stuffed into a pocket and her belongings crammed in a sack, she summoned the girls.

"Miranda, dear, you suggested a tune this could be set to. Would you sing it for the warlocks?"

She read the updated ballad. "Sure, Mama."

"Good. After we've done that, you and Gillian will return to your room and pack your bags. It's time to go."

"But Mama," Gillian whined, "we like it here."

"Stop right there. You will not argue. The Rehsavvys have been kind to us. We must not tax their generosity." Her voice held steady, but her hands shook. "Come, Miranda. Let's get this over with."

Irene and Miranda stood at the door to the warlock's study, but Irene's hand would not rise to knock.

"What's the matter, Mama?"

"Nothing, dear. My nerves are frayed, that's all."

The door opened. "What, pray tell," Quicksilver said, "arouses such a storm of anger and resentment on this fine autumn morning?"

"Mama, are you angry?"

"I am a little upset, but not at you, sweetheart."

Quicksilver's eyebrows arched. "You do have a talent for understatement. Your timing, by the way, is excellent. We were discussing you. Please, come in. Sit down."

Lucinda gestured for Irene to sit beside her on the sofa, but Irene handed the first paper to Quicksilver and walked over to the window. "Adapting the king's oath as you asked, Your Wisdom, was trivial. It needed pruning and smooth transitions, but this will work for a person of any rank."

He read it through and smiled. "Indeed, this is exactly what we need. Thank you, my dear."

"And as dissemination of news is the Air Guild's responsibility, a few words about the recent events seemed in order. These days most news travels through pamphlets and newspapers…"

"Leaving the illiterate peasantry high and dry. As well as many aristocrats, who can read but have no interest in doing so. I have long argued that abandoning the traditional minstrels and storytellers was a mistake."

"Yes, sir. Oliver used to argue with the Air Enchanter about that, among other things. A song may reach a wider audience. It you have time, Miranda will sing it for you."

"We will make the time. Let us hear it."

Miranda stepped into the middle of the room, went rigid, and covered her face with the page. "I can't sing. You're all staring at me."

Lucinda said, "You've been serenading us for days, and you have a lovely voice. What's the matter?"

"Stage fright," Irene said. "As long as she isn't asked to sing, no one can stop her."

"It might help," Quicksilver said, "if we gazed out the window instead of watching you sing."

"Yes, sir," she said.

Quicksilver joined Irene at the window. Behind them, the paper rattled, and a nervous voice began, "This is the Ballad of Master Sven."

Master Sven went up to Abertee,
His Grace, the White Duke, for to see…

Miranda finished, in a stronger, surer voice, to applause.

"Very good. I like it," Lucinda said.

"Well done. Both the execution and the composition." Quicksilver first bowed to Miranda and then to Irene. "This ballad will be more effective than dry commentary in the broadsheets."

They praised both singer and song more than Irene thought either deserved. It would be dangerous to let their flattery cloud her judgment. "Thank you, Miranda," she said, ushering her out. "Go pack your bag. I'll be along in a few minutes."

"You're packing?" Lucinda said. "Good. But we hadn't said anything…"

Irene's throat tightened. "We'll leave at once, ma'am. Overstaying our welcome wasn't my intention."

Lucinda blushed. "I didn't mean that."

Did everyone in the Fire Guild display their emotions so publicly? Irene wondered if she had ever blushed. She couldn't recall.

"You've been lovely guests," Lucinda said, "and you're welcome to stay with us as long as you like. But we won't be in this house much longer."

"Pardon? You've not been packing."

"Come, sit down," Quicksilver said. "No, I insist." A firm hand on Irene's shoulder steered her to the sofa. He sat opposite, frowning. "As news of the verdict on the White Duke's family spreads, their friends and associates will be out for revenge on everyone involved in their downfall. We will be moving into the Fortress for our family's safety, and for Alexander's…"

The greatest wizard of their time couldn't protect his own family? The room spun, and darkened. Irene recovered her senses to find Lucinda had an arm around her shoulders and was crooning to her.

Quicksilver said, "A direct attack on either Lucinda or myself seems unlikely, but given an opportunity they would attack our son or Alexander in retaliation, and while he is in the Fire Warlock's service, Alexander is unshielded. After your involvement in the charter search, and with no magical defences, you are at risk. Further, if it becomes public knowledge what else you have done—the oath, and this ballad…"

"Please, Your Wisdom," Irene said, "don't tell anyone who wrote that ballad. The Air Guild will be furious with me for bypassing them, but they would reject anything from me."

"Your relationship with the Air Guild concerns me. Perhaps now that Enchanter Paul has acknowledged we are in the midst of civil war, he will take the dangers to you seriously."

She handed him the Enchanter's letter; his wife read over his shoulder. Their faces darkened as they read.

"What rubbish." He handed it back to Irene. "I recommend you toss this on the fire. Now as to your safety, of the four centres of guild activity, Airvale has the highest proportion of nobility. I regret I must say so, but without Enchanter Paul's support, a safe return to Airvale is not in your near future. Perhaps never."

"Don't apologise for good news, Your Wisdom."

One eyebrow angled upwards. "A moment ago you seemed eager to leave."

"Not eager, sir, and not to return to Airvale. Please, sir, you said you would help. If you would write a letter of recommendation for my services as an editor and proofreader, surely the scholars at Oxford who knew Oliver would give me a chance…" Irene's voice died at his emphatic head shake.

"The university is too open and densely populated, with too few members of the Fire and Earth Guilds in residence to guarantee your security."

"But then, where?"

"Come with us to the Fortress. If you are not safe there, you are not safe anywhere."

The Fortress brooded over the town. Safe, there? How could Irene reconcile Warlock Quicksilver's assurances with Winifred's warning? The Fortress would, no doubt, protect her and her children from the vengeful duchess, but not from that murderous staircase.

Winifred had not said how soon the Fortress would kill her.

Oliver had exacted a promise that Irene would stand up for herself for the children's sake. Mother and the Air Enchanter gave orders. The warlocks gave advice.

They had gone to supervise packing, leaving her to ponder their offer. "It is high time you present yourself to the world as the accomplished witch you are," Quicksilver had said. "The Fire Guild will use you in a fitting capacity, if you let us. You have proven your worth, and we need you, but I will not order you to the Fortress. You have the right to make your own decisions. If you will not come, you are welcome to stay in this house, but we cannot spare anyone to guard you."

Gillian climbed on the window seat beside her. "Mama, where are we going?"

She was adorable. What mother could forgive herself if her children were injured in retaliation for her actions?

Irene pulled her daughter onto her lap and pointed at the Fortress. "The warlocks are moving up there, and taking Alexander. We're going with them."

Quarantine

Two days after the trial, the four magic guilds' council members crowded into the Earth Guild's amber chamber.

"We have imposed a selective quarantine," Mother Celeste said. "We've defined the contagion as bad ideas about governance, affecting the aristocracy. If someone in quarantine shows they've recovered from the disease by taking the oath or acknowledging the terms of their charter, we'll lift the quarantine on them. We can't block all communication with other nobles, but we'll feed them a steady stream of news about Lord So-and-So taking the oath, or Baron Somebody's charter coming to light, or Earl Whatsit's appearance before the Frost Maiden on charges of misuse of taxes, et cetera. That should counter whatever they hear from each other about noblemen hunting witches and wizards.

"Most will give in and take the oath before long, since they don't have the patience to endure a long quarantine. Once they hear about the White Duke and Lord Geoffrey, most will be more scared of the Frost Maiden than of King Stephen."

Lucinda studied the room. The Earth and Fire Councils had intermixed, but except for Lorraine and Charles, who sat next to her, the Water Guild Council kept their distance from the Fire Guild.

The Air Guild Council sat together, closest to the door. Watching the four of them—Enchanter Paul, a middle-aged enchanter, and the two enchantresses—Lucinda experienced twinges of guilty conscience for berating Paul over the Air Guild's foot dragging. The older enchantress should have been in bed, not sitting through a long meeting. Compared to the Earth Guild Council, three times the size and not even including all level-five earth talents, he was justified in complaining they were understaffed.

Beorn said, "Since the Earth Guild's enforcing the quarantine, the rest of us will have the time we need to talk to them, one by one, and explain things. We can target the ones most likely to give in early, and pressure them. The worse offenders we can leave till later. We can also sweeten the deal for the first few taking the oath by promising rewards the later ones won't get. There'll be some bullheaded holdouts, but keeping them in quarantine shouldn't be a problem, since they already rely on clerks and stewards to run things for them. Any questions?"

Warlock Sunbeam asked, "Won't this be a strain on the Earth Guild?"

Mother Celeste said, "We've handled quarantines before, and always have to be prepared to handle another one if necessary. If—as we expect—the quarantine means fewer people are hurt in riots and other violence, we'll be better off. If the majority of the lesser nobles give in within a few months, we could keep the worst offenders—the dukes—in quarantine indefinitely. Years, if necessary."

When the meeting ended, Beorn motioned for Paul to stay. The other three Air Guild members bolted, as if they couldn't wait to escape the stinking hordes of the lesser guilds. Lucinda gave herself a mental slap. Repeating that old slander, even silently, wouldn't help.

Beorn said to Paul, "Enchantress Carla doesn't look so good."

Paul said, "She's been ill ever since the reforging of the Water Office. I'm reluctant to use her if we don't have to."

"Don't blame you. What'll Winnie do? She shouldn't do any of the 'explaining to nobles' bit."

Lucinda stopped to listen. Sven and Lorraine did the same.

Paul said, "I agree. She has no interest in contracts, oaths, charters, or anything of that nature. The lower-ranked wizards and witches who normally work on contracts can make the explanations, paired with your fire wizards for their safety. Winifred is capable of protecting herself, and will assist with the charter search. I've asked her to study the spells on searching for and recreating contracts."

Sven said, "How long will it be before she can use them?"

"A few days, I imagine. Why?"

Conscious of Jean's admonition to not further antagonise the Air Guild, Lucinda frowned at Sven and shook her head.

Sven shot her an apologetic look. "Winifred lacks the grasp of theory needed to easily acquire new, complex spells. She'll need time to understand them, or tutoring by someone familiar with the theory, or both."

Paul said, "I understand she didn't learn as much theory as she should have at the guild school, but she should have no difficulties with the spells on the contracts. They are no more complex than the spells in the Water Office, which she handled well enough."

"She didn't understand those."

Lorraine murmured, "I see he has been taking diplomacy lessons from Warlock Snorri." Lucinda strangled a laugh.

Paul glowered. "I heard no complaints about her work."

"Enchantress Carla covered for her. Winifred executed most of her spells correctly, because someone who did understand them coached her thoroughly, but when Sorceress Lorraine asked for changes in a few spells, Winifred couldn't handle them. Carla did them for her, in addition to her own spells."

"Master Sven is correct," Lorraine said. "She was in over her head."

Father Martin chimed in. "I attribute Carla's poor health to overextending herself on the reforging."

Beorn had a faraway look in his eyes. "I guess that means," he rumbled, "we can't rebuild the Air Office until your granddaughter's old enough to do her share."

Paul's eyes went wide. "Are you saying one of Irene's girls will be an enchantress?"

Beorn started, and focused on Paul. "You got other grandchildren?" he snarled.

Paul went red. "None that I know of. Which one did you mean, Miranda or Gillian?"

"Doesn't matter. If they were mine, I'd treat them both like they're going to be powerful witches."

"They're not yours, and it matters to me. Don't hold out on me, man."

Beorn pushed himself to his feet. "No, burn it. I said too damned much already." A column of fire sent Paul reeling backwards. Beorn disappeared.

Paul sneered, "What a convenient way to end an argument you're losing." He glared at the faces surrounding him. "And as for you lot, I expected better of you, than to criticise a talented witch for having less mental acumen than yourselves." He turned on heel and stormed out.

Sven's shoulders sagged. "I didn't mean it like that."

"Of course you didn't." Lorraine reached up and patted him on the shoulder. "You were trying to warn him of her limitations, since he does not seem aware of them. Keep in mind he needs to view her in a positive light, as we do not have the luxury of not using her, however we may view her abilities."

Father Martin said, "You certainly started off tactfully enough. I didn't think you were trying to belittle her—I'd noticed the attraction between you during the rebuilding."

Sven flushed. "I'm tired of people assuming I'm interested in women who throw themselves at me. Why can't the ones I want do that for a change?" He stomped out and slammed the door.

Father Martin wilted. "Oh, dear, I didn't mean…"

As Jean and Lucinda walked towards the tunnel to the Fortress, she said, "I'm worried…"

"I do not blame you. Our effort to work together has had a less than stellar beginning. Perhaps the wizarding guilds are the ones that should be quarantined."

Winifred Comes to Call

A shadow fell across the papers on the library table. "Well, Irene, you look remarkably comfortable for a woman in peril."

Throughout the main floor of the Fortress's library, men stared. One man at the nearby central catalogues leered. The voluptuous brunette outlined against the window ignored them. Scholars didn't interest her.

Irene said, "Winifred, what are you doing here?"

"I should ask you that. I'm not the one in danger in this place."

Irene couldn't blame her for being irritated, but wasn't about to apologise for ignoring her advice. "How did you get here? Aren't only the Fire Guild allowed in the Fortress without a warlock's permission?"

"Oh, that." Winifred flicked a hand. "Paul dragged me to a meeting at the Warren, and while I was there I asked the Locksmith if I could see you. Said I was concerned about you. She said she was glad somebody in the Air Guild was, and I could visit whenever I liked, as long as you didn't mind. You don't mind, do you?"

"Of course not. I'm glad to see you."

"So tell me what it's like here."

"It's only been two days." Irene had crept into the Fortress in the Rehsavvys' shadow, expecting to be scorned as a wanton airhead, only to be greeted by a pair of enthusiastic scholars primed by Sven's praise, each begging for her attention to his groundbreaking work of exceptional erudition. She accepted both dry, derivative manuscripts, but warned them the Fire Guild would soon require her assistance.

She would never have had the audacity to claim the Fire Guild would be assisting her in the search for the charters, although that was closer to the truth. Lucinda would be directing the efforts of several dozen

Fire Guild talents, and even more mundanes, in finding and securing the targeted noblemen's records. They would leave the ledgers and other similar documents on site for Sven, and box the rest for shipment to the Fortress, where Irene would conduct the search without leaving the safety of its walls. Sven and a trio of mundanes were at work in the Red Duke's family seat. The first crate should arrive before nightfall.

Winifred wouldn't be interested in that. Irene described what little she had seen of the Fortress and Blazes. When she paused, Winifred said, "It's good you're enjoying yourself, even if you are insane to come here. But honestly, Irene, I need your help."

Irene heaved a long sigh. Of course Winifred needed her help. She always did. She wouldn't make a social call just for Irene's benefit.

"Help with what?"

Winifred glanced around the library. "Could we find somewhere more private?"

Private they certainly were not. While Irene waited for the crates to arrive, a table not far from the librarian's desk had beckoned. The Fire Warlock had offered her a room like Sven's, but a private study would encourage her tendencies towards isolation, and do little to convince the scholars to trust her with their work.

They retreated to a quiet corner, hidden among the stacks. Winifred said, "Paul's insisting I help with this fuss over charters. He gave me a copy of the spell to recreate a charter from a scrap, and I expect I can handle that—it's the standard spell for recovering a document mangled by accident, right?"

"Not quite. Spells on the charters prevented normal wear and accidental destruction. The owners inflicted these damages deliberately, so the recovery spell is a bit different."

"Then you'd better review it for me."

An hour later Winifred could snap her fingers and recreate a charmed paper thrown on the fire. Irene felt sucked dry, as she always did after one of these sessions. Memories from their school days crowded in: the spells she had grasped the principles of at once, the hours she'd spent explaining them to Winifred, and the better marks Winifred had received, because she could make the spell work.

Irene swallowed her resentment again. Frankland needed their help.

"You'll do fine," she said, and rose.

"That wasn't all I need help with," Winifred said.

Irene returned to the chair and groaned. "What else?"

"How do I find the obnoxious things in the first place? Paul gave me a spell to find contracts, but he said it would find lots of them, not just the charters. He seemed to think all I need to do afterwards is read through them, but I can't read as fast as you, and I despise Latin. I wouldn't recognise a charter if you waved one under my nose. Irene, I need your spell."

"My talent isn't a matter of training. You know that."

"But aren't there spells for finding charters?"

"To find contracts, yes, but to find a specific charter one needs some distinguishing characteristic—who wrote it, or when, or some specific clause in it. There's no spell to find random charters. In the early days they would never have been lost, and later, the nobles weren't eager to let anyone search for them."

"But couldn't you write a spell? You've written complicated spells before, and you found the charter—you know what's in it."

"In that specific one, yes, but there's no guarantee the same clauses would be in another. Searching for the protective spells might help, and even that would identify many contracts, not just the nobles' charters. There might be ways to distinguish them from other contracts, but anyone writing a spell would need to understand a fair amount about contract magic."

"Well, don't you?"

"Some, but my expertise lies more in sensory manipulation and weather magic."

"You could learn."

Irene mulled it over. The world's greatest collection of books on magic was at her fingertips, and her requests for texts on contract magic would not raise eyebrows, as they would in Airvale. The problem appealed to her, and Warlock Quicksilver would be pleased if she made the search easier for everyone without endangering herself.

"Yes," Irene said, "but the research and spell construction will take time."

"How much time? A couple days? A week?"

"Several weeks, probably."

"Several weeks?" Winifred's voice rose, her nostrils flared, but after a few moments' struggle she managed a smile. Irene almost applauded.

"You'll do a great job." Winifred patted Irene on the shoulder as she left. "Let's not tell anybody what you're doing. It'll be a nice surprise when you're done."

"**M**ind if I join you?" Lucinda hovered over the chair across the dining room table. Irene's mouth was full; she waved for the warlock to sit.

Lucinda said, "When I first came to the Fortress, sometimes I'd feel about to burst. I'm not surprised you had a lot to share." She reddened under Irene's blank stare. "You and Enchantress Winifred talked for most of the afternoon."

"Thank you," Irene said, "for the reminder to guard my privacy."

Lucinda's blush deepened. "I'm sorry. We are nosy and we do gossip, but the Fire Guild's rumours usually have some facts behind them."

Unlike the Air Guild's. The comparison hung unspoken in the short, awkward silence.

Lucinda blurted, "Didn't you say Oliver was planning to marry Winifred? It's unusual that you two stayed friends after he jilted her for you."

"You've gotten the wrong impression. That match was Paul's aspiration, not theirs. Winifred thanked me for relieving the pressure on her. She values her freedom, and says she intends to never marry." Irene kept her suspicions to herself that Winifred's predatory eye made married men attractive sport. Little evidence supported that supposition. Even Irene's mother, an inveterate gossip, had never passed on more than hints at misconduct, while Irene, faithful wife turned lonely widow, had had her name dragged through the mud. It wasn't fair.

Lucinda said, "I bet she never bothered to tell Paul that."

"Of course not. But after Oliver died she did try to persuade the Air Enchanter to pay attention to my unusual talent. It didn't help. She has been kind to me, but it is aggravating that she's his favourite."

"Why? That's what I don't understand. She seems rather dim."

"That's not quite accurate. She's an accomplished practical witch, of average intelligence. If you give her a plan with specific instructions to follow, she'll do a terrific job, no matter how complicated. She's great with weather magic, and manipulating individual people—"

"Oh, wonderful."

"She's an asset in an emergency. She can talk someone out of hysteria almost as well as a healer, or into taking necessary but unpleasant action."

"Fine, I'll accept that as a useful talent."

Airvale's gossips had not reported any dissatisfaction with Winifred's work on the Water Office. Telling the Fire Guild she didn't have the capacity for the sustained abstract reasoning required for the charters, treaties, and contracts in the Air Guild's domain would poison Irene's relationship with her. Besides, the challenge of making the air magic spells in the Water Office concrete enough for her to understand had saved Irene's sanity over the past year.

And she'd given Irene another challenge. Lucinda's company was pleasant, but Irene hurried through her supper, eager to return to the library.

The Oath

"Who else has taken this oath?" Before the drawing room's crackling fire, Earl Eddensford rubbed his hands as if they were cold.

Lucinda resisted the urge to grab and warm them. "No one," she said. "You would be the first."

"We came to you," Jean said, "because you have proven a man of courage and integrity. We trust you will see the honour it is that we approached you first."

"Honour, perhaps," the earl said. "But a great risk, certainly."

"And rewards commensurate with the risk. The first five noblemen taking the oath will gain greater power than all who follow. All four magic guilds have agreed to offer concessions to the first man taking the oath— concessions that will put his house amongst the foremost of Frankland's great families." Jean handed the earl the roll of parchment adorned with the seals of the four officeholders.

The earl's eyes widened as he read. Claire watched without moving, her needle poised in mid-air.

"The first five men," Jean said, "will be remembered by future generations as the greatest noblemen of our time."

A hint of humour glinted in the earl's eyes. "Which is fine for our grandchildren, but little consolation for our families now if we don't survive the next six months."

"True," Jean said, "But not everyone in the nobility will be against you. Queen Marguerite will be pleased, as will Prince Brendan. They will take note, and remember who is willing and who is not."

"And the prince will someday be king. But again, that is in the future, and in the here and now, King Stephen is angry over her interference, and suspicious of my ties to you. If I swear this oath, he will act as if I am his sworn enemy."

"I will not deny that, but as you say, he already distrusts you, and as you see," Jean waved at the parchment, "he will have little hold over you."

The earl reread the parchment. "Yes. This is astounding. Overwhelming. I need some time to digest this."

Claire set down her embroidery and took her husband's hand. "Richard, will it help more if I leave you alone or if I stay?"

"Stay, please. I value your opinion."

Claire escorted Jean and Lucinda to the door. Lucinda whispered, "Don't try very hard to persuade him."

Claire raised limpid blue eyes. "Why not? This matters to you—a lot, I think."

"Very much, but it has to be his decision. The magic won't be as effective if he's pushed."

She pursed her lips. "All right, but can I at least say I wish he would? He'll do it anyway, without me telling him to. He wants what you've offered. That's obvious."

Jean and Lucinda strolled along the gallery over the mansion's great hall, passing antique statuary and paintings by old masters—a collector's dream—without a glance.

Lucinda said, "You're more worried about the queen than you are about him, aren't you?"

"Yes. I am convinced he is our best choice, and the power he will gain will protect him and his wife and son, but the dangers to Queen Marguerite are mounting, and this will not help."

"Is it worth it then? As long as the king listens to her…"

"Which he does less and less. Lord St John and his cohort have driven a wedge between them. Her usefulness to us is nigh over, but we cannot abandon her to the king's wrath. I do not want her blood on my hands."

Lucinda had wearied of the art on display before the earl emerged from the drawing room and approached them, parchment in hand.

"I have one question, Your Wisdom, and I hope you will not take offence." The earl eyed Jean for a moment before continuing. "It is no secret the king despises you. Are you forcing change on him strictly for love of Frankland, or is personal spite involved as well?"

Jean hesitated.

Never, ever, lie to a warlock, Lucinda whispered. *Including oneself.*

He threw her a sharp glance before turning a smouldering eye on the earl. "King Stephen, like his father and grandfather, is a misguided fool. As Fire Warlock, I considered him an unavoidable nuisance, no worse and no better than his predecessors. An unteachable man, made dangerous by the power he holds without understanding, but one not impossible to outwit and outmanoeuvre. But now…"

Jean walked to a window and gazed out over Gastòn rooftops. "But now, Frankland has changed, and he has not. If the king had been willing to work with the officeholders for Frankland's greater good, instead of opposing us at every step, we would not be in our current straits. We could have delayed rebuilding the Water Office for another year, perhaps two, until Lucinda could wield the lightning on her own."

He returned to Lucinda's side. She held out her hand and he clasped it with his. "These last four months"—he continued—"since we returned from the Orient, have been the most difficult of my life. Stephen's actions have put at risk everyone and everything I hold most dear. My wife and my best student both nearly died. Other men and women have died, and more will die before Frankland is at peace again, and I hold him responsible.

"So, yes," he said, turning to face the earl. "Despise me if you will, but I cannot deny my animosity towards this man Stephen. Nothing would give me greater pleasure than to force him to abdicate, and watch his son swear the oath he refuses. That, now, is my goal. Will you help or will you refuse, now that I have admitted to such human frailty?"

The earl answered with a weak smile. "I will help, Your Wisdom, and I'll feel more secure knowing there's more at stake for you than the good of Frankland, however much that means to you. If you're after revenge, you're less likely to abandon me when things go sour."

The dignitaries—Gastòn's city council, influential merchants and craftsmen, and even a few lesser nobles—jockeyed for position in the rows of chairs. Standing, the earl's staff and tenants, from butler down to swineherd, filled the remaining space in the ballroom. Jean and Lucinda sat in the last row. Between them were Alexander, and a woman so heavily camouflaged by the magics of four guilds that even knowing who she was, Lucinda could not recognise Queen Marguerite.

Lucinda said, "Has your husband indicated any suspicions you are using the earl to contact us?"

"No," she said, "not to me. But if he no longer trusts me, he wouldn't, would he?"

The captain of the guard called for silence. The earl and Claire, followed by the four officeholders, filed in. The crowd gawked. The Fire Warlock made a brief speech, thanking the earl. The Earth Mother described his new privileges and responsibilities. The Air Enchanter administered the oath. The earl repeated the oath, with diffidence at first, but ending in a ringing, "for all my people!"

The crowd cheered, stamped, clapped, whistled, tossed hats in the air. Alexander twisted around and goggled at the jubilant commoners.

Lucinda's eyes widened. *I bet he's never seen any commoners so enthusiastic about a nobleman before.*

Jean smiled. *Neither have I.*

The earl raised a hand for silence. Lucinda stared. This was a man transformed. The melancholy, the guardedness, the slightly hangdog aspect of a man waiting for news of the next disaster, were gone. The man addressing the room, thanking his people for their support, was a man in control of his fortunes, with a straight back, noble countenance, and commanding air. A man an army would follow into the gates of Hell.

The prince gaped at his cousin. Over his head, Jean winked at Lucinda.

"Good gracious," the queen breathed, "if my husband looked like that…"

Afterwards, while Alexander suffered an emotional farewell from his mother, the earl said to Jean, "You haven't asked me to talk to others you approach about taking the oath, but if I can help, I am happy to do so."

Jean gave him a warm smile. "Thank you. Your assistance will be invaluable."

The earl bowed. "My time is at your disposal, Your Wisdom."

Claire and Lucinda escorted the queen to her tunnel.

"If only Stephen would understand," she sighed.

"It isn't safe for you to tell him," Lucinda said.

"No, I will not give away my presence here. He would hear that I disobeyed, and not listen to the rest. He will be very, very angry with Richard, and he will blame me."

"His advisors will be furious, too. Your Majesty, do you have someone tasting your food?"

She paled, and reached for the doorframe with a trembling hand. "Yes, my earth witch. I thought—hoped—I was being a Nervous Nellie, but if you... I trust her. There are few others I can trust."

"Is there anything I can do to help?"

"I don't see how you could. Pressure from the Fire Guild would make my situation worse. Only, I beg you, continue what you are already doing. Take good care of my son."

She walked into the tunnel and disappeared.

Duncan on the Causeway

"**D**o you want the good news first, or the bad news?" the Fire Warlock asked.

Duncan kept swinging while he thought that over. "Good news, I guess."

"The king's not going to appoint a new overlord for Abertee."

Duncan dropped his hammer. "You're putting me on."

The Fire Warlock grinned and leaned against the smithy wall. "Quicksilver and I had a fight with the king. He wanted the Red Duke, and I nixed him as too dangerous. Quicksilver suggested a southern baron who would never come anywhere near Abertee, and the king nixed him for being too lazy to show you rabble what a real overlord was like. We argued back and forth for weeks until finally King Stephen lost his temper and said, 'Fine. Let them rot without an overlord. When Abertee falls apart and they come to me begging for a master, then you'll have to take who I appoint.' So you've got a chance to show you don't need a nobleman in charge, and that's what we wanted in the first place."

"What you wanted, or what the old Fire Warlock wanted?"

He shrugged. "It was his idea, but I like it. Of course, we'd never have gotten there if the king had known that's what he wanted."

Cousin Jock and the lads were listening, too. Jock said, "Wily old fox, isn't he?"

Duncan struggled to make sense of it. Everybody in Frankland had an overlord. What would it mean to not have one? Nobody'd be threatening hardworking people for the fun of it. Nobody'd be badgering people to collect rent and taxes.

"Hold on," he said. "If nobody's collecting the taxes…"

"Oh, they'll still be collected. But you folk living here will decide what to use them for. You can fix roads and feed orphans instead of throwing parties and decorating the duke's manor with gold leaf, if you want. That sounds like a better use to me."

Duncan beamed. "When you started talking, I wasn't sure we'd have the same idea about what was good news. But you're right—that's damned good news. Now tell me the bad news."

"The king's not going to appoint a new overlord for Abertee."

"How's that?" Jock said. "You said that was the good news."

"Well, see, the duke didn't do much for you, but he did hire guards to patrol the roads, and kept the docks on the river repaired. Some things got done. Somebody has to make sure they keep getting done."

If the Frost Maiden hadn't warned Duncan not to hit anybody, he would've swung at the Fire Warlock. "It's bad news, all right. This son of a bitch is saddling me with all that rubbish."

The son of a bitch grinned. "You've been saying anybody with a little sense could do a better job than the duke."

Jock and the lads laughed. The oldest journeyman said, "You'll do a fine job, Master Duncan."

"Back up a minute," Duncan said. "No overlord? Those shields for the nobles are to make sure there's always somebody ready to take over when some duke or baron or whatnot died. How's the Fire Office letting you get away with this?"

"It's simple enough. We've had lines die out before. The Office lets me—the Fire Warlock, that is—appoint somebody as interim lord until the king names a permanent one. Since the king's decided he won't decide, you're it. The nobles you might've gotten stuck with haven't been honouring their charters, so the Fire Office isn't pushing me to give it to any of them. More important, between that oath you swore the other night and being a swordsmith, as far as the Fire Office is concerned you're as good as a noble anyway."

Duncan yelped. "You can't demote me to duke. I'm an honest man."

Jock laughed and pounded him on the back. Duncan cursed. The Fire Warlock had warned him they were cooking up an oath for his agents to swear, so when Master Jean had dropped in with his little poem, Duncan hadn't been surprised. It seemed simple enough, and sensible, like what somebody in charge of other people ought to say. Hazel had liked it, and Duncan had trusted the old fox.

He should've known better.

The Fire Warlock thumped him on the shoulder. "It's not as bad as you think. Come on, I've got a couple things to show you. Grab your coat."

He had one arm in when fire flowed around them, then the fire died. He and the Fire Warlock were standing beside the White Duke's manor house.

"Frost you," Duncan said. "Warn me next time. My dinner hadn't settled good."

"Forget that, and look at this place. It's huge. And, as far as I can tell, you've got to use some of the taxes and rents to keep it in good shape."

"And we ought to. It's the grandest house in this end of Frankland."

The Fire Warlock rolled his eyes. "Right. You going to be proud of it, standing empty? Or are you going to do something with it?"

"I hadn't..." Duncan leaned back and took a good look. After a moment, he paced along the walk, counting windows. "A lot of people could live here. We've been talking about a home for widows and orphans."

"That's the spirit. And you've already got staff there to run it. Remember, the duke didn't spend much time running things. He had staff do that for him. They can keep on doing what they've been doing, only working for you now, instead of him."

Duncan considered that. "How many of them can I trust?"

"About half the guards and most of the rest, except for a few at the top. The clerk that helped with the search proved he was on your side, and I hear he'd be happy to come back. The steward's got to go, but you can hire another one to run things, and spend your time doing the stuff I really wanted an agent for: keeping an ear to the ground and making sure everybody's treated fairly."

"Steward, eh?" Duncan scratched his chin. Being responsible for everything in Abertee stunk, but putting the tax money to good use might make up for it. "What else did you want to show me?"

The Fire Warlock grabbed his arm. "Get ready, we're going through the fire again." When the fire died they were on the causeway between Quays and the coast road. Duncan didn't bolt; the Fire Warlock stood between him and dry land. Facing the Fire Warlock, Duncan didn't have to look at the Crystal Palace. He peeked over his shoulder. He'd walked in and out again alive, but it still gave him gooseflesh. "Tell me why we're here."

"Imagine you're leading an army to attack the Water Guild. How defensible is this place?"

"What the hell? You're joking."

He wasn't joking. If he hadn't been grinning a few minutes earlier, Duncan would've sworn he'd never cracked a smile or gotten a good night's sleep. Duncan pulled his collar up around his ears against the cold wind, and tucked his hands in his armpits. All the stories about Fire Warlocks ended with them burning out. He'd hate to lose this one. God help them if they got that sour lemon, Flint, next.

The Fire Warlock said, "Answer the question. How would you attack it?"

"I couldn't. Your gates funnel armies towards the Fortress."

"That's invading armies and rebellions. Not even Warlock Quicksilver knows if the magic will work on an army led by our own nobles. Things have never gotten this bad before."

"*Frostbitten hellfire!* Hazel told me you were keeping the nobles tied down so they couldn't talk to each other—good idea, that—but I thought you were worried about little packs of hotheads burning down Water Guild halls here and there. I never thought about something that... that..."

"That pathetically asinine? That murderous? That contemptuous of our own people? Yeah, I'd rather not consider it either, but I have to. Answer the question. How would you attack it?"

"The Fire Office will make you strike me dead for answering that."

"Not when I'm the one asking."

Despite the cold wind, Duncan wiped sweat from his forehead. "Fine. Let me think. That palace is pretty new—four hundred years old, maybe. They weren't planning for defence when they built it—look at all that glass—but they built it in a good place. There was a castle there earlier..."

"There've been at least three, maybe four, forts on that same spot. Yeah, it's a good strong spot."

"There's water all around, except for this one spit of land, and it's under at high tide. The Water Guild never go overland—they all go by boat. But it'd be nuts to attack it from the water—those witches and wizards would drown everybody coming that way."

"Right. Go on."

"The army would have to cross the spit, and if they're trying to murder the Water Guild, the first thing they'd do would be fire all boats within reach so nobody could escape. They'd cross at low tide, on a night with a full moon. They'd either come up from the south on the coast road, or go through Crossroads and along the king's highway to where it meets the Tee. There isn't any other way. The coast in the other direction is too rough… *Frostbite!*"

"Yeah. You ought to see now why we didn't want Abertee in the noble's hands."

"Aye. And why you want somebody you trust keeping an eye on the manor. But what the hell do we do if they do start making trouble?"

"You're in charge of keeping the peace here now. You can arrest anybody coming through armed to the teeth and spoiling for a fight."

"If they come in ones and twos, sure, but you said an army. I can't arrest an army of mounted swordsmen when all I've got is a few guards and farmers with pitchforks and smiths with hammers."

"I'm not expecting you to. Don't play *Soldiers and Wizards*—and if anybody does think that'd be fun, you've got my permission to knock some sense into his head. But keep an eye open, and let me know about anything funny going on. Spread the word to the folk along the highway and along the coast to keep an eye on the Water Guild, too."

"Eh? Just because those aristos have decided the Frost Maiden's their enemy doesn't mean the common folk think she's our friend."

The Fire Warlock leaned closer and growled, "She did all right by you with Lord Geoffrey and the duchess. What more do you want?"

"Hey, whoa. Don't yell at me. I'm happy. But it'll take longer to convince folk who aren't talking to witches and wizards day in and day out that things really are changing."

"Then tell 'em to keep an eye open for me, and if they think it's because we're still enemies and I'm spying on her, I won't mind."

"Aye, that'll work. Now, if you're done showing me stuff, tell me how to find that clerk."

A Spell for Winifred

"Irene, didn't your mother warn you that someday your face would freeze and you'd wear a scowl for the rest of your life?"

"Hi, Winifred." After a brief smile, Irene resumed frowning at the papers, pens, and open books littering her table in the library. "You shouldn't have come for a few days yet. It's not finished."

"You've already put me off twice. It's December. I need it."

December? Weeks had slipped by without her notice. Irene bounced out of bed before first light and was soon turning pages in the vaulted chamber set aside for the charter team's use. Clerks and porters flowed through, unpacking and repacking crates, and bringing her stacks of documents as fast as she could fly through them. Several scholars worked alongside, although reading at a much slower pace.

Late afternoons, after her magic gave out, she spent in the library, researching contract magic. In the evenings, after reading to the girls and Alexander, she returned to the lamplit library, leaving only when Master Thomas ordered her out, or her eyes would no longer stay open.

With the girls under a mundane tutor's competent supervision in the morning, and in the afternoon, under Katie or Mrs Cole's watchful eyes whenever Gillian chivvied Miranda into leaving the music room, worries about them didn't trouble her. Neither did worries over money. The amount the Fire Guild offered for her services left her gasping. She accepted without demur, and ordered a gown in pale yellow, her first silk dress in a decade.

But as gratifying as the work and money were, a significant and unexpected component of her happiness was the sense of inclusion in a team focused on bringing fairness back to Frankland. The fire witches and wizards involved in the charter search teetered on the edge of exhaustion. Tempers were lost and curses thrown on a regular basis, but there was also a sense of mutual trust and respect, foreign to the Air Guild's unbridled individualism, that was strong enough to encompass even an air witch.

The only thing lacking was an occasional private conversation with Sven. They talked often, touching on many subjects, but nothing personal, and never alone, as if constant chaperonage could undo the damage already done to their reputations.

Lucinda had warned her he was an anomaly among fire wizards. "He values intelligence, but he's cautious," she had said. "Terrified of making promises he can't keep."

As well he should be. Irene's own history said so. Why should she mind?

"That spell," Winifred prompted. "I need it."

Irene corked her ink bottle and handed Winifred the smudged, scribbled-over draft. "It will help, but it will still find more documents than it should."

"But less than the spell I've been using?"

"Yes, but it could be better. Warlock Quicksilver would help. It seems silly not to ask his advice."

Winifred lowered the paper, frowning. "Did you tell him about it?"

"No. He's been so busy, he's had no time for me."

She shrugged. "Perfect it later. Teach me how to use it now."

Three hours later, she had wrung Irene dry and was still baffled.

Irene said, "Leave it for tomorrow. We've had enough for one day."

"I suppose you're right. My head hurts." Winifred made no move to rise. "You've been here in the Fortress for almost two months. Do you like it?"

"I love it, except for those diabolical stairs. I'm happier here than I've been since Oliver died."

"Is it true that fire wizards never have cold hands?"

"Pardon? Don't you know?"

Winifred glared. "If I did, why would I ask?"

"How would I know?"

"Aren't you sharing your bed with that handsome bore, Sven? Everybody says you are, so why not? What's taking you so long?"

"None of your business," Irene said, and walked away.

The service stairwell was narrow and airless. Winifred would never enter it. Irene sat on a landing, hugging her knees and listening to the silence.

Soon after they had moved in, a scholar, after leering at her for several minutes from the catalogues, began whistling the tune to the slanderous song about her and Sven. The librarian slammed a book on his desk, shoved his chair backwards with a screech, and stalked towards them. She held her breath. The librarian grabbed the whistler's ear and marched him from the library. On his return, he nodded to her.

"Sorry, ma'am. If anyone else is rude to you, let me know."

The whistler never reappeared.

The Fortress was a small island of civility in a sea of spiteful gossip. The respect shown Irene here threatened to make her forget the rest of Frankland considered her an object of derision or hatred.

Worries about the future did not ruin her present pleasures, but sometimes in unguarded moments, they pushed her towards panic. Marie Richardson could not touch Irene in the Fortress, but someday Miranda and Gillian would leave and become targets for the former White Duchess's revenge. Compared to that threat, damage to Irene's reputation was of small moment. She shouldn't have let Winifred's questions upset her. They certainly shouldn't have surprised her, coming from Winifred.

During their school days, all Winifred had ever talked about was men. After Oliver began courting Irene, she had probed for more details than Irene had been comfortable sharing. In return, she had told Irene too much about her schoolgirl infatuation over Warlock Arturos. Those confidences had stopped, to Irene's relief, after he married an earth witch, but vague hints and guesswork had led Irene to believe the infatuation had grown into adult obsession rather than withering.

Irene had assumed Winifred had gotten what she wanted. She always did.

She didn't know if fire wizards had warm hands? Irene's respect and affection for Arturos rose several notches. She owed him an apology, but didn't dare admit her suspicions. The rumours Winifred had made a serious play for Sven's affections seemed to be baseless also.

That made no difference. Sven kept his distance; nor did Irene need any further entanglement with a fire wizard. Her mother would…

Her mother could go bury herself.

"Mama," Miranda pleaded at bedtime, "will you please stop singing?"

After two more sessions, Winifred finally understood the spell. An earl's charter, one Irene had found, served as a test. Winifred found it hidden in the storeroom housing boxes awaiting shipment back to their owners. She also found three guild charters referring to it. They deemed that good enough.

"The search will progress quickly with several people using the spell." Irene reached for the paper. "I'll make a copy—"

Winifred held it out of reach. "I'm not sure that's a good idea. You knew where the charter was, so this wasn't a fair test."

"Why not? You didn't know."

"You told me there was one in the room somewhere."

"That's true, but—"

"It wasn't a fair test. I should try it on my own."

"All right, but I should still make a copy."

Winifred patted Irene's shoulder. "You've done a great job, Irene, but forget it—I'll take care of it."

Master Sven, Hero

Two workmen were loading the last of the sorted boxes onto a cart. The rows of incoming crates stood chest high. A box of papers labelled *Green Duke* waited on Irene's desk.

She had been almost done with him three days ago. Hadn't she?

She yanked papers from the box. The text was black; her magic was gone for the day. Her head pounded. What had happened to her?

Her eyes wouldn't focus; the Latin was meaningless squiggles. She put her head down in her hands and moaned.

Matt, the Fire Eater overseeing the movement of crates, came running. "Mrs van Gelder, are you all right?"

"No, no...I'm just...I don't know...tired."

"I'm not surprised, ma'am. You have the patience of a saint. That enchantress gave me a headache, and I got off easy, compared to you."

Enchantress. Did he mean Winifred?

"Although I have to admit," he said, "it's easier now to understand why the Air Guild hates you. You show her up just saying 'abracadabra', and if she's the next best witch they have..."

She blinked at him, confounded. "Pardon?"

"Sorry, ma'am, you look beat." He steered her towards the door. "You'd better quit for the day, and get a good night's sleep."

"But I'm so far behind..."

"Don't worry about that. Mrs Rehsavvy said not to disturb you. The time you spent teaching Enchantress Winifred to find a charter would pay off later."

"Oh. Thank you, Matt." Irene wandered away, head full of fog, and lurched out onto the ramparts with only a light shawl over her dress, in hopes the frigid air would cut through her confusion.

Winifred had asked for help and she didn't remember? Had her anger with the Air Guild become so fierce she tried to block their existence from her memory?

Today's headache was the first she had experienced since abandoning her job at the guild school. The voices on the wind had ceased to torment her, too. The whispers about promises were clearly a schoolboy prank, although she still could not fathom how they had known what to say. But the other, stronger voice…

The wind howled but carried no voices. If Oliver's rich baritone never came again, would she be sad, or relieved? As much as she had loved him, part of her recognised him as an arrogant, domineering rogue. They had eloped because he had decided they would. She had raised no objection, but he hadn't asked what she wanted. He should have gone to the Company of Mages as soon as he understood she was a javelin, but he had wanted the reflected glory of that book of spells.

Bury the Air Guild, the whole lot of them.

After ten minutes of roaring silence, she went inside to get warm.

Three books on contract magic stared at Irene from the library table. Tucked underneath were several pages of notes, in her handwriting, on charters and identification spells.

Had she been sleepwalking? Or were the kinder rumours true, and she was going mad?

"I thought I'd find you here." Sven's voice made her start. He pulled out the opposite chair and leaned on it, grinning. His eyes sparkled; he fidgeted like a schoolboy. "Would you mind my company?"

"Of course not."

"You look preoccupied."

"Confused, rather. Maybe you can help."

"Glad to if I can," he said. "And if you don't mind listening to me first."

"You do look about to burst. Go ahead."

"I found the Black Duke's charter."

"Well done!"

"And even better, I've signed a contract with a London publishing house for a book of poetry."

She shoved the books aside. "That's wonderful news. I'm so glad for you."

"Thank you for helping me find the nerve to approach them. I haven't thanked you properly, either, for writing that ballad, although you made me sound more heroic than I am."

"How did you know who wrote that?"

His grin broadened.

"Oh," she said. "You didn't."

"You proved my guess correct. And another thing: the Water Guild is sponsoring a party at the Warren on Yule Eve for everyone involved in reforging the Water Office. I'd like you to come with me."

"A party? But with everyone so busy with the quarantine…"

"Things have been going well, especially after the news spread that Earl Eddensford had taken the oath, and even the worst troublemakers would have to think twice about disrupting Yule. Sorceress Lorraine said after all we've been through, we need to relax and celebrate."

"But a party with Frankland's highest ranking witches and wizards? After all the rumours, think what taking me will do to your reputation."

"Those rumours are rot. No one whose opinion matters to me believes them. But if you won't let me escort you, go on your own."

"Don't be silly. The Water Guild won't invite me."

"They will after I tell Sorceress Lorraine what we owe you for tutoring Winifred."

"Sven! How did you…?"

"That was glaringly obvious even before you spent the last three days coaching her on charters. You told me to write about what happened in Abertee—and I have been when I can find the time—but I also have in mind writing the truth about you."

The truth. Something nagged at her. Winifred. Charters. These books.

She pushed the stack of books towards him. "You said you'd help with my problem…"

He shoved them away. "Leave that for a moment. Irene, what's wrong? You've been running away from me ever since coming here."

"Pardon? We hardly ever have time to talk—"

"When we do, you make sure we're chaperoned. Your children, Fire Eaters… And you always switch topics whenever I bring up anything personal."

"You must be mistaken."

He frowned. "You're shivering."

"It's December. Picking a table close to the windows wasn't clever."

He reached across the table and grasped her hands, warming them. Blue eyes bored into her. "You're confusing me," he said. "You act warm towards me one day and cool the next. I sense strong emotions at work, but I don't understand them."

Her sense of propriety fought with the pleasure of having warm hands. Propriety won, but he wouldn't let her pull them away. She said, "Air witches don't have strong emotions."

"Rot. I thought you had warmed towards me while we were working together at the White Duke's, though I had no reason to expect that. I mean, you'd been married to a hero, and I...wasn't one."

She wrenched her hands away and stood, knocking over her chair. "And then you proved you're one, too," she shouted. "Frost you men wanting to be dead heroes."

He lurched backwards as if she'd slapped him. Scholars' heads turned.

"I hate you!" With that burst of illogic, she fled. And, naturally, ran the wrong way. He was between her and the service stairs. An empty alcove by the outer door provided shelter. In a few days, it might be safe to emerge. Her breathing was still shallow and rapid when he followed her in and drew the curtain.

"I was right about the strong emotions," he said. "Go ahead and yell— they won't hear." When she didn't respond, he said, "You don't really hate me, do you?"

She shook her head. He gripped her shoulders and pulled her around to face him. "Talk to me when you're angry. I can't do anything if I don't know what's wrong."

"You can't do anything about it anyway. If the Fire Guild demands heroics again, you'll respond. You heroes are all alike." She knocked his hands away and turned her back. "I'd rather marry a nobody than be widowed again."

"And I'd rather not take second place—again—behind Ollie, but you can't do anything about that, either."

"Sven, you don't have to pay court to me. You could find dozens of women who'd be thrilled to attend the Yule party with you."

"I don't want them." He put his hands on her shoulders again, and turned her back around. She didn't resist. He said, "We've been dancing around each other for weeks now, afraid to say what we feel." He slipped a hand under her chin and tilted her face towards his. "But I'll say it. I want your company."

He bent down. She was suddenly breathless.

The outer door slammed. A child's voice wailed, "Mama." Instantly they were a yard apart. Sven swept the curtain aside. Gillian flung herself into Irene's skirts. "Mama, Miranda's done something naughty."

Irene didn't dare look at Sven. "What did Miranda do, dear?"

It took a few moments to calm Gillian enough to tease a comprehensible story from her. Sven grasped it first.

"Alexander ran into a tunnel, and Miranda followed him?" Gillian nodded.

"Good God." His eyes unfocused.

Irene clawed at the curtains. Sven had told her about the traps in the tunnels. Her daughter might already be caught in one.

Sven focused again abruptly. "You'll have to tell Lucinda—she's in her sitting room. I'm going to the Warren for help." He bolted for the stairs.

The Rehsavvy's apartment, two tiers down, lay directly underneath. The inner stairs were slow and far away. The moving staircase would be much faster. For a moment, terror for Miranda warred with terror for Irene's own life.

She followed Sven toward the outer stairs. With one foot on, Gillian slammed into her and she pitched forward, grabbing the handrails with both hands. The stairs responded, shifting from a leisurely glide to a plummet. The landing zoomed towards them. Irene bit down a scream. The descent ended with a hard jolt, knocking her onto her hands and knees.

Gillian tugged at her arm. "Come on, Mama. Do that again."

They ran for the next flight. Irene lunged for the rail, and closed her eyes. They plummeted again. They left the stairs and crashed through Lucinda's sitting room door, shouting. Warlock Snorri vanished in the fireplace. Lucinda fanned the flames.

The fire dimmed. They heard shuffling, and Miranda whimpering, "I'm scared, I'm scared."

Alexander said, "Stop whining. The tunnels are safe."

"They're not! They hate us. Can't you feel it?"

"No. We're lost, that's all." A quaver in his voice belied the confident statement. "When we find a door we'll open it and get out."

Lucinda sucked in her breath. "There are doors all over those tunnels."

Miranda's whimper changed to a wail. "We've been in here for ages already and haven't found any. They're hiding them. They want to bury air witches."

Alexander said, "Don't be silly. The warlocks will come for us. Look! There's light, that way."

The shuffling noises increased in velocity. Light outlined a door at the end of a sloping side tunnel. The dim forms of the two children started down the incline. Feet skidded on gravel. One fell, knocking the other down. They slid the rest of the way together and thudded into the door.

"Are you all right?" Alexander asked.

"I want my mama." Miranda beat on the door with her fists. "Open up!"

Alexander skidded twice on loose gravel before grabbing the latch and pulling himself up. He struggled, but the latch wouldn't budge.

"What's the matter?" she said. "Is it locked?"

"I don't know. It's hard to tell in the dark."

"Let me try."

"What makes you think you can open it if I can't?"

"I'm a witch."

The prince sniffed, but gave her a hand up.

Miranda got a solid, two-handed grip on the bar of the latch, and shoved. The door swung open, and pulled her into empty air.

The Prince of Air
and Darkness

The tunnel door swung in the wind, dangling Irene's screaming daughter over a thousand-foot drop. Irene savaged her knuckles. Lucinda screamed.

Alexander clung to the doorframe. He stretched out an arm, but couldn't reach Miranda. He braced himself against the doorframe's lip and, with one hand firmly on the catch, eased out over the void. He reached for her, almost had her, and the door swung out of reach. She stopped screaming, and hung on with her eyes closed, whimpering.

Warlock Quicksilver leaned over Irene. "Oh, dear God."

Lucinda said, "Rescue them!"

"I cannot jump into empty space, or into a tunnel."

"But we floated down from the top of Storm King."

"Air magic—Paul…" Fire licked Irene's shoulder.

Alexander inched further out, waiting as the door swung closer. It reached its nearest point. He lunged for the latch, caught it, and hung motionless between the door and the frame, then grimacing, pulled the door closed, inch by hard-won inch. When Miranda's legs touched the lip, he said, "Let go. You'll sit on the floor."

She fell backwards onto the tunnel floor, grabbing at a toehold under the lip. She pulled her feet in and scrabbled up the slope, sending gravel cascading out the gap. Alexander seemed frozen. The tension in his face increased; the door opened wider. Irene grabbed Lucinda's arm and shook it as he leaned further out.

A hand reached out of the tunnel and caught his shoulder. "Earth grips you," a woman said. "You will not fall."

A healer on the Earth Mother's staff treated Irene's bloody hand and lip, and the burn on her arm. The bite marks were self-inflicted, but when or why her sleeve had caught fire was a mystery to her. There were other mysteries: Why had the children been in the tunnel? Why was the swordsmith, Master Duncan, among those gathered in the Earth Mother's drawing room? Irene ignored those questions and hugged her crying daughter tighter.

The chatter died as the earth witch who had rescued the two children refused the praise and gratitude the Air Enchanter and others heaped on her. "I'm sorry, Your Wisdom, but it's my fault. I meant to bespell the latch to let only someone in the Earth Guild open it, but I must have left out the part saying which guild. I'm so sorry."

Sven said, "It's not your fault, Granny Hazel. I read your spell when I investigated the trap. That is what you said."

"But then, why did it open?"

"The magic on the trap must be strong enough to override yours, although I don't understand why it behaved as it did."

Quicksilver laid a hand on the witch's shoulder. Her vivid freckles faded as colour returned to her ashen cheeks. He said, "We will pursue that question another day. For now, be assured you are not responsible for the near calamity. Indeed, we owe a considerable debt to you and Master Duncan for your effort to defang that trap."

Master Duncan said, "Aye. If you hadn't put that spell on the latch, the door would've flown open like it did when I hit it. They wouldn't have gotten stuck, like I did. They'd've gone sailing out into the blue, and we'd've had a right royal mess to clean up."

Irene's 'Dear God' was lost amid a chorus of exclamations. Warlock Arturos buried his face in his hands and groaned.

The royal person, wedged into a sofa between Arturos and Lucinda, regarded the smith with wide eyes. "It happened to you, too?"

The smith related his encounter with the traps, and his conjecture they had been laid to protect the Warren. "And that's why the earth guild won't let anybody else use the tunnels." He added with a growl, "So just what were you two doing in there, anyway?"

The two children exchanged guilty glances.

Quicksilver said, "A good question. And, no, you need not negotiate how much to tell." He waved towards the fireplace. "We shall have it all. Watch."

Alexander rode the moving staircase to the top, scowling. His scowl deepened as he stood on the balcony watching the two girls rise towards him.

He greeted them with a curt, "Why are you following me?"

Miranda said, "We knew you were upset about something, and Miss Underwood said nobody comes up this far unless they're in trouble with the Warlock. She let us follow you because I said you shouldn't have to see him by yourself."

"I'm not in trouble. I've been here by myself before. I like it here. It's quiet. I can think without anybody bothering me."

Gillian said, "Doesn't the Warlock yell at you for coming up here?"

The boy shrugged. "He doesn't seem to mind. He told me not to fall down the stairs, that's all."

Miranda said, "But there is something wrong. We can tell. Can we help?"

"I doubt it. I'm just trying to decide what to do."

Gillian said, "Sometimes, when I don't know what to do, Miranda tells me a story. Then I know what to do. You ought to let her tell you a story."

The boy sat on the marble floor, pulling his knees up to his chin. "It won't do any good, but go ahead."

The girls sat beside him. Miranda said, "Once upon a time, there was a clever prince. The prince worried about the kingdom, and about his father, so he walked the challenge path to see the Fire Warlock."

Alexander turned his head to stare at her. "You're not supposed to know I'm the prince. Did your mother tell you?"

Miranda's brow wrinkled. "You're not the prince. His name is Brendan."

Gillian said, "Go on, Miranda."

"No one knows what the three challenges are, but since the prince passed them all, he was brave as well as clever."

"That's not so," Alexander said. "Not brave nor clever."

Gillian said, "The prince was brave. Miranda said so."

"Thanks for trying to make me feel better, but it's not working."

"Stop interrupting. I want to hear the story."

Miranda said, "The Fire Warlock set him to work and promised to teach him what he needed to know. And so he did. The prince learned many things, but the most important thing he learned was that there was a blight on the kingdom because the kings had stopped taking the oath to

231

be fair to all the people. And he learned a secret: an older version of the oath made the kings more powerful.

"He wrote his father a letter because he thought this secret would please him, but his father hated the Fire Warlock, and didn't believe the letter, and was angry with his son for believing the Fire Guild. So the prince gathered his courage and went to see his father, to convince the king the secret was true. I…I don't know what comes after that."

Alexander prompted, "The king believed the prince, and took the oath, and they all lived happily ever after."

Miranda paled. "No! That's not how the story goes."

He grabbed her shoulder and shook her. "Tell me what happens."

"I don't know."

He scrambled to his feet and shouted, "You're lying! You know how it ends and you're not telling me because I won't like it."

She backed away from him. "I don't know. I haven't heard the story yet either. I just know it's bad."

"I shouldn't have let you tell me a story. I hate you!" She blocked the stairs; he ran away from her, towards the tunnels.

Miranda ran after him, shouting, "Alex, wait! You can't go there!"

They disappeared down the corridor, leaving Gillian, thumb in mouth, staring after them with wide eyes.

Master Duncan cleared his throat. "I…uh, I knew I'd seen the lad, but I didn't remember where. I was joking…"

Warlock Quicksilver said, "Do not imagine you can divulge his identity to anyone outside this room."

The smith gave Quicksilver a scowl that would have made most men quake. Quicksilver ignored him, and regarded Miranda with concern. The Air Enchanter sported a less benign expression. Irene stroked Miranda's hair, unsure whether she had hatched a swan's egg or a cuckoo's.

"Mistress Irene," Quicksilver said, "were you aware of your daughter's talent for 'story-telling'?"

"Her stories seemed an unusually polite manifestation of a big sister's normal desire to order her younger sister around, Your Wisdom. Nothing led me to suspect magic was involved."

"Miranda, you are very young to have been cursed—I cannot say blessed—with such a strong and dangerous talent. Have you learned anything from today's adventure?"

"Yes, sir," she whispered. "I shouldn't tell a magic story if I don't know the end. But, sir, I don't know how any of them end when I start them."

"Then you must not start any such story until you have gained enough control over your talent to foresee how it will end, and even then, you must keep the stories to yourself far more often than you tell them to the people involved. It is not a blessing to know one's future, even for minor things, and what you consider a good ending will not always please your listener. Yours is a talent requiring both good sense and emotional maturity to use well. If it were offered me as a gift, I would not accept it."

She raised her head from Irene's shoulder and blinked at him.

The Enchanter said, "Now, surely, Jean—"

Arturos said, "He's right. Knowing what's coming is a curse. Visions piss me off. Cause more trouble than they help."

Lucinda said, "I could put a lock on that talent, blocking her from using it until she's older. It wouldn't affect her other talents."

Irene said, "You could make it unlock when she's, say, sixteen?"

"Yes, that's easy."

"Expiration at eighteen," Quicksilver said, "would be better—"

"Don't be ridiculous," the Enchanter snapped. "This is Air Guild business, not Fire Guild, and I'll not allow—"

"Eighteen, then," Irene said. "Do it."

Sven knelt beside her. "Is that what Ollie would have wanted?"

Irene glanced at the Enchanter. He was arguing with Quicksilver. He never heard what she said, anyway. She turned back to Sven. "Absolutely. Oliver despised being a seer, and feared it would trouble our children. His father pushed both him and Winifred to use their talents too young, and then wouldn't heed Oliver's warnings over what he foresaw. Oliver begged him to discipline the guild before it tore itself apart, but now it's too late. That's why he didn't speak to his father for the last five years of his life."

She looked up, and met the Enchanter's eyes—the first time he had ever looked directly at her. He was livid, and swelling.

Frostbite!

"Done," Lucinda said.

The Enchanter turned his fury on her. "You can't overrule me on my own guild. You know that."

"You can't overrule a parent's judgment on a minor child," Sven said. "You know that. At least now Miranda will have an almost normal childhood."

Miranda said, "Thank you, Mama."

The Enchanter hesitated, then glowered.

"And now," Irene said, "Supper and an early bedtime are in order. Sven, the tunnels… Would you…?"

"It will be my pleasure to escort you back to the Fortress." He lifted Gillian. She threw her arms around his neck and clung to him.

"Mama, wait." Miranda shot across to the sofa, and curtsied to the prince. She held her hands together behind her back and looked down, toeing the carpet for a moment, then mumbled, "Thank you." She leaned forward and kissed the prince on the forehead, then backed away. "Now I'm ready."

Irene winced at the breach in royal protocol, but Alexander's red face held embarrassment and a trace of pleasure, not anger. She added to his confusion by making a deep curtsey and saying, "I am in your debt, sir, for saving my daughter's life."

The Air Enchanter said, "Irene, you don't understand. Let me explain." Polite words, but his voice held tightly controlled fury. "Tonight, after the children are in bed at your mother's. It is high time you came home to Airvale."

Half a dozen voices competed for attention. The girls protested. Paul expressed outrage over their reluctance to return to Airvale. Warlocks talked about safety. Sven asked what Irene wanted. Over the din one voice stood out—a voice that didn't frighten her, because it came from her memories.

"Stand up for the children," Oliver had said. "Don't let Paul or your mother or anybody else make decisions for you. Promise me that."

She had broken that promise once. Never again.

"Hush," she said. "We're going home."

The clamour died. For a moment, all was still. The Enchanter shot a smug glance at Quicksilver, who looked dismayed. Lucinda chewed her lip. Sven watched with intent eyes and held breath. He did not set Gillian down. She jammed her thumb in her mouth and glared.

"But mama," Miranda wailed.

"Hush," Irene took her hand and pulled her to the door. Sven held it open for them. "Airvale is not my home. Ready, Sven?"

The Call of Gravity

The door of Mother Celeste's drawing room closed behind Sven and the three van Gelders. Enchanter Paul turned on Jean.

"I have wanted," he said, "to take you at your word, and believe Irene fled to the Fortress for her safety. But it appears there is truth to the rumours she followed her lover."

Jean's eyes glittered. "Mistress Irene has been widowed nigh on three years. It is ungenerous of you to begrudge her another chance at happiness."

Lucinda said, "Her romance with Sven isn't a slur on your son. It's obvious she loved Oliver."

Paul turned his glare on Lucinda. "I am concerned about the effects of such a lewd and public love affair on impressionable children."

"Sven, lewd?" René hooted. Jean gave him a quelling look. René shook his head and grinned. *Hey, big sister, does the Air Guild always fall for its own lies? Seems that way, doesn't it?*

"If either one exhibited any impropriety," Jean said, "you may be sure everyone in the Fortress and Blazes would know of it. Indeed, Miranda and Gillian would do well to learn from their mother's example of how to conduct a discreet and dignified courtship."

Paul said, "Perhaps I am mistaken. Clearly, I am no longer needed here," and stomped out. Lucinda wasn't the only one who breathed a sigh of relief.

"Excitement's over," Mother Celeste said. "Supper and an early bedtime is good advice for all of us."

"Yes, ma'am," Hazel said. She started for the door, but Master Duncan said, "Hold on a bit. I've got something to say."

He squatted before Alexander, bringing them almost eye-to-eye. "You're worried about not being brave, eh, lad? Stop worrying. You had the gumption to lean out and grab that door. Everybody here knows that took guts." He looked around the room. "Tell me I'm right." They did. Even René voiced agreement.

Alexander flushed. "But I was scared."

"That door scared me, too. If you hadn't been scared I'd think you were a fr... er, dammed fool. Being brave isn't about not being scared. It's about keeping your head and doing the right thing when you are scared. Remember that."

Alexander nodded, and a slow smile spread across his face—the first smile of genuine, unadulterated pleasure Lucinda had seen him wear.

Miranda asked for an old favourite, *Ella Air Witch and the Enchanted Eagle*, for her bedtime story. Sven hovered at the door, watching. When the story ended, he slipped in and ordered both girls into dreamless sleep.

Irene followed him out into the sitting room and crept close as he replenished the fire.

He said, "You're shaking."

"My daughter almost died." Her voice shook, too.

He gathered her into his arms, and pulled her down onto the sofa with her head against his shoulder. He pressed his cheek against her hair and warmed her. Her trembling abated. She watched the fire, almost in a trance. He shifted his grip to finger an errant curl.

"Tomorrow," she said, "I must apologise to Arturos and Quicksilver."

"What for?"

"For presuming to call the Fortress home. I'm here on their sufferance."

"Don't be silly. The Fortress, like the Rehsavvy's house, has its own magic. If it's claimed you, neither of them will gainsay it."

"Claimed me, an air witch?"

"You're not the first person without fire magic to take refuge here, and you won't be the last. You're free to stay as long as it suits you."

She lifted her head, and for a moment they were cheek to cheek. They both moved a little. Their lips met. She broke off the kiss, only to have the pleasure of meeting his lips again and again.

A log broke and fell in a shower of sparks. His lips travelled across her cheek, down her neck. "You're trembling again," he murmured.

"Not from cold." She lifted a hand to stroke his hair. "I thought no one but Oliver would ever quicken my pulse. I was mistaken."

"It's true, what they say—an air witch's breath is sweet and she can enchant with her words."

"Is it true, what they say—a fire wizard's hands are never cold?"

He tensed. "Why did you say that?"

She drew back. "I had heard…"

He drew a deep breath, held it, then let it go. "I know, everyone's heard that. The last woman who asked me that question had only one thing on her mind, and she was damned annoying."

"Who was that?"

He shook his head. "It's not important. I shouldn't have said anything."

Irene rose to throw another log on the fire. "It was Winifred, wasn't it?" He frowned, and reached for her. She sidestepped and jabbed at the almost-consumed log, breaking it into glowing fragments. "Did you kiss her, too?"

"No. Stop that." He took the poker from her. "You're making a mess, and you're running away from me again."

"I am not." She sank down on the footstool with her arms folded tightly across her chest. "Winifred's the only friend I have in the Air Guild, but she's been thrown in my face for so long I'm sick of her. I understand about always being second best, and she doesn't have nearly as many redeeming qualities as Warlock Quicksilver."

He snorted. "That's an understatement."

"She's always had everything she wanted, and I've had so little."

"You had Ollie."

"She didn't want him, thank God. It's hard to believe she wanted you, and you didn't respond."

His lips thinned. He knelt and reached into the fire, building pyramids of burning firewood. "The truth is, I did. She attracted and repelled me at the same time. I'm sure she used a glamour spell on me, because she enthralled me when she was nearby, and when she wasn't, I felt nothing but a muddle of relief and anger and…"

"Lust?"

He flushed. "Yes, that too."

"I shouldn't have said that."

He avoided her eyes. "But it's true."

"Most men would have welcomed her attention."

"I'm a mage, remember. I know something about the bonds that form when two highly talented people couple. Decoupling from an enchantress—assuming she wants out—is much harder than falling into bed with her in the first place, and the thought of being stuck with Winifred... Even while I was enthralled, she bored me silly. Not like you." He turned his head to look at her. "You always have something interesting to say, and thinking about you makes me happy. If I see you at breakfast, my whole day is brighter. Irene, you don't need to be jealous of her."

"But, Sven, if she used a glamour spell on you—she could, and I can believe she would—how did you resist her?"

"She hates the Earth Mother's amber meeting room. She would arrive late and bolt when the meeting ended. I dawdled. Even so, I escaped more by luck than willpower. I made her angry and she dropped me."

"What did you do?"

He ducked his head like a schoolboy. "I offered to tutor her on the theory behind the Air Guild spells."

"Oh, dear Sven, you are indisputably a mage. No, she wouldn't have appreciated your offer—not one bit."

"Would you have? Irene, what do you want?"

"Pardon?" She stared into the fire. "No one cares what I want."

"I do. It's obvious what Winifred's after. You, I can't figure out. Those kisses... Now you're not even looking at me."

If Winifred hadn't come between them, would the heat of the moment have melted her resolve and let her indulge in what rumour said already occupied them? Climbing alone into a cold bed was a hateful prospect, but some misguided sense of pride insisted that since Winifred would have slept with him, Irene would not.

"If," he said, "you want someone to run your life for you, forget it. I'm not interested in those kinds of games."

She swung around to face him. "Sven Matheson, whatever gave you that idea?"

"I've asked you what you want, and you've never given me an answer. Have you ever listened to yourself? You're a capable, intelligent witch, but you hardly ever claim credit for your own actions. You talk as if things just happen to you."

"Don't they? That's what my life has been like."

"The Air Guild mistreats you; I understand that. But inanimate objects don't throw themselves—"

"No? No one bullied by the Air Guild believes in inanimate objects."

He winced. "I hadn't considered…"

She turned towards the fire. "Sven, Mrs Cole will be annoyed if you make me cry. Go away."

He sat very still for several breaths before going to the door.

Without taking her eyes off the fire, Irene said, "Oliver told me to stand up for myself, but I don't know how."

"You just did, and rather well, I'd say."

"But you listened. The Air Enchanter never does."

"More practice might help. Start by telling me what you want."

He waited a moment, then growled and yanked the door open.

"Sven?"

"Yes?"

She turned to look at him. "I want—all I've ever really wanted—is respect from my guild. You can't do anything about that."

He stood in the open doorway, staring at the floor, the excitement from earlier in the day gone. "What you need is a guild you can respect. I can't do anything about that either. Good night."

"Sven?"

The almost-shut door swung open. He leaned back in. "Yes?"

"And, I want… I want to go to the party with you."

The hard line of his mouth relaxed. "See, that wasn't so hard. And thank you—I'm looking forward to it."

"Morning, ma'am. Ma'am—I know you air witches don't like being cooped up, but are you sure you want to go out on the battlements today?"

Irene said, "Is there a reason not to? We haven't been out since the storm began—air witches don't care for stinging sleet and freezing rain any more than most people do—and we need fresh air. It's snowing now, and it's beautiful."

"Yes, ma'am, it is pretty." The grizzled sergeant in the watchtower scratched his chin. "But there's ice out there in spots, and you can't always tell where through the snow."

"Ice on the walk? Doesn't the Fortress melt the ice and snow?"

"It does, but there's been no letup in stuff coming down for more than three days, and the Fortress sometimes gets a bit behind."

"Oh." The van Gelders had been miserable for three days. How could anyone have lived through the last war's siege without losing their sanity?

Gillian tugged on the guard's coat and turned big, sad eyes up to him. "Please, sir, I want to go out. Won't you let us?"

He shrugged. "I'm not saying you can't. I'm just saying be careful. Wouldn't want you to get hurt."

The other guard said, "You'll probably be all right if you stay clear of the stairs."

The exposed stone stairs with steep risers and no handrail were nightmare fodder. Irene said, "There is no weather that would induce me to take those stairs. Thank you."

He grinned and held the door for them.

The clouds were breaking up, and the falling snow glistened in slanted shafts of light. They laughed in delight at being outdoors, being alive. They caught snowflakes on their tongues, threw snowballs, and sang silly songs. They joined hands and danced in the snow, the sergeant's warning forgotten.

The children ran Irene out of breath. She stopped to watch them dance, standing guard in front of the stairs.

Behind her, Oliver said, "Aren't they precious?"

She whirled. Her feet slipped on ice and she pitched forwards. She grabbed for the parapet, missed, and fell headfirst down the icy stairs.

The Murderous Stairs

Irene's body hung in mid-air, arms outstretched. The girls screamed. Guards yelled. Snowflakes settled on her arms. If this was a dream, it was unlike any dream she'd ever had.

The guards grabbed her legs and pulled her back onto the battlements like a fisherman reeling in his catch. They set her on her feet, but her legs wouldn't support her. The next few minutes were a blur of faces and voices, and only steadied and began to make sense when they had wrapped her in a blanket and set her before a warm fire. Miranda pressed against her on one side, crooning a favourite melody. On the other side, Gillian sucked her thumb noisily. Several guards crowded into the small room. Someone pushed a second glass of whiskey into her hands.

Second? The warmth in her throat and stomach proved one downed, but she had no memory of it. Whiskey at ten o'clock in the morning? What would Mother say?

Irene lifted the blanket and took in the girls. "What happened?"

"I want to know that, too, ma'am," the sergeant said. "I was watching you, and you were just standing there. Then you whipped around, sudden-like, and went down. Why'd you go spinning around like that?"

"My dead husband spoke from behind me." *Frost it, they'll say I'm mad!* "But of course there wasn't anyone there."

"No, ma'am, there wasn't."

"What kept me from falling?"

"There's magic on all the stairs in the Fortress. You can't fall down and get hurt on any of them. They won't let you."

"What?" The glass slammed down on the table, splashing out half the whiskey. "I've been living in terror of the stairs in this place for three months now, and they're harmless?" Frost it, her voice was shrill.

The sergeant patted the air. "Whoa, now, ma'am."

She drew a deep breath. "Why didn't anyone tell me about this magic?" Not much better. She sounded like an angry fire witch.

"Nobody told you, ma'am, because nobody's supposed to know. The two Fire Warlocks—the old one and the new—they both know, of course, and a handful of us guards, but nobody else."

Another guard said, "I betcha Mrs Cole and Master Sven know."

"Well, yeah, they know everything going on here."

Sven knew? Of course he did. Hadn't he said she wouldn't fall? "But why keep it a secret? There are others frightened by the moving stairs."

"They didn't use to have that magic on them, ma'am. After Granny Verna died in a fall some five, six years ago, the Fire Warlock—the retired one, that is—went around with an earth witch putting spells on all the stairs. But he said he didn't want people knowing about them. He was afraid they'd get lazy and cut corners, and get into bad habits. Then when they left here and went someplace else without the spells, they'd be more likely to do something stupid and kill themselves there. And he said he'd feel damned rotten if that happened."

Despite her fury she laughed. "Warlock Quicksilver said he'd feel 'damned rotten'?"

"Well, not those words, ma'am, but that's what he meant. He was feeling damned rotten anyway, about Granny Verna."

"She was married to Warlock Arturos, wasn't she?"

"Yes, ma'am."

She swallowed another mouthful of whiskey, and leaned back with her eyes closed. "Of course Warlock Quicksilver would have good reasons for secrecy. Forgive me for yelling at you. I am very, very grateful for those spells."

"It's all right, ma'am. You've had a bad upset. Maybe you ought to lie down and rest for awhile."

She agreed that was a good idea, and staggered to their apartment with the sergeant's support. Once in bed, sleep wouldn't come. Oliver had called the girls lots of things—impossible imps, fetching little fairies, half-pint hellions after his own heart, but *precious*? Not his style.

Whatever, or whoever, had spoken to her, it was not Oliver's ghost.

Although Marie Richardson and several other highborn Air Guild parasites could throw their voices a short distance, and had the venom for such a murderous stunt, they were not familiar with Oliver's distinctive timbre, nor were they welcome in the Fortress. But if one of them hadn't spoken to her, who had?

Fire and Air

"If you have a moment, Madam Locksmith, may I please have a word with you?"

Father Jerome plucked at Lucinda's sleeve as the ranking witches and wizards involved in the quarantine left the Earth Guild's amber meeting room. Her arm ached, the meeting had taken three times as long as she had expected, and she had a million things to do in the three days before Yule, but she didn't hesitate to step out of the queue moving through the small antechamber.

"Of course, sir. What's the matter?"

"I am still waiting," that most tactful and considerate of men said, "for word the Fire Guild has defanged the trap in the tunnels that nearly killed those two children. I understand your guild has little time to spare—I just don't want you to forget that diabolical device."

She glanced over her shoulder, but Jean was still in the amber box, talking to Mother Celeste. What could she say? She could not tell Father Jerome, the senior earth mage, it was none of his business.

Master Sven stepped in. "I'm sorry, sir, but the Fire Guild Council met, and decided not to dismantle the traps. At least, not yet."

The earth father's eyes bulged. "Good heavens. Why not?"

The departing queue stopped to listen. Enchanter Paul, frowning, loomed over the shorter earth wizard's shoulder. Lucinda tensed. In this gathering of formidable talents, few would be unaware of the simmering antagonism between Paul and Sven.

Sven said, "Both Warlock Arturos, an acknowledged seer, and Warlock Quicksilver, our history's most seasoned warrior, believe the traps still have a part to play in Frankland's defences. Given the current crisis, they are reluctant to part with a weapon protecting the Earth Guild without active assistance."

Enchanter Paul said, "Does your guild's paranoia know no limits? We have been at the Fire Warlock's beck and call for months now. Your interference with the other guilds' business is becoming intolerable."

"Defending the nation's healers is certainly Fire Guild business," Lucinda snapped, though she agreed with him that Jean and Beorn suffered from delusions of danger from every compass point. Jean had gone into the Guild Council meeting expecting a strenuous argument, but once he and Beorn discovered they agreed, her arguments about the safety of innocent wanderers carried little weight. Flint's dismay on finding himself on the same side of an argument as Jean was the only bright spot in that rancorous meeting.

Paul ignored Lucinda. "I will inform Mother Celeste myself. When she orders you to remove the traps, you cannot refuse."

"Paul," Mother Astrid said, "she knows. Warlock Quicksilver told her they didn't want to remove them, and she concurred. I've heard her reasons, and I agree with her."

Enchanter Paul and Father Jerome both blinked at her. The earth father said, "I didn't know that."

Mother Astrid glanced at the circle of avid listeners with a wry smile. "It's on the next council meeting's agenda. She didn't want the decision widely discussed until then."

Father Jerome flushed. "Oh, dear. I'm sorry."

Paul sniffed. "Frankland's citizens are in more danger with the traps than without them. I insist on hearing her reasons."

Sven said, "And you said you disapproved of interference in other guilds' business."

Paul glared. "As an officeholder, I have the right and responsibility to question the others on matters affecting the nation. I certainly wouldn't do so for the fun of it. Had I any spare time, I would concentrate on our own urgent affairs."

Sven flushed. "If the Air Guild is so short-staffed—" he didn't acknowledge Lucinda's yank at his sleeve " —how can you afford to ignore the javelin in your ranks?"

Paul's face went blank. "Javelin? What javelin?"

Father Jerome said, "An unrecognised javelin? What sort of talent?"

Lucinda rocked on her heels. She sympathised with Sven, but Jean had insisted they couldn't afford to further alienate the Air Guild. Her elbow in Sven's ribs had no effect.

Sven said, "The most accomplished wordsmith we've had in centuries. As the Air Guild deals with contracts and trade agreements, that has to be a useful talent."

Paul said, "Yes, absolutely. Are you suggesting some youngster in the school is showing talent the faculty doesn't recognise? Who? You should have informed me as soon as he came to your attention. Don't hold back on me, man."

Sven snarled, "I'm not talking about some boy in the school. This is someone who graduated a decade ago. Your daughter-in-law, Irene."

Paul gaped. "What nonsense. Irene has very little talent. That's obvious to everyone in the Air Guild."

Sven said, "She's a level three witch. That's obvious to anyone with half a magical eye. That power has to go somewhere."

Paul sneered, "Apparently it has gone towards a glamour spell to enchant you, sir."

Sven's flush deepened. "If she could—and I don't believe she can—that would still take more talent than you've given her credit for. Maybe you should have sent her to the Empire as a spy, since all you think she's good for is deceiving people."

Paul's face was as red as Sven's. "Keep such ridiculous ideas to yourself, sir, or I shall give credence to the rumour Warlock Quicksilver thought you unfit to join the Company of Mages."

Lucinda gasped. Sven went white. Behind him, the door to the amber chamber crashed against the wall. Jean shouldered through the queue, spitting fire. "How dare you!"

Sven's wand tip, glowing red, danced before Lucinda's eyes. She grabbed his hand and forced it down. He tried to shake her off, but she put her weight into it, hissing, "Don't threaten an officeholder!"

Mother Astrid grabbed his other arm. "Calm down."

Jean pushed past them to poke Paul in the chest with his own wand. "What right have you to repeat such a base canard?"

Paul retreated before the shorter warlock. "I beg your pardon, Your Wisdom, but you can't deny there was such a rumour."

"I do not deny its existence. I can and do deny its substance. I had, and have, no qualms about Master Sven's worth, and I said so in the letter I wrote to the company while on my honeymoon. Did you not read it?"

Father Jerome laid a hand on Jean's shoulder. "Your Wisdom, Enchanter Paul wasn't at the meeting where we voted on Master Sven. We may have been lax and not forwarded your letter to him. I don't remember. It didn't seem important."

Jean turned a glittering eye on the earth wizard. "And why, pray tell," he said, overriding Sven's snarl, "did it not seem important?"

Father Jerome threw an apologetic look at Sven. "Because you had, on several occasions, already expressed your frustration with Warlock Flint's little games. The rumours were preposterous; I ignored them."

Jean turned back to the enchanter. "Indeed. No mage should be so gullible."

"Gullible?" Paul said. "I'm not the one taken in by someone calling herself a javelin."

Jean had been roaring a moment earlier. His voice was now as soft as velvet. "Taken in? Am I to understand the argument is over Mistress Irene? Then you must also accuse me of being gullible."

The colour drained from Paul's face. "What, she's enchanted the entire Fire Guild Council?"

"Not Flint," Lucinda said, "and Sunbeam doesn't care, but five of us believe she's a javelin. Including the Fire Warlock, who, as you know, is protected against enchantments and glamour spells by your guild's magic."

"Ollie believed her a javelin, too," Sven said. "But you never respected his opinions, either, for all you pushed him to be a mage."

Paul's glance flicked between the three angry faces confronting him. "But it's impossible. I did ask Enchantress Winifred to substantiate Oliver's claims about Irene. Winifred assured me she had no talent."

Irene had said Winifred had supported her. Lucinda and Sven exchanged a startled glance.

Father Jerome's voice carried a distinct edge. "I gather from all this that this woman—Enchanter Oliver's widow, the same air witch involved in the charter search, is that right?—is either an enchantress-level wordsmith, or is an adept with glamour spells of such power and quality that she must be a javelin in that respect. Is that so?"

Paul deflated. "I hadn't considered…"

"One responsibility the Company of Mages bears is to identify and support young witches and wizards with unusual talents who would otherwise be overlooked by the less sophisticated men and women running the guild schools. If you'll allow me, I'll investigate and report on this witch at our next meeting. I don't know her—I have no reason to either praise or condemn her." Jerome turned, searching for someone among the onlookers. "Would one of the water mages assist?"

Sorcerer Charles said, "I'd be happy to."

Father Jerome shot a look filled with venom at Paul. "Thank you, Charles. I'm sure you can think for yourself." He turned, facing the Fire Guild trio. "I trust that will that satisfy you."

Jean bowed to the earth father. "Of course, sir." Lucinda nodded, and curtsied. Sven, his lips a thin line, hesitated. Mother Astrid pushed on Sven's shoulder. He followed suit with a jerky bow.

Father Jerome turned to Enchanter Paul. "And you?" His tone of voice brooked no argument.

Enchanter Paul nodded slowly and bowed, then turned and walked away. The noncombatants moved aside to let him through, then followed him out. Sven, looking a trifle dazed, joined the queue.

Lucinda said, "Jean, didn't you say we shouldn't antagonise the Air Enchanter further?"

He grimaced. "You must remember, my love, that I am a fire wizard. Sometimes I lose my temper."

Mother Astrid said, "Not just you. That was as close as I've ever seen Jerome come to chewing someone out."

Lucinda huddled against the door of Winifred's cabin, but the narrow porch offered no protection from the biting wind. A few feet beyond, the ground dropped, providing a vertigo-inducing panorama of snow-covered mountains. If she ever came to this frostbitten mountaintop again, she would walk through the fire into Winifred's kitchen, good manners be damned. Why not? The entire Air Guild, except for Irene, already seemed to consider Lucinda the rudest person they'd ever met.

Poor Irene. With friends like Winifred, no wonder she'd fled Airvale.

Lucinda pounded on the door again. She already had Winifred's attention; an enchantress would have to be on her deathbed to not notice a warlock's fiery arrival, even without the alarm spells Lucinda had triggered.

There were no other humans for miles, but the cabin had more spells against eavesdropping than the Rehsavvy's house on the Blazes town square had. What was Winifred hiding?

The door swung open. "Come in, come in. I'm sorry to keep you waiting, but I wasn't expecting you."

As Lucinda crossed the threshold, her mind's eye caught a glimpse of someone—man or woman, she couldn't tell—climbing out a rear window. Then the image blurred, and she could not see out any better than she had earlier seen in.

Fine. Let Winifred's visitor enjoy the cool breezes for a while.

Lucinda explained politely, and at length, that they had expected Winifred at the meeting. "I don't mean to be a bore, but we need everyone in the Air Guild helping out. Is there anything a mundane could do for you?"

Enchantress Winifred let out a long sigh. "I will not have a mundane in my house. I'm sorry, I've done nothing but work for weeks, and I couldn't take it any longer."

She was complaining about being overworked? Lucinda tried not to let her annoyance show. "It is hard. I've barely seen my baby or my husband for weeks. We…"

She stopped. Winifred's face had gone slack, her eyes unfocused. Lucinda ground her teeth. Dread crawled over her.

The slack expression vanished, replaced by an intense stare. Winifred grabbed Lucinda's wrist and shook it. "Warlock Locksmith, be careful. Don't let the Fire Warlock's demands steal this precious time with your family. You can never recover time lost with young children."

As if Lucinda didn't already know that. Her polite mask slipped. "My son is in good hands. This crisis can't go on forever. When it's over—"

"Do you think you and your husband will live into old age together? Go home and love him as a wife should, while you still have time. You may not have another Yule."

Without Winifred's grip on her wrist, Lucinda would have run for the fireplace. She retreated a step, but stopped short on catching a whiff of a glamour spell.

She advanced on Winifred, and probed. The enchantress went rigid, and let go of Lucinda's wrist. They stared at each other without moving, locked in a battle of wills and spells as intense as a sword fight. Winifred radiated trust and goodwill, but malice glinted underneath. Her glamour was the most subtle Lucinda had yet encountered. If she hadn't been the Fire Warlock's apprentice and covered, though to a lesser degree, by the Fire Office's shields, she would never have noticed.

Winifred spat, "You'll earn a mention in the history books you love, all right. Your reign as Fire Warlock will be the shortest on record."

Lucinda fell into the fireplace and rolled across the hearth in her bedroom in the Fortress, covered in ashes. She didn't bother dusting herself off—she lay on the floor and wept.

Lucinda blew her nose and stuffed the sodden handkerchief in her pocket before entering the dining room. She had washed her face, but couldn't find her Earth Guild charm to hide her red nose and eyes. Maybe no one would notice.

Sven was telling a story, making the van Gelders laugh. Good, Lucinda could use some cheerful company. The two adults looked up as she approached. She gulped and backtracked. She should have realised that with Sven away from the Fortress so much, they had little opportunity to enjoy each other's company, and wouldn't appreciate an intruder. Too late; they had already donned their polite faces.

"Lucinda, what's wrong?" Sven was on his feet, pulling out a chair. "Sit down; you look ghastly."

"Trust a fire wizard to say what no one wants said." Irene held out a clean handkerchief. "Do you need this?"

Lucinda took it and thanked her. "Irene, I don't like your friend Winifred. If she hadn't uncovered Baron D'Armond's charter, I'd be tempted to lock her in a closet so I'd never have to see her again."

"Winifred found a charter? How did she do that?"

Sven's forehead creased. "You hadn't heard?"

"Tom reported that the Air Guild found a baron's charter. I didn't ask for details. You've been too busy the past week to give me more than two sentences at a time."

"The Fire Warlock's been running us ragged getting everything locked down and peaceful for Yule. We've—"

"Wait," Lucinda said, "Didn't Winifred tell you about the charter? She came here to deliver it."

Irene said, "What day was she here?"

"Three days ago? Four? The day it snowed, after the ice storm," Lucinda said, and watched an air witch turn to stone.

Friends and Enemies

"Irene, are you all right?"

Lucinda's question seemed to come from the far distance. She had stopped crying, and both she and Sven were staring.

Irene's own voice seemed to come from someone else. "Girls, if you're through with supper, return to our rooms and prepare for bed. I'll be along soon." She forced herself to focus on Lucinda. "Didn't you say Winifred could enter the Fortress any time, as long as I didn't mind?"

Lucinda nodded.

"I mind. Don't let her in again."

"Good," Sven said, "because she's not your friend."

"Is she anyone's friend?" Lucinda blushed and stared at her plate. "I've spent the last hour spying on her, and I can't find out anything."

"No," Irene said, "You wouldn't. She values her privacy, and she's a virtuoso at keeping secrets. She won't give anything away."

"Would you let me spy on her through your life?" Lucinda's blush deepened. "It's an awful imposition, and I've no right to spy on her. I'm an interfering busybody of a fire witch, but..."

"Don't apologise," Irene's voice said. "I want to know."

Sven followed the two women to Irene's apartment. Lucinda turned to glare at him.

He said, "I don't like her either. I can't help Irene if I don't know what Winifred's done."

Lucinda shrugged and let him come along.

For Irene, the next hour was a week long. Attempting to read *The Fire*

Warlock's Pet proved a disaster—the girls complained about her flat and dreary voice, and the skips and repetitions when she lost her place. Sven pulled the book from her unresisting hands and voiced the dragon with dramatic vigour. The girls giggled in delight, became more alert, and begged for another story. He promised a story on another occasion and ordered them to sleep.

Sitting by the fire and answering Lucinda's questions brought no relief.

"Where did you first meet Winifred?" Lucinda asked.

"At the Air Guild School," Irene said. "We were twelve. She believed in my talent, and always kept me company during the tests."

A scene bloomed in the fire. A younger Irene, spine straight and rigid, perched on the edge of a chair by the headmaster's office. "I wish they would hurry. I don't like waiting."

The other girl put a hand on her shoulder. "Doing the testing late in the afternoon isn't fair. Nobody does well when they're tired. It's been a long day already, and you're tired, aren't you?"

Irene's head drooped; her shoulders slumped. "Yes, I'm tired," she mumbled.

The door opened, and Irene shuffled into the headmaster's office. Winifred followed, smiling.

⚜

The image in the flames disappeared. Sven growled like an angry dog. Irene seemed, once again, to be a long way away from her own body.

Stop it, she thought. *I don't want to know any more.*

You already know, it said. *You just don't want to believe.*

"Go on," her mouth said.

More scenes followed, Sven and Lucinda taking turns. A recent one in the Fortress's library, with Irene teaching Winifred a spell to find a charter, and Winifred telling her to forget it, shocked her from her daze.

"I spent weeks working on a spell and don't remember it?"

"We need that spell," Lucinda snarled. "What's the worst you can do to an enchantress? Bury her and let her suffocate? By God, I'd like to do that."

"But, why? Why did she do this to me?"

"Envy," they said together.

"But she's an enchantress."

"A level five talent, with a level two mind," Lucinda said. "You have a level five talent, and a level five mind."

Sven said, "She needs you, and hates you for it. If you hadn't helped her, she'd have been a laughingstock in the Air Guild—the enchantress who didn't have a clue about magic."

"She doesn't have your courage or strength of character either," Lucinda said.

"Me? I'm a coward."

"Rubbish," Sven said. "Lucinda, all we've seen has been between Irene and Winifred. Can we find out what happened between Winifred and Paul? He said she told him Irene had no talent."

Lucinda sucked in a long breath, and blew out between pursed lips. "That's harder, and I'm already tired. I'd have to evade her privacy spells without alerting her that I'm snooping, and I can't draw on the Fire Office without a reason to snoop."

"Deceiving an officeholder ought to do."

"Er... Fine. Give me some time."

The Air Enchanter unpacked boxes of Oliver's papers with no enthusiasm. Winifred watched.

He said, "I asked you to re-examine Irene's talent. What have you found?"

She sniffed. "She has a high opinion of herself, but I've never seen her do anything I'd consider interesting."

"Oliver seemed to think that she had talent no one else in the guild was aware of."

She shrugged. "He was in love, and they say love is blind. I know his opinion of her talents changed after they married. It's a shame he never came back to Airvale to talk to you, but then she didn't encourage him to come. I do know she has a secret she doesn't want the guild to find out: she hears voices. She's convinced she's heard Oliver's voice since he died."

The Enchanter's head snapped up. "Is she going mad?"

Winifred waved her hands. "I'm not a healer."

"Hearing voices is not healthy. I didn't realise she was so distraught. I must visit her." He started to rise.

Winifred laid a hand on his arm. "I'm sure she's not a danger to anyone else, and Granny Beatrice knows about the voices. She's been treating Irene as well as anyone could. If you barged in asking about the voices, she'd be upset that they aren't a secret any longer. And if she does talk to you about her problems, you won't hear anything other than narcissism."

"I suppose you're right." He sank into his chair, the worry lines in his face smoothing out.

"But there is something you could do. There's a manuscript for a book of spells somewhere in these boxes. Oliver was proud of it, but she's not in any shape now to handle publishing it. Imagine how she will feel seeing it in print with Oliver's name in gold leaf on the cover."

"Really?" He thumbed through the papers with more zeal. Bent over the boxes, he could not have seen Winifred's contemptuous smile.

"Impressive," Lucinda said. "That was a masterpiece of deception, and not a single lie."

"Impressive is not the word I would have chosen," Sven said. "One more scene."

"Sven, I'm exhausted. We've already proven Winifred is a lying vixen. What else is there? We should all go to bed."

"One more," he said.

Dozens of kites bobbed and weaved, forming a kaleidoscope of shifting patterns in rainbow hues above a deserted beach. The only people atop the sand dune were the muscular man Irene knew so well and the air witch gliding to a graceful landing beside him.

"Hello, Oliver. Don't you ever get bored of these childish games?"

His eyes remained fixed on the kites. "Hello, Winnie. No, I hope I never do. Creating something beautiful is worthwhile, even if it is fleeting. What brings you here?"

She ran a hand along his biceps. "Have you reconsidered my offer to play more adult games?"

He didn't move. The kites danced. "Forget it, Winnie. I'm not interested."

"You've been married, what, four years now? Aren't you tired yet of that colourless mouse you married?"

"My grey-eyed Athena has more depth than you can comprehend. I'll not risk what I have for you, Winnie. Your charms are all on the surface, and what's underneath is shallow and not very pretty."

She dug her nails into his arm. "Don't insult me. I can make your life hell."

He shrugged. "I'm a seer, too, remember? My life's already hell."

"I can make her life hell."

He turned towards her then, blue eyes as cold as the winter stars. "How many women's lives will you ruin? Be careful, Winnie. Someday the women you've hurt will exact revenge. I'm sorry I won't be here to enjoy it."

The wind rose and he flew out to sea, pulling the kites in a long train behind him.

Unmerry Yule

Dawn found Irene walking the ramparts, staring out into grey emptiness. She had abandoned her bed after drifting in and out of dreams of inanimate objects whispering vicious rumours or hurling themselves at her.

What nonsense. Sven was right; objects don't fly through the air of their own accord. Voices don't arise from the ether. She would have admitted that sooner if she hadn't been afraid of what she would uncover when she probed.

No more. It was long past time to call Winifred to account. High time, too, as Quicksilver had said, for Irene to take responsibility for her actions and convince the world of her worth. If only she knew how.

She was in no mood to party, but was unwilling to disappoint Sven. When the time came, she slipped on the yellow silk gown, but it brought no joy. Her reflection in the looking glass was wan and lifeless. She pinched her cheeks and plastered on a smile for Sven's sake.

Sven and three male warlocks—Arturos, Quicksilver, and Snorri— waited with Lucinda by the stairs. Clad in an elegant dress with gold embroidery on the collar and sleeves, she looked more regal than most noblewomen. The burgundy velvet complimented her high colour; next to her, Irene would look like a wraith.

Irene's envy gave way to shame on closer inspection. Lucinda's red-rimmed eyes suggested she had spent the night in tears. In Irene's distress over the evening's revelations, the fact that Lucinda had been crying before coming to supper had slipped her mind. She was tempted to ask what Winifred had predicted, but afraid Lucinda might answer. The four wizards looked tired and apprehensive.

"What will we do when we see Winifred?" Lucinda asked.

"She won't attend," Irene said. "She hates crowds. She never goes to parties."

"She'd come today, out of spite," Sven muttered.

"If she does, let's link arms and form a tight circle around her, to show her we care."

That elicited a bark of laughter from Quicksilver and a snicker from Snorri.

"I'd rather not see Enchanter Paul, either," Sven said. No one said anything for a moment.

"Are we waiting for someone else?" Sven asked.

"Yep," Arturos said. "Here he comes now."

Alexander hurried towards them in clothes befitting a prince. Katie quickstepped behind him, fussing with his collar.

"Several others will be bringing children," Quicksilver said. "I thought it would do him good to see us having fun for a change."

"Fun?" Lucinda said. "We look more like we're going to a funeral than a party."

"I'd rather get some sleep," Arturos said.

They rode the moving staircase in silence.

Holiday scents of cinnamon, nutmeg, fresh-cut spruce, and roast ham wafted over them as they entered the Warren's Great Hall. Irene's spirits lifted with the Frost Maiden Emerita's gracious acknowledgement of her contribution to the reforging. The Earth Mother's hug, no less generous than to anyone else in their group, gave her spirits another boost.

She whispered to Sven, "Mother Celeste does know I'm an air witch, doesn't she?"

"Of course. She approved of your defying the Air Enchanter for your children's sake. She said, 'For an air witch she has her feet planted on the ground'."

Master Duncan ambled over with the earth witch who had rescued Miranda and Alexander on his arm. He jerked a thumb at the Frost Maiden Emerita. "What's that she's wearing? I've never seen anything like it."

Neither had Irene. Apparently one long length of blue silk shot through with silver, the garment rippled in fluid motion, and was utterly feminine. Her left arm was bare; fabric cascaded over her right shoulder.

He said, "If you didn't know, you'd never notice she only has one arm."

Lucinda said, "I ordered it shipped from Delhi for her. It's a sari."

"That can't be right, ma'am. There's nothing sorry about it."

Irene laughed. Sven smiled down at her. With her hand tucked into the crook of his arm, they watched the gathering crowd. The Fire Guild's gloom had dissipated. Snorri was inspecting the buffet. Lucinda gushed about her son's latest accomplishments to Master Duncan's earth witch. Arturos and Master Duncan traded bad jokes.

If Sven were as muscular as either of those two men, Winifred would have forgiven him for suggesting she needed tutoring. Someone should warn Master Duncan's earth witch.

Irene walked out into the middle of the Great Hall and gazed at the decorations while regaining control over her breathing. Winifred had damaged her life for too many years; she would not let her ruin the holiday, too. Or destroy Irene's respect for the men she encountered.

Lucinda laughed at something Master Duncan said. Someone offered Irene a glass of wine, and her hand rose by reflex. The quality of the bouquet drew her out of her preoccupation. Sven steered her towards the buffet table, introducing her to a pair of earth wizards along the way. They both acted pleased to meet her. As they loaded their plates, the intoxicating magics of Yule decorations, delicious food, superb wine, and pleasant company soothed her soul.

The Air Enchanter arrived and started towards them. She and Sven turned their backs on him. A water wizard waved them over to a nearly empty table and Sven performed the introductions.

"I've been looking forward to talking to you," Sorcerer Charles said. "I understand you're responsible for that spellbook with Oliver's name on it."

Sven reddened. "Don't look at me like that. Yes, I gave away your secret, and I won't apologise. The other mages needed to know."

"Quite right," the sorcerer said. "Intriguing little book, but I've had questions about the spells on weather magic ever since I acquired my copy. Would you indulge an old bore and talk about them now, or would that be too tedious a topic for a party?"

"Tedious?" Irene said. "Not at all, sir. It will be a pleasure."

Irene should have known what was in store when agreeing to discuss weather magic with the senior water mage. He dissected the most complicated spells, pointed out problems, and stitched them back together with improvements. Two hours later, five pages of notes, filled with new sources to consult and suggestions for other spells, formed the nucleus for a second volume. Her head was as light as the altocumulus lenticular clouds they were discussing. The Air Enchanter had left early, without coming closer. Winifred had not entered her thoughts since meeting Sorcerer Charles.

The Rehsavvys were dancing in the middle of the hall. Sven had long since wandered to another table, where he was shooting sparks into the air for the children.

A light voice said, "May I interrupt?" The Frost Maiden Emerita was at Irene's shoulder. "I have been awaiting an opportunity, but Charles has the look of a man settled in for the day."

"I'm sorry, Your Wisdom." Irene stood. "I shouldn't have monopolised him."

"No, sit, please. I want a few words with you, Mrs van Gelder. The thanks I expressed while greeting guests were inadequate appreciation for all you have done for us."

"Do you mean finding the charters?"

"Among other things. Yes, we are grateful for those, and for the evidence you found in the Archers' favour. And it is of no small moment that Quicksilver's Fire Eaters speak highly of you. Nerves are frayed, and open warfare might already have erupted between the Water and Air Guilds if such a prominent air witch had not shown herself firmly on the side of law and order."

"Prominent? I beg your pardon, Your Wisdom, but you're mistaken. I'm the least important witch in the entire guild."

"Nonsense," the two water talents said in unison.

"You're a fine witch and scholar," the mage said. "The other guilds have taken note of you; it confounds us that the Air Guild spurns you. And, while you may not appreciate it now..." He paused and glanced at the sorceress.

She nodded. "Go on."

"The Richardson's attempts at character assassination have inadvertently made you Frankland's most famous air witch."

Irene's hands flew to her face. "Oh, no. No. Mother... My children..."

The sorceress's fingers brushed Irene's arm. "Take heart. The Fire Guild, with its reputation for speaking the truth, even—"

"Or especially," the mage said.

"—when it hurts, assure us neither you nor Master Sven have embarrassed your guilds. We are fortunate indeed that the first of these vicious attacks were against you two. Your dignity and decorum in such trying circumstances have rendered the slanders laughable, and easier for the rest of the talented community to bear. I cannot overstate what your example has done for the Water Guild's morale, particularly in the lower ranks."

Irene lowered her hands and stared at the sorceress over her fingertips.

"Ah," she said. "You have been living in the Fortress, amongst the Fire Guild's more civilised members. I gather they have not repeated the other rumours."

"What other rumours?"

"The nobles have subjected every witch and wizard involved in the quarantine to allegations of sexual misconduct."

"They've gone overboard with it," the water mage said. "It hasn't done anything for the Air Guild's reputation for mendacity."

"Indeed," the sorceress said. "If one believed a quarter of the tales, one would infer that three of the four magic guilds have overnight become houses of ill repute where the sole activity is drunken debauchery. Few in Frankland are that gullible."

"I hadn't heard any of this," Irene said.

"Thank the Fire Guild for their restraint. Did I say that? Ah, me, the world has changed. I thank you for the impeccable behaviour you have exhibited. No one with a drop of sense credits the gossip, and our witches and wizards can be proud to be in your company."

"Of course they can," Sven said. Irene hadn't noticed him approaching. He smiled at her. "Haven't I been saying the truth about what you're worth would come out eventually?"

"A good deal of truth has already come out," the sorceress said. "About your worth, too, Sven."

"Oh?" He slid into a chair with a slight frown. "I meant to ask Irene to dance, but perhaps you should explain that statement."

"I am happy to. For your work on the charter search, Sven, and the great conspiracy's destruction, the commoners—"

"Don't forget his defence of the Archers," the water mage said.

"Yes, that too. For those, the commoners have taken you to heart as their hero. You are the most loved mage Frankland has had in centuries."

He gaped at her. "You're joking."

"She is not," the water mage said. "In the past month, several dozen babies, scattered across Frankland, have been christened Sven—not, heretofore, a common name."

"To be fair," she said, "there were more Duncans."

"True, but if I dare make a prediction, I'd say that within five years, every village and hamlet in Frankland will have a Duncan, a Sven, a Lucinda, and an Irene."

Sven and Irene stared at each other. A slow smile spread across Sven's features.

"You meant to ask me to dance?" Irene said.

"Yes. Will you?"

They walked onto the dance floor, but Irene's mind was not on dancing. *Famous? A role model?* She was stupefied, is what she was.

From the damage Sven did her toes, his mind wasn't on dancing either. "Naming babies after us. I'll be... I'll be..."

"Frostbitten?"

He laughed. "I should tell you to watch your language, but it does seem appropriate. The finest Yule present I've ever received, and to have it come from the Water Guild..." He shook his head, smiling.

Warlock Arturos disappeared in an echoing column of fire, sending a group of earth witches scrambling. Sven's smile faltered. Warlock Quicksilver and Lucinda jogged across the dance floor towards the new Frost Maiden. Irene and Sven turned to stare. A second, smaller blast by the buffet table followed. Snorri was gone. Unease rippled through the room. Sorceress Lorraine joined the huddle around the Frost Maiden.

Sven strode towards the water mage. "What's going on?"

The sorcerer shook his head. The two men, fire and water wizard together, watched the whispered conference with identical frowns. Then Sorceress Lorraine glided towards them.

"Charles," she said, "Our guild house in Blacksburg is under attack, with several people reported injured or dead."

"I'm on my way." Water flowed across the floor. He stepped into it, and was gone.

The gathered crowd made a show of resuming its merriment, but the bubbling chatter had given way to nervous whispers and furtive glances towards the two warlocks. Dancing resumed. Sven and Irene joined in, without evident enthusiasm on either side.

Sven frowned at her. "I have a bad feeling about this. If things turn nasty, go back to the Fortress and stay there. Don't do anything heroic."

"Me? I'm a coward. Why would I—"

"Don't fool yourself. You're no coward. You're as much a hero as—"

"Don't be ridiculous." She pulled from his grasp. "You're the hero. You'll go wherever the Fire Guild sends you, won't you?"

"I have to. Irene—"

She stalked away, tossing over her shoulder, "If you get yourself killed, don't expect me to ever speak to you again."

"Irene—"

Warlock Quicksilver disappeared in a quiet tongue of fire. Lucinda ran towards the two Frost Maidens. Sven swore under his breath and followed. Irene ran after them.

"…another attack," Lucinda was saying. "On a Water Guild house. Jean was right; this can't be coincidence. There has to be a conspiracy at work. Tell the Water Guild to go to earth—we don't know where they'll attack next." Her voice rose. She was ashen against her wine-dark velvet. "The Fortress is shutting up—we can't go home. Oh, dear God. We can't go home!"

Mother Celeste swept past Sven and wrapped an arm around Lucinda's shoulders. "Stop it. We need you sensible. I will not let you panic. Hear me?"

Lucinda hid her face in trembling hands. "Yes, ma'am. Sorry. Eleanor…"

"Hush. She's already at work."

The Frost Maiden sat rigid with her hands on her knees, staring into space. Mother Celeste steered Lucinda through the agitated crowd towards the fire, talking to her in a low voice. Sven followed.

Sorcerer Charles reappeared, carrying a girl drenched in blood. Arturos followed a moment later, carrying two more wounded witches, one in each arm. Healers surged towards them as Arturos bellowed orders. Irene backed under the balcony.

Master Duncan joined her. "With the whole Earth Guild on hand, I figure they'd tell me to get out of their iced way if I offered to help."

She said, "At least they wouldn't ridicule your offer."

Arturos headed towards them. "You, Duncan—forget what I said about not playing Soldiers and Wizards. Any man you can deal with tonight is one I won't have to. Hotfoot it home, raise the alarm, and block the roads to the Crystal Palace."

"You want me to talk folk in Abertee into fighting for the Water Guild? On Yule? Are you nuts?"

Arturos clamped a hand on the smith's shoulder. "I am not nuts and don't give me any backtalk. These attacks aren't angry commoners running riot—they're organised squads of guards with the worst nobles leading them. We've got a full-scale war on our hands. Tell your folk you're doing it because I ordered you to. Tell them they're not defending the Water Guild, they're defending Frankland, or that the Scorching Times are coming back, and Abertee'll get scorched if the nobles attack the Crystal Palace. Hell, I don't care what you tell them. Just do it."

"Yes, sir."

"And when Lucinda—the Locksmith—when she's Fire Warlock, don't give her any backtalk either." Arturos thrust out his other hand. "Sorry to do this to you, Duncan. I've got to say, it's been nice knowing you."

The smith looked at the Fire Warlock's outstretched hand for a moment, then reached for it, and pulled the other man into a hug that would have done an anaconda proud. With a solid thump between the Warlock's shoulder blades, he let go and ran for the tunnels.

Irene yanked on Arturos's sleeve. He leaned down; she kissed his cheek. He saluted, and ducked into the fireplace.

"Mrs van Gelder?"

Alexander, an Earth Guild child in tow, dodged between running wizards and came to a breathless stop beside her. "I can't stand this. I'm going to the palace, like Miranda said. I should have done it already. Mrs van Gelder, my father trusts the Air Guild more than he does the Fire Guild."

Irene backed against the wall with her hands over her mouth as this terrible child said, "Come with me, please, and convince my father to take the oath."

Trapped

Alexander, erect and rigid, waited for an answer.

"No one listens to me," Irene croaked.

"The warlocks do, and I do. You're wise."

"Are you ordering me to go, Your Highness? The king's advisors hate me."

His shoulders drooped. "No, ma'am, I won't order you. Warlock Quicksilver said I shouldn't order anyone other than guards into danger. He said asking for help would have better results with everyone else." He turned away. "I'll go by myself."

The quaver in his voice tore at her conscience, but she couldn't abandon the girls. *Promise me*, Oliver had said, *you'll stand up for them.*

Rubbish. Above everything else, what they needed—what all Frankland's children needed—was a king who would take the Great Oath and end this class warfare. Until then, her children would be targets for Marie Richardson's revenge whenever they left the Fortress.

Warlock Quicksilver had said Alexander was unshielded. She, the adult, had no right to let a child, especially one she owed a debt to, walk into danger alone, and aside from her private, petty concerns, accompanying the prince to confront his father made good sense. If they could persuade King Stephen, it would be worth risking her life. Sven's warning and her own terror were insufficient reasons for refusing. Winifred's prediction of her death in the Fortress eliminated that excuse. Or did it? Dying in the Fortress didn't eliminate the possibility of receiving fatal wounds elsewhere and being carried home to die.

Her body caught up with the prince while her mind was still making excuses. "I'll go with you, Your Highness," she heard her voice say.

The Earth Guild child led them through a tunnel and within minutes, while Irene's intellect was still coming to grips with her conscience's decision, they were following a shocked servant through the palace. They skirted a courtyard where squads of guards were forming into marching order. Alexander found the sight cheering. "Father will help the Fire Warlock stop the riots," he said. Irene could not share his optimism.

King Stephen scowled at them. He dismissed the servants carrying his helmet and sword with a wave of a gauntleted hand. "You're timing is terrible," he said to his son. "We should have guessed the Fire Warlock would send you to disrupt our plans."

"The Fire Warlock didn't send me. It was my idea to come. If you'll listen to me, we can use magic to stop the riots, and—"

"What riots?"

Irene's hand covered her mouth, stifling a scream.

Alexander stammered, "The…the attack on the Water Guild in Blacksburg, and…"

The king drew himself up, chin in the air. "That was not a riot. The Black Duke on our orders led a military strike against them. We are teaching that frostbitten Guild a long overdue lesson. When we've captured the Crystal Palace they'll take orders from us from now on."

Irene fell on her knees, babbling. Alexander yelled. The king shouted orders. The king's personal guard swept through the room, manhandling the prince and Irene, hauling them away.

At the door, they came face to face with her tormenter from Airvale, the new White Duke. His eyes bulged. He stabbed a finger in her face, and shouted, "You! I'll get you, you brazen viper."

The king's men saved her the need to answer as they hustled their two prisoners along the corridor and up a flight of stairs. The men gripping her arms were not unkind, but they left bruises.

The men dragging Alexander were not so gentle. Alexander fought, and the captain, a minor lord, cuffed him across the face. The boy yelled. The captain said, "Stop that noise. You're not getting what you deserve, you traitor. You're shielded—I can't do you any real damage, and we both know it." He hit the prince again, harder, for good measure.

The men dragged them through a room filled with guards, then shoved them through a set of ornate double doors. The doors slammed shut behind them, and they turned to pound on the doors, yelling.

Behind them, a woman said, "Brendan, darling, what are you doing here?"

The tiny princess clung to her nursemaid's skirts and watched Irene with enormous eyes. The child reminded her so much of Gillian she had to turn away.

"We are prisoners," Queen Marguerite said. "The dukes have been pressing the king to charge me with treason for disobeying his orders, but he won't. Stephen would rather destroy the Water Guild than me. We are safe enough for tonight."

A violent argument playing out between King Stephen and the White Duke in the courtyard below, with the duke shaking his fist at the queen's apartment, led Irene to doubt her prediction.

The queen took her son's hands in hers, looking him in the eye. "Brendan, my son, we must be prepared. You may be king before the night is over. Are you ready to be king?"

The prince paled. The king was an idiot for condoning an attack on the Water Guild, but his life wasn't in danger, was it? Would the Fire Warlock call the lightning down on a king? Irene leaned on the window frame for support.

A bugle sounded. The massed guards began marching from the courtyard.

Irene said, "Where are they bound? The king said the Crystal Palace, but that's across the channel and hundreds of miles north."

The queen and the prince joined her at the window. The queen said, "Armed men from all over Frankland are converging on the Crystal Palace. They're using the Earth Guild's tunnels to get there. An earth wizard drew maps, and breached the quarantine."

A nearby chair caught Irene when her knees buckled. She leaned her head against the wall, torn between desires to rage and to laugh.

Alexander evidently did not find the situation funny. "That's stupid. They can't. They'll all die."

"I know that," Irene said, "And so do you, but few others do. The Earth Guild Council have not allowed the truth about the tunnels to spread."

Alexander said, "Mother, don't you have a tunnel of your own?"

"No longer. The earth wizard found my tunnel and closed it, and

Stephen took away the witch who'd cut it."

"Why didn't the Fire Warlock know? He's supposed to know everything."

"I've wondered that for weeks, too. The White Duchess—Marie Richardson, that is—told Stephen they could keep it secret, but it didn't seem possible."

Ice water flowed through Irene's veins. The warlocks had worried about a conspiracy after the October riots, but she had not believed it.

She put her head down in her hands. No, the truth was, she hadn't wanted to believe. It made no sense. There was a way to hide a conspiracy, but Marie Richardson, level two witch, couldn't do it. An enormous amount of power, power only an enchanter or enchantress could command, would be required to keep a secret this vast.

At the trial, Winifred had floated down from the top tier in Justice Hall to stand with the White Duchess—an air witch, but a poor one. One who was no rival to an enchantress.

The Air Guild Council's older members had never done Irene any favours, but they had reputations as honourable people, and the demands of the guild and the quarantine had been exhausting them. They wouldn't notice Winifred, with Irene's spell for finding a charter, pretending to spend her time on the search while conserving her power for something else.

But why would Winifred be involved in this? She wasn't a noblewoman. She didn't care about politics. All she cared about was wizards.

Queen Marguerite clapped her hands to her mouth and retreated from the window, gasping. The king was no longer in sight; the White Duke had ordered the last squad to do an about-face, and was pointing towards the queen's window.

A thunderous pounding on the doors to the outer chamber accompanied shouts. "This is the White Duke. I order you to hand over the air witch."

The captain of the queen's guards returned the shout. "The king said to keep her here until he comes back. We take orders from no one but the king."

"Then we'll come get her!" A ferocious pounding began. Irene cowered behind the thick bedpost, and flinched with every blow on the outer door. This palace's architect had not had defence in mind; that door would fail before long.

"I hate this." The prince turned a pleading face to her. "If I take the oath when I'm king, will things go right again?"

"It will take the country a long time to heal, but yes, Your Highness, it will put us on the right path again."

"Then I'll do it." He lifted his chin and inhaled deeply. "I won't do what the warlocks want. I'll take the more powerful one. But I will be king for all the people. I swear it."

Irene gaped at him. He was sworn; he had to keep this promise.

The noise coming from the outer chamber tripled in volume. The door had been breached. Men yelled. Steel clanged on steel.

She knelt before the prince. "Your Highness, call on the Fire Warlock for help. You've heard the old stories—you know the words."

"But I'm not king. I'm a prince, and the Fire Warlock's busy."

"You're royal, and the heir to the throne. You have the power. The Fire Warlock will come if you call. He has to."

If he didn't come, they were doomed.

The double doors burst open. The White Duke's men drove the guards into the breach. The queen screamed and clutched at her son. The White Duke glanced at Irene and then at the windows in the outer wall.

She screamed at the prince, "Call for help!"

The windows bulged as a blast of air hit them, then shattered in a hail of glass. The bed provided some shelter, but the windblown glass swirled around it, and flew through the hangings, hunting Irene. She curled into a ball, burying her face. The fragments, small at first, sliced into her exposed arms. Larger splinters followed, scoring her scalp and carving into her shoulders and back like knives. A dagger of a shard lanced into her thigh, and she screamed. Another one stabbed her shoulder.

Throughout, the prince was shouting, a weak treble at first, inaudible over the noise of the wind and clashing swords, but quickly becoming stronger and deeper, more resonant. "By the power of the people vested in me, I order you to stop. These women are under my protection. I call on the Fire Guild—put down your arms or die!"

Swirling shards bounced off Irene with a clatter. Seconds later, flames engulfed them as the very air caught fire.

Airhead

Lucinda and the two sorceresses were issuing orders from Mother Celeste's drawing room when the call for help blasted through Lucinda's mind. She plunged into the fire mid-sentence, emerging into a maelstrom of fire, wind, and flying glass as all four Fire Warlocks—past, present, and two future—poured fire into the queen's apartment. Faster than speech, four minds met. She grabbed Alexander and Queen Marguerite, and pulled.

They tumbled out of the fireplace into the Warren. René followed a heartbeat later with the princess and her nurse. The gathered witches and wizards had barely had time to register Lucinda's disappearance. Mother Celeste shouldered them aside to wrap her arms around the refugees. Alexander twisted out of Lucinda's grasp, shouting. "Mrs van Gelder's still there. You have to help her."

"Quicksilver's taking her to the healers," Lucinda said. "Why were you there? What happened?"

It took some time, and a good deal of Mother Celeste's calming influence, before they told a semi-coherent story. When Lucinda had heard enough to convince her the attack on the queen was a combination of bad luck and poor timing, unrelated to the evening's other events, she left them in the Earth Guild's competent hands and returned to relaying orders.

Despite her arms shielding her closed eyes, white lightning dazzled Irene. Scorching flames licked her skin. She wept from pain and terror, the glass knives digging deeper into skin and muscle with each racking sob.

Warlock Quicksilver thundered in her head. *Do not move!*

Lightheaded with relief, she relinquished muscular control, and let his magic hold her rigid. After an eternity lasting only seconds, the flames died, leaving darkness and a profound silence.

It couldn't be silent. The blast had deafened her.

Glass fragments on her skin rose like a swarm of gnats. Longer shards began to slide out. The dagger in her shoulder caught on bone, snapped, and stabbed afresh. She fainted. Awareness returned with intense cold. Blood and tears poured down her face.

Hands slipped under her arms and lifted. Quicksilver, his face a mask of fury, supported her on one side. On the other, a royal guard turned his head away and vomited.

The outer wall had vanished; sleet poured in on the wreckage. Lightning flashes lit the burnt-out shell of the queen's once-luxurious bedroom. Prince Brendan and Queen Marguerite were not there. Several dazed guards huddled together; charred bodies sprawled around them.

An instant later, flames rose. The wreckage vanished, replaced by the Warren's great hall, swarming with distraught healers and stunned casualties. Quicksilver snapped out orders her ears couldn't hear. An earth wizard cupped his hands over her ears, and her hearing returned. A witch dispelled the blood and slapped bandages on the wounds in her shoulder and thigh. Another smeared ointment on her arms and scalp. Someone else shoved a mug of something warm and delicious, smelling of cinnamon and nutmeg, into her hands. She gulped the potion, and the throbbing in her back and shoulders subsided into a dull ache.

With the most pressing of her bodily needs tended to, she began to recover her wits. "Where's Warlock Quicksilver?"

A witch shrugged. "Gone."

"Where's the Locksmith?"

Another shrug. "Don't know. Why?"

"I have news to tell them. Now." Irene stood up.

"Sit down," the senior witch snapped. "We're not done with you yet. You're still bleeding."

"It can wait."

She grabbed at Irene's bodice. "Sit down, you silly airhead." The new dress, already shredded, ripped. The silk slid down her arms, exposing her corset.

"Uh, sorry," the earth witch said, "I didn't mean…"

Irene stalked away, fuming. She looked more like a harlot—or a noblewoman—than a respectable witch. She yanked a blanket from a stack on a table and threw it over her shoulders. A Fire Eater threading through the crowd caught her eye; she followed him to the command centre where the generals were marshalling their troops.

Lucinda huddled over the fire in the Earth Mother's drawing room. The Frost Maiden Emerita directed two porters in the placement of a large, freestanding mirror. The Earth Mother was calming the agitated queen and prince. Irene retreated to the far end, out of the way of a scurrying stream of witches and wizards, and leaned against the wall. The royals were uninjured. The queen would have told the witches about the men massing to destroy the Water Guild. Irene could return to the Great Hall and have her injuries tended to.

Alexander careened towards her. "Mrs van Gelder, help!" He skidded to a stop, staring. "Couldn't the healers help? You look…"

"Bloody awful," she said. With a split lip and blackening eye, he didn't look good either. "What's the matter?"

"We can't tell anyone about the army in the tunnels or the danger to the Crystal Palace. Lies come out of my mouth. You have to tell them."

Liquid sloshed from the mug the healer had given her. "I have to?"

"You can, can't you?"

She opened her mouth, then closed it and swallowed. Licked dry lips. Her breathing sounded ragged to her own ears. What happens when talents in other guilds break their oaths? Do fire witches drown? Do water witches burn? What even frightens earth witches?

Don't be ridiculous; no one ever breaks their oath. The Fire Warlock would find out, soon enough, about the threat to the Crystal Palace. If that was all…

"Please." Alexander tugged her into the drawing room. "You have to tell."

Promise me, Oliver had said, you'll do what's best for the girls.

Spilling Air Guild secrets could kill her. Not true; Winifred had predicted Irene's death in the Fortress, and she was in the Warren. She had no excuse, but her guess about a conspiracy still made no sense. Winifred despised politics; she cared about men. Wizards. But the wizards she wanted in the Fire Guild had spurned her.

She hated the Water Guild. Had always hated the Water Guild, for as long as Irene could remember.

Pieces of the puzzle shifted, rearranged themselves, snapped together. Irene slammed the mug down on an end table. "Make that an order, Your Highness."

His forehead puckered. "What? But you said…"

"Wait." She gulped four big mouthfuls of the healer's potion, and set the mug down. It was still full. "Order me to renounce the Air Guild, Your Highness. I'm not strong enough by myself."

"Oh!" His eyes widened. "Mrs van Gelder, I… We order you to renounce the Air Guild."

Irene swam through air as thick as molasses, and could not draw breath. She elbowed through the crowd, Alexander following in her wake. Even in her frantic state of mind, enough self-detachment remained to amuse her; her mother would be appalled by her bad manners.

Lucinda's back was to her. Irene's chest burned, her vision darkened as she lunged for the other woman's sleeve. Lucinda turned, her expression changing from annoyance to alarm.

"Irene, what's wrong?"

"Fire Warlock…" An invisible troll yanked on Irene's corset laces. "Needs to know." The room spun; her vision darkened. Bright orange letters streamed into the gap between them: Air Guild Conspiracy.

The troll's fist slammed into Irene's back, knocking more air from her chest than she would have believed possible, and the world went dark.

Counterattack

"**B**reathe in, damn you."

The troll's fists constricted Irene's rib cage. Her ribs creaked from the strain of obeying the order.

"Breathe out." The air rushed out in a gust. "Not so fast. Breathe in. And stop bleeding, for God's sake."

The disembodied voice, time after time, ordered Irene to breathe. Her vision cleared. She lay on her back before the hearth. The Earth Mother, her face glistening with sweat, knelt with her hands on Irene's ribs. "Breathe in," she ordered. "Breathe out."

Others crowded around—Lucinda, Arturos, and a ring of ghostly faces. The two warlocks were flipping through stacks of papers. "It's here." Lucinda sounded on the verge of tears. "I've seen it. I just don't know where."

Irene wiggled her fingers. A breeze lifted papers and carried them past her face. One, two, three, dozen pages, then bright pink flashed past. She snatched, and shoved the page under Arturos' nose.

"By the authority invested in me," he read, "as Fire Warlock, if any oaths or spells binding you constitute threats to Frankland's peace, I declare those oaths and spells null and void."

The troll released its grip. She wheezed like a leaky bellows, drawing in lungfuls of life.

"Great smoking piles of dragon dung!" Arturos snarled, flinging the papers into Lucinda's lap. "Why can't I say 'You're free', and be done?"

"King Stephen," Irene croaked. "Army…Crystal Palace…through the tunnels."

"How? They'd not—"

"Earth wizard made a map."

"Frostbitten rocks!" Shocked faces turned towards the Earth Mother. Irene cringed away from her savage expression, but her eyes were focused far in the distance. The floor shook, the wooden panelling reverberated with her voice. "When I lay my hands on that cloud-addled pebble-hearted renegade, I will gut him alive and feed him his own entrails."

"Celeste!" The queen rapped the Earth Mother on the shoulder. "Stop that."

Mother Celeste refocused on the staring faces. "And now, I will shut up before I embarrass myself any further."

A grin flitted across Arturos's face. Irene wasn't sure she hadn't imagined it. He leaned over her. "Who's behind the conspiracy?"

"Air Guild kept secrets." Breath came more easily now, but her throat and chest burned. "Built hidden channels into the Air Office."

"Son of a bitch! You mean any of you lot—sorry, them—could…"

"No. Has to be council member. Winifred. Trying to kill you."

For several heartbeats the two warlocks gaped. Then Arturos surged to his feet, bellowing. "That two-faced little weasel. I should've given her what she deserved ten years ago. I'm gonna…" Flame sprouted.

"No." Lucinda and Irene grabbed for him through the fire. Irene screamed, but hung on. Mother Celeste grabbed her, healing the burns, and swearing.

The flames died. "Drown you both. Let go."

"No," Lucinda said. "She's ours."

"Listen," Irene wheezed. "Keeping secrets is Winifred's strong suit. If you burn her, the channels will disappear and you won't find out who else is involved or their other targets."

Arturos glowed in orange and red; fire danced along his arms and around his head, and heat radiated out from him. "I'll get it out of her."

"No, you won't," Lucinda said. "You can't believe anything she says. She'll tell you one truth after another and it all adds up to a bald-faced lie."

"Air Enchanter," Irene said. "He can spy on the channels without letting them know."

Arturos said, "That conceited bastard treats her like a teacher's pet. He won't listen to me, and I'd rather punch his face in."

"He'll listen to me." The Frost Maiden Emerita leaned into the circle. "My people are dying."

"Fine. Go."

She disappeared. Water splashed Irene's face, and hissed into steam where it lapped at Arturos' feet.

Lucinda said, "If I put a lock on Winifred so she can't use her magic, will the channels disappear?"

Irene said, "Not if the lock only affects future magic use."

"Right. I can do that." Lucinda's eyes lost focus.

Irene grabbed someone's arm and pulled herself upright. The Earth Mother tried to push her back down. Irene shoved her hand away.

The Earth Mother barked, "Lie down. You're not fit to move."

"I didn't hold onto him just to keep those channels open. I'm going with Lucinda."

Irene focused on the boy whose arm she'd yanked on. Alexander. Frostbite. She'd probably broken half a dozen royal protocol rules. She pushed on his shoulders, stood, and tugged the blanket into place. Her torso was a single, massive bruise.

Lucinda said, "Ready?"

"Ready." Irene grabbed Lucinda's outstretched hand, and followed her into the fireplace.

"**D**uncan, you mangy cur," Master Walter yelled. "You didn't say we were coming here."

"If I had, would you have come?"

"No, frost it."

The two dozen men, all he'd had time to rouse between Nettleton and Crossroads, had gone through the tunnel before the ones in the lead realised they'd come out in Quayside. Six had bows, the rest carried hayforks and hammers. Not much good against shielded and mounted aristos armed with swords. Duncan didn't care to think about that.

"Mildred," he yelled over his shoulder. "Close and lock that tunnel door."

"Aye," she called. "I'm heading to Edinburgh."

If Edinburgh couldn't spare a healer, they'd be in deep trouble. They'd need more than one healer before the night was over.

The men turned on him, yelling. He shoved through them and they followed him onto the coast road. An hour short of low tide, there was no moon. A few glimmers southeast marked the town of Quays, but the

Crystal Palace was a coal-dark blot where the stars met the sea.

"Listen, you lot," he shouted. "We're here on the Fire Warlock's orders, so no backtalk. That thing out there is no threat to us tonight." He told them what was going on further south, and what the Fire Warlock had said.

"I don't like it, Dunc—er, Master Duncan," Cousin Jock said. "I don't want—"

"I don't give a rat's arse what you like, or what you want, Jock. We're not here on holiday. Frankland's at war, and whose side would you rather be on, the Water Guild's or the aristos'?"

"Neither."

"Too bad. Shut up. We're—"

Billy Martin tugged at Duncan's sleeve. "They're coming, Master Duncan. I can hear 'em."

The men went quiet. Horses, lots of them, clattered on paving stones. Torches raced towards them from the south.

"*Frostbite!*" Duncan said. "They're going to beat us to the causeway. Get moving. Billy, stay at the rear. Prod anybody not moving fast enough."

Billy's teeth showed as he brought his fork down and waved it in Jock's direction. Doug was already running. Duncan ran, and hoped the rest would follow.

The lead horses were on the causeway before they got close enough to pick out one rider from another. Duncan stopped and nocked an arrow. "Aim for the wizards," he said, and started shooting.

"How do we know—?"

"Hats," Doug grunted, and let fly. "Not helmets."

The riders never saw them. They punched a few holes in the line, but there were too many. Horsemen were still coming up the road when the leaders had crossed the causeway and were firing the nearest boats.

The thunder of hooves was lost in a rising roar. From both sides of the causeway, dark walls as tall as church towers rose, blotting out the stars. For a moment Duncan stared, wondering, and then forgot the riders, the Frost Maiden, the Fire Warlock—everything but saving his own skin. He grabbed little Billy Martin by his collar and ran for high ground. He couldn't hear his own screaming over the roar.

The two walls met with a boom that shook the ground. Moments later the first wave hit him between the shoulder blades. He went under, and was dragged face down over shingle. He fought to his feet, and came up in froth full of screaming men and horses.

The water rushed back down the beach and he went down again, rolling in the surf. Salt water filled his head, and he was sure he would drown, but then the water picked him up, carried him ashore, and spat him out on solid ground. He struggled to his knees, coughing and blowing, as the waves tossed horses and the other men from Abertee ashore like driftwood.

Panicked horses running for the hills kept him jumping. When the stampede was over, Duncan counted heads with his teeth chattering. They were lucky—they hadn't lost any men, despite getting kicked, stepped on, knocked down, and scraped raw. They sorted themselves out with the strongest carrying those that couldn't walk, and staggered towards Quayside.

Billy Martin had been mangled the worst. Duncan stooped beside him. "This is going to hurt."

Billy said, "Duncan, the next time you ring the alarm bell, I'm sticking my fingers in my ears and pretending I didn't hear it."

"Can't blame you, lad. You've done your share."

Billy groaned and went limp when Duncan lifted him. Duncan took one long look down the shore and muttered, "I hope the Fire Warlock won't mind us taking care of our own before we go looking for aristos."

A woman's voice beside him said, "There are no survivors."

He yelped and whipped around. "Frost—sorry, ma'am. Your Wisdom. Ma'am, you could scare the sh— You could scare a man to death doing that."

"I beg your pardon. I did not intend to frighten you." She glided along beside him as he trudged towards the inn. "I came to thank you and your men for protecting my people and my home. Tell them the coming year will be a golden one for the valiant men of Abertee. Your crops shall flourish, your herds shall grow fat, and your craftsmen shall not want for work."

"Thank you, ma'am, but you didn't need us."

"No, but neither you nor the Fire Warlock knew that, nor was I certain what would happen. Let your men return home. The townsmen will gather the horses."

"Ma'am, you said 'No survivors.' But their shields…"

"The Water Office has executed summary justice. The Fire Office's shields do not protect against execution for treason."

"But if they were obeying the king's orders…"

Against starlight off the water, he saw her head shake, her shoulders rise. With her arm gone the shrug looked unnatural, lopsided. He winced and looked away.

She said, "I do not fully understand either. Perhaps because you broke the bonds between the Water Office and the king. Perhaps there is another explanation. There is much magic at work tonight. Frankland reeks of it, and the war is not over yet."

She disappeared. Duncan hurried for the inn, and warmth.

Winifred's Secret

Lucinda and Irene emerged from a fireplace into a draughty, single-roomed structure, large and high ceilinged, as rustic cabins go. Across a table strewn with dirty dishes, Winifred and Marie Richardson stood with their backs to the fire, studying a map of Frankland pinned to the wall. They whirled. For an instant, terror of the snarling aristocrat washed over Irene. It vanished, leaving her gasping, while the cringing ex-duchess retreated into a corner.

A ladderback chair beside the hearth offered support for Irene's swaying body. The Earth Mother had been right; she was too battered for this.

After one startled glance, Winifred had concentrated on Lucinda. Now she recoiled, her eyes flying open.

"I've hidden your magic," Lucinda said.

Winifred bolted for the outer door, and was swinging it open when Lucinda said, "You can't fly."

Winifred stopped dead in a blast of frigid air. Outside, a black void gaped. She had boasted about her private aerie that only a level five witch or wizard could enter or leave, once the autumn snows fell. She slammed the door and swung around, screaming, "Get out of my house."

"You're in no position to make demands," Lucinda said. "Your house, your goods, your life—they're all forfeit. I'm charging you with treason and attempted murder."

"Not attempted," Irene said. "Murder."

The cowering woman in the corner shrieked. Winifred turned and stared. "What did you do to her?"

"Mirror spell," Lucinda said. "She's scaring herself, and this time I have no sympathy for her."

Winifred bared her teeth. "Fine. I don't care. She's not pleasant company. But I do care for my privacy. Your blather about treason is nonsense, and you're trespassing. Get out of my house."

"Never, ever, lie to a warlock, Winifred," Irene said.

Winifred seemed to notice her for the first time. "What happened to you? You look like a mouse the cat mauled."

"Are you surprised I'm siding with the Fire Guild?"

Lucinda said, "We know about the covert Air Guild Channels. We know about the conspiracy to destroy the Water Guild—"

The woman in the corner shrieked again. "The king. His orders—"

"Shut up," Winifred said.

"Talk," Lucinda said. "As the Fire Warlock's representative, I order you, talk."

"The king gave us orders." The words were barely intelligible through sobs. "He won't let the Frost Maiden freeze us."

"No? The Fire Office won't let treason go unpunished, even if the king would. Assuming Stephen survives the night. If he doesn't..."

"If he doesn't," Irene said, "King Brendan will swear the Great Oath. He has no sympathy for his father's foolishness."

The ex-duchess turned wide, staring eyes at Irene. She jabbed a finger at Winifred. "It was her idea."

"Shut up!" Winifred strode across the room and around the table. The duchess scrabbled around the other side and ran for the door. She flung it open and sprinted through. She seemed to hang in mid-air for an instant, then vanished. In Winifred's cabin the three women stood frozen, listening to her extended scream, abruptly silenced.

Lucinda exhaled a long sigh. "Well, that's a relief. Putting a duchess, even a former duchess, on trial for treason could be dangerous. A commoner, on the other hand—even an enchantress—"

"You're mad," Winifred said. "I have no idea what Marie was involved in. You can't use what she said in court, because everyone knows someone being tortured will say anything to stop the torment. You haven't a shred of evidence, and never will. As for secret channels, that's rubbish. Ask anyone in the Air Guild. They'll tell you."

"Anyone except me," Irene said. "You shouldn't have alienated me from the Air Guild, Winifred."

Her hands twitched convulsively. "What are you talking about, Irene?

I'm your best friend in the guild. You'll never desert me."

"I already did. I've renounced the Air Guild. All four guilds now know its secrets."

Winifred blanched. "You? You're scared of your own shadow. You don't have the nerve."

"You gave me the courage. We were in the Warren, and you said I'd die in the Fortress."

The other woman's face went blank, then livid. "I shouldn't have spared you the nasty details. You'll—"

'Shut up!" Lucinda barked. Winifred went rigid and silent, nostrils flaring.

Irene said, "Thank you. I've no interest in anything she has to say—ever."

"Me, neither. Except I did want to ask *why*."

"She wouldn't give you an answer you could believe."

"True."

"But I can guess. You hate the Fire Guild, don't you, Winifred? You couldn't seduce either fire wizard you wanted. You didn't relinquish hope for Arturos until he became Fire Warlock. When you realised you could never have him you decided to exact revenge for spurning you."

Winifred ignored Lucinda's expression of revulsion. She stared at Irene, breathing hard, fists clenched.

"And you hate the Water Guild, too, don't you?" Irene had so far been on solid ground. Now she ventured out into thin air. "You never said why. Did you, years ago, foresee your own death by freezing? You would do what you damned well pleased until then. When you saw an opportunity for revenge on both guilds, you grabbed it. If it harmed innocent people, you wouldn't care. You never have."

Lucinda's eyes bulged. "She foresaw her own death for treason and didn't try to avoid it?"

Winifred edged closer, snarling. Irene slid her hands down the posts of the chair to let them rest on the lowermost rail. "The treason didn't matter. Her life has been forfeit for years. Granny Verna's death on the stairs was no accident."

Winifred snatched a butcher's knife from the table and lunged. Irene swung the chair up. Lucinda slammed into Winifred from the other side. The enchantress hit the chair full on, knocking Irene into the wall. The butcher knife clattered onto the hearth. Winifred sprawled on the floor, moaning.

Irene set the chair down and leaned on it. Her ribs ached. The wound in her shoulder throbbed.

Lucinda dusted off her hands. "All those games of Soldiers and Wizards were good for something. Are you all right, Irene?"

"Will be," she gasped.

"Then let's go. I'll send someone to fetch her after this is all over, if we survive. If we don't..." Lucinda nodded at the inadequate stack of firewood beside the open door. "She may freeze to death anyway." Her smile was ferocious. "Can't say I'd care."

Guildless

Matt, Fire Eater, died defending two screaming water witches. Lucinda wanted to hide in a corner and cry, but didn't have the time. She would weep for him later, she promised herself, shoving aside the images of his hacked body.

The generals huddled together for comfort. Alexander was wedged between his mother and Lucinda on a sofa shoved close to the fire. Nearby, Eleanor and Lorraine directed and comforted their guild through their magic mirrors. Enchanter Paul, ashen-faced and shaking, sat with them, meekly carrying out their orders.

Lucinda conjured images in the fire, and a small army of witches, wizards, and royal guards paraded through the sitting room to receive their orders. Warlocks popped in and out of the fire. After the third time, Queen Marguerite stopped screaming.

Alexander listened without comment as his mother issued instructions in the king's name for churches and guildhalls to open their doors and take people in. She avoided anything that could be construed as taking sides, but she could, and did, find shelter for the poor mundane souls left homeless by the fires.

Warlock Flint walked through the fire into an open plaza with his back turned to a line of archers. They shot him dead for his arrogance. Lucinda was furious with him for letting himself be taken by surprise. She wanted that disgrace to the Fire Guild revived so she could torch him for his stupidity.

She had just abandoned her third fruitless search for news of King Stephen when Father Martin came in and dropped on one knee before Queen Marguerite. "Your Majesty, we found King Stephen. I am very sorry. He died in one of the traps."

Her hands were clenched together, the knuckles white, but her voice, though low, did not quaver. "Thank you. I am not surprised." That was all she said, then.

The rebellion completed its collapse as the sky lightened. A handful of troublesome nobles had been herded into the Fortress's dungeon or the Crystal Palace's prison, but most were dead or dying—burnt, drowned, scalded, or caught in the traps. Mother Celeste went with the two sorceresses to survey the wreckage of the Water Guildhalls. The flood tide of incoming wounded slowed to a trickle. Bandaged fire wizards stumbled into the parlour one by one, settling down behind Lucinda to watch in grim silence. Sunbeam collapsed into a wing chair and snored within seconds. Tom, Matt's best mate, sat with his elbows on his knees, staring at the carpet. René lay against Lucinda's legs on the hearthrug, pretending to sleep to hide his tears.

Queen Marguerite consented to let an earth wizard carry her son— asleep for some hours already, despite manly efforts to stay awake for the duration—to a guest room a few doors away. She saw him safely settled with two trusted guards on watch and fire and earth witches on call nearby, and only then did she allow herself to weep.

Lucinda would be desolate if she lost Jean. Her heart ached for the queen, but she could not find it in her to grieve for the king.

All Irene wanted was rest. When she and Lucinda had returned to the parlour in the Warren, the Earth Mother was gone, overseeing the Earth Guild from the Great Hall. Irene shrugged and settled onto a sofa to one side of the fireplace, sipping from the mug that never emptied or grew cold, no matter how much healer's draught she drank. The pains in her shoulders and ribs eased, and finally vanished.

She huddled under her blanket, watching the images Lucinda conjured in the fire. An air wizard threw a knife at Sven, slicing through his leg. She splashed brown liquid across green carpet, and wondered how she could repay the earth wizard that tended him, at risk to his own life. For a long time afterwards, tears slid unchecked down her cheeks and into her mug.

That interminable night gave her plenty of time to reflect on her actions. Winifred would no longer poison her relationship with the Air Guild, but

Irene had pushed the fracture to complete breakage. She had become a witch without a guild, an abomination that had no place in Frankland.

Warlock Quicksilver eased onto the sofa beside her with a deep sigh. A servant offered him coffee and a beef pie, and he thanked her with a smile.

"Even a warlock must occasionally sit and rest," he said, downing the steaming coffee in a few gulps. "And I want to thank you for what you have done."

It wasn't fair to burden him with her trivial problem, but Irene's confusion spilled out. "Your Wisdom, Winifred once predicted I would die in the Fortress."

"Yes, Lucinda told me. Under its protection, you should experience a natural death of old age. Do not let her spite dishearten you."

"I would like to live there, sir. It feels like home, but…"

He studied her for a moment. "If you fear being a burden on the Fire Guild, your concern is ungrounded. For what you have done for Frankland tonight, you may, if you wish, live the rest of your life in idle luxury in the Fortress's finest apartment, and the Fire Guild will still be in your debt."

"Thank you, Your Wisdom, but no work would be as bad for me as the wrong work."

"Then we shall give you suitable work, as much of it as you wish. That, my dear, is a promise."

"But, sir, will the Fortress let me in?"

His brow furrowed. "Why would it not?"

"Because I've renounced the Air Guild."

"Ah…indeed. No, it will not tolerate an unaffiliated witch." He frowned, and finished his pie without speaking. "It would not do for you to rejoin the Air Guild."

"No, sir."

His eyes gleamed. "Nevertheless, you need not be guildless long. Leave that to me." Rising, he made her an elegant bow before vanishing in the fireplace.

The sun was well above the horizon on that bitter winter morning, the year's shortest day, when a loud voice demanded, "Is Irene here?"

Sven, pale and fierce, stood in the doorway with a tight grip on each doorjamb. "I heard she—oh, there you are." He hobbled towards her, leaning against the wall for support. "There's a rumour you'd been hurt. I've been out of my mind with worry. What happened? You look…"

"I'm fine." She gazed into the mug. "You should know better than to pay attention to rumours."

"You're right; I should." He pulled a footstool close and eased onto it. "Thank God you stayed here."

"You shouldn't have worried about me." She waved at his bandaged leg. "You had enough to worry about."

"This? A scratch. You should know better than to pay attention to rumours."

"It wasn't a scratch, and it wasn't a rumour. I watched blood fountain out."

"Burn it, I didn't want you to see that." He threw a glare at Lucinda's back. "You're still talking to me."

"You're not dead."

"Yet." He smiled. "But I am a fire wizard, Irene. I can't avoid trouble. You can." He put his hand on her shoulder, and she flinched. He snatched his hand away. The palm was wet and red. "What the…?" He yanked at the blanket around her shoulders. It came free, and he stared. "God almighty." He shouted, "We need bandages here, and hot water," and threw the blanket over the sofa back. "Tom, move your drowned butt out of the way." He shoved the other wizard off the sofa, then pushed Irene face down. Her mug landed on the rug, and spilled out a fragrant stream.

"What are you doing? Stop it." She could draw only enough air for a whisper.

He ripped away her bodice remnants while yelling, "What the hell happened? Why didn't anybody take care of her? Look at this!"

Fire wizards crowded around. She cursed Sven without sound.

Lucinda picked up the fallen mug and sniffed at it. "Were you drinking this? How much?" Irene waved two fingers, then three. "More than two cups? Not a good idea."

Irene pulled her elbows tight to her sides and pushed up to draw a good breath. Her ribs creaked. She wheezed, "Didn't want to make a fuss."

"For God's sake, woman," Sven said. "Stand up for yourself. Don't let airhead manners make you bleed to death."

She twisted her neck. The bandage on her shoulder was soaked through, and oozing.

Lucinda said, "If she drank more than a mugful of this potion she'd be so numb she wouldn't notice, but she shouldn't be bleeding. I heard Mother Celeste order her to stop, hours ago."

Snorri said, "Maybe she did something to tear it open again. I've done that."

"Could be. She clutched at her shoulder after she threw the chair at Winifred."

Tom, sitting cross-legged on the floor by Irene's head, goggled. "She threw a chair at an enchantress?"

"I didn't throw it." The fire wizards' chatter overwhelmed Irene's whisper.

Sven said, "Will somebody, please, for God's sake, tell me what happened?"

"Irene might," Lucinda said, "if you'll stop yelling long enough to listen."

"Sorry," he mumbled, and started cutting her corset laces.

Irene hissed, "What do you think you're doing?"

He yanked at the laces. "I'm getting rid of this mess so we can clean and bandage your back. And see where else you're bleeding. Lie still and be quiet."

"I will not! You can't undress me in public."

That brought hoots and catcalls. Tom grinned. "You want him to undress you in private?"

"Yes!" Tom's grin broadened. "No! That was not what I meant!"

"No?" Tom said, "You want me to undress you instead? In public or private?"

Lucinda's fiery roar rode over the noise. "Enough! Sit down and shut up."

Wizards scrambled away amid a chorus of "Yes, ma'am... Sorry, ma'am." The charged silence of a dozen people holding their breaths followed.

"That was uncalled for. You know she's a respectable woman." Lucinda turned on Sven. "And you—have you taken leave of your senses? Or are you trying to prove the Air Guild's rumourmongers right?"

The ripping stopped. "I, uh... Drown it! I never thought..."

Irene looked over her shoulder. Every inch of skin, from Sven's neck to his hairline, one ear tip to the other, was the brightest red she had ever seen on a human face.

"Obviously not." Lucinda's voice blistered. "If you had been thinking you'd know you have no right to manhandle an unrelated female."

"I have a right," Sven bellowed. "I'm going to marry her."

The Fire Eaters roared and surged closer. Irene buried her face in the sofa cushion and moaned. Shouts from a dozen members of the Fire Guild battered her ears.

Two-foot high orange letters hung in the air.

BE QUIET

The cacophony stopped. Now, really, she should have thought of that years ago. She added:

Contrary to rumours,

having one's clothing ripped off,

in public or otherwise,

is galling.

"Youngsters," Warlock Sunbeam tut-tutted. "Don't know how to treat a lady." He draped a lap robe across her. She mouthed a thank you at him.

He said, "You needn't worry, my dear. A noblewoman at a ball would exhibit more flesh, and your back is not exactly erotic right now, either. Trust me."

"No joke," Snorri said. "But it is interesting. That's the biggest bruise I've ever seen, and I've seen some good ones."

"Irene, I'm sorry." Sven sounded near tears. "But you said you were fine and you're…not. You need a healer."

"That's us." The Fire Eaters moved aside to let Master Duncan's earth witch and another woman through. "We heard shouting and thought we'd better investigate. Oh, my." Tom crabbed aside. The healer knelt, peeled back the bandage, and frowned at the gash. "I'll stop the bleeding, for now, but both this wound and the one in your thigh need to be stitched, or they'll tear open again. You're not bleeding anywhere else, but your ribs are a mess. You're not doing yourself any favours lying face down."

Sven dropped his head in his hands and groaned. With help from the two witches, Irene sat upright without further embarrassment, the lap robe providing cover.

The healer said, "Your ribs, the bruises… I've never seen anything like this. What happened? No, don't talk yet." She rummaged in her basket for needles. "You wizards, go somewhere else—"

Fire wizards howled. Sven shouted them down. "We'll not have her treatment delayed any further. Granny Hazel said go; we'll go."

"Maybe you should marry him, Irene," Lucinda said. "He's obviously gone berserk over you, and with an avowal as public as he made, he'll have a hard time weaselling out of it."

He said, "I don't want to get out of it."

Tom looked wistful. "If you won't marry him, I'm available."

Sven grabbed a fistful of his shirt and hauled him towards the door. "Tom, don't be an ass."

"Irene," Lucinda said, "If you don't mind, I'll show them what happened."

"I don't mind."

"Good. Sven, if you hadn't lost your head and made such a fuss, you could have called for a healer and taken her somewhere private…" She shooed fire wizards out of the drawing room, still scolding, leaving Irene alone with the healer and her assistant.

She whispered a summary of the evening's events to the two astonished women while they stitched, bandaged, peeled away sodden undergarments, and spread salve on her bruises. They left her clean, clad in a high-necked, long-sleeved robe, and under orders to avoid corsets and enthusiastic huggers for a month.

Sven had said he was going to marry her. Talk about rash promises! She had made a few herself; who was she to complain? A mage's promise is a serious matter; what kind of fool would she be to reject such an offer?

The fire brigade returned, bringing with them Warlock Quicksilver. Sven had been pale before; he was now ashen. They regarded her with awe.

Tom said, "Lady, you are one mighty witch."

"Yes, ma'am," another one said. "No wonder the Air Guild aristos are scared of you."

She opened her mouth to protest, but Quicksilver winked and shook his head. "A formidable talent, indeed," he said. "The new year will be a better one than I had imagined possible."

"Yes, sir," a fire wizard said. "I was sitting here thinking we'd taken care of one lot, but our children would have to do it all over again with their children. Now, maybe not. Maybe things will go right again."

"They will," Lucinda said. "We have something to celebrate this Yule, after all."

Irene closed her eyes and relaxed into the sofa cushions, warmed by their praise. She had made changes in the outer world—significant changes for the better—through the power of her mind. What could be more magical than that?

A few minutes later Warlock Arturos, more intimidating than ever with his eyebrows and three-quarters of his beard burned away, emerged from the fireplace and staggered to the nearest chair.

"It's over," he said. "The Fortress is open again. We can go home."

Lucinda kissed him on the forehead. "And you're still with us. Thank God."

The wounded wizards queued before the fireplace, waiting their turn for a warlock to take them home. In a few minutes only the snoring Sunbeam and Sven, beside Irene on the sofa, remained.

"Sven," she said, "you can't just tell the world you're going to marry me. I won't have it. I release you from your promise."

He hunched over, staring at the carpet. "Irene, I'm sorry. I…I love you. For you I would take being second, but I can't blame you for not wanting to marry me after I've shouted at you and embarrassed you and ordered you around."

"Sven, I—"

"It's just that I was so shocked. You could have died."

"Sven, you—"

"You gave me grief for being a hero, but you've gone and been one, too, and it scares the hell out of me."

"Sven, I—"

"And I hope you don't think I'd do something as ridiculous as ripping your clothes off to take advantage of you. I could undress you without ruining your clothes. Oh, drown it! You're going to slap me for being suggestive, and I deserve it."

"Sven, stop it. Why would a witch marry a man who didn't want to strip her naked?"

He raised his head. He was scarlet.

"Sven, you're the first person in my life who's ever asked what I wanted, and meant it. There's nothing second rate about you. All I meant was, a unilateral dictum is bad contract magic. It should be a mutual decision. Why don't you start over and do it right?"

He reached for her hand, and raised it to his lips. His hands and lips were warm; a shiver ran through her, but not from cold.

"Irene, will you marry me?"
"Yes, Sven, I will."

The Company of Mages

A quartet of warlocks emerged from the parlour's fireplace.

"I call this Fire Guild Council meeting to order." Arturos nudged Warlock Sunbeam. "Wake up, old man."

"Council meeting," Sunbeam repeated without opening his eyes. "I heard you."

"Council meeting?" Irene groped for the sofa arm's support. "I'll go—"

"No, you won't," Arturos said. "This is about you. Everybody in favour of inducting Irene into the Fire Guild say aye."

Six voices said, "Aye."

"Any nays?" There were no nays.

Sunbeam said with satisfaction, "That's a poke in the eye for the Air Guild," and resumed snoring.

Irene sagged against Sven's shoulder. "I can go home."

Quicksilver smiled. "Before we return to the Fortress, the Fire Warlock has a question for you."

Arturos said, "I do?"

Quicksilver said, "The one you asked me earlier, about King Stephen."

Arturos looked blank. "Well, yeah, I've been wondering about him all night. The Fire Office should've saved him from the traps. I'm damn glad they got him, and I didn't have to, but still…"

Irene said, "The Fire Office didn't protect him, because he was no longer king."

Arturos gaped. Sunbeam opened his eyes and sat up. The other four exchanged triumphant glances.

She repeated the prince's vow, word for word, and added, "Prince

Brendan didn't promise to take the oath. Whether he intended to or not, he swore the heart of oath itself, to be king for all the people. He then cemented his claim on the throne by calling on the Fire Office, using the magic phrases accorded the king."

Quicksilver said, "And as King Stephen had never taken the oath, the Fire Office transferred its allegiance to him, even as Stephen and his guards were entering the tunnels."

"Huh," Arturos said. "It could do that?"

Quicksilver said, "Tell me who issued that call for help."

The Fire Warlock's "Oh" was a long, drawn-out sigh. "The king did. It never occurred to me he wasn't Stephen. I'd wondered about that since he wasn't there, but I didn't have time to think about it."

Quicksilver's expression turned sombre. "This unexpected blessing must remain a Guild Council secret. That poor boy must shoulder a heavy burden. Learning the role he played in his father's death, unwitting though it was, will not help."

His expression lightened. "Now let us return home, so our newest member may have a well-earned rest."

The clarity of mind Irene had maintained on Yule eve disappeared, and she spent the next fortnight in a near trance. Her body moved like an automaton, feeding itself, bathing, dressing, and dealing with the mundane matters of everyday life, but fog engulfed her mind, turning the world indistinct shades of grey. She noted her new friends in the Fire Guild cosseting her—if Katie had not minded the girls, Irene could not have coped—but their words of comfort flew past without touching her.

The Fortress staff moved the van Gelders into a large suite of sun-filled rooms with a private balcony and space for a growing family. Crates of their belongings arrived from Airvale, but she could not muster the energy to unpack.

The Water Guild did not require her presence at the trial; the tortures Winifred had inflicted on her were of no import next to charges of treason and murder. She spent the day pacing the Fortress's ballroom, watching tears of sleet slide down the windows. She knew she mourned the phantom friend her head said never existed, not the real woman facing execution, but her heart still insisted on believing in the phantom.

Afterwards, Lucinda summarised the trial for her. All Irene remembered was a vivid image of Arturos glowing red and orange, turning Justice Hall uncomfortably hot. Lucinda said he never once looked at the defendant.

The next day, Father Jerome and Sorcerer Charles reviewed Irene and Winifred's entwined histories with the Air Guild Council. The formal letter of apology, signed by all three remaining members, was no more effective at staunching a bleeding wound than the bandage on her shoulder had been. She filed it away and did not look at it again.

Several days later, Warlock Snorri bounded from the dining room fireplace, yelling. Arturos and Quicksilver, both grinning, followed on his heels. Within seconds scholars and wizards were crowding around, reaching to shake Irene's hand or pat her on the back.

"Stop, please." She held up her hands. "I don't understand. What's the fuss about?"

Arturos squelched Snorri's reply with a hand on the boy's head. "For your services to Frankland on Yule eve, you'll be the first commoner in three hundred years to be promoted into the nobility."

"Pardon?"

"It was King Brendan's idea," Quicksilver said, "but one with which we heartily concur. Further, the Company of Mages will hold a long overdue meeting, and you are invited."

The fog numbing her began to dissipate. She clutched at the table. "Will I have to demonstrate my talent? I've never done well on practical tests, and—oh, no—before earth wizards, too. Oh, no."

"Relax, my dear. The wording implies Father Jerome and Sorcerer Charles have already reached a conclusion, and expect no dispute."

"What? Oh, no."

"Oh, yes. Here, read for yourself."

He handed her the invitation, and in golden letters she read, "… to introduce Frankland's javelin wordsmith…"

Irene floated across the battlements, savouring a light snowfall and the sound of Miranda singing, somewhere in the distance. The frigid air blew away the remnants of her mental fog, and she inspected the corner stairs without fear. Her ears would never hear Oliver's rich baritone again, but that knowledge brought relief, not sorrow.

Even if the voices had been his shade, rather than Winifred's doing, now, with recognition from the mages, his promise had been fulfilled. As for her promise to him, she was getting better at standing up for the children, and for herself. Her new guild would encourage her to do so.

"Rest in peace, Oliver," she whispered into the wind. "I will always miss you, but I don't need you any longer."

She turned and went inside.

Enchanter Paul exuded the air of a man shocked to find he has become elderly. He watched Irene and Sven approach the Warren's conference room with a muscle in his cheek twitching.

"Are you sure you can handle him?" Sven said.

She nodded and squeezed his hand, then let go and went to meet the Air Enchanter with Lucinda's coaching still fresh in her mind. After exchanging greetings, there was a moment's awkward silence, then both began talking. His voice rose. Hers did, too.

He held up a hand, "Please, be quiet and let me speak—"

Three-inch-tall letters the colour of cold steel hung in the air between them.

I AM A WITCH.

You *will not* silence me again.

You lost your son.

If you want your grandchildren's respect,

You will listen to me.

The Enchanter shrivelled. "I'm sorry. I should have realised how that would sound, but I meant to apologise for mistreating you. I am listening. Speak. Please."

"I couldn't hide my unhappiness in Airvale from Miranda and Gillian. They've seen the Fire Guild's respect and the Air Guild's disrespect. They will need training in air magic, but the guild school frightens them. Their willingness to go depends on you."

"What should I do?"

"Come to the Fortress and tell them what happened. Admit you made mistakes. Tell them why I've been mistreated, and that you won't let it happen again. Arturos said the Air Guild lost a third of its members in the Yule War. The ones gone were the troublemakers and deadwood. You'll never have a better opportunity to reform the school. If you do, I will do my best to keep my anger from spoiling the Air Guild for them. I've already told Quicksilver I don't want the mages issuing a public reprimand. Further embarrassing the Air Guild won't help me."

He stared into the distance, the muscle twitching faster.

Her tone sharpened. "The Air Guild was already understaffed. You can't afford enemies in your ranks."

He flushed. "No, of course not. That wasn't... You are right about the school. I will do what you ask. I was thinking that you are very generous. You are treating me far better than I deserve."

Irene agreed, but chose not to say so. "This isn't for your sake—it's for theirs. They need a guild they can be proud of."

She turned to enter the conference room but he stopped her. "About Sven—he's your fiancé, isn't he? Congratulations. He's a decent man; he'll be good for you."

Warlock Quicksilver reviewed for the other mages the spellbook's history, and Winifred's malicious interference in Irene's life. Father Jerome and Sorcerer Charles presented their findings, showing scenes from her life in a magic looking glass. They did not demand any tests, but sounded so thrilled and eager to use her talents, that when Quicksilver suggested a demonstration of the sort she had done for him, she agreed. The *oohs* and *aahs* that followed were quite gratifying.

They sent her and Enchanter Paul away while they discussed disciplinary action. On being summoned back to the conference room, the Company's verdict surprised them both.

"We won't strip Oliver of the title of Mage," Father Jerome explained, addressing the Enchanter. "The spellbook is a fine example of a collaborative effort, with the quality of Mistress Irene's spells demonstrating Oliver's teaching abilities and grasp of theory. Jean and I will write an account of today's presentation for our records, but that account will not be made public until twenty years after your death. The spellbook's next printing will have both names on it, with Mistress Irene given prominence. That's all."

Paul bowed his head. "That is much kinder than I expected. Or deserved."

"That may be," the earth wizard agreed blandly, "but the Air Guild must be given a chance to recover, and further insult would not help."

He turned to Irene. "We have two more items of business to discuss this afternoon. We are expecting the Fire Warlock momentarily, and he asked that you stay, as they involve you."

"Me?" She glanced at Sven. He looked baffled. Traces of tension lined Quicksilver's face.

Arturos strode from the fireplace, and after answering a chorus of calm greetings, said, "Queen Marguerite asked the Earth Guild to cut a tunnel from Alex—sorry, King Brendan's rooms directly to the Fortress, so he can consult with us whenever he wants."

"Certainly," Father Jerome said. "Excellent idea. Long overdue."

"It is a revival of an ancient tradition." Quicksilver said. "The previous tunnel was closed about two hundred years ago on the king's order."

"She also asked," Arturos said, "for a mage to take on the job her father had supervised, overseeing the rest of the king's formal education. Whoever does it won't have to do all the tutoring himself, but he will have to spend a lot of time with the boy to make sure he's on the right track, and that his tutors are thorough."

"Any of you could handle that," he said, glancing around the room at nodding heads, "but since he's shown an affinity for the Fire Guild, a flame mage would make the most sense."

Sven and Quicksilver tensed, neither one looking at the other. Irene caught her breath.

There was a slight pause. "We haven't had an opportunity like this in centuries." Father Martin frowned, speaking slowly. "I agree. It should be a flame mage. Sven is the youngest, and has had fewer encounters, good or bad, with the nobles, particularly the ones at court. Jean has dealt with them for more than a century. I am sorry to disappoint you, but…"

Sven's expression was a hard mask, but it didn't hide the rising red. Quicksilver rubbed his temples like a migraine sufferer.

"Yes," Sorcerer Charles said. "We can't afford a misstep. Jean is well versed in that contentious history." He surveyed the other mages. One after another, they nodded. His tone changed to a brisk pronouncement of their verdict. "Jean's regular appearances at court would be too painful a reminder. We must award Sven this singular honour."

Astonishment and delight flooded Sven's features. The mages were grinning. Quicksilver and then Irene laughed. Arturos's chuckle added a deep rumble. The mages laughed at their gentle joke, and reached to shake Sven's hand and offer congratulations.

Quicksilver soon called them to attention. "You have seen what Mistress Irene can do, and she has proven beyond a doubt she is a true daughter of Frankland. I trust you will agree with the Fire Guild Council that we need her involved in the eventual Fire Office reforging. I want her to review the spells in the Office for errors, and to understand enough to offer corrections. She should study advanced fire magic, under my supervision, along with Lucinda, René, and Sven, but the Company of Mages must lend our council your authority to override the strictures preventing all but council members from seeing the secret spells in the Fire Office. "

Irene held her breath, dazzled and overwhelmed. Her heart overflowed with joy, too deep for laughter or words.

"Splendid idea," Sorcerer Charles said. "I approve."

"You know, Jean," Father Jerome sighed, "against my better judgment I'm beginning to accept that it is time to reforge the Fire Office. You're collecting the talent needed to do it—first a locksmith, and now a wordsmith."

Quicksilver said, "This is, of course, if she is interested."

"Interested? Yes, sir, please!"

"Good." He smiled. "I promised you suitable work. This will keep you busy for years."

They left with the Company's endorsements ringing in her ears. As they stepped into the fireplace, Warlock Quicksilver said, "I trust you will indulge me. It is a clear day, and you might enjoy this, as I do."

They had not arrived in the Fortress, as she had expected. They stood on the small rise south of the town square in Blazes, facing north as the setting sun lit the Fortress's western face.

"I do, Your Wisdom. Thank you." Taking her fiancé's arm, she floated along the path towards the shining citadel, and home.

The story continues in
The Forge, Reforging, Book 5